More Than I Can Say

More Than I Can Say

Colin Bellwood

JANUS PUBLISHING COMPANY LTD
Cambridge, England

First published in Great Britain 2018
by Janus Publishing Company Ltd
The Studio
High Green
Great Shelford
Cambridge CB22 5EG

www.januspublishing.co.uk

Copyright © Colin Bellwood 2018
British Library Cataloguing-in-Publication Data
A catalogue record for this book is available from the British Library

ISBN 978-1-85756-877-6

Cover Design: Janus Publishing Company Ltd

Cover Illustration by Colin Bellwood

Printed and bound in Great Britain by
KnowledgePoint Limited, Reading

Contents

Michael

(*The Highwaymen 1961*)

– Death and youth is the worst mixture –

Aunt Annie did laying out and so when she spoke of such matters she was offered respectful ears. She also decorated interior rooms, not with any great deftness or precision, but at speed and very cheaply. The 1960s had begun, but in the terraced houses of Castleford there still remained the attitude of earlier decades (alongside the economic restrictions) that, as far as interior decoration went, how it was was how it stayed; men might fix sinks or sideboards and women cleaned and tidied and set out ornaments, but transforming an inside living space for the sake of change itself would still have been an eccentric indulgence. Only when there was real peeling and stains too large for pictures to hide was Aunt Annie called in.

– *It's brightened it up* – I remember my father saying after Annie had spent her usual two days with the focus of a storm's eye slapping paste onto patterned wallpaper and climbing up a stepladder to hang and arrange the sodden strips. My mother looked less sure, but as ever held back her thoughts on her husband's decisions. As a 10-year-old, I was only pleased when the kitchen table, which had been used for Annie's pasting, was returned to its proper place and we no longer had to eat off stools, but even then I noticed that some of the wallpaper flowers had been badly matched here and there, a segment of a rose growing out of a thorn or a curling stalk suddenly becoming a petal, and it was this which came back to me when it was explained what 'laying out' meant and that Aunt Annie had

1

performed the operation on my grandfather. I could not rid myself then of the thought of his arms being segmented down to chest level, or of an ear, like that rose, forced into unnatural partnership with a neck.

– Yes, death and youth. I have dealt with those in my time, said Annie.

– You remember the Tordoff boy? The group of female mourners Aunt Annie was holding forth to gave a kind of squeezed hush of remembrance. Came off his motorbike, recalled Aunt Kath and Annie nodded: Well, that is what you don't want to see! You don't want to see someone who should not be dead dead. *You want to see someone who should be dead dead!*

I found it hard to define my unease with this as I heard it and as I recalled it later. It was the *should* perhaps which played on my mind, and the image of Aunt Annie casting her focussed eyes down on a corpse and nodding with something like satisfaction – this one *should* be gone! This disturbed me more than any idea of the injustice of mortality and from that day I avoided Aunt Annie; before then she had seemed just another of my aunts, with more presence than some, quite manly in a way, with a muscle tightening in her jaw, but from then on I avoided her and her strong gaze, feeling I might suddenly see in this gaze a recognition that young as I was, an example of the sad injustice of mortality though I might be, I actually *should* be dead.

– And have you heard about the card?!

Aunt Beryl said this with the sly leaning forward of the gossip, perhaps automatically, for gossip she was, but also perhaps wanting to shift the conversation from the dark and the insoluble towards the altogether more convivial whisperings on other people's failings. *Poor Irene!* she said and the group turned towards my grandmother in her usual chair in the black netting of a bygone age, her face rouged, but as blank and expressionless as the pot spaniel standing beside the fireplace.

– Are you earwigging? My mother came up behind me and I indicated the shovel in my hand and the coal which, following my father's instructions, I had just transferred from the coal house to the heaped blaze in the fireplace. I had lingered there, however, caught by the snippets of adult conversation. What was this about a card? I looked along the line of condolences set out on the mantelpiece above the fire, but then it was clear I could linger no more amongst the women who had gathered in the living room. The men for once had congregated in the kitchen where my mother's brothers had opened some bottles. The children and some other adult mourners, who were neighbours rather than family, were standing in the yard, the adults against the fence which faced the outside coalhouse, the children down towards the end of the yard where the hump of ground which had once housed a small family air-raid shelter provided an interesting contour.

I had not seen my grandfather in death, although I had been taken to see him soon before in the bed brought down to the front room in which he now lay in his coffin. A *stroke* had laid him low they said and, as my previous acquaintance with this word had been when it related to fondling pets or tied to the word *luck*, there was an element of confusion in my mind. There was nothing of fondling or happy chance in the figure I saw in the bed on that visit; the face seemed hardly to be the face of my grandfather, or it was his face as if it had somehow been sucked to one side and when he tried to smile at his young visitors (my brother and me) it seemed as if he were trying to lift a weight with the corner of his mouth. I was tongue tied and only wanted a childish release, feeling, as children can, the vague sense of irritation at adult weakness and disorder. My love for the man was an altogether cloudier affair and only later did I get any really clear pictures of him, of throwing snowballs at him when he came home from the pit and him bending to scoop up snow and return the missiles, and the white snow on his grimy miner's clothes. His ubiquitous grin came also, the same grin he had tried to manage on my last sight of him and that some unforgiving force had rendered grotesque. He could make us laugh. He could always make us laugh, although (again I clarified this later and after I had found out what I found out) never like the clowns in the circus; the circuses which came to our area were poor affairs in those days, travelling shows with weary-looking animals and road-hardened, businesslike performers who brought

3

their magic in the same way as carts brought coal. As a little child I no doubt marvelled at the elephants and laughed at the clowns, but even by the age of ten I was beginning to find these latter merely silly and my grandfather was never that; even with children there was always an element of detail in his humour, the facial expression, the cleverly placed emphasis, the subtleties of the best comedians. *He was a jolly fellow!* I heard this from another of the adult voices as I went out to join the children at the end of the yard. From Mrs Butterfield, the next-door neighbour, who had reason to revere any kind of jolliness; her husband was like a humourless lump of slag, as we called the useless slate which encased the coal seams. Even when he had washed off the dirt of the pit, his features had the resistant solidity of something mined, his infrequent words fell like chippings and his whole presence and manner was of some half monster come from the ground, cursing his coming and the ground on which he was condemned to stand. My grandfather used to rag him a little through the fence. *Coughing better there, Tommy!* he said once as he led me and my brother down the yard on an outing to the welfare and I remember the sad slab of a man turning his indistinct eyes towards us and not even replying, but coughing again with the heavy depth of the mine and then growling up a thick ball of spit. *Yes, a bit of toenail in that one, Tom!* My grandfather had grinned at him and then winked at us boys. It seemed a dangerous thing to me, ragging this monster, and I pulled my grandfather's hand onwards, but he seemed fearless. I had been told that as a young man he had lied about his age and gone as a soldier to the Dardanelles, a commando, my mother said proudly. He had landed as a commando in a boat and had been shot at and wounded; there were papers my grandmother had to prove this. In the Second World War he had been an air-raid warden and there was still the tin hat he had worn for the office, which he would let us play with, although he would never put it on himself.

I looked at the humped remains of the air-raid shelter as I walked back towards the group of children gathered next to it and something of the fathomless weight of other people's histories pressed even on my self-centred child's mind.

– We've made a boat, said cousin Michael, who was a couple of years older than I, almost a teenager. – I'm going to row it, like that song. My brother and two other male cousins nodded appreciatively in the direction of the three-sided orange box set out near the end of the yard, two sheets of cardboard jammed into the open end as a semblance of a prow and two building bricks to fix the structure and to act as a seat.

– What we need is oars. Michael looked around. *You shouldn't be getting dirty!* came the call from cousin Cynthia amidst the circle of girls which had formed a few paces away to echo the adult females inside and to cast the occasional disparaging look at the idle play of the boys, but Michael ignored her and when my brother said there was a bunch of old sticks and other strips of wood in the coalhouse, Michael said he should show him them. You can't go in there in your clothes, said Cynthia, but Michael ignored her and ushered my brother on.

– What's this about Grannie and a card? I asked of Cynthia, who was the oldest of the girls and might well have been taken into confidences; girls were offered more of these earlier than boys and in general were more likely to seek them. Cynthia turned away, however, although it seemed to me she didn't know. I looked beyond her at the high latched gate to the yard where so often I had seen my grandfather's grimy hand reaching over when he came back from the pit and through which we had gone so often to the welfare, but in truth I made no real sense of his death; no reality attached to it or to the idea I would never see him again, nor go with him through that gate. Those were closed and laconic times and the veins of feeling which ran like seams of worthwhile fuel in a greater mass would only appear from time to time in blazes of sentiment, in obvious songs and simple romances, in drunken chortling and senseless fights. The times of the individual's importance were still to come (in the North of England at least) as was their obverse: few people felt meaningless or without identity, but like those seams of coal they could be trapped and crushed and never brought to any blaze. My grandfather at least had been a flame, I thought – or rather again I thought this later in the apparent release of a poetic

5

adolescence – at the time I could not absorb his extinction and my unthinking heart would not accept it.

– These'll do.

Michael came back with two strips of wood he was going to use for oars. They're too thin, said Malcolm, who disputed most things with his brother, often to the extent of blows. And they need flat bits at the end. How could you row through water with those?! Michael ignored him and sat himself on the seat of building bricks then arranged the wooden strips on either side as they did in the boats on Ponte Park lake. I watched him begin his journey singing in a quite tuneful voice – *Michael row the boat ashore, Hallelujah* – at which the group of girls turned again towards him. You'll get dirty! they said. And you shouldn't be saying *Hallelujah*. Salvation Army say that and this is a church we're going to. Proper church.

– Piss off, said Michael, who was noted for his bad language, and the girls turned away in disgust. I turned away myself, also vaguely feeling the play inappropriate, although I knew my grandfather liked to sing and one of the songs he sang had been by the black man who had visited mines in Wales, which song was also about the River Jordan. – *River Jordan is chilly and cold, Hallelujah. Chills the body but not the soul.* I knew the lyrics of Michael's song better than Michael, who it seemed only knew the first lines containing his own name. I looked again at the latched gate (there had been a song from that black man which my grandfather also sang which made some mention of a latch) and this time I did imagine his coal-dirtied hand and the gate thrown open and him appearing in its frame with a broad grin for his grandson.

The mystery of the card was cleared up for me a few days after the funeral. One evening after my brother and I had just had our supper and were having our last time downstairs which I in particular pleaded for, my mother's brother Ron and his wife, Aunt Kath, arrived, I think unexpectedly, with some update or other on my newly widowed grandmother, and my brother and I were banished to the kitchen and the door was closed, but I could still hear most of the conversation; the television was turned off as my father was already developing his opinion that this new technology was a conversation killer. – So she's getting herself upstairs … I heard him say and Uncle Ron's reply that yes his mother was getting up to bed, although a check still needed to be made on whether she had done so and did not spend the night in her chair. It's as well, said my father, who considered himself a source of strength and practicality in the matter. It helped of course that he and my grandmother had disliked each other. As was the way in those days, my mother and father had spent the first years of their marriage in the house of one of their own parents, usually the mother's, and my father, yearning to be the master of his own hearth, had come up against my grandmother more than once. At the time, of course, I hadn't recognized this dislike, nor my father's satisfaction at seeing a rival reduced; at the time it only sounded as another beat of the tough realism all northern men were supposed to show. *Poor thing*! said Aunt Kath. She's been going through those old boxes over and over … Only to be expected, said my father and I heard the pipe he had recently taken to smoking, tap tapping. Going over old photographs and all, Aunt Kath went on. Well, not so much photographs as old cards. She must have kept all the cards she was ever sent, birthdays, postcards … My ears began seriously to wig at this. The mystery of the card might finally be solved.

– There are postcards from Nellie, from Scarborough, weddings, all sorts.

– She's always done that, said Uncle Ron. She's always kept cards. There was a silence, which my father, as was his wont, filled.

– Have to accept she's gone a bit in the head, your mother. Have to accept this has knocked her off a bit. Look at what she did on the mantelpiece. Setting that card out like that.

– I don't think she knew she'd done it, said Aunt Kath.

– Well, that's what I'm saying … I heard my father's pipe tapping. That's what I'm on about. She doesn't know what she's doing. Gone she is at the moment.

– *You would say that*! This was my mother, a strange, challenging volume and sharpness to her voice, and then there was the unmistakable sound of a sob and a silence like the end of days.

A few minutes later my father appeared at the kitchen door, his face fixed with the fury of minor humiliation. You two should be going up to bed! he snapped, trying to make it seem as if he were taking the responsibility of what should have been my mother's office as a favour to her in her time of need, but even then I sensed his intervention was an escape from the sudden and uncharacteristic confrontation his wife had offered, and in front of visitors. He needed time to dampen his surprise, gather his thoughts and consider his reaction. It was as part of this reaction perhaps that he solved the mystery of the card.

– What did Grannie do with a card? I asked him as he came upstairs to see we two were in bed, which was what my mother would normally have done. Downstairs I could hear the indistinct voice of Aunt Kath offering consolation, although I hoped never to hear my mother sob again and so I made no attempt to listen closely any more. What did she do with a card? My father was staring blankly at my brother as he rolled over under his blankets and then he turned to me and gave out a sound which was half a grunt, half a chuckle. She put out a birthday card with the cards on the mantelpiece, he said, paying back his mother in law and his newly, briefly, confrontational wife with this revelation to a child.

– There were all the cards you get for funerals, those you get when somebody has died, all set out on the mantelpiece and then right at the end of the line there was a birthday card with a clown on it and *Happy Birthday Grandad!* I heard in his voice the echo of the more genuine laughter the grown-up men must have shared at this.

– A card from you and your brother it was, with a clown on it, kicking up his big boot ... My father even lifted one of his slippered feet in a mime of this, which was quite strange to see as he had none of the comic qualities of my grandfather or my mother's brothers. *Happy Birthday Grandad!* Your Gran had set it out at the end of the line and nobody noticed until a fair few people had arrived and then ... he tailed off, conscious perhaps of revealing too much to a minor, and looked down towards the voices, thinking he should get back and re-establish himself.

– This has made an old woman of her this has, he said and with that final barb for his old adversary he turned away. You get off to sleep.

I found doing so hard, however, not only because of the blurred sounds of conversation continuing downstairs, but also because of the image of the birthday card, which I remembered: big, painted lips around a grin, a battered straw hat with a little flower in it, chequered trousers and big orange boots, one of which was lifted towards the birthday salutation. Other night-time images came as usual, pulsing in and out of the shadows made by the little battery-powered nightlight set on the table between my brother's bed and mine, and then in the darkness of closed eyes and the rim of the blanket pulled tight over them came the terrible imaginings, although in their midst was a new and more benign image, one which grinned at the monsters and reduced their malevolent capacities, one which might even place its outsized orange boot in their rear. What are you laughing at, Grandad? I remember asking him once when his grin became a laugh for no reason I could see and he just shook his head, still laughing. *At all of it, lad,* he said. *At all of it.*

I slipped into sleep that night hearing these words of his and then came a genuine dream in which he rowed his boat across black and chilly water and disembarked on some foreign shore, smeared with coal dirt as a commando and (here the image was confused with the fleeting mix of dualities which occur in dreams) grinning and laughing as a clown.

Everyday

(Buddy Holly 1957/Bobby Vee 1960)

After chemistry we had a rehearsal for Armageddon. It was done by forms, but not by form teachers, so in our case it fell to Punch Ambler to pass on the instruction as an extension to his lesson and he seemed ill at ease with it from the beginning, although, given the essentially scientific nature of the dark matter, one might have expected him to be more comfortable with it than, say, the English or the foreign languages staff. We heard later that Nosreap Pearson, the physics master, actually drew some diagrams and wrote out some equations on the board as part of his instruction, but Punch seemed altogether more diffident, even vaguely annoyed with it all; perhaps as a scientist he recognized the basic inefficacy of the exercise. For us, although no-one actually said so, it was just another fearful layer on the fear which had been building for some time: having adult authority confirm the worst of possibilities meant that it was still harder to consign the issue to the realm of imaginings, alongside books and movies or those things which only really happen elsewhere. What goes on at school, in one way or another, is always a great reality for its pupils.

– There will be a siren, said Punch, still in the white lab coat he wore for the lessons, and turned towards the window – from the fire station – he fingered at the rubber pipe of the Bunsen burner and tapped other fingers on his long desk, which was raised on a dais and on which he conducted his demonstrations. We gathered around the desk for these, but for this extra instruction we had been sent back to our tables.

10

– This will give you four minutes … He drifted off, his features silhouetted by the blackboard. It was the notably hooked nose perhaps which had given him his nickname, but he was one of the oldest members of staff and the name had simply been passed on to us when we arrived at the school; for all we knew it related to a blow he had thrown in some distant past; certainly there was nothing other than the nose to bring out any resemblance to a hard, long-chinned puppet; his was a crumpled, dishevelled figure, if anything more like the soft tin can he had once shown us slowly imploding when it had all the oxygen inside it removed. Nor was he any great source of authority in the school; he was not Reichsführer Wood, the German teacher and senior master who had interviewed Rudolf Hess when he landed in Scotland, nor lame Ma Naylor, who could shrivel a student with a look, and, as far as there was indiscipline in those Grammar School days, he could suffer some of it in his classes, although you had to be careful as from time to time he would suddenly turn on someone and give them a detention, perhaps more as a culmination of something in himself than anything specific to the offence. Brian Brown had recently received one from him just for lifting a pipette too high. Inattention, however, was by and large something of a norm in chemistry, apart from those who were keen on the subject, and I had already spent most of the lesson idly putting tiny reflected windows on all the bubbles of the bell jar diagram we had drawn. Moreover, it was a standard joke that Punch's chemistry demonstrations tended to go wrong: lack of preparation on his part perhaps, given the mechanical quality which might set in after too many years of teaching, contaminated materials maybe (the classroom laboratory was not the pristine environment it would become), bad luck, or the genuinely myriad possibilities of experimentation. Whatever the reason, there had been a number of occasions on which we had been told to write up the experiment as if the particles had turned blue or the gas had ignited; enough for the lampooning urge to outweigh the other occasions when the conclusion of the demonstration had been just as expected.

– This will give you four minutes –

For all this absence of authority, particularly when the class had dispersed back into the laboratory, which was larger than a normal classroom, at that moment Punch had everyone's attention; even Dave Poole, who had brought in some pages of *Lady Chatterley*, sellotaped and thumbed, followed the teacher's gaze as it went to the window and back. – In this time … Punch pushed the half-moon spectacles back up his beak … you will be able to get yourselves onto the floor and under desks … his absent gaze drifted out towards us … or the tables if it happens when you are in here … Was there even an indistinct lifting of the indistinct corners of his mouth at this? I was too far back in the room to be sure, but there was certainly something perfunctory to his manner, as if he were even more past caring with this extra instruction he had been instructed to give than he was with his chemistry, with which there were still occasional traces of the weight of truth he had once been excited to discover and pleased to pass on. We heard later that Bronco Lane, the English teacher, had actually treated the whole thing as a joke with the class he had – *You get under a desk in a foetal position and put your fingers in your ears and you'll be completely safe!* he was reliably reported to have said. It was also reported that he had later been carpeted by the Headmaster for saying it. Levity was one response of course, particularly amongst one's peers: Bogey Collins said he was not going to get under any desk, but he was going to stand on it and sing 'Goodbye Cruel World' as the nuclear blast came through the school, and Pooley said that the minute the siren sounded he was going to rape Jane Nodder, although the general opinion was that he wouldn't have time, particularly if she ran for it. Also it might happen during PE, which the boys and girls did separately.

The levity was all fairly hollow, recognizable as bravado even by adolescents. In general the underlying mood was of terror and we clung to routine as to an invisible lifebelt in a rising, invisible flood, and it was perhaps a mistake to have this little talk (a drill as it had been called); we would probably have been better going on as if world matters were separate from our real lives as in most cases for most people they generally are (although at least we were not asked actually to assume the under-desk positions as were some third years), but it had been decreed the drill should happen by a decent and equally terrified local authority as one of the few renditions of practical response on offer.

Jim Dobson had another, however, and he told me about it as we walked home from school that day. *I know someone who has made a shelter!* He looked over his shoulder to make sure no-one else was listening. Someone he knew had made a nuclear shelter in the cellar of his house and he was going to go down into it to survive the blast and he had invited Jim to join him. *Tomorrow.* It will be tomorrow for sure, said Jim. There was some agreement on this. Greggy Gregg, the most studious of our group, turning to his studiousness as his own lifebelt, had read all the newspapers and watched the TV news, all of which I had been avoiding, the fear they induced being too great: the Russian ships were sailing towards Cuba with their missiles and there was a blockade of American ships to meet them and as soon as this meeting occurred, which would be tomorrow, missiles would be fired and then the whole network of intercontinental rockets would be released, mushroom clouds would rise from all British cities and the bright light and the wind blast of the short film we had all seen would come, shattering and flattening buildings like the matchwood models in that film and reducing people to globules or to seared and misshapen corpses as in the worst of horror movies.

– It'll be tomorrow, said Jim. So there'll be no point coming to school. I mean *getting under a desk*! That's just stupid! We all agreed on this. The Grammar School had not even had its windows whitewashed as it was rumoured would soon be the case with some civic buildings so the Mayor and his Councillors could be saved. (Although the windows of the Town Hall, which was quite near to the Grammar School, still seemed as they had always been; there were other rumours of sandbags inside, however.) Rich southerners would have nuclear shelters, was the general opinion, and the richest of them would reappear when the storm had passed, some no doubt thinking it was as well for an overpopulating world that there should be a cull of the less useful. Ideas of nuclear fallout and radiated afterlife were hazier and there existed the notion that if one could just live through the blast we had all seen modelled on TV, if

13

one could just duck under the blow, then survival was a possibility. There were after all survivors of Hiroshima and Nagasaki, none who had found themselves in the bull's eye of the target of course, but, staring in a daze at the camera, there were those who had been on its outer limits, in shredded clothes, but with no more burns than might be suffered in a bad pit accident. They had at least survived. And in our particular case the bull's eye of Leeds was ten miles away. Not enough, said Greggy, with his good student's precision. The blast will spread out as far as us. Everything above ground in a radius of ten to twelve miles will be gone.

– *Everything above ground!* Jim repeated this for me as he told me about his friend's shelter. *And this is a cellar.* Right underground. I'm going there tomorrow. I'm not coming into school, I'm going there. It's a cellar and Mr Lassiter has set it up with lights and some beds and some cans of food and such so he can stay down there until it's over.

– Have you seen it? I asked and Jim nodded yes, looking around again to be certain no-one else was listening. I had heard Jim mention this Mr Lassiter before, he was some kind of preacher at the church to which Jim and his family belonged, although it was not really a church as such; they met together in a local hall which had once been a dance hall and from time to time went to each other's houses. *Christadelphians.* I knew the name, although nothing of how they differed from the Church of England to which my father said we belonged, although we never went. They were not Jehovahs, I knew that; they did not appear on your doorstep to try and convert you and Jim had once been quite scathing about Jehovahs and their many wives for one man.

The denigration of the established church was gathering momentum at the time: it was just another arm of political control, was a charge which came alongside questions with longer histories as to how a good God could allow so much suffering; how could He let mass murder happen and so on; that any divinity might be separate from or subliminal to the fractious mix of human organizations which use its name had not occurred to us and it had all become bound up with the teenage years which were also setting in, where youth seemed closer to veracity than any grey-headed experience. The logic seemed inescapable: if God was omnipotent, He had brought World Wars and the Holocaust; if He was the Prime Mover then He had moved the world towards annihilation. The simple obverse of this was being expressed also, of course, particularly as the threat became more real: the Apocalypse was coming: it had been predicted many times before, but never with such scientifically effective back-up; of course the sinful world was about to be destroyed. The wrath of God would be nuclear.

I knew, although he had never actually said it, that this might well be Jim's opinion. Greggy and I (when we were apart from the intimate triangle he and I and Jim usually formed) put this down to parental influence. Greggy's father knew Jim's and he had told Greggy the man was an odd bird, a Bible basher, who had once given him a fat pamphlet to read called *The Exegesis of Daniel*, which had passages in it about A Great Beast coming and the world all ending. Jim himself said nothing about such matters, although he would join in our dismissals of the standard church: scoring points for his side, we thought, not simply deriding the whole institution as we were. And yet as the reflected light of our tiny speck in the cosmos seemed about to be extinguished or turned to flame for a still briefer moment, as the good earth seemed about to become a scalped and barren sod, (as ever at such times) what would otherwise be fantasy or exaggeration can become well-spoken truth and broader gestures and dark remnants no longer mere personal demons or public theatre.

– Do you want to come? Jim asked me then.

– What, down the cellar?

– Yes. Tomorrow.

– But this bloke doesn't know me.

I have to say the invitation surprised me. Jim and I were great friends, but I was no Christadelphian and there was something about Jim's manner, as if he were asking me to accompany him as someone might who just didn't want to be alone.

– What about Greggy? I asked, but Jim said he couldn't turn up at Mr Lassiter's with two companions; one he thought would be all right, two excessive.

– And does he know I'm coming? I asked, to which Jim was evasive, even furtive, simply repeating that he thought it would be all right.

We left the matter in the air, but after I had involuntarily caught snippets of the late evening news, which were all about the American blockade, and after another half sleepless night anticipating the end, I resolved to join Jim in Mr Lassiter's shelter. There were some thoughts for my family, but I was a teenager and my father had recently clouted me for spending too long on my hair in the bathroom and my mother had given me no great sympathy. It would be sad also not to have Greggy along, but then there was a suspicion he would find some Socratic comfort in his calculations even as he was being obliterated. Besides, there was the element of having been chosen: Jim had asked me and not him, perhaps because I had always been rather less dismissive of God, perhaps because I had always allowed more spiritual possibilities than our more cerebral friend.

– Have you decided? asked Jim, when we met as usual for the morning walk to school. Greggy lived nearer and besides had been charged with accompanying his first-year sister. So when I nodded and said that yes I had decided to come there was only Chutney Pickles who usually tagged on to us to call *where are you two going?* when we turned off towards The Malts instead of carrying on as usual towards school.

– Brilliant! Jim seemed very pleased and we turned down through Valley Gardens and out towards Beancroft where he said Mr Lassiter lived.

– I've brought some food. He opened his school satchel to show me: banana sandwiches, which he knew I liked, and I sensed in this another aspect of invitation. He was walking quite quickly also and although of course the blast could come at any time and we needed to get on, I could see he didn't want to give me much time for second thoughts as we departed further and further from our usual route and the reality of the truant excursion became more and more apparent; neither of us had actually played truant before. We passed a few other pupils heading in the proper direction and received a few querying looks, but only one other group echoed Chutney's question and then we were too far along Smawthorne Lane for there to be anyone to see us, other than some stragglers preoccupied with their own timing, and for all any adults who saw us knew we were going to the school dentist which was also located in one of the big houses on Beancroft.

It was a strange mixture of emotions I felt as we walked on in that lively fashion and in silence: the wild break from routine seemed a full confirmation that this was my last sight of the world as it was and as it had been and the incipient poet in me wanted to pull a flower from the ragged beds in the Valley Gardens and feel some velvet petal, gaze at some sweet colour before it all became blackness and ash. The child in me also wanted its mother, but then I was fourteen and I had known for some time that if I suddenly regressed ten years or eight or six or even three and threw myself into my mother's arms she would have only been confused and concerned and almost certainly a little condemnatory; I was supposed to be becoming a man.

– Whereabouts is it on Beancroft? I asked, just to break the silence in which we were walking and Jim said it was not far up and we went on, into a chasm it seemed to me; less familiar streets, wider and quieter than the ones I really knew, with far more trees. – We could dump our sacks. Jim pointed at a clump of bushes. We don't need them any more. We both had school satchels, loaded with text books and exercise books, which in my case at least I carried back and forth more as a gesture to the possibility of study rather than its essential tools, but I felt an ill-defined reluctance to do this; bunking off from school was enough it seemed to me. How many gestures did utter alteration need? And so I clung to the satchel (which all but the styleless wore over one shoulder instead of the far more sensible manner with the strap across the chest) as if clinging to a strap for standing passengers in a bus. You've got the sandwiches in yours, I said, but Jim shrugged: I can take them out. I shook my head, however, and walked on, not as committed as my friend, and still, despite all the clear evidence to the contrary, retaining some faint hope that the world, the Grammar School, might continue, and I did not want to be in trouble for ditching my sack. In fact I nearly turned around at that moment, feeling I would rather have the minor bind of a late arrival, with a form teacher scolding me like a mother, and all the other saving details of the everyday than this exegesis of Daniel. To hide from a Great Beast, you must first acknowledge its existence and the comfort of ages has so often been ignorance.

– This is it – still with his satchel on his shoulder, Jim indicated a shadowy house, smothered it seemed in bushes and trees, and then it was the council house boy in me who wanted to turn away; not only was there a large double gate, but there was a pathway leading to the house; one covered in shale and pebbles such as wealthier people had. Big house, I said and Jim nodded – We sometimes have meetings here – which was one of the very few times I had heard him make mention of the church or the sect or whatever it was he belonged to, and yet, although he had been there before, Jim seemed no more comfortable than I as we went through the gate and up the pebbled path. The whole house seemed as if it were closed up, even abandoned, with dark curtains drawn on all the windows, and I noticed great clumps of weeds in the front lawn and a couple of tubs hooped with rusty metal which should have had plants or flowers in them, but which were filled in fact with nothing but soil. Round the back, said Jim and we went across the tree-shadowed frontage to another gate and through this down a narrow path running along the side of the house.

– Does he live here alone? I asked, looking up the bleak bricks, but Jim didn't answer; he seemed more in a daze than I was and the empathy which is quite naturally seldom more than an inkling for adolescents began to deepen in me and I realized – actually realized – that my friend had suffered similar terrors to my own, that maybe they all had, Bogey Collins certainly with his transparent bravado of standing on a desk and singing, but maybe even Punch Ambler, maybe even the Headmaster.

We came around to a conservatory extension to the house, half brick, half glass, which again defined the setting as quite alien for me; conservatories were no more frequent in my world of homes than dressing gowns and again I thought of turning away, but the cool, shadowy atmosphere held me as in some kind of conservatory, some kind of greenhouse itself; a specimen in some roomy but lidded jar.

Jim knocked on the conservatory door and a figure appeared beyond it, garbled at first by the glass then framed by the door it opened. Mr Lassiter was smaller than I had somehow expected; generations of mining and malnutrition meant height was not a notable feature of our area; the tallest boys at the Grammar School were barely six foot. Somehow, however, I had expected Mr Lassiter to be at least the size of the Headmaster or of Torchy Walsh. Instead he was actually no more than my own height, a little less than Jim's, and quite a similar boyish build, in a grey cardigan and grey neatly pressed trousers rather like those of our school uniform; only the face gave away his greater, middle age, flecked with marks as it was and lined along the forehead and down the cheeks as if the years had begun to cross out the clear portrait of a young man. His hair was still the even brown of youth, however, parted with severe neatness, and my practised eye could see that even at this comparatively early hour and even though he was staying in, he had already used some Brylcreem on it. It was quite long into the neck also – a youthful style which was only just beginning and, with the disapproval of youth faced with inappropriate renditions of itself, I looked with distaste at the brown strands hooking out like tiny claws around the ears.

– James, he said to Jim and then with a change of tone which was unmistakable to me later, but which in that moment was rendered merely glassy *Who's this?* Jim explained who I was and although at first Mr Lassiter only moved the door of the conservatory back and forth as if he were trying to create a draught, he finally opened it fully and beckoned us both in. It was at this point I should have turned away. Given such an ambiguous welcome, why would I go on into an alien, brooding mansion of a place? But then there was nothing but death and destruction waiting outside, although in truth I followed Jim less from this logic than as one prisoner might follow another.

– Brought your friend. Well, welcome friend! said Mr Lassiter as we went through into a kitchen, and then he turned towards me: *A new brother!* Joining us on the great day. The great day which has finally dawned! I avoided his eyes although they soon went from seeking any contact with mine and on to Jim, who seemed more dazed than ever, even as if he were in some kind of trance. *As we always knew it would,*

James! A smile came as another line to the little man's face and as he glanced again at me I looked away and around the kitchen, which, like the exterior of the house, had nothing but the alien trappings of the middle classes: a thick wooden table with no cloth and long expanses of wooden-fronted cupboards above and below a gleaming sink with taps which had thick, faintly jewelled glass handles.

– And is your friend in the same year as you? The man seemed keen to elicit a verbal response from Jim and I did nothing but nod as Jim gave the answer for me. Mr Lassiter glanced quickly again at me. So, we should be getting ourselves ready, he said, making an effort it seemed to gather himself into a more habitual manner; I did manage this perception; he was clearly used to being listened to, in that setting at least, even followed, and Jim and I followed him across the kitchen with Jim's own trance-like motion drawing me on as the invisible strings of adolescence will. There was a glimpse of a darkened sitting room and then we went through another door and down some concrete steps into a brightly lit cellar, sweetly musty as if dampness and scent had been mixed, vaguely reminiscent of the detergent my mother used. Unreality sounded for me then like some distant thunder and there was a strangeness as if there had been snow outside so heavy it had closed the world into one house and then one room. *What was I doing here?* The answer seemed no more real than the setting itself, the supposed hard truth outside no more than a tasteless trick to place me in this still stranger mixture of immediacy and dream.

When we were all at the foot of the steps, Mr Lassiter pointed at a pile of metal panels stacked against the wall. Those go on the door when we have settled in, he said and then swept his pointing finger all around the white ceiling of the cellar.

– That's plastered. But above it is all stone, all stone ... I followed the arc of his finger ... The light is from upstairs ... he indicated the two illuminated circles almost flush with the ceiling ... But when it becomes necessary – his finger fell to one corner where a patterned rug covered some kind of box – there is the generator.

I looked from this machine to the furnishings: a table with crossed struts which probably meant it could be collapsed and two sturdier chairs on either side; there was a black book in its centre and beyond it two canvas camp beds with neat piles of blankets on them. There were also a number of plywood packing cases, some of which had still more blankets on them. Mr Lassiter, perhaps noting my examination of all this, said – We have all we need. Then he turned again to Jim. – *Do you not feel joyous?* The absence of abbreviation in his question spoke of theatre or of church to me and although Jim nodded, he did not seem to me to be feeling any such thing. Mr Lassiter took a step towards him, before turning suddenly to me and I could hear, I thought, the distant strangled irritation I had heard before in adults as they transmuted some mood into instructions or questions.

– Do you know what the Apocalypse is? he asked, and I said that I did, that it signified the end of the world.

– The end of the world *as we know it* – he gave this as some kind of correction. – And do you know what eschatology is?

This I admitted I didn't know.

– Well that is the study of final things. It comes from the Greek for 'last', for last things.

I nodded as at a teacher and then flinched back a little as the man took a step towards me. *Apocalyptic eschatology*, he said, the first word of which my mind converted to 'apoplectic', the meaning of which I did know, which I had used more than once in essays as I liked its popping sound; although as the second word of the phrase brought 'chat', the strangeness of the whole situation began to be tinged with a certain nonsense – you could not at once be 'apoplectic' and 'chatting' – and this had its impact on the whole setting, and although I still avoided the older man's eyes I felt myself becoming a little more solid and conscious, as if the nonsense might spread still further, perhaps into the Apocalypse itself. This is the way the world ends, with no more than a pop. And with this there was nothing sonorous for me in what Mr Lassiter went on to say, even more so as I felt sonority was his intention.

– There is really only one true apocalypse in the New Testament, he said and pointed at the book on the table, and the absurd neologism 'apopalypse' came popping in my mind, and when he

21

said – That written by the prophet John – I heard it as poppet John. *The Revelations!* He pointed again at the book on the table.

– Written in John's own name! There is only one other written by a prophet under his own name and that is the Shepherd of Hermas.

I actually met the man's eyes then and I knew he could see the unbeliever in me, perhaps even the nonsense popping in my head, and he turned abruptly back to Jim. We will see now the truth of those revelations, James, he said. The truth of those prophecies.We will see at last the lie, the emptiness of the Trinity!

Did this refer to me? I wondered, and to the unwelcome threesome I had made, when the man had only been expecting my friend? And where, I wondered, were all the other Christadelphians? The nonsense became strangeness again, flooding out and around a litany of spoken words and unspoken thoughts, and more chasms opened, more strange settings and threats half known and unknown. – *We will see all this now, James* – the man lifted his hand to Jim's shoulder as if to wake him and then he moved his older face almost to Jim's neck and his voice softened.

– *We will see the truth of the One God as our own John Thomas has predicted* –

The flooding in my head stopped abruptly with this and the bubbling and the popping solidified it seemed into clarity. Mr Lassiter was transmuting: the clawlike hair strands were in motion, the lines of his face shaping up into what when it turned to me would be the face of a fiend. I had read some D. H. Lawrence other than *Lady Chatterley* and I knew what *John Thomas* meant. *I'm off!* I said and I turned back up the concrete steps, pulling on the strap of my satchel as if to assist me in the climb. My movement seemed to bring Jim out of his trance. *Where are you going?!* I heard him call after me as I quickly retraced our steps through the kitchen and the conservatory and along down the side of the house. This was my escape it seemed then. No care or brotherhood could save me if they involved anything really different and my spirit called out to the everyday as if to some deity.

– *Wait! Wait on.* As I reached the big double gates I realized Jim had come after me and I turned to him, and I also saw (although

I wondered later if my melodramatic mind had actually created this) a curtain lifting at the front of the house and the face of Mr Lassiter appearing. Only years later did I consider how accurate or not my fearful teenage perception had been in those terrified times. In those moments I was moved by quite simple, quite learned reactions and I had soon gone down Beancroft and out onto Smawthorne Lane. Looking back then I saw Jim was still coming after me and I paused to let him catch up.

– That bloke! I said as he did so. *I mean … that bloke!* But Jim closed his eyes and gesticulated that he didn't want to hear anything more. We're going to be really late, he said, seeming less in a dream now, and as we hurried on I looked at my watch and reckoned we would only miss form time and assembly.

– We'll get there for first lesson, I said and Jim nodded agreement. I also added the reassurance, although of course I knew Jim himself would be well aware of it, that it was three lates before you got a detention.

Johnny Will

(*Pat Boone 1961*)

Kershaw Avenue was the worst of the streets in which I did my collecting, worse than Park Drive, which for all its fancy-sounding name was also bad. It was certainly worse than Crewe Road or Sheepwalk. The best in fact was Gallows Hill which, despite the echo of black and solemn retribution, had better houses, none of which was council owned. I didn't mind that part of my route; it was on the periphery of Fryston Woods and there were pleasant gardens to walk through and people who usually paid what was owed; there were a couple of addresses with folk who occasionally questioned the amount, as if they themselves kept records, but in these few instances both I and Stevo presumed the Gallows residents were right and so we simply took their word. This would never have happened on Kershaw: if any query or alternative amount was offered we presumed it was a fiddle. One Gallows resident had once given me more than I had in my collection book, saying we had clearly forgotten he had now begun to take a weekly magazine. This would not have happened on Kershaw; there they would simply have kept quiet if they were asked for less than expected and then watched me go with the suppressed grin of the sneaky winner. More likely on Kershaw was that they wouldn't pay at all, alleging the newspapers had never arrived, or – as they were far from being all dishonest – that they would pay the following week. Or they would attempt to pay part of the total, which negotiation Stevo specifically forbade me to enter into saying it made a complete linnet of his books (Stevo employed this word regularly as a catch-all term for a mess or for a foolish person and I never found out why; it made no sense and seemed to have no derivation from or assonance with any other term for such matters, nor to my knowledge did anyone else use it this way, or use it at all; specific knowledge of any species was not a characteristic of our area). Others on Kershaw would simply not answer the door; there were no radios suddenly switched off or a hushed silence heard through the letter box as might happen with the council rent collectors; this after all was only the weekly collection for the daily newspapers (no-one took magazines on Kershaw) so there was no need of deep-seated evasion; on the other hand if even a shilling or so could be saved or its payment deferred, so much the better.

Worst of all, of course, were the houses of the very worst families, the Deans or the Harwoods, where a gorilla of a man or woman would open the door to the knock and give out a territorial challenge to anyone, particularly anyone asking for money. Gordon Dean himself might appear, always in a singlet vest, his big face twitching and his muscles and his stomach rippling and bulging as if the violence had already started somewhere within him. And this was if you got through the ragged guard of children and animals who inhabited the yards and who might throw an old wheel at you. The Harwoods had a particularly fierce hound, which after a visit from the police, was permanently chained to a metal pole beside its kennel, but its menacing bark, its staring eyes and the slimy leathery mouth of a face stretched around bared teeth were still enough to dissuade a visitor. I only occasionally ventured to the doors of the Harwoods or the Deans (and this only under duress from Stevo) and the delivery boys began to throw the newspapers as far as they could up the yard in the style of American movies, even though Margaret Dean appeared at Stevo's shop, made up heavily for the outing and fuming like a gas cylinder, to complain about the practice. Stevo took her on well, we all agreed on it, and mentioned non-payment and threatened to discontinue deliveries altogether, a few days after which, Kevin, the Dimmer Dean as he was known, turned up at the shop with a lump sum. Stevo was quite fearless in matters of business. A sixpence was a sixpence to him and a penny a sixth of that, and he would probably have faced death, certainly a beating or a dog, to defend any coin which was rightfully his.

So Kershaw was hardly my favourite part of the collection route. The Avenue itself was reasonably paved and tarmacked, unlike Hillcrest Avenue, which led off from Gallows Hill and which the better-off residents of the big detached houses there kept unmade to dissuade access, and which in winter could become something of a quagmire. Nor were the houses on Kershaw slums; they were not even the old lines of terraces which could be found in Castleford; many of them were semi-detached and those which did run into three always had a ginnel to separate the third. And they were all brick and pebble dash, there was nothing of the corrugated metal or the thin wood of the post-war prefabs still standing in Ferry Fryston (and which would stand for a number of years to come); they all had space for gardens and yards. And yet, in one way or another, the residents had rendered it all at worst squalid and at best unkempt: there were disabled prams, broken chairs and occasionally a larger piece of discarded furniture in the garden yards, litter which had become as embedded as stones and rusting ill-defined relics of some brief and long gone burst of activity – a broken go-cart or half a bike – which stood as more organized folk might stand garden gnomes or water features. A smashed Santa Claus had once remained as a pitiful centrepiece in the front garden of one Kershaw address for almost a year, with dandelions climbing over the faded red of the costume and the shattered sack of presents.

Also, the vicious circle of notoriety had done its work and anyone with even the faintest of aspirations would turn down the offer of a council house on Kershaw and might well receive an understanding nod from the council official making that offer. It was generations before anything like substance abuse put its confused, sharp edge on any such area and there was nothing of the cramped hovels of Dickensian London, but the Avenue had the bedraggled mournfulness of a working class which was only half working and that half at grinding work it detested. The atmosphere was at once tough and listless, of people who were not past caring, but who had never been raised or induced to care to any consistent effect. There were none (or at least there seemed to be none) there who had developed a consciousness and even a pride in their underclass and perhaps also in their dwellings, as the very few who did attempt to maintain their garden or their fences or hedges soon succumbed to the prevailing atmosphere. Or they left.

So, although I was very much a council house boy myself and even the child of a broken home, which was still unusual and still stigmatized at the time, I followed my mother's lead and that of all those on my own street in looking down on Kershaw and its residents and I never went down it except for the professional obligation of the weekly newspaper collection, and its name sounded of nothing but lowliness to me. This changed, however, in the late March of 1962 when I first saw April McPhilomey.

The family was new to the Avenue. *Geordies*, said Stevo. Down from Newcastle so the father could work at Wheldale pit – Seem all right, he added, which was high praise from him – The fella came in. Accent and that, but he seemed all right. *Daily Mirror.* I paid no particular attention, but then on my first visit to the address, collection book in hand, *she* opened the door to me and Kershaw was suddenly and in one way or another immutably transformed, both its name and its setting.

– Papers, I said and she smiled, illuminated not just by the light in the little hallway but by the drizzling greyness of the early evening which threw its own faint gleam inwards. I always made my collection early evening on a Friday, around half six or seven, a time, said Stevo correctly, when you could be fairly sure people were back from whatever they did during the day, but before they had begun their tea and definitely before they had gone out again for the Friday night. That day was also still pay day for most and that pay in cash, and so it was the time to catch them, when one and six or two bob or whatever it was would seem less than it did on Monday and certainly than it would on Wednesday or Thursday.

– Newspapers, I elaborated awkwardly, seeing a faintly quizzical expression appear. I'm collecting newspaper money. And my heart flew into her features, into the shapely lips and the pronounced cheekbones and eyes which fluttered like birds themselves. Also,

I noted approvingly, there was no beehive to her hair such as my most recent girlfriend had erected and over which we had fallen out. April's hair simply fell like flat gold on either side of her face and shone as if crowned by the light above her and the faint rainbows being thrown inwards. *Dad!* she called, which word from her lips was just another bird rising. There was nothing loud or harsh to her voice, as was usually the case on Kershaw, and when she added – Somebody here for newspaper money – I heard the lilt of the unusual accent, decorating these two last words which may be amongst the hardest words to beautify – and it was another indication of the exotic and a reminder that even on a journey through a land laid waste you may come upon a shrine.

As her father came into the hallway, she turned away and this time the image for me was of a bell; the full blue skirt (in my memory it was blue) swayed like a bell as she turned and the hand she waved towards me had in its movement the very sound of that bell, a pure peal of femininity. – *Newspapers* – I bumbled through my exchange with the father, who as Stevo had said, seemed all right, but around and beyond him I saw nothing but the traces of the daughter who had flown, who had pealed, away and I went back out onto Kershaw with nothing but music in me. ''*Til I Kissed You*' in particular.

My group allowed the Everly Brothers into the limited canon of what should be listened to. The Everlies had begun in the fifties; they attempted something like rock from time to time and their quiffs were very acceptable renditions of the one worn by Elvis himself. Although increasingly even Elvis was not immune from the purists amongst my group; his films had begun to confuse the issue, the black and white purity of 'Jailhouse Rock' and 'King Creole' had given way to colour and it was certainly Brian Hopper's opinion that a sell-out was under way and that those of us who were truly rock should focus more on Eddie Cochrane, Gene Vincent or Jerry Lee Lewis. These, he said, were the truth and the fact that the first of them was already dead meant nothing more than that he had gone the full distance down the rock road. I had to admit to being ambiguous and confused even before that Friday as part of me agreed with Spike Ellis who said Hopper the Bopper, as he tried to get himself known, and his great friend Beesley were just old Teds trying to hang on to something which was passing or past; they still wore beetle crushers where Spike had begun to sport a pair of winkle pickers. I hung along, not really taking sides, but even before April I had to admit to a secret and guilty liking for Tab Hunter's old 'Young Love'. (Hopper was even dismissive of Buddy Holly's slowest, sweetest songs.) And then I found out that the McPhilomey girl on Kershaw was called April and this it seemed sealed my transition, my movement away from the simple black-and-white beat to an equally simple but emotionally more colourful world. 'April Love' came, by Pat Boone, the very mention of whose name would have had Hopper gurgling the smoker's cough of a dismissive laugh he had worked so hard at cultivating. In fact the name might well have been the one which aroused most bile throughout the core of my old group; Como and Crosby could be consigned to earlier generations, but Boone, though older than us, was younger than them and from time to time he tried to launch himself at more insistent rhythms with an embarrassment akin to seeing old people in leather. And yet it was his song which came into my head and my heart as that April of '62 began and as I thought of April McPhilomey. Too much of a coincidence it all seemed to my young heart; the fates themselves drawing the strands from words and sounds, from times and places, into one perfect knot.

Those fates then continued their work: they gave me a first disappointment as should be the case with any love story: April did not answer the door when I turned up the following Friday for the newspaper money, my whole week having been devoted to my new beginning, my new music, all wrapped and knotted around her name; but then the following Sunday, with the kindly expression of amused gods, those fates put April directly into my path. She was outside Stevo's shop, which was just up from Kershaw and to which I had been sent on an errand for my mother as the only shop open on Sunday. There she was, standing with two other girls, one of whom I recognized from the top of my street. These two were looking at something in a magazine they had just bought and April, I felt, quite deliberately stepped away from them and towards me.

– You collect the newspaper money don't you? she said and I said yes I did, holding myself steady, as if all the dreaming and musings and songs of the days since my first sight of her had been a rehearsal, as if all that cloudiness was suddenly being brought into shape and then into a point, as moisture comes into a drop. The gods and fates of love were smiling down on me it seemed, moving their pieces, offering their phrases as they do when they create destiny. *Musical Express* they had me say, indicating the folded paper in her hand, as if her hair, which though darker in daylight was still flaxen gold, as if her lips and cheeks and fluttering eyes were not my real concern, as if her flowered dress and pale cardigan were not the glades of paradise itself. *Talk music* whispered the gods and again it seemed that all the weeks and months and years I had devoted to this were no more than appropriate preparation.

– What's Number One? I asked, although I knew and she smiled real interest and we talked about the charts as the April breeze of the Sunday morning lifted tiny wisps of the flaxen gold and salved the heat on my burning cheeks. The other two girls seemed to have been moved motionlessly to one side and it was only after a time I glimpsed one of them slyly looking. They went to the Modern School in Castleford, whilst I was at the local Seniors, and so although I knew them by sight, I didn't know their names.

– Are you at the Modern? I asked April after seeing this sly look from the friend, although still the other two came no closer as if, as pawns of the gods, they were allowing my great encounter its space. April said she was: she had come down from Newcastle with her family and she had just started at the Modern. A vague shadow passed through the bright moment for me as I knew there was some opinion that Airedale Senior School was lesser than the Modern and of course I did not want to seem lesser. I went back to the safer ground of pop music.

– The one I really like is Lance Fortune, April said then. Do you know 'Be Mine'?

I had heard the song I said and I dissembled liking it. For all I knew, I did. Or at least the newness in me would, the fresh and modern spring of richness and colour.

30

– He's on in Wakefield next Saturday, April glanced at her friends as if in confirmation of the information she was giving. Next Saturday. I nodded as if I already knew and then the gods it seemed gave me the words and I said I would take her if she liked and her face fluttered beautifully open. – *Really*?! Of course, I said. If she really wanted to go, and it was as if her two companions had been slid still further off, although I did notice them huddling briefly and then as they came out of that huddle I glimpsed that they were grinning. But this would be the standard behaviour of anyone caught on the edge of such arrangements. Can you get tickets? asked April and I nodded another of course, feeling the strength of destiny; it would be just another movement of the gods, just another tick of their inevitable clock, and so it was arranged. April and I had a date for the following Saturday and I turned into Stevo's as happy as I had ever been and all the trappings of Stevenson's Newsagents, all the newspapers and the magazines, all the lines of cigarette packets and the jars of spice, were suffused with this happiness. Even Stevo himself, hunched in his usual posture at the counter, was briefly a part, even his lumpen face with its greying tash and the thickly rimmed spectacles which had been repaired on one side with a strip of Elastoplast, even these seemed elevated, although he soon re-established his earthlier presence by cataloguing the money still owed after my last collection and I wondered how anyone could care about money at such a time.

It was money, however, which became my own preoccupation in the days which followed. Lance Fortune was indeed on in Wakefield the coming Saturday evening. I even saw a poster for the show, to which I would previously have paid no attention. Tickets it said were available from the Wakefield theatre itself but also from the Kiosk in Castleford and they were seven and six each, which posed me a problem (the slimy coin underside of almost every realized dream): two tickets would cost fifteen shillings (which seemed excessive; Wee Willie Harris had performed at the Kiosk for half a crown on the door). There would be the bus fare to Wakefield and a few more pence at least for pop or whatever sweetmeat my new love desired. I calculated that my collector's wage, plus the half a crown pocket money I also received on Friday, would be enough for the incidentals, but the fifteen shillings ticket money was another matter altogether and another and far less lovely Pat Boone song pushed its way into my head, a trite, novelty number with some lament about having to get enough money to take a sweetheart to a dance after an ultimatum from that sweetheart that if the singer couldn't take her then somebody called Johnny would. It was a daft little song, but it ate into 'April Love' as woodworm might eat into a glorious devotional panel or as lice might crawl in golden hair. *That Johnny, that no-good Johnny* – It helped that Sam Carr had worked out a comic rendition of it which played on our usage of the name as a colloquialism for a prophylactic, but there was no getting around the reality which faced me. I had to get that money and get it right away.

I offered my old leather jacket for sale, but even at ten reduced to seven and then to five shillings, I found no takers; the times were moving on and it would be years before leather, even the poor, padded affair which was my jacket, made a reappearance as desirable wear. I also tried to sell some other things, a few 45s and a torch, but again there were no takers and even if there had been, the sum garnered would have been nothing close to what I needed. Nor could I approach my mother or my so-called uncle (there was a growing tension between him and me anyway and what money he had he mostly spent on beer and betting). My mother herself was out of the question; I was increasingly looking forward to the day when I could leave school and earn a proper wage so I could alleviate some of the strain which was more and more evident in her face. It had even become quite hard to take the pocket money from her, although I did. More than ever before, I began to think of having enough in my pockets so all the women of my life might live in ease, even luxury, and in my gift. Without doubt, other forces were beginning to shift and grow in me alongside the sense of musical alteration and it was hard to tell how far these were the movements of nature and how far they were those which mere events and environments make. They were all focussed in that week, however, as into a moment of conception or death. I had to get that brass.

My friends had no more funds or access to funds than I had and even if they had – as with the friends of Boone's song – they would probably have said no and I would have needed a number of loans anyway for such an amount. And so it became clear (as an early dark answer can, rejected for its darkness but then hanging in the background, watching other answers come and go like a grinning devil who already knows the outcome), there was only one real option: there was only one time when I had in my possession the necessary amount and this was after my collection round. I usually returned with as much as five pounds to Stevo's shop. Approaching Stevo himself had hardly featured in my thoughts: had I asked him for a loan he would have stared at me as if I had asked for the moon, as if I had come from the moon, and the request might even endanger my job, which was a privileged post, a position of trust, a cut above the delivery boys, and faced with any such request Stevo might begin to wonder whether his trust in me was misplaced; and for reasons I couldn't really define, I did not want him thinking that. Ernie Stevenson could hardly be described as an attractive or even a sympathetic man, but he was straight and for all the hardship in our area, I had been brought up to respect this. *And yet what choice did I have?* I began the rationalizations of every crook and betrayer since the beginning of civilization: the amount was a drop in Stevo's ocean, I was underpaid for what I did, my background was poor, my peers uncaring and besides, this was a matter of the heart and God Himself knows how many crimes and betrayals have been assigned to the heart.

I closed off the internal debates and moved to the how. I thought of saying I had lost the collection bag, or better that I had had it stolen and I even toyed with bringing Spike into the scheme, having him put on his balaclava and grab my collection somewhere where we could have witnesses and could make a great show of the incident. We could then share the money. I soon discounted this; Spike, though wild and immoral enough to participate in such a scheme (he had already been up in juvenile court), was, by dint of those same qualities, untrustworthy. Also I had seen a number of films and telly pieces where the weakness of the criminal scheme had been in the number of participants. Mine, I concluded, must be a solo affair, which conclusion increased the sense of isolation and the weight of the guilt and I wondered whether those accomplices and gangs had not been solitary, not only because the scheme needed more than one, but because this weight itself is shared.

There was no other way, however, and that Friday before Lance Fortune on the Saturday, as I left Gallows Hill, where I was most likely to receive a note, I transferred one of ten shillings from my collection bag into my trouser pocket where I had already dropped six sixpences and then I moved the whole hoard into the still more secret recesses of my mac, where it all burned like tiny cinders. My final scheme was simple: I would just not tick payment on a cross section of people who had actually paid, so the amount I gave to Stevo was accurate as to what it was in the book, but short in actuality. And I chose this cross section from people who normally paid, to whom Stevo would give at least another week of grace and credit. Somewhere in my fevered and focussed mind this offered me the possibility of replacing the money in the next week, or in the next fortnight, making the matter right: the embezzler's myth – *it was a temporary matter, a secret loan, no theft.* And yet as I walked from Gallows Hill along the edge of Fryston Woods, the darkening branches waved at me like fingers of accusation or spread thick and firm like gibbets, and the wood beckoned like the unlit caverns of all banditry. Not for nothing is the myth of the Greenwood made sunny and hearty and not the sodden briar it undoubtedly was; not for nothing do outlaw validations come like carousing encouragements – *people deserve my trickery, my cleverness in itself renders my crime worthy, these are the times and everyone is doing it* – all of it was Fryston Wood, trying as such woods have in times ancient and modern to render the poor child of honesty lost.

I tried to find some consolation in the music in my head, but by the time I had arrived back at Stevo's nothing was coming, as if the music itself needed the space of a clear conscience. I was even trembling and I sought to hide this in movements which were more sudden than usual and then a bout of false coughing, and then I saw I was actually wringing my hands and I pulled them apart and brought one up to bang at my chest for the coughing and buried another in the deep pocket of the mac, although there it touched the cinders of my sin and the hand bounced back out again as if burned.

– You all right? asked Stevo, looking over his spectacles and I cleared my throat and shook my head – Got a cold coming I think – at which he gave his habitual sniff at young people. – You should wear something on your head when you're out. You kids never have nothing on your heads. You want a cap or something on your head, you linnet! I nodded nervous agreement and as he turned his back I stared at the honest brown of his working man's smock.

I went towards Kershaw as soon as I had left the shop, needing to see the prize for which I had perjured my soul, the meaning the gods had given which was greater than any value systems transient society erects. I went past the Deans' house and the Harwoods', which had one of the new panda police cars outside it, causing my stomach to leap and the stolen note and coins to burn in my pocket as if that burning might show through. I hurried on to the McPhilomeys' and knocked on the door, which was opened by a rounded, quite jolly looking woman with curlers in her hair. I asked if April was in and she actually chuckled at me as if I had said something funny and then she called out – *April!* – keeping the chuckle in her voice, which I might otherwise have found disconcerting, but dark and fugitive as I was, it seemed to help to have someone lighten the mood. And then there was April, her hair tied back in a pony tail, but still a vision.

– All right, Mum, she said as the woman moved away only slowly, shaking her head as if she were still savouring a joke, and I noted April's use of the word 'Mum' rather than 'Mam' as would have been the norm in our streets, and this in itself spoke of greater things and my heart fluttered with the fluttering eyes which briefly met mine. So, tomorrow, I said. We can get the Wakefield bus from the top of Sheepwalk … I went into the speech I had rehearsed for the arrangements (these were the days when only a few in our area had telephones). There's a bus comes up from the Magnet about six … April was resting both her hands on the door and even as I was speaking I could sense a certain unease in her and the door

35

was never fully opened and her eyes went down and the dark wood closed in and the birds came falling from the skies.

– I didn't think you'd got tickets, she said and I shook my head as if against some hood those dark forces were trying to force over it.

– Well, I haven't. But I've got the money. We can get in on the door.

Her eyes came up then and for the first time since I had first seen her they were caged.

– What it is, she said and leaned her head into the thick edge of the door. – What it is, is I didn't think you'd got tickets and, well, another friend has got some. He's already got some tickets and so I said I would go with him. I didn't think you'd got tickets.

– I haven't, I repeated as if it were some kind of incantation against the dark. – But I have got the money.

She leaned still more heavily into the door then to bring it partially closed.

– But he's already got tickets and so I said I would go with him.

– Right, I said. *Right.* There was still enough of the brooding rocker in me, the leather-coated rebel, careless of girls, for me to turn on my heel, and as I turned I felt the door quickly close behind me as a blow that knocked me senselessly along the path and out through the gate, which I left open.

I walked along Kershaw then with as much challenge in my gait as I had ever shown on the Avenue, and had the little group of kids I went past offered me any opportunity I might have gone into them with the blind fury of a Samson. I looked at the Harwoods' dog, quiet for once and gnawing on some meatless bone, and I looked around for something to throw at it. Another layer of darkness rolled down then and I thought of the money I had stolen and all for nothing and a panic came and I wondered if I should hurry back to Stevo's and say I had just found some extra collection money in the pocket of my mac and I needed the collection book again so I could cross off the payments which had been made, but which for some reason I had forgotten to indicate.

I set off in the direction of the shop, but then thought better of it: hard and straight as he was, Ernie Stevenson would see straight through me. He would see the crime and he would see the weakness of someone unable to see that crime through and he would feel contempt for both. So, instead I brought my turmoil into bitterness. *Cow!* I spat. *Tart!* And then *Gold digger!* This was how she coloured her hair – with the gold from the pockets of men! *The hell with her and her Lance Fortune!*

I did put the matter of the collection money right in the following week; only briefly did I think of keeping the money anyway as a gesture against the fates and against her and then I found out she was not called April at all, but Avril and she had made the change herself and insisted on it with her friends and family because she disliked Avril and this allowed me to sneer at her vanity as was the manner of our area. Nor did I see her again much; only a few months later I heard she had moved to live with relatives somewhere further down south, where she might have more opportunities. *Yes – of gold digging!* I thought privately and bitterly and allowed no dialogue as to why she should not use her looks as men might use their strength. *She was a stuck-up cow!* was my comment in the brief exchange I took part in with regard to her leaving. *She thought she was too good for round here!* And there was some agreement, although as someone else remarked you couldn't really blame her for wanting to get out of Kershaw. And perhaps at that point, for all my bitterness (which extended to a denigration worthy of Hopper the Bopper of anything by Pat Boone), there were some ill-defined and unexpressed thoughts in me as to the links between aspiration and manipulation, the dark roots of crime and the sad sameness of any betrayal.

A Scottish Soldier

(*Andy Stewart 1961*)

Jean stared out at the view, the panorama as they called it in the cinema, but sweeping and panoramic as the view was, she could not bring up those cinema titles over it as she had done as a girl and as a younger woman, with her name in the same gleaming letters as the title. Sometimes she had simply added her name to the real names. Sometimes she had created others (mostly composites of real stars' names) to go with hers above an imaginary title, although she knew her imagination was not good enough to think of any titles to match the best of the real ones: *Gone with the Wind* or *Written on the Wind*. 'The Wind on the Water' or 'Over the Hills' had been typical of her efforts and she knew they were poor and more often she had simply let the title blur illegibly. She needed their sweeping music also as she had no capacity for making up any tunes of her own. One of the best openings, she thought, had been *The River of No Return* with Robert Mitchum, whom she liked, and Marilyn Monroe of course, and the other film with Alan Ladd riding down through grassy hills to a ranch which had mountains in the distance. *The Big Country* had wonderful music, but its opening had disappointed her, focusing on galloping horses rather than the sweeping country of the title as it surely should have done.

It was strange that many of her favourite openings had been of cowboy films as she didn't particularly like cowboy films or films with any kind of fighting in them. Apart from anything else none of the fighting was true to life; Jean had seen men fighting and there was nothing of the clear dance of clean blows shown in films: in real life it is more a swirl or a stalemate of wrestling and grappling, a mess of parries and butts and kicking and swearing. One of her earliest memories was of her father and his brother falling upon each other and her mother screaming and clawing at their heaving unity. She had peeped through the window then as the two men rolled outside and seen her father getting on top, hissing and spitting at the form beneath him, slapping and strangling at it until next door's and some others came and blocked her view. Sometimes if there was fighting in films she just closed her eyes. Len had noticed her doing this in one of their earliest dates at the Picture House and whispered:

– What are you shutting your eyes for? This is the best bit!

Why men were excited and interested and even comfortable watching fighting and uninterested and uncomfortable watching a kiss was a mystery to Jean. Just their nature, she supposed, and she gave it as little thought as she gave to any such matters, although she recognized that, as Alice had said, not all men were like the men she had grown up with, the men of her family and the man she, Jean, had married.

– That's why you married him, her daughter who was very clever had said, because he was just like them … although the more detailed explanation Alice then went into had been difficult to follow and Jean's mind had wandered rather as it did at such times, as it had used to wander at school. Her daughter would undoubtedly be right, she thought: unlike her, Alice had listened attentively and done well at school and then even gone on to university in Manchester. Certainly Jean herself could not offer any explanation as to why she had married Len. He looked a little like Alan Ladd perhaps; he had asked her and then the whole system which moves such things had been activated and she had gone along with it. She had never expected anything of films and their titles in her real life.

She had not expected Len to turn out as violent as he had, however. He had seemed attentive and when he started at the steel works and Alice was born, their lives seemed to be taking the appropriate shape. There was even a possibility he might be made a supervisor and so would be able to work just days and not shifts. Jean could not remember anyone discouraging or even questioning the marriage, although there were some signs even when they were courting: Len had once turned up for a date with blood crusted under his nose and she had heard of him fighting, and once he had got hold of someone who had spoken to her, not knowing she was with him. Again she had put all this down to natural male behaviour and in truth had it been otherwise her friends and what remained of her family might have looked askance at him. Len's favourite film star was John Wayne, whom Jean herself didn't particularly like. He was not good looking like Tyrone Power or Robert Taylor and he was always ordering everybody about. And he was usually in cowboy films.

She stared across the rippling water, which on that day was less attractive than it was when the sun shone; the sails of the many little boats were less colourful and the movements of the boats themselves seemed more sluggish and aimless. The bigger green-and-yellow ferry took its line as purposefully as ever, but the wake it left had a brownish tinge as if the boat were ploughing through soil, not cleaving blue water and leaving white foam behind. There could be nothing for Jean of the old film panoramas that day, nothing of Castleford Park's hill which she had always gone to, looking out over the spread of houses to the fields of Ledston and Ledsham. There were the winding wheels of the pit heads of course and the distant egg cups of the power stations, but there were more fields and hills than people who didn't know mining areas might think and the River Aire could glitter and the fields and trees of Fairburn beyond it could be varied and vivid greens. It was the spot where she had dreamt the most. She had even stood there with Alice as a baby in her pram and then on a few occasions when her daughter was a little girl, although the child had impinged on the dream as children will, calling for more practical applications, and Jean had thought, without ever cohering the thought, that her clever child might have more opportunity to make a real film of her life, to make the dream into a reality as they say, although any thoughts as to the consequences or the logic of this were even more incoherent. Park Hill was the spot of her solitary, her true panoramas, linked to girlhood and youth of course, but even as a fully grown woman she had gone there; she had even gone there on the day after the incident which had marked the last eleven months of her life and which had brought her here, as far away as she could be, so far away that if she went any further she would be going back. Alice had told her this as if it were an advantage, as if she were as far removed from her troubles now as she could be, and again Jean accepted that her clever and strong-willed daughter was probably right.

She shifted on the stony seat as it and the grey reality of the day worked to sharpen the specific recollection. It was always there anyway, like some physical characteristic which has to be accepted, a deformity which needs strength and practice to be accommodated, and so she made no attempt to ward it off. Len had slapped her that day, just before he went out to the pub. She had complained about the clothes he had left piled on one of the good chairs and he had slapped her. *How difficult was it just to carry the clothes to the basket in the bathroom?* She had not even asked this and on another occasion he might simply have shrugged at her, but that morning he was just that way out and she had received a slap across the face for her tone. It was nothing to what he had inflicted on her before: he had cuffed her around the head, kicked her on the legs and in the back and on the backside and once grabbed her by the throat as her own father had grabbed his own brother, spitting the same fury. But the belt had been his favourite, the leather belt he slid out from his trousers and looped and flogged at her whilst she huddled away from it; he liked using the belt, it even excited him; Jean had heard of such things although she had never understood them, but once as she peeped out from under her protecting arms she saw the bulge she had come to feel disgusted by was appearing, and on another occasion he kept the belt in his hand but forced her down and forced himself on her. She had hated him then more than she had ever done before. Before this there had been at least a vague feeling in her that such outbursts, sporadic as they were, were the inevitable manner of things. The grinding shifts Len worked and the necessary money he brought in gave him an entitlement which she had to accept and to suffer just as she accepted and suffered the night-times. The attentiveness of their courting days was soon gone and any softer gesture was offered as he might offer a gift and she was grateful for them, but the gratitude itself became another layer of hatred, more subtle and finally more potent, and by the time their daughter had grown and left and they were alone together in the house in Three Lane Ends and the attacks were far more casual, her hatred was not an open wound but something closed over, festering and seething and waiting its moment of release. The slap to the face that morning had brought this moment. It had been nothing; Len undoubtedly thought so and what had become mechanical in Jean would have thought so too, but it was as if that flicking hand had taken away the covering and broken the mechanism.

–*I'll drop my clothes where I bloody well like!* he shouted and Jean stood back, not even lifting a hand to her stinging cheek, and watched him hitching up his trousers and then his shoulders as he did. He would have gone as a sailor during the war, he said, if he had not been drawn out as a Bevan Boy, and from time to time she saw a sailor's walk in him; and in their early years she had felt sympathy for him shut up as he was in that warehouse and doing those shifts and the necessary overtime, dreaming of his own seascape, his own panorama. For a time she felt for his disappointments and his frustrations, but even before Alice explained it far more clearly, she had recognized how she had become the soft and proximate target for all these frustrations. Nor had she provided him with a boy which he could be proud of himself about (and then, as Alice also said, a boy he would no doubt have been further frustrated and then irritated by and belt as his own father had belted him). In the confines of the thin terrace, there was only his wife. Len had never really struck his daughter; there had been the occasional prods and cuffs, but no real blows, for which Jean was again ambiguously grateful, and Len was never verbally capable enough to take Alice on as she grew. *You just hit things to try and make them simpler!* the adolescent daughter had once said to her father and even then Jean remembered Len glancing angrily at her for any trace of agreement or any participation in this victory of a female voice. In the end he had quietly surrendered and even took to boasting about the achievements of his only child. So there was only Jean to belt.

Jean had accepted this, just as she accepted her husband would not let her work (in those days this cast aspersions on the male breadwinner and brought still more ambiguity and complexity into the home); she could make her escapes in her head. And yet with that slap that morning it was as if one mechanism had been broken and another activated and she prepared herself as she might prepare a meal.

The poker would be her weapon. She had thought of this before, although again her imagination was not enough to see the act played out or to go beyond it to any aftermath. She would use the poker and she also knew when and where. When he came back from the Sunday lunchtime drinking he had his dinner, a Yorkshire pudding soaked in gravy and then the beef and potatoes and vegetables, and then he would sit in his chair by the fire and his head would roll back and forth and his knee would sway out. How she disliked these movements: the extremities lolling away like things which had been badly pinned on and the face drawn down by the weight of food and drink, the jowls sagging, the eyes half lidded and the damp mouth drawn open. From time to time in this state Len would continue whatever diatribe he had been conducting over the table although the words were mostly lost as he fought with sleep. Jean had tried before to get him to go to bed on those Sunday afternoons, but he considered this to be an admission of a defeat of some kind and he rolled and twitched on in the armchair by the fire until finally he dozed off, still perhaps mouthing unintelligible complaints and challenges. Sometimes, during this stage, his hand would go down to his groin, like a child, but disgust had long since outweighed any softer reaction Jean might feel. The truth was Len could never really hold his drink. Jean knew other men would not necessarily be made into this mumbling mess by three or four lunchtime pints. Others would go home to their own Sunday dinners and be revived by the food, some might even be rendered happier by the drink and then go sensibly to bed or even simply shake off the effects, other than the fattening flesh. Again, however, Jean's sympathy for a man caught in a culture of beer but with no capacity for it had been short lived and she had no understanding as to why anyone would persist with something which in his case only brought unhappiness and confrontation to the surface. Drowning cares with drink was not what occurred with her husband; there were moments, no doubt, which she hadn't seen, moments even of careless laughter; but what she saw were only those drowned or desperate things floating fully to the surface.

All this again was more thought than she gave to the matter. It was a simple act of retaliation, the blow which would finally be returned for all those she had suffered. She did not even consider whether the poker's strike would actually kill him or whether she would follow it with another. It would stop the lolling at least – she was certainly pleased at this prospect – the blow would at least have its impact on those stupid, swaying movements of the head and the knee. She was pleased also at the prospect of closing up the damp, lolling mouth and the half-lidded eyes, or of tightening them into a cry or a yelp, but other than this she had no anticipation or planning, other than knowing that when he adopted his usual position in the fireside chair she would take the poker from the companion set and as his head lolled forward and offered itself she would smack the poker down on it. She had more physical strength than she sometimes pretended to have; on a few occasions she had warded off his attacks, although she had learned that this just drew him on to greater effort and it had seemed more sensible not to offer the resistance. But she could certainly hit hard enough to cause him damage. More than once, suffering her own unworded frustration, she had brought some kitchen utensil hard down on the kitchen table or against the sink, although she had finally broken a ladle doing so and after this it had seemed sensible to show restraint or merely to mimic the blow. There would be no mimicry on that day, however. Her commitment was mechanical and real and even as Len came back into the house, trying to turn his incipient staggering into a sailor's gait, working hard with his words and his facial expressions so neither sagged completely away from him, she glanced repeatedly at the fireside utensils.

– Beef's gristly, he said. And a few lumps in the mash!

She was pleased by his complaints; there had been the odd occasion when, as a residue of some good humour in the pub, he had seemed more amenable on those Sundays and she did not want this on that day. *You've got all bloody morning*—! The rest of what he said was drowned in a slaver of gravy and Jean, who as usual had eaten earlier, felt she could get away with no response, although her silence itself sometimes set him off and she had a catalogue of stock phrases she used. He seemed particularly incoherent that day, however, and made no demands for responses, mumbling more to himself than he normally did, and she noticed his hanging lip was even more pronounced than usual; and then came a series of noisy eructations and he clutched at his stomach.

– Hard bloody carrots! he said and Jean kept on with her knitting, waiting her moment, still far more mechanical than excited, more determined than wild, and as he crossed the room from the table they set out on Sundays, and swayed for a time looking into the fire and then at his fireside chair, she stood and looked again at the poker. – It's cold as well … He was making an unusually long pause before taking to the chair and Jean wondered if he was going to take up the poker himself and stoke at the fire. He tottered backwards slightly then and hunched forward, mumbling a curse at his discomfort, and then his body stiffened a little and strained and he looked as if he were trying to break wind and she saw him glance in the direction of the lavatory and then his eyes lolling upwards as if discomfort would send him for once to bed.

– Get yourself in front of the fire, she said and he looked across at her, struggling to find something he could be harsh about even with solicitousness. *Damn carrots*, he said. *And 'taties*! And again he looked as if he were trying to let out some relieving wind, but all that came was a gurgle and he brought a closed fist tapping at his chest. To Jean's relief then he did sit down, letting his head go back at first, but then it came forward and for the first time the mechanism in her seemed to speed up and hurry her on. For the first time since she had realized what she had to do, she made some excited movements and she dropped her knitting and went across to take the poker from its set, all behind his back as she had thought she would, but even though he was not half sleeping as she had also thought, she knew she was not going to wait. There was her target and she was going to bring this metal bar down upon it. Still excited, even trembling, she lifted the poker high above her own head.

Her blow never came down, however, as at that moment Len rolled forward out of the chair, clutching at his gurgling throat as she had seen her father clutching at a throat all those years ago. Jean brought the poker slowly down and rested it and her other, empty hand on the back of Len's armchair as her husband sank fully onto the fireside rug, bringing both arms around himself as if against the cold. She made no movement towards him, but stood leaning on the back of the armchair as someone might lean on a fence to watch a beast in a field. Her husband's form tried to sway and struggle upwards and she heard him trying to say something and then gasping for breath, and then there was almost a baby's cry from him and he sank down and struggled and gurgled again as she watched until he was finally still.

She went and stood over him then and lifted the poker, ready to strike if he made another move. There was no further movement, however, although she did hear what sounded like a thin trump and then she thought she saw the faintest of shivers run through him, although this could have been the flickering light from the fire. *Len*, she said finally and pushed at his mound with her slippered foot. There was no answer and after she had stood for some time longer in a silence which was still quite thoughtless, still quite mechanical, she stepped over his inert form and replaced the poker in the fireside set.

Jean looked at her watch. She had said she would be back at the house before Alice and Graham came home from work and although she had sorted out the stations she had to use, it would still be better if she could avoid the busiest times at Circular Quay. She lifted herself from the stone seat; this was the vantage point which had been created by some early governor for his wife so she could look across the expanse of water which came out of the harbour and went on to the Pacific Ocean. It was certainly a nice spot, thought Jean, although she preferred to be higher up. But then there were places nearby which you could climb to, some lovely spots again with trees and grass; Alice had walked her to the area quite soon after her mother arrived.

– Because I know you like to sit dreaming, her daughter had said and Jean had smiled again at her cleverness. She it was who had taken charge of her life now. As soon after that Sunday afternoon as she could, Alice had come all the way home from Australia where she now lived with her husband. He seemed nice enough, thought Jean, although he had a smile which went strangely downwards and she had caught a few snippets here and there and wondered if he was wholly happy she had come to live with them. Alice had been insistent, however and as she said, given the meagre widow's benefit, and that her mother was still some years from her pension, she would have had difficulties. Jean had been unsure; it was all so far away and she could probably have found some kind of work, cleaning or something, but Alice was insistent.

– You've got rid of him, she said. Now you need to get out of this place.

So in the end Jean had gone along (strangely in a way, she thought, as Alice herself had always complained to her that she, Jean, *went along* too much). Alice had made all the arrangements, as she had for Len's funeral, even beginning some of those by telephone all the way from Australia, although the daughter hadn't wanted a last look at her father in the funeral parlour. *He was a swine!* she said when they were left alone after the cremation and the little gathering in the upstairs room of the tea shop on Temple Street, and Jean had felt the need to balance this out, if only a little.

– He didn't have much of a life, she said. Pit during the war and then shifts at—

– He didn't have to treat you the way he did! was Alice's sharp response, although the daughter had not actually known about the worst of it, and Jean shrugged.

– It was how he was brought up … And her daughter, recognizing the charity, had embraced her and for the first time since her return shed a tear, which then, quite inexplicably to Jean at that particular moment, became a flood.

Jean looked at the water lapping against the smooth rocks as she walked on. Convicts had been brought here. They had been the first people from England to look out over these waters, although in those days of course you could be sent away for very little. Would she have been sent here, she wondered, if she had actually brought the poker down, if Len had waited just another moment before he fell forward? Was that in some strange way why she was here anyway? Certainly she would not have come had it not been for her intentions that day. Had it not been for what she had been going to do, which of course nobody else knew about. Had it not been for that, she would have resisted even her daughter and stayed in Three Lane Ends. Had it not been for that Sunday she would not be here, and not because it was the day Len died, but because of what she herself had been about to do. Was it some kind of guilt? This vaguely occurred to Jean but she gave the matter no more elaboration in her mind and she never considered telling anyone, not even Alice. Although she did think that Len himself should have been sent here for what he did to her. She let such considerations fade as she usually did, on this particular occasion into the slapping of the water. Len would have liked to come here as a sailor, she thought.

She lifted her watch again and quickened her pace, looking across at the great bridge as it came fully into view. It was far more impressive than anything she had ever really seen. Part of her knew this and the same part of her could even cohere something as to how people feel attached to places simply because it is where they have grown up, where they have had their hopeful youth and its inevitable romance. After a certain age it may be that the heart is always elsewhere; Jean did not really make this conclusion, although she could not help but recognize that even this beautiful and famous harbour and the splendid bridge of which she had seen so many photographs and which was now actually in her sight, even this magnificent panorama did not bring her any dreams.

Wheels

(String-a-Longs 1961)

There were four young men in the car: Dixon at the wheel with his new friend, Jan, who was half Dutch, as his front-seat passenger, and his older friends Arundel and Tonks in the back seat. The car was a recent acquisition of Dixon's, acquired soon after his full licence, a Morris Minor for which he had paid the princely sum of twenty-five pounds; a solid black hump of a vehicle, which he had been assured had the reliability of that classic machine and which to him as his first car had all the glamour of a Maserati. He stroked the steering wheel from side to side and occasionally leaned back in the seat as if he could feel propulsion surging throughout when in fact what power there was came from the old horses wheezing and pulling from the front. The climb up the hill on Ashton Road had already proved something of a challenge, particularly with a full load of passengers, and both driver and passengers had found themselves unconsciously leaning forward as if to give those old steeds assistance and encouragement. Going downhill, however, with the same load, provided Dixon with a little more of the smooth speed of his dreams and he had even been moved to exclaim – *Look at that! It's a real runner!* And neither of his old friends in the back seat, who knew even less about cars than Dixon, had offered disagreement. Jan, the half Dutchman, perhaps with the extra knowledge of his wider background, had looked a little more sceptical, but he had let the scepticism dissolve into the expression of indulgence which was his standard. He, after all, had lived in Rotterdam.

That expression of indulgence had come to be something of an irritation to Arundel, who had every intention of going abroad himself in the very near future.

– Seats are comfy, said Tonks and this irritated Arundel also; his old friend had a tendency to repetition. You've already said that, he said and Tonks shrugged.

– Well, they are.

– So where's it to be, boys? Dixon sat back in the driver's seat as the car settled into an easier pace on the straight. *Anywhere you like, boys. We're on the road!*

– What about that place we went to … Tonks looked out of the window and the scenery sliding by seemed to wipe away the end of his sentence even more readily than usual.

–Which place? prompted Arundel, but Tonks still seemed dazed by the movement and, again as was fairly usual, Arundel had to read the subject matter himself in the blanks of his friend's mind. You mean that pub in Whitwood? At which Tonks nodded as if he had said this himself. With the tables outside?

– That's it, said Tonks.

– We can get further than that! Dixon lifted a dismissive hand briefly from the wheel. I mean we can get to Wakefield or Leeds. He grinned at his front-seat passenger, who had recently joined him as an employee of the carpet store. Jan also had a full driving licence, had it for a full year, he said, since he was old enough to have one, as if such things came automatically for the more cosmopolitan. His father had taught him, he said, whereas Dixon had had to stump up for lessons from the miserable married couple who ran the Airedale School of Motoring, suffering the old man's contempt for learners and the vagaries of the old woman, who more that once during a lesson had made him wait for her outside Woolworth's. Dixon's own father could not have taught him, however, as (like many of the fathers in the Castleford area) he had never learned to drive. Neither Arundel nor Tonks could drive, although the former said he was on the verge of taking out a provisional licence. So Dixon looked at Jan as one driver to another, as one who had mastered something of modernity, as one ready to face this newer world, ready to drive towards its dawn, and hoped the half Dutchman (although he was only called Smith; it was his mother who was Dutch) was appropriately appreciative of their common skill. Certainly he saw nothing but indulgence on his front-seat passenger's face.

– What about heading for Wakey?

Dixon glanced back at his other passengers. Wakefield was nearer than Leeds and as far as he could picture the terrain, there were fewer hills. Going to Leeds would entail the steady climb near Rothwell when even the bus seemed to struggle. Not that Dixon allowed this any more than a fleeting calculation amidst his excitement. On the wings of this excitement it seemed his Morris Maserati could climb Garroby Hill.

– They've got that strip club there. The driver was determined to show his new pal a good time on this Saturday night and given they were motorized this would be more than the usual session at The Junction. They were all 19 years old now and the pastimes of boys should be properly past.

– *A strip club!* The surprise in Tonks' exclaimed response was not what Dixon had been looking for, but at least his old friend followed it with a manly guffaw of enthusiasm. *I'm up for that!* Arundel again made a finer estimate of the motives for Dixon's suggestion, but whatever these were, even he could not deny the specific sexual attraction.

– Is there a strip club in Wakefield? asked Jan and Dixon clicked his tongue O yes! – I knew there were some in Leeds, the front-seat passenger went on. But I didn't know there were any in Wakefield.

– *The Cigany*, said Arundel; the friends had discussed a trip to it more than once. Dixon pressed on the accelerator.

– That's it then is it, boys? The Cigany it is! And there was general agreement as the image of a buxom lass taking off her clothes engineered as much common feeling in the quartet as there had been since they met up. *Up for that!* said Tonks and grinned at the female image undulating across the scenery undulating past.

– It'll cost … Arundel tried, but found himself unable to stop himself from saying this. He knew that, for all his recently acquired motor vehicle, Dixon was not earning a great amount at the carpet store and Tonks was working on his father's milk round and tipping up even more than he and Dixon were for their continuing stay at home. Of the four of them it was Arundel's estimate that he, Arundel, earned the most.

On the other hand it was Saturday night and when Dixon, with a little impatience, reminded him of this, he threw up his hands – *Right. Right* – and allowed himself also to relax into the movement of the car and the image and prospect of the buxom lass.

The car seemed to gather in smoothness as it ran through Cutsyke and Normanton out towards Wakefield, although when flecks of rain began to appear the windscreen wipers Dixon activated came up like things hauled out of a trench, dragging smears of dirt with them which further obscured rather than cleared the screen. The arm of the wiper on the passenger's side managed a few tortuous arcs then gave up its functional ghost and fell to final rest a few inches up. The other, seeming to recognize its partner's demise, kept doggedly going, even clearing some of its own dirty streaks and flipping back and forth more quickly as the wet flecks became rain.

– Can you see all right? asked Jan, peering over the thin dead arm on his side, and Dixon reassured him he could, although for a time there was nothing but blur.

The road was not as heavily used as it would become, however, and the driver's wiper finally did its duty and Dixon's affection for the machine overflowed and it was his turn to feel irritation with a friend as Arundel cut into this with – Where are you going to park? Ever the practical sod, he thought. Ever the civil servant. Could he not learn the sophistication of their new friend? There were no new horizons in Arundel, thought Dixon, nothing of the risks and adventure of modernity; a Town Hall operative to the end. Arundel considered himself a cut above and in some ways he was. He read more than most and he had garnered four O levels, but in the end, thought Dixon, Keith Arundel had gone out to work just as they all had and in the end he would stay in Castleford just like Freddy Tonks, in Townville rather than Airedale perhaps, with the snotty girlfriend who was as thin as a wiper blade. Arundel would get a provisional licence, thought Dixon, and he would probably get a full licence and a car, but he would use it for nothing more than getting to work and transporting shopping and his wiper blade of a wife. He would never drive towards distant horizons.

– There'll be parking by the club, he said and Arundel sniffed.

– They'll charge you for that!

– Where is it anyway, the club? Was there something of the diplomat in the half Dutchman? Neither Dixon nor Arundel was sure whether his question at this point was partly to smooth out the hint of altercation.

– It's near Belle Vue, said Tonks. There's that waste ground there. There's that waste ground where they park when there's a match. Dixon turned the car into the side streets, grinding a gear in the change down but still glimpsing nothing but indulgence from his front-seat passenger. Any driver knew what it was like to grind a gear. Although he began to feel he should stop now, the concentration of it all was getting to him a little and it was time to take a pause, particularly with an audience of passengers, particularly as the rain was now quite heavy and the solitary wiper blade seemed to be gathering into a slapping frenzy, as of someone in water waving for help. He and his new vehicle had got to their destination and Dixon had no doubt the vehicle would get them home. It was time to stop and revel quietly in his achievement.

He turned the car onto the waste ground, which reassuringly had a few other vehicles parked on it although two of these were lorries and another what looked like the remains of an ice cream van. This was not the time to let concerns get the upper hand, however, thought Dixon. This was not the time to say I want to find a less-exposed spot for my fine new motor. This was not the time to act like Arundel. This was a time for coolness with possessions, the casual daring of one young man for others.

– Don't know if this is the waste ground I meant. Tonks was peering out of the window. Not sure this is the waste ground I meant.

– Does it matter? asked Arundel. Belle Vue is just up there. Dixon heard that irritating touch. *Now* Arundel was being throwaway! Now, when it was not his property in play, his new car exposed. Had it been his car, thought Dixon, they would be looking for a safer kerbside harbour, maybe even a car park. But then had it been Arundel's car they would not even have come as far as Wakefield.

– So are we near the club? asked Jan, seeming quite keen to open the door, and the young men all clambered out, hunching against the rain.

– Always rains in Wakefield! said Tonks, a Cas lad not about to miss a chance to blacken a rival locale. *Always bloody rains here!* And Dixon, having assured his new friend the club was not far away, gave out his own exclamation as he saw Arundel reaching into the bulging pocket of his suit. *Not the pacamac!* Arundel shook out the blue-tinged plastic, however, and proceeded to haul it over his shoulders, seeking out the armholes, and Dixon glanced at Jan and felt that he and his new friend shared a moment of smiling indulgence at his old friend's dated excess of protection.

– You're as bad as my dad! he said as he locked the car as carefully as he could. The handles and the locks themselves all seemed rather loose. *It's only a bit of rain!*

He hurried to catch up with the quick pace set by Tonks, who knew his quiff would not stand much in the way of adverse elements. They all bent against the weather then, finding no shelter until they reached the bleak block of buildings which had once been warehouses and in the centre of which, as its limited Las Vegas frontage announced, was The Cigany Club. Tonks paused then to take stock of his hair in the first reflective surface he could find and the others straightened themselves also, faltering a little around the entrance. Dixon adjusted the knot in his black leather tie and looked again with distaste at the billowing plastic mac Arundel was carefully taking off and refolding, although he had to admit that underneath it Arundel's suit seemed less rumpled than his own now felt. His old friend always dressed well, better in fact than his new one, who was wearing an unfortunate pair of fawn cavalry twill trousers, mottled now with damp steaks. Jan's jacket was a little baggy also and he was wearing a shirt which seemed to be a pale yellow, perhaps with some memory of tulips. Dixon wiped the raindrops from his own suit and allowed himself to think with pleasure again of his new car and his competent drive.

– *In we go then*! Tonks led the way through the door and up to a table behind which sat a woman of indeterminate age, heavily made up, who the friends all agreed later was probably an old stripper. She sold them first a membership to the club and then entrance tickets and told them wearily that the first act was not until nine. To Dixon's relief there was no challenge as to anyone's age and also to his relief, Arundel made no comment as to the amount they paid to get in. Arundel, he felt, was also feeling the simple excitement of it all, particularly as the buxom lass of their imaginings was given more specific form in the large photographs which met them in the passage to the interior.

– *Crimey*! Look at that! said Tonks in something of a church whisper, indicating one of the photographs, and all four nodded. *Look at that*!

– So, boys, what's it to be?

Feeling himself the instigator and promulgator of the whole evening, Dixon stood the first round, knowing Arundel's comment was coming but too excited to preempt it – You can't have more than a couple – and he agreed that as he was the driver he would go to shandies after a couple, maybe even after one. The price they were charging for the drinks would provide its own restraint anyway, the friends agreed on this.

– Anyway I'm here to see some— Tonks mimed pulchritude. I'm here to see some of that. I can get sloshed at The Junction.

The friends began to laugh more readily with the drink, and when they had settled themselves around a table quite near to what was clearly the performance area, conviviality settled over them like a warmth at once cradling and expansive and Dixon felt the sweet moment of the first drink and comfortable, bright society when it seems there is nowhere else you would rather be. *Now this is a Saturday night*! he said, overflowing with the moment and his car and his call of venue, and even the bulge of the pacamac in old Arundel's pocket was just another detail of the pleasure. He told the joke he had been saving and received a response over and above its merit, although Tonks, as usual with jokes, laughed as much for fellowship as full comprehension. Then came the hilarious moment at this

55

same friend's expense when the conversation turned to journeys and
Tonks said he would like to see a real mountain, preferably abroad,
in the Alps or such, but if not then the highest mountain in Great
Britain, which he called Ben Hur. Dixon felt his sides might split
and Arundel gagged on his drink. Even Jan, who had been laughing
less uproariously than the other three, joined in, although when
he came out of his own paroxysm, Dixon thought he saw a hint
of recrimination in the half Dutchman: laughing at jokes was one
thing, but simply laughing at another's ignorance … Tonks didn't
mind, however, thought Dixon; he might even revel in his mistakes,
even repeat them as his contribution to the fun and as some kind of
triumph of comic simplicity over febrile knowingness and created
information. He was not the type to go home and weep at being
laughed at. At least that was Dixon's estimation.

– It's Ben Nevis, you donkey! said Arundel and to illustrate Dixon's
estimation it seemed, Tonks shrugged:

– Well Ben Nevis then, Ben whatever it is, I'd like to see that.
Whatever it is I'd like to see it. I like the look of mountains.

– No mountains in Holland are there? Dixon turned to Jan,
perhaps a little provocatively; he was not going to have a newcomer
wax condemnatory about relationships he had only just come across.

– Flat as Susan Sykes! Arundel was quick to jump in on this and
Jan looked both quizzically and indulgently one to the other.

– No. None at all, he said and Dixon dropped his hint of a
challenge. He could not have his first friendship with someone who
had not lived their entire lives in Castleford threatened. He had
known someone of Irish extraction and another who it was said had
actually been born in Kenya when his father was stationed there,
but he had hardly been able to call those friends. I'd like to get over
to Holland and visit it some day, he said. I like the look of those
windmills. At which Jan smiled indulgently.

– It's Paris for me, said Arundel, placing his beer carefully on a
mat. See the Eiffel Tower …

– It's like the Blackpool Tower, said Tonks. It looks like the
Blackpool Tower.

56

– Well, it would, said Arundel. They based it on it. Tonks dabbed at his quiff, which he shaped carefully up at the sides so it formed a fine brown furrow down the centre of the crown. The trick he said was to have a half crew and then let it grow and shape it from this base, and whatever else there was about Tonks, his hair was generally admired.

– What, they based the Paris tower on the one in Blackpool?

There was some exasperation in Arundel's chortle at another faux pas from Freddy.

– No, you donkey, it was the other way round. And it's a lot bigger, the one in Paris than the one in Blackpool. Jan offered agreement.

– And do you know, nobody liked the Eiffel Tower when it was first built, he said. Everybody hated it. People thought it was ugly and a lot wanted it pulled down …

– Really? Dixon nodded, but he hoped this tendency to offer information, which he had not noticed before in Jan, was not going to be persistent. You had to be careful how you offered information in Castleford. He even caught the briefest of glimpses from Arundel: this new member he had brought along was something of a know-all, dressed like somebody's dad, and when Arundel said, *you know, I didn't know that*, Dixon caught this element in his tone.

– Has it got a circus in it like the one in Blackpool? asked Tonks. The one in Blackpool has a circus in it, and Dixon recognized Arundel's smile of affection for their old friend's simpler manner. More *genuine* he would say: the Castleford preoccupation which Dixon had begun to think could lead to as much mummery and posturing as any pretension. And yet he could not deny his own feeling of warmth and occasionally envy for a thicker, simpler skin and he too grinned affection as Jan said that no, there was no circus in the Paris tower and Tonks waved his hand at Blackpool's superiority.

– They've got a circus in the one in Blackpool.

– I want to see the Follies Bergers, said Arundel, certain his pronunciation was correct; he had kept up with some French even after school. Where they Can-Can. He leaned towards Jan with another ambiguous look.

– Hasn't that got a windmill on it?

The entry of the first stripper took all their attention then. The background music in the club had been provided by loudspeakers hanging visibly amidst the garish ceiling lights and there had been some unrecognizable upbeat tunes, nothing worthwhile or current for the friends, but just before the first buxom lass stepped out a combo of drums, base, saxophonist and guitar set itself up in the corner of the performance space and this it was which now provided the accompaniment. *The Cigany's own Charmaine* came the announcement from the Master of Ceremonies, who had also only recently appeared, dressed in a glittering jacket and a big bow tie. *Here she is Running Bear!* And the combo went into a laboured version of that pop tune, heavy on the drums. It was a disappointment, Dixon could not help but feel this; the young woman was dressed as a Red Indian squaw, which spoke more of theatre than of sex to him, and it seemed a long time before she slipped off the decorated blanket she was first wrapped in and then the Red Indian waistcoat and the frilled skirt. Also, she was barefoot and for Dixon heels of some kind seemed essential to overt sexuality; barefoot brought the shape down to something more real, even vulnerable, and although when the fawn-coloured bikini was finally exposed and the top half removed it was more of an excitement, he could not get past this flattening effect. Moreover, the friends were close enough to the performance area to notice the young squaw's nervousness; she seemed uncomfortable with her movements and clearly mistimed some of them, and the bright lights shining on her even showed a few facial tics of anxiety. Dixon was reminded of another experience on the Golden Mile of the aforementioned Blackpool when at the age of 16 he and Arundel and Tonks and a couple of others on a day trip had gone into what was advertised as a Girly Show to find nothing but a few tableaux of tired and rather tubby women. One of those he remembered had also seemed nervous as she held her pose.

The disappointment with the first act was unanimous, although Tonks observed that she had been a good-looking girl. How old do you think she was? asked Arundel and Jan said he thought it might have been her very first time. The musical combo was given its spot then and the Master of Ceremonies stepped forward to offer a rendition of Michael Holliday's 'Story of my Life' and then a terrible attempt at 'Long Tall Sally', which prompted some response from a larger and nosier group of young men, who had already made something of a disturbance by pushing two tables together.

– Bloody Wakefield lads! said Tonks. Always like that, bloody Wakey lads! Dixon felt his euphoria fading a little and it was only the thought of driving his car again which prevented him from salving this with more beer. The Master of Ceremonies took on his audience with some expertise and this reassured and lifted the mood and then the second stripper was older and more expert and wore knee-length silver boots as part of what was supposed to be some kind of flimsy space suit, whilst the combo went into a slow, bumping version of 'Telstar'. Dixon noted how Jan was nodding appreciation.

Sex itself was another foreign land Dixon intended to visit in full: there were things they did in Holland and France, he thought, which had not yet been thought of in Castleford. There were high-heeled boots and costumes as from outer space. He would drive into it all: one day a sports car maybe and a woman in boots posing on its bonnet. In the vague inebriation he felt, which had to be as much from the atmosphere as from the pint and a half he had drunk, he even managed to picture the woman they had just seen posing against his Morris. He took one of the John Players Tonks was handing round and he noticed Jan did also, although he had not seen the half Dutchman smoking at work. Arundel refused the fag; the health risks were quite obvious, he had said on a number of occasions. Dixon compromised by not inhaling as often or as deeply as Tonks, which technique he also seemed to see in his new friend. He looked at Jan Smith's profile wreathed in smoke, and imagined them setting off together, towards the south coast and the ferry and on to Rotterdam where Jan had relatives, although he had grown up in Dewsbury. Perhaps the two drivers could go on then to Paris where they would see the smoke-filled Follies.

After another spot from the Master of Ceremonies and something of a hiatus during which the nosiest of the audience groups began to sing its own songs, the third and last act came out and as they were now well on towards dark night she was the most explicit of the three, flicking the tassels from her breasts and making` her bikini bottom into a thin strip that she pulled on suggestively. Male tumescence rose like heat in the room and there were fewer shouts from the audience, and in the midst of his own response Dixon gave some brief thought to the power such a performer must feel and how simple things and people could be.

– Hell's bells! said Tonks as the last act made her final bend and exit. *Hell's bloody bells!* And Dixon felt his own Master of Ceremonies pleasure in his Saturday night arrangements. The friends would remember this Saturday night for some time to come, he thought. Next time they would head for Leeds and then maybe even London where the women on show undoubtedly went still further. The world was opening for him it seemed, like those dark female mysteries themselves.

– Good was that! said Tonks as they left the club. That was good! This was agreed by all as they made their way along the wet, empty streets.

– That Mike ought to be more choosy about what he sings though, said Arundel, and Jan, who was picking his way a little, considering his next step as someone does who is feeling the effect of drink, laughed out loud, as loudly as they had heard him laugh.

– He wasn't called *Mike!* he chortled. That was a joke with the microphone! Arundel was nonplussed.

– What was he called then?

– God knows, but it wasn't *Mike!* The half Dutchman sent out more loud laughter and it was Dixon this time who moved against any chance of the exchange sharpening. I think he was called Danny, he said. It said it on the poster. Danny something or other.

– Well, whatever his name was, sniffed Arundel, he needs to be more careful about what he tries to sing. Jan Smith took another careful step and laughed out loud again.

– Who cares anyway! – definitely less indulgent than he had been – we're only there to see the fanny! The three older friends exchanged a glance at this; the newcomer was clearly less capable of holding his ale than they and he indicated as much by lurching to one side.

– You all right there, Jan-O? Arundel called, pressing home his advantage. We're not going to see your basket coming back are we? The meal provided as part of the entrance fee had been of scrawny chicken pieces and chips served in a little wicker basket.

– Don't be saying that! said Dixon. You know what talking about it does.

– Talking about what? asked Tonks, checking his hair even in the darkened shop windows. Talking about what?

– About throwing up, said Arundel, not to be denied. How talking about heaving makes you more likely to heave. So careful, Jan-O! Don't be talking about your basket! Don't be thinking about those chicken bits, boy-O!

Dixon shook his head. This was what he must leave, he thought, this discomfort with strangers, this nervous assertion of a tiny patch of earth, this freemasonry of the known. He thought again with pleasure of his car and he was pleased he felt in no way drunk; he had soon come through any early effects and he could now give full concentration to the dark roads. He had only driven a few times at night and he was well aware this offered its own challenge. He felt ready for the challenge, however, and the rain had stopped and there was a mellowness to the dark, the dampness softening outlines and spreading lamplights, almost like the Cigany's curtain itself, velvet and sequinned and about to be drawn. He would go through this, thought Dixon, and leave other things behind, even dear old Tonks who was reiterating his enthusiasm for what they had just seen, certainly Arundel, clever in detail but with nothing of breadth, and now it seemed even his new friend, who had just come to rest against a pillar box, retching and allowing Arundel a joke about not posting anything from any basket.

– You all right? Dixon asked and Jan lifted a hand to indicate he was, but he seemed no more than a road sign to Dixon now, pointing to others who could dress well and carouse all night and who had been to Paris and beyond.

– Shit beer in Wakefield! said Tonks. Shit beer here.

– It was John Smith's! said Dixon with some exasperation, but his old friend brought down the finger and thumb he had just been using to bring the strands of his quiff forward and swirled the finger around. They mess with it somehow, he said. They mess with it somehow here. It's never the same!

Dixon looked from one to the other of his companions. He would get back in the car and drive them all competently home, and drop them off one by one and then he might go on into the night; he was neither tired nor drunk and he might just go on. He had filled the tank before they had set out so he would have enough fuel. He might even drive to the coast. He might even get as far as Filey. It was early May and so quite warm enough to spend the night in the car and then in the morning he could see the dawn breaking over the glittering infinity of the sea's horizon. Yes, he thought, the world was opening for him, the great mystery, the great fanny of the world. *Where's the car?* he heard Arundel ask as the foursome arrived on the waste ground, and he looked around the dark expanse and there were the old lorries and the derelict ice cream van silhouetted against the sky, but there was nothing but space, absence, where his Morris Minor had been.

– *Arseholes!* exclaimed Tonks. *Bloody, thieving Wakey arseholes!*

It's Now or Never

(Elvis Presley 1960)

The Star Fisheries was on Bridge Street and the window of the back room which was used as storage space looked out onto the river itself. In fact when the foam created on the river by Hickson's Chemicals and by the flour mill a little distance upstream reached its thickest, this window could be blinded by the creamy bubbles, some even squeezing in at the edges as they might at the portal of a poor washing machine. Maureen didn't like this blinding effect, although she didn't really mind the foam; it seemed like snow out of season to her – it tended to be at its worst when the weather was warmer – although just like snow it was only a visual pleasure in its clean early stages and less so when it took on the yellowness and torpidity of scum. In general, however, Maureen preferred to look out onto the foamless river, moving quickly as it did over the stretch between the weir and the road bridge. There was something hypnotic about quickly moving water for her, something in the movement itself, and she could simply stare at this, although there was also that in her which occasionally imagined bodies being brought along by the flow; she had heard stories of suicides and mishaps along this very stretch: some anguished, hopeless, love-crossed soul or some foolish drunk who had tried to walk across the weir. There was one time, crossing the road bridge with Joe, who lived out towards Allerton, when she had been convinced she could see a body tangled amidst the branches of the bank, caught in the eddies there, given only a last semblance of life by the swirling of these, although it turned out to be a clump of material somebody had dumped, thinking it

63

would be washed away. Another time, this time alone, she had been convinced she could see some kind of fish or serpent lifting above the swirling surface, which on closer inspection she could see was only newspaper.

On that early summer evening the river she looked out onto from this back-room window was comparatively clear and the current quite sedate and after a time her eyes drifted upwards to the thin strip of countryside of the opposite bank which was also visible. The waitresses at the Star took their breaks in this room; amidst the old boxes and disabled furniture, it had a table and a chair such as were used in the café itself and a couple of the same black plastic ashtrays. Peter Brizalleri, who with his brother owned the café (although his brother was seldom seen), insisted, however, that there should only ever be one person on a break in there at any one time, which was why Maureen was very surprised when Rita pushed aside the coloured strips of the doorless doorway and stepped in. *What are you doing?* she exclaimed, but Rita lifted a hand for reassurance.

– Cannonball's gone over 'road, she said. *Cannonball* was their nickname for Brizalleri, based on his squat, fully rounded shape and a moustache which was the only feature of a face that was otherwise simply one shining end of that roundness and which hairy adornment gave him something of a resemblance to the TV character called Cannon (in fact, Brizalleri knew of the nickname and rather liked it, hearing in it more of a reference to his dynamism).

– He's gone over to Martin's for some change.

Rita looked over her shoulder and through the curtain of coloured plastic strips and Maureen moved around like a river eddy herself to indicate that if Rita were not quick with whatever this was, she would be the one to leave. Apart from the regulation with the back room, if neither she nor Rita was serving there was only old Doris out there and she was quite capable of making mistakes even with the limited menu the Star Fisheries offered. Nor could they be certain of the underling loyalty of Mikky and Grif as they called the two young fryers and wrappers, although both of these would often say how they hated Cannonball's guts. Rita lifted her hand again for calm.

– It's got to be now! she said. I know it! I know he's got it with him.

– Got what?

– For Christ's sake, Maureen! I told you. Pauline Lane said he was in Ascombe's last Saturday. And now Ranky's sister has just told me Ranky told her he actually bought a ring and he was going to ask me on Sunday. He was going to give it to me on Sunday.

– But he didn't. Maureen moved nervously from one foot to another although Rita was actually blocking her way out.

– No, of course he didn't! Rita almost snapped this. I would have told you wouldn't I? I didn't know he had actually bought a ring. I knew he had been in Ascombe's, but I didn't know he had actually bought a ring! But Ranky's sister has just been in. She's just told me just now!

Rita's rather chiselled features were as animated as Maureen had ever seen them and, without really bringing the picture fully to mind, Maureen thought again of the swirls and eddies of the water she had just been staring at. She was aware of the image of life as a river although she couldn't see how it really worked: a river rises and runs to the sea just as life begins with a spurt and a trickling and ends in some vast unknown; but too often, it seemed to her, life was more like a pond. In all she preferred the river just as a river. Again she looked nervously beyond Rita at what she could see of the café, but she could not help but be concerned by her friend's agitated manner. Rita was usually the one with her feet on the ground. She would not stand staring at rivers, she would certainly not bring to mind any images of what life was like; normally she brought her hard gaze onto anything *airy fairy* as she called it and onto anything which was clearly more a state of the mind than an actual state and yet here she was, working herself up into a state, her fists clenching and opening and the hands going up then down to lift her apron and waft it as if she were fanning a flame.

– He's got it on him right now, she said, her words also clenching and her voice going up and then coming down for the recollection. *He had it with him on Sunday.* And he'll have it with him now. He wouldn't leave it at home. Not with his bloody family. He must have had it with him on Sunday, but I didn't know and we had all that palaver with my mother and I wasn't in the best of moods and I didn't know he had actually gone and bought the bloody ring!

Rita's eyes narrowed as onto a bad memory and for a moment, Maureen thought she was going to cry. She had seen Rita cry before, but not often and not as they had grown older. Rita didn't cry as Maureen herself might, sometimes for no particular reason and then at other times for something more specific; she had cried quite recently when Cannonball shouted at them both. Peter Brizalleri frightened Maureen, just as many things frightened her, far more things than frightened Rita, although at that moment Rita was in a state which had something to it which at least seemed like fear. And only with an effort, it seemed also, was she holding herself back from a flow of tears. – *Dumbbell! Bloody dumb bloody bell!* Maureen had seen Rita turn on men before, on her boyfriend Geoff, but also on men in general for their stupid ways. She offered a gesture of agreement and consolation, but looked nervously again towards the café. One of them needed to get back out there soon.

– *And I know him, Maur!* Rita looked directly at her, pinning back any movement. – I know the pillock and if he doesn't do something at some set time, at the time he's got it into his thick head it's when he should do it, then there's a good chance … She brought her hands out from under her wafting apron and clapped them together. *There's a good chance he might not do it at all!*

– Do what? asked Maureen, genuinely confused, and suffered, at least briefly, the hard stare Rita usually reserved for men.

– *What do you think?!*

Realization came to Maureen then and she said, O, O, I see and Rita's stare clouded once more.

– It's got to be now, she repeated. I just know it. If it isn't, he'll just drift off again. I know him. It will all just drift off again. And who knows when the dumbbell will work himself up to it again. He might even take the thing back. Ascombe's will take it back. They'll charge him, but I bet they'd take it back.

There was something like desperation in Rita's voice and again there seemed to be the threat of tears. Maureen sought some tough and practical advice for her normally tough and practical friend.

It was strange to see her in this state, not least – *It's got to be now!* – speaking of certainties which could hardly be seen as such, as Rita herself would normally surely have seen. Maureen could see no inevitable necessity in the situation. The only real inevitability she saw was that if Cannonball returned and found them both together in the back room he would shout at them.

– Geoff's picking you up later isn't he? she said. Maybe then …

Rita smoothed out her apron and straightened herself. She was quite tall, taller even than a number of the men they knew, which was one reason why she liked Geoff, who was taller than she, although he was hardly good looking and, as was generally agreed, as Rita herself would say, he could be quite gormless. There had always been an undercurrent of question as to what Rita and Geoff were doing together, although others nodded their heads at how a woman like Rita would want a wholly malleable partner and how the last thing the clever and the practical need is someone equally so. Maureen quite liked Geoff; he said so little and seemed quite gentle, where her own Joe was always on and he could be quite brusque; although those same whispering currents observed another and probably stronger tradition of a pliable and easily intimidated woman needing what looks like strength.

– Yes, he's walking me back, said Rita and it was her turn to glance at the coloured strips and the café beyond before coming to the point and the plan which had brought her into this risky encounter. Look, you're off before me, she said. One of the girls always stayed for the tea time shift and that evening it was Rita's turn.

– I can switch if you want, said Maureen. I'll change if you want and you can go and find Geoff.

– No, it isn't that … There was a wildness in Rita's eyes such as Maureen had not seen before; she had convinced herself of some destiny here it seemed, she had wound herself up into thinking that somehow this was now or never, just like the song.

– No, what I want you to do … Rita stepped forward, leaning her head down to the smaller, daintier figure and lowering her voice as much as she could ever manage… What I want you to do is go and find Geoff and tell him … She paused over the favour she was about to ask and Maureen glanced at the window where just a few minutes earlier she had been thoughtlessly watching the river. She tried to avoid involvement where she could; she disliked the tensions of relationships, even looks and moods troubled her and raised voices of anger or anguish were always frightening. She felt her insides beginning to swirl and eddy as Rita outlined what she wanted from her and after she had listened she timidly tried for an out.

– *You want me to go and tell him that?* The plan seemed another aspect of Rita's unusual state, almost as wild as coming into the back room when Cannonball was only across the road. Rita was insistent, however.

– Yes, you tell him Tom Garbutt has been chatting me up again and that he even mentioned us getting engaged.

– Did he?

Rita looked down on Maureen then like some bird of prey deciding whether whatever it was looking down on was worthy of the effort of a swoop, but as those same wholly focussed eyes cast around there was nothing else and so they came back.

– No, he didn't. Well at least not today and not engagement. *No!* Exasperation sounded in her voice. – But I know Geoff and he needs a push and if he thinks Tom Garbutt has been around he will get on with what he was going to do on Sunday if things hadn't … She tailed off and both young women glanced towards the café. Rita turned back then for a final and forceful reiteration of what clearly seemed to her to be an absolute essential. *You just find Geoff!* He'll be in the Mallard. You just tell him that Tom Garbutt has been around and that I told you he had mentioned getting engaged to me. You just tell him that.

Although she had no wish to do what she was being asked to do, Maureen could find no words of objection or any way in which she could withstand the fixed eagle eye and the wild, focussed eagle's heart of her best friend's current state. Also it seemed Rita was not going to step out of the back room until she got an agreement and Cannonball's return must surely be imminent. So Maureen agreed and saw a briefer calm pass across her friend's face although for the life of her she could not see how the plan had the guaranteed outcome Rita seemed to think it had. All right, I'll go to The Mallard, she said, and Rita's thank you was a little pleasure for Maureen and her friend's turning back through the coloured strips of curtain a relief.

Leaving the Star Fisheries at the end of her shift, Maureen walked up towards Carlton Street more slowly than usual. Usually when she left work her pace was as determined as it ever was, directed at getting home as soon as she could so she and her mother could watch television in comfort and maybe even finish their tea before her father and her brothers came home from work. As she walked, it occurred to her that she was a little annoyed with what she had been asked to do (apart from anything else it would mean she would have to go into the Mallard alone) and half-thought excuses began to float through her mind. She could tell Rita she had not been able to locate Geoff or that she had met her mother on Carlton Street and her mother had not been feeling well and so she had had to go home with her. Such excuses were easily overtaken, however, easily outweighed by the image of Rita's eagle eye focussed on her as she made them. In the state Rita had got herself into another image came into Maureen's mind of her friend winding herself up still further until the firmly grounded feet actually left the ground and she became the tall, beaked thing she sometimes seemed to be and flew fully upwards, flapping her apron and squawking fury at all those who had disappointed her.

With this Maureen brought herself into her normal after-work stride. The sooner it was done, the sooner it was over and she would at least have done what she had been asked to do. Barbara Fowler hailed her from the other side of the road, but Maureen called – *can't stop* – and used a garbled version of the mother excuse and went on along Carlton Street, which was more or less shut down, with just a few others who for some reason or other had stayed after closing time and were now heading home with the same directed step Maureen herself usually employed. She looked at them with envy. The pubs had opened, however, and there were already shadowy heads beyond their windows, nearly all of them men, and she knew Geoff's head would be one of those. Rita was right about her boyfriend; he and the other drivers and conductors walked up from the bus depot to the Mallard and when it was Rita's turn to work until seven-thirty, it had become a routine that Geoff would stay in the pub and then meet Rita when she finished and walk her back along Wheldon Lane. Geoff would be in the Mallard. Maureen knew she could have no excuse here. But then she thought, all she had to do was what she had agreed to do; she could do that and get away in fairly quick time. It was no aspect of her office to ensure an outcome.

She paused at a bus stop and stood there as if she might be waiting for the 155 as she did when she went to her grandparents'. She would rather be doing that, she thought. She would rather be doing anything but this. She turned towards the estate agent's window and looked along the photographs of houses. Joe had been going on recently about something called a mortgage which you got to allow you to buy a house, so you didn't have to rent from the council. This, he said, was what he was going to do when the time came. There was no chance he was going to rent from the council, he said, he was going to get his own house. Maureen couldn't really see the difference; as far as she could grasp it, this simply meant you were paying out to a bank rather than the council and you had to do any repairs and such yourself rather than waiting for the council to come round. Although she had drifted off rather when Joe was explaining it all. In some distant future it seemed you stopped paying, but then Maureen didn't like to think too much of the future; she found no excitement in it and her imagination almost never turned in its direction. She preferred stories and dramas to be on television or radio and although at times they were forced upon her (witness her walking towards the Mallard now), in truth she wanted nothing of them in her life. She was only attracted by movement outside herself. When any such movements affected her, when they invaded her, as they had in the recent risk of the Star Fisheries back room, she was simply unsettled. It seemed quite clear to Maureen that with any such movements the potential for awkward or even bad things happening increased and with this the discomfort and the tension and the fear. And yet she knew one day she would have to go on into the future – just as she had to go on now – one day she would have to leave home just as she had left school, one day she would have to marry Joe, although as yet he had made no mention of any ring. This did not trouble Maureen, however, as it clearly troubled Rita. Again she rather preferred it; any ring, any definite declaration on Joe's part, would be a clear indicator that the future, with all its fearful potential, was imminent. Yet this was what Rita seemed to want; she actually seemed to want to hurry it on.

Maureen brought her gaze from the photographs of houses to her own image in the glass. She had often felt herself almost as flimsy and transparent as that reflection. And small; there were other girls as small or smaller, but they seemed to have more confidence than she had, more solidity. She had never given herself the significance some others seemed quite naturally to give themselves. *You will get more confident as you get older*, a kind teacher had said to her once, but in truth she was still waiting. She had been told recently she looked like Brenda Lee and this had helped a little, and she had tried to get her hair into the style of the picture on the LP she had, but, she thought, there was really nothing in her of Little Miss Dynamite.

She made herself set off again. The sooner it was done, the better. She could not help but falter, however, as she saw her reflection reappear, still fainter, in the Mallard's windows, which were dark tinted to half way up. The pub's front doors, only one of which was open, had some small and prettily coloured glass panes, almost like the big window of Trinity Church, and she looked at these as she went in, thinking vaguely how she would like to be like stained glass, caught in some lovely, coloured movement, light only ever passing through her, only ever brightening and enriching, never really disturbing, as separate as any river. She went on in and the male heads turned to look at her and there was another and quite definite feeling of irritation with Rita, who knew just as well as Maureen herself that a woman going into a pub alone would cause a reaction. But Rita, it seemed, currently at least, was willing to sacrifice anything and anybody. And here I am (Maureen even snapped her fingers softly at this thought), being moved on as usual, pushed into motion by other forces. If Joe heard of her going in the Mallard alone, he would be annoyed; she could tell him about Rita and so on, or part of it at least; tell him she was looking for Geoff as a favour to Rita, although Rita and Joe did not get on particularly well and Joe would still be annoyed at any impetus for her other than his own.

Maureen looked around the interior of the pub, her terrors rising, but thankfully Geoff's head was quickly visible beyond one of the thick wooden barriers and half-Confessional walls which divided the pub's space; a comparatively new management had attempted to relieve the shadows these caused with a number of wall lamps, uncovered at first but then, after complaints, muted by green, frilled shades. The same management's attempts to establish a small platform so groups could play on certain nights had also received complaints from the regulars and it had been abandoned, and the group which for a brief time did play on Fridays had to squeeze into a shadowy corner. The overall colour and impression of the place was of beer; the ochre of bitter running into the darkness of mild, the ceiling a low, chalky head, and throughout there was not just the smell, but the vague moisture of drink like the damp touches and reduced light of incipient rain. The male heads turned back to their beer as the young woman, who had come in on her own, went over to a man, although there was an invisible shaking of some of the older heads for another crack in the world.

Maureen sat down on the fixed wooden bench Geoff was occupying, relieved he was alone and that any others he might have been with for an after-work drink had gone. She was relieved and quite pleased also to be greeted by a smile from him, a strain of puzzlement in it of course, but it seemed to her a genuine smile. Geoff was a tall man by the standards of Castleford, with a thin mat of fair hair which he had tried but failed to shape up. The Brylcreem he used only worked for a time early on and as he was more careless with his appearance than some, it only ended by creating a collapsed mixture of thicker and thinner strands, as of a half-finished, suddenly abandoned nest, and by giving a gleaming emphasis to the receding which was beginning at the temples. His father was bald as a coot and Maureen knew this caused Rita concern, although Rita had read in some magazine that baldness comes down to men via the mother's line. As Geoff's mother's father was dead she had no idea whether he too had been bald. Geoff had said that he would find some photographs, but as yet he had failed to do so. Beneath this, the young man's face was a quite open affair, with large brown eyes which were his best feature and which from time to time Rita eulogized upon; this large and open quality extended also, and less fortunately, to the rest of the features, with a broadness in which the cheekbones were lost and the nostrils exposed and within which a wide mouth could too often be found hanging ajar. It was this last, thought Maureen, which made Geoff look a little slow, this and his tendency to limited conversation. She, however, had always found something quite pleasing in the young man's overall appearance and from time to time she had defended her friend's choice to others, saying she could see what Rita saw in him. There was the height of course and there were quite broad shoulders, and hands which were large but which seemed quite careful, even delicate, in their movements. Also he had an undeniable solidity to him; the very slowness of his manner and his reactions gave him this and Maureen was particularly grateful for it at that moment when it seemed that she was being moved along by some current.

– What are you doing here? Geoff asked and Maureen shrugged and smiled. She knew she needed to get on with things, but her mind had rather emptied. She should simply say what Rita had told her to say, but in that moment this in itself seemed an emptiness to her and she was grateful again for the slowness in the man; there was no alteration to his body shape to accompany his question as there would have been in Joe or in Rita; both of these would have leaned forward like interrogators when there was no immediate response; both of these would have wrinkled their brows and narrowed their eyes and, if there was still no answer, they would have begun with gestures of burrowing. Geoff's wide eyes and features gave her space to drift off a little from the main direction and to contemplate the bus driver's tunic jacket and its badge. *It's the glamour of the uniform!* was Rita's joke, but Maureen realized in that moment how this tunic gave him still extra solidity and that it was not just in that particular moment she had felt this. Those big and careful hands could manage a big double-decker bus; she had been on a bus Geoff was driving more than once and she realized now how she had always felt some admiration for him. Just recently she had suffered the silly chatter of Eric Hicks, the conductor, who lived two doors up from her, and she had looked towards Geoff in his driver's cabin and wished she could sit in controlled silence next to him, rather than having to find at least some responses for silly Eric. Geoff waited, still smiling, as these half thoughts and memories passed across the blankness of Maureen's mind. She forced herself to concentrate then.

– It's Rita, she said and Geoff's reaction was no more than a recall of the puzzlement he had shown when Maureen appeared, as if, like another slowness, this expression had not had the time it needed to dissipate. He said nothing, not even filling in with a questioning repetition of the name. – *Rita* – it was Maureen who did this and then she managed to impart something of the fabrications her friend had charged her with – *Tom Garbutt has been into the Fisheries, talking to her. He came into the Star* ... The lie which all this was swirled around Maureen and she was able to recognize how few lies she actually told. A few to her mother of course, perhaps even to her father on the few occasions they spoke, but in general lies were more dialogues of otherness for her, redolent and ripe with the fearful possibilities of discovery and repercussion, better left to radio and television and films, better left to the fiction in which they had their proper place. – He was chatting her up again, she said, thinking that at least she could use something of other occasions, simply time transfer a little. This helped with the lie. *He was getting quite serious though.* This was a direct reproduction of one of the phrases Rita herself had used and as Maureen went on she found herself able to reproduce others her friend had suggested, almost watching herself and listening to herself as she might listen to the radio or watch television.

– He even said they should get engaged. He even said perhaps they should get *engaged*. Having used and repeated the crucial word, Maureen fell silent, turning her eyes guiltily away, but then looking back for Geoff's reaction.

– He said that? The big young man's puzzled expression intensified and then spread into a rather more complex confusion and Maureen nodded, unwilling to repeat the falsehood again. Geoff lifted his drink slowly and took a draught and Maureen's heart went out to him with a sudden and quite strange strength. Not once before had she thought of Geoff as anything other than Rita's boyfriend, not once had she seen him as anything other than this, and in that strange moment, forced out of her normal routine by the wild scheme and the uncharacteristic behaviour of a friend, finding herself in a completely different and uncalled-for setting, she half recognized that nothing has inevitability: the shadowy walls around them could have been built differently or in a different place, the Mallard and even Carlton Street could have been called something else, somebody's hands had chosen to place the framed photograph of the cricket team on the wall and Geoff could have been her boyfriend and not Rita's.

A strange thrill went through her with this and it was all she could do to hold herself steady on the bench, squeezing herself to do so, squeezing her arms into her sides, her fingers into her palms and her knees into one another. Then an even stranger impulse came up through all her squeezing and burst it seemed all over her. Why had she never seen Geoff before as she saw him now? His large steady shoulders a firm base for those big strong features and the brown, steady eyes like those of some fine, faithful animal, more a bear than a dog. Maureen's thoughts were as half formed as ever, but they came in a real flow and swirled out some television scene in which Geoff said: *Well, to heck with her! Let Tom Garbutt have her!* And then he was no longer Rita's Geoff and then somehow she and he, Maureen and Geoff, would find themselves sitting beside each other as they were now, but not as they were now, for he would reach out his big hand and take hers. The part Joe might play in this vivid but spectral scene was indefinite, a distant threat as of distant shouting or drums, and in that thrilling moment it seemed to Maureen that the man beside her could manage any such threat, just as he could manage any threat at all, just as he could manage a big double-decker bus.

– Tom Garbutt, said Geoff, placing his beer carefully back on its mat, and it was all Maureen could do not to tell him the truth. *No, that's just what Rita told me to tell you. He has chatted her up before, but you already know that, but it has not been recently and not today in the Star Fisheries and there has certainly been no mention of engagement.* The moment was passing for her, however, overtaken by a weightier crowd of half thoughts, as a steady group of marchers would catch up with one of their number who has recklessly thrown off his hat and his shirt and run ahead too quickly. They march on past him then, sitting exhausted and dazed on the roadside, and some of their sullen and sober group haul him up and haul him along until he is fully absorbed again into their number and going again in their direction.

– She finishes at seven thirty, doesn't she? Geoff lifted his watch and Maureen nodded. She could go now, she had done her part, but somehow she was reluctant to leave this man's side. She even wanted to slide closer to him. She could even take his hand as they might in a television scene, particularly if it was American, as a gesture of comfort and encouragement. It wouldn't mean this in Castleford, however, as Maureen knew, and yet she still found herself leaning at least a little closer and looking at the face which had turned slowly away from her and wondering why she had not seen this face before as she saw it now, so strong in the shadows falling across it, the parting in the mouth a very line of strength.

There was no discomfort for her in the silence which followed then, a silence which went on for some time, and Maureen could not help but think how Joe would have broken that silence, how he would have been flicking at the beer mats as he did, how he would have been fidgeting from side to side and how he would certainly not have let any silence persist.

– *Right.* Finally Geoff finished off his beer and stood and Maureen stood with him, dainty Brenda Lee and the great uniformed bear. I'll get on down there, he said and Maureen wondered again whether she should tell him everything, tell him about the scheme of which she had been made a part. *Had he got a ring? Had he got it with him?* She would never have done such a thing to him; *she* would never have resorted to lies to draw him on. And then came another strangeness in which, as they stood together in that shadowy, church-like space, it occurred to Maureen that he might be feeling a strange and similar moment; neither of them could think things out fully and clearly, but in that moment there did seem to be a feeling between them which was quite clear. Perhaps it was wholly her – Maureen could not escape half thinking this – perhaps this was wholly her feeling, but as they stood there together she could not help but feel there was something shared. *Or was it just the deception of the river? Showing so many lines, so many movements when in truth the whole thing is only going one way.*

– I'll get on down to the Star then, said Geoff and Maureen nodded and went with him out of the pub, walking beside him towards the little stained-glass windows of the door, letting him usher her through as the gentleman he was and then standing beside him as under a great tree, reluctant to leave its shelter. She had to get away, she thought. She had done her part and now she had to let the matter take its course. The potential for fear which was usual in her and which had been banished by the strange thrills, came back and with it other vague spectres: Rita's angry face for one and then those of her mother and her father and then looks and whisperings swirling everywhere.

– *Right.* Geoff turned away from her slowly, rather as a boyfriend might at a parting it seemed to her, still not able to subdue the strangeness completely. She was prettier than Rita, she knew that, and now she remembered Geoff once saying how she looked very pretty. *Very* pretty he had said. She turned her heel on every thought then and said goodbye and walked away, although as she looked back at his retreating figure, as she found herself unable not to do, it seemed to her that his head was turning slowly, as if he also had taken another look at her. It was all in her mind, she told herself as she stopped to gather her thoughts. But then how could this be? She was not someone who could ever have it all in her mind; there were only ever partial thoughts, how could she ever have it *all* in her mind? She should go home, she thought. Sort herself out.

She was unsettled even at home, however. Her mother noticed it and asked if she was unwell and Maureen said she was all right, but undeniably the strangeness was persisting and she couldn't settle as she normally did and, when her father came in she said she had to go out. – On a Tuesday? exclaimed her mother, and it seemed briefly that her father might speak up against it, but he had knocked his thumb back at work and was focussed on what his wife could do to alleviate his suffering. So Maureen went out along Wheldon Lane and even stood for a time staring up at the evening sky, before setting off again. Men could stand in solitude, but a young woman alone had to look as if she were going somewhere. A man could stand staring at the river, perhaps throwing contemplative stones into it, but this was no posture for a woman. So Maureen walked back towards town, only glancing at what was visible of the water off to one side, walking as if she were going to meet someone and then when she came to the road bridge she stood looking at the river passing under it for as long as she could before turning again and adopting the same purposeful pace, this time as if she were going home. The sky had begun to darken, although a few late, brighter streaks broke through as indicators of a clearer night. One of these even had the shape of a staircase, she thought as she walked. She was drawn on then, past her own street and on to Rita's house which was beyond the rugby ground. Geoff had played some rugby she remembered, as had Joe, and she remembered Joe saying how Geoff, being the size he was, might have been quite useful if only he had half a brain and a bit more bite. This was what Joe had said, she remembered, and again it was as if there were still whisperings and murmurings in the gathering darkness around her and these spoke of likeness, of unity. Neither she nor Geoff were considered smart. Rita was and Joe thought he was, but she and Geoff were thought of as dim. Maureen knew this, although the word 'dreamer' might be used more often for her. *Dolly daydream*! Rita called her, but as Maureen paused again in her walk, the whispers were of how like should be with like and how half and half make one and some other revelation seemed to be rising until it was just beneath the surface, as if the next movement, the next step would make it clear. Maureen went on with the quality of a sleepwalker, turning into the gate of Rita's house and going up to the door as she had so many times and lifting the ornate brass knocker. *What are you doing?* came the whispers. *What are you wishing for?*

Rita opened the door, which was a relief for Maureen as Rita's mother could have an even fiercer stare than Rita. It was a relief also that her friend did not ask what she was doing here, with no prior arrangements on a Tuesday night. Naturally Maureen would want to know the outcome of the wild scheme in which she had been called upon to play a part, and these were the days before everyone had a telephone.

– How did it go? she asked, but she had her answer in a glance and without doubt her spirit sank and then was caught like rags in the eddies of a river bank or like the blackened daily newsprint she had once thought was something else. The old fears were there also, however, a young lifetime of them, and there was an element of thankfulness as the old order came marching along and gathered her up and as the heavy lines and the persistent patterns of the river drowned out the strangeness and Maureen was able to feel at least some genuine pleasure for Rita as she stepped forward, smiling and tall with triumph, and extended her left hand to show off the engagement ring.

Mrs Mills' Medley

(*Mrs Mills 1961*)

As the Wallace Arnold finally pulled into Bridlington it had begun to rain and this did not help the mood of any member of the family Cresswell. Indeed, apart from 8-year-old Linda, who had gone into the private world she shared with the selection of dolls she had brought, the father, the mother and the 13-year-old son all had, as the Yorkshire phrase had it, a monk on. The father's was the grimmest, a veritable black and tonsured mood of disenchantment. During the lavatory break which was scheduled an hour out of Castleford and an hour from the coast, his son, against his specific instructions, had wandered out of sight of the coach and had been the last back on it, causing a few minutes' delay and receiving a cuff from the father for his disobedience. This had meant that the family's male–female arrangement of their seating on the coach had been altered at the mother's insistence so she and the father sat together behind their children and the father had spent most of the second part of the journey feeling his wife's disapproval for the cuff and finding his eyes brought repeatedly back to the length of his son's hair as it bobbed its provocation in front of him. Billy had been told to have it cut for the holiday, but again had shown quite specific disobedience, although he had attempted to cover this with a lie, saying Clarence Powell's barber's had been too full for him to have it done, an obvious, almost nonsensical falsehood. The lies and the disobedience of the young sounded like the solemn bells of the monastery then for Don, the father, who, although he was not yet forty himself, had begun to feel the weighty disillusionment of age. Was this why they had fought a war? (Don had served as a navy stoker in the last months of the second world conflict.) Was this why he went day after day to Glasshoughton pit? These had been the recent questions raised amongst a peer group drinking. So young men could grow their hair long and show nothing but lies, disobedience and a facial expression which in their fathers' presence at least was either as monkishly sullen as Billy's was now or had the faint flickering of a sneer? And yet those holidays at the coast with his children, particularly his son, particularly when the boy was old enough to hang on his father's words and copy his father's actions, had been perhaps the happiest of Don's life. In those times it seemed everything had validity and the now and the future were as open and as lovely as the sea and the sky. The shadows of the monastery had surprised him and he still had the quality of a man surprised and sinking into his own sullen confusion, only superficially alleviated by phrases and actions he had learned to be standard as if, like prayers, only they could put some hold on what is passing, fix some certainty within some seascape of hope.

The mother's monk had less of this; hers could still be half dismissed for the misery he was, half replaced by someone smiling and even handsome, a doctor perhaps, who would know not only how to cure, but how to make a patient smile. For her, the cloaked figure was more of a gloomy and annoying presence, muttering *I told you so*. Every year for the last six they had come for their summer week's holiday to the same boarding house in Bridlington and as June had told Don, it was probably time for a change, if not of the resort itself then perhaps of the accommodation they used. There are times, June had said, when it is time for a change. She had even suggested this year they should go to a caravan. Her cousin had done so and it gave you more freedom, said June. None of those gongs for breakfast and tea. She had known Don would not agree. But, as her own monk kept muttering, they would have been better in a caravan. They would also have been better without Billy and this also had been a possibility; he could have stayed at his grannie's; June had spoken of it with her son and, tracing reactions the father was no longer able to see, she had recognized Billy's enthusiasm for the possible arrangement. Certainly they would have been better with

81

just the three of them, her and Don and little Linda, who lived in a world of her own anyway. They would have been better just the three of them and in a caravan; with this, apart from anything else, she could avoid the stiff old biddy who ran Rosedean Guest House, to whom June had never taken. In a caravan they could make their own timetable, they could come and go as they pleased. Although again she had known Don would never agree – *In a caravan?* he had said. Like gypsies?! – ignoring whatever she said about how good the caravan camps are now. It had to be what it had always been for her husband, what he had fought for in the war as he occasionally said and what he worked for day after day down the pit as he said more often. To have someone else prepare and present their breakfast and their tea – didn't the mother want that? And to be so near to the front, to be able to see the beach from the bay windows of the Guest House! June had found no way of counteracting this, even though she recognized the relationship between her husband and her son had become such that the holiday simply could not work. And she had been proved right no more than an hour out of Castleford, when they were no more than half way to the sea. *I told you so* muttered her monk, but the invisible hood which she had drawn over her own face was more of frustration and resentment. Let her husband stew in his juice was her mood, in the monastery atmosphere and the poor monastery food of the Rosedean Guest House.

So, after the Cresswells had pulled out their suitcases from the hold of the coach, it was a monkish little procession which made its way through the rain from the coach station and across the familiar roads of the seaside town.

Mrs Mills saw them arriving from the window of the second-floor rooms she used as her own. The Rosedean Guest House was one of the white-fronted terraces of four- or five-storey buildings which had originally been residences for Victorian families enriched by northern industry and colonial trade, but soon converted (such Victorian plants and their scions quickly uprooted at the earliest influx of the working class) into guest houses. *Guest House* was Mrs Mills' favoured title for her establishment and her home; she did not like to have Rosedean referred to as a hotel and in season at least she never accepted visitors for less than three nights. A week was the norm, although there were some who might stay a fortnight and, certainly at the height of the season, most of her guests were those who had stayed with her before. And there was a weight on the word 'guest' for Mrs Mills; she had none of the qualities of the professional hotelier which time and competition and shifts in deference were beginning to introduce; for all that they were paying, whoever occupied the rooms in her house still had the aspect for her of people she had invited and who she expected would show all the manners and responses appropriate. Sand not being brought into the hallway and the stairs and certainly not into the rooms was a prime example of her expectations and she had a bucket and brush placed just outside the front door under a card with clear instructions as to the removal of sand. This front door was meticulously opened at eight during high season and always left open until ten-thirty at night when it was equally meticulously locked. Any guest wanting to exit before eight would have to wait and any guest wanting to enter after ten thirty would be forced to ring the bell, which disturbance was not what would be expected of a guest. Other neatly printed cards on the Guest House notice board above the glossy half table in the hallway set out other expectations: guests should make sure no sand was brought into the hallway, stairs or rooms (this repeated, as Mrs Mills, for all she had spent all of her life by the sea, had a particular aversion to sand); guests should be considerate of other guests and there should be no undue noise; guests should be aware that breakfast was served between eight-thirty and nine-thirty and the evening meal between six-thirty and eight-thirty and there would be no culinary exceptions to these timings. On both occasions a gong would be sounded to indicate serving had begun. No other food was to be brought onto the premises: Mrs Mills was aware other establishments had relaxed this last rule and others had even begun with something they called 'self-catering', but she would have nothing of such developments and as she said, she had removed any strictures as to drinks: flasks and even some bottles could be brought into the rooms as long as they were properly managed and the bottles properly disposed of. No towels were to be taken from the rooms, however: this expectation Mrs Mills had considered worthy of the main notice board, given the association and temptation of beach and towels, and it was repeated in the cards posted in the rooms themselves, alongside other room-related instructions.

In Mrs Mills' eyes it was all very neatly and very clearly done; clarity was all she saw in such things; had it been feasible she would have done the same with all the matters of her life. Her husband, for example, had been laid to rest in the graveyard of the nearby church for some twelve years now, but it did seem to Mrs Mills that during their life together it would have been no bad thing if she had been able to post a few clearly printed expectations for him.

She watched the Cresswell family processing, hunched, through the gate and up the path and then climbing the front steps, the woman and the girl in macs and hats, but the man and the boy bareheaded. (Umbrellas were not common in mining communities.) Mrs Mills turned to the mirror then to make sure of her appearance. The young Irish woman she had recently employed would be waiting as instructed in the hallway to greet the arrivals and show them to their designated rooms; the girl had already done as much for the Phillips couple, and Mrs Mills considered whether she herself should make an appearance on the landing or wait as she had with the Phillips couple until the guests had settled in. She decided to show herself. She had welcomed the Cresswells for a number of years now and watched the two children grow, and she felt a strain of affection for the family, particularly the man and the boy, the first being properly deferential and in her opinion properly manly and the boy, quiet and quite good looking. The woman she liked less, being a little brassy as Mrs Mills' own mother would have called her, rather too full of herself, at least in potential, and the little girl wholly unresponsive, perhaps even somewhat simple. Through these years the children had not really made their presence felt, however, unlike another brood which Mrs Mills herself had been forced to admonish and which, had there been an attempt on its part to return, would have found her saying she was full. In general the guests at Rosedean were those whose offspring had grown and were no longer with them or others who, like

Mrs Mills herself, had none. In general also, her guests were orderly and quiet people and hers was a quiet and orderly Guest House. Even the meals could be taken in something approaching silence and the few who did avail themselves of the sitting room and the magazines she had set out there did so with a quiet appropriate to the setting. Her guests were here to get away from the banging and the hissing of factory machinery (this was her thought, although she could do no more than imagine such a setting), the hurry and the noise of some production process or the darkness of a coal mine, and where other guest houses had installed a television in their sitting rooms Mrs Mills would never do so.

What she did, however, was hold the Friday Evening Social, the evening before the Saturday which was habitually the day of arrivals and departures, at which Social she would play the upright piano set against the sitting-room wall and invite, indeed expect, all her adult guests and selected staff to join her. There might even be some singing. Mrs Mills had been particularly pleased by the gathering of the previous evening when Mr Smith and Mr Devonshire had done some Flanagan and Allen and Mary, the Irish girl, had sung a Ruby Murray song quite nicely; and this year's newcomer to her invitations, Mr Teale, had shown he had quite a nice baritone in a rendition of a song Mrs Mills did not know (and so he had had to sing it unaccompanied), but which had been quite appropriate in its sentiments and its tune. She was pleased that Mr Teale, who seemed quite a hearty fellow, was here for a fortnight with his fat, quiet wife: he could sing again at next Friday's Social, she thought, and having heard his song she might be able to pick out a few notes of accompaniment this time.

Quiet and order and expectations fulfilled had been the tenets of Beryl Mills' life, but within such a framework she was aware there were times when a heart and its heartiness should show. The problem was that if the framework does not dominate, then people do not know when to stop. Mrs Mills could see this in Bridlington itself, where the amusements and the shows which had once been this occasional heart, this appropriate and occasional heartiness, were enlarging and expanding and becoming every year more brassy;

when heartiness outweighs order, when it is persistent or expected or even demanded, then it seemed to her the beast may well be loosed.

She straightened her cardigan and the string of pearls her husband had given to her for an early anniversary. The dress was appropriate, she thought, the little red flowers on it not too pronounced. She kept her brighter dresses for the Friday Social or for her visits to the Spa Theatre, although it was some time since she and her two widowed friends had found anything appropriate to see there and now as it was high season there was a brassy summer show on, with some comedian or other who had been on television. She touched at her permed hair, more a manual echo of its shape than a touch, and then more definitely at the brows she had just plucked that morning and which had reddened a little with the operation. She considered another brush of make-up, but then leaned back and found her appearance acceptable. She was older now, this was undeniable, but as the plain heaviness of her features had never allowed her or others to think them pretty she did not feel any great loss. She had even been more content with her features in middle age than she had been with them in her youth; she had been able to make something more statuesque of what had been mere weight, something more sculpted of hair which had simply been dull. She was past that prime now, she recognized as much, but the 63-year-old woman who appeared before her in the glass, the strong and orderly widow who made her own way in the world, who ran her own Guest House and had six people working for her, was not unpleasing to her. She brushed herself down, again with no more than a ghost of the movement, and went out onto the landing to offer her usual words of welcome to the new arrivals. Those and a few carefully phrased reminders as to what was expected of them.

The rain persisted in the following days, even more persistent than the August rain which can plague northern England; there were not even the breaks in the cloud which more usually come around evening when the rain clouds, having worked their disbursements for most of the day, seem to tire a little and an obliterated sun can force through something of its light and the grey sky can become at least silvery.

By Wednesday, however, the rain had become thinner and then it subsided into spits and spots, as was the phrase, and by Thursday it had stopped and there was even some spectral sunshine behind higher and whiter clouds. If the sun had got through properly on the last two days of the Cresswells' holiday week there was a chance it might have provided some mitigation to the overall assessment of what the weather had been like; rather as the hour-long pleasure cruises on the *Bridlington Belle* or the *Thornwick*, which went up along the coast as far as Dane's Dyke in chugging silence and then ten minutes from their return to the harbour struck up with an accordion to give a semblance of merriment for the potential customers watching the return; rather as the sitting room of Rosedean Guest House suddenly burst – or at least lifted – into music and song on the Friday evening. The weather, however, continued to be defiantly dull and this did not help to lift the mood, dismiss the monks, with which the family Cresswell had arrived.

There were times of some alleviation for Don; he had found his usual pleasure in staring out at the infinity of the sea; he remembered his excitement at being brought as a boy himself to this same coast (only on day trips at that time: Miners' Outings, with his own pit-working father) and the unmitigated thrill it had been for him to see the unmitigated space which lay beyond the white buildings on the front. It must be hard for those who have never been lowered in a cage down a pit shaft, heard the dull, dusty thud of the safety doors closing or crawled along a trepanner tunnel to the hot cavern of the coal face to realize what such unmitigated space might mean to a miner. Don had even managed a few walks along the cliffs towards Sewerby (his wife had used Linda as an excuse not to come, particularly in the rain, and although, with a gruff awkwardness, an aching pathos which he could not recognize himself, but which had in it an echo of that same space, Don had asked Billy if he wanted to come along, the boy of course had not done so). Even under the wet clouds, however, Don had found something of this old pleasure and for a time his disappointments took on their own cloak. But when he turned back, the monk came out again from under this, shaking his head at how a son who had once looked up to a father was now avoiding his father's eyes or almost levelling a gaze at them which had nothing in it but refusal, rejection and barely disguised insolence. Space became loss for Don then, infinity a nothingness, and he found himself unrefreshed by his outings, coming back not as some soul brightened by a glimpse of heaven, but as a man reminded of mortality and trapped by the circumstance of life. He was mining coal for other people and those others it seemed had no thought or sympathy for his efforts, whatever they mouthed; they would see him lowered into the bowels of the earth and have him work and sweat there and what had seemed the purpose and the hope of this – how often had he vowed that his son would not follow him down the pit, how he would get an education and not even have to see a trepanner – all of this seemingly had turned to mockery. Don felt himself wanting to strike his son again, simply for his manner, simply for the look on his face and the part he was playing in this great deception. In the blackest of the coastal cloud the father now felt he saw the primal lie of the family; the cloak, the shroud of verbalizing humanity which presents the mere persistence of a species as something relevant and reverberant in the individual itself, as something somehow of salvation.

His wife's mood had not fallen quite so far, but not having done so there were not even for her any particular moments of alleviation. Her monk, although not as miserable as her husband's, had kept up a steadier insistence, reminding her again how she had not even wanted to come on the holiday, or at least not in the form it was taking, how she had seen all this coming. Just what had Don expected of a 13-year-old boy? What had Don himself been like at thirteen? Although there had been a war which began in his teenage years, a focus which had overridden many things ... June could give such answers, but she could see also that these were changing times; she could see this where her husband could not; her husband, it seemed to her, especially with the monk on her shoulder, was incapable of seeing anything but himself in others and even in the world itself. Perhaps it was motherhood; this had been her thought more than once. It could not just be by being a woman (although these were male sparks being struck between father and son); being a woman was part of it, but were it just this then the bossy old biddy June was having to suffer in these days would have an understanding similar to her own and if anything Mrs Mills seemed to June to want to project herself quite as much as any man. The old landlady did not seem to see any of the stupidities of her ways; she did not seem to see she was as much a relic of the past as the antimacassars on the chairs or the thick-glass-fronted case with its china and its ornaments.

June's own mother had something of the same, but, thought June, she had been a mother and so had more breadth to her vision – *I'm just out of touch!* her own mother would say. *I'm just so out of touch with it all.* At least she would admit this where this Mills woman did not seem to realize she was the unnatural pose of an old photograph, the thick hemline of an outdated skirt, the last smell of chintz in a modernizing world. June bit her tongue during their very first exchange and again at breakfast the following day when the old biddy had passed amongst her guests like the Duchess of Wetwang as June had christened her, not to Don's amusement, although Billy had smiled. – How is it all? the landlady had asked and June had wanted to say *poor! It's all poor!* The toast is barely browned, the bacon sloppy strands of fat with no more than slivers of meat and the fried eggs' glassy yolks shimmering around in a slime which reminds me of something post natal. Have your kitchen staff thought of flicking some cooking fat onto the top of the eggs? Or is it all, as I am beginning to suspect, quite deliberate?! (June had amused herself with this, but she had not shared it with Don.) Are you going back into the kitchen now to share the joke with your staff and say *they are actually eating it!* Are you watering the milk? It seems so. And creating the cereals yourself from the broom you have carved? *Or are you not a woman at all?* This last had been the young mother's most outrageous thought with regard to Mrs Mills, trying to throw something of its excess into the mournful cowl at her shoulder. *Mrs Mills was a man!* Dressed up as men dress up as women to get a laugh: Old Mother Riley or the other one who came on *Sunday Night at the Palladium.* It didn't really work, June admitted this even as she thought of it; for all she had a substantial form and the face and hair of an embalmment, there was some undeniable femininity to Mrs Mills, in her voice and in the movements of her hands and in the way that, if only from time to time, June had read her responses to men. Any amusement, secret or otherwise, was welcome to June in that week, however, particularly at the landlady's expense.

– *Fine. It's all fine.* Don had given his reply to the breakfast query and June looked at him with a mixture of frustration and irritation. He was a boy from the forties or the fifties answering an elder and a better. There was some sweeter feeling which came through also as she looked at her husband, like the brief silvering of a raincloud.

As for Billy, his week was lifted only by Roy Orbison and other current voices and tunes which he could hear in the amusement arcades and those he could get, fading in and out of his hearing, from the portable radio which more than once his father had threatened to confiscate and destroy. The son had to be careful how he used this little transistor on holiday; at home he could even switch it on quietly at night when reception was at its best, even listen to it under the blankets of his bed, but on holiday here there was no possibility of that and had his father known it had been Billy's efforts to retune the radio which had caused him to be late for the coach on the outward journey then the threat of confiscation and destruction would undoubtedly have been carried out. So the monk which followed the 13-year-old boy around Bridlington was a less specific figure than the one which accompanied his father and even the one muttering vaguely at his mother's shoulder; it was more an eminence of muted, youthful anguish, a compilation of girls' faces and mournful tunes which strangely could be as pleasing as they were mournful. Why would Orbison's songs about loneliness and weeping loss, 'Blue Angels' and 'Running Scared', fill and not empty his heart? (Although the last of these had a happy outcome.) Why would a song about a girl who should be an actress because she played her faithless part so well be something he listened to with undisputed if also undefined pleasure? Why would Del Shannon's 'Runaway' be more a thrill than a tale of woe and a story of loss? The teenager had even been able to walk in the rain with something of this ambiguous excitement thanks to Shannon's lyrics or the more wistful celebration of the falling rain's rhythm from The Cascades.

In all, his monk was far less of an imposition than was his father's, for all that the young man's face seemed more of a reflection of the sullen and the downcast. His monk was a nebulous figure which had in it some sense of a future, however confused, some possibilities of realization and fulfilment when, in some indistinct maturity, cloaks and cowls would be cast off and pure love and bright being would be revealed. The teenager's moody friar had nothing to it of ending.

The little girl, meanwhile, had played with her dolls, incorporating a new addition to their number which had been bought for her on the front and altering the clothes of some to match the setting. She seemed untroubled by the weather and the change of sleeping arrangements and only reacted with awkwardness or tears as a reflection of the moods around her. The family went down to the beach on the days when the rain had stopped, but a strong, cool wind had mitigated against any lengthy stay there and Billy of course no longer wanted to play cricket with the little beach set from previous years which his father had brought along more in hope than expectation. Billy had tried to listen to his radio until his father told him to turn it off as it would disturb the others on the beach, even though in such conditions the beach was only sparsely populated, and the youngster had gone moodily off to the water's edge on his own, refusing to wear any kind of bathing costume. June had seen her husband fuming at this and had tried to calm him, and there must be no other blows she had said. Striking a child for misbehaviour was one thing, but hitting out simply because of the boy's mood would entail her own immediate departure; there were coaches every day to Leeds and trains to York, or if necessary she would have her brother come out and get her in his van. These threats had had the desired effect of restraining Don, but his mood still irritated his wife as did his dreamy simplification of the past. She too remembered those family circles which had been formed on the beach when Billy was small and her mother and her brother's family and on one occasion Don's mother came along, but Don seemed to her now to be making something more of these than they had been; he seemed unable to recall the cool wind blowing then just as it was blowing now and the children's teeth chattering as they got back into their clothes. There had been some fun, of course there had, but there had also been other things which Don now seemed to have put out of his mind. He now seemed incapable of remembering the atmosphere between his mother and hers or the arguments between her brother and his wife or that wife sitting on a knitting needle she had left on a deckchair, or his sister's son, perhaps as a result of the beach exposure, starting with the whooping cough. As she had tried to say to him, those days of connected families all holidaying together were probably going, perhaps gone. Her brother was even talking about going abroad. And had Wilf and Don ever really got on that well? Only, it seemed to June, in her husband's memory, which rubbed off edges, rounded out awkward details as if it were smoothing out a statue.

The week's holiday then was hardly a good one and June was pleased when the final full day arrived. Even her husband would not be able to pretend to himself it had been a good holiday, she thought, although she made no great matter of this, happy to have got it over with and saving for later any plan as to how it could be altered or avoided next year. There was Christmas to come before that. The usual rejoinder from Mrs Mills – *So we will see you again next year, Mr and Mrs Cresswell* – could be nodded at and dealt with later. The old biddy might even be gone herself by then. Although, thought June, she was one of those who looked as if she would make very old bones, one of those who looked as if she had been born old and so not subject to the usual processes, some kind of sea rock or cliff herself; but then June had been reading about erosion in the local paper and how there had been a sudden fall of rocks and soil in the coastline out towards Primrose Valley, about how the whole coastline was steadily receding. Even Mrs Mills would suffer the tides: June was thinking this as reluctantly she joined her husband for the Friday Social on that last day (Billy for once quite content to babysit his sleeping sister) and as she watched the old landlady moving around her sitting room with all the airs and graces of the Wetwang Duchess, ordering the men about like boys, treating all the women as she treated her employees, who, apart from the occasional appearance of some handyman or other, were all female.

– So, Mrs Cresswell here you are, my dear ... said Mrs Mills, condescension dripping off her, it seemed to June, as rain might drip off a tent. And that was what the old girl's striped dress reminded her of, with its broad red and yellow stripes, or as if someone had decided to paint wide, festive lines on a brick kiln. The younger woman smiled and nodded and bit her tongue again, knowing that here on the old girl's home ground, she could find no way of being a verbal match for her even if she had spoken out, and with no friendly female ears to whisper into she had to settle for the relieving amusement of her thoughts. In other settings she could share these with Don, in other settings some of her thoughts made him smile, but this, she knew, would not be the case here; certainly not in the mood he was in.

– Have you had a good week?

The landlady turned as soon as she could to the man of the family and June watched her husband reduced to a boy, shifting from one foot to another as he said O yes.

– The weather could have been kinder, said Mrs Mills and then, in truth without any intention of rubbing any noses in it, rather as an apologist for her home and her business – *It was quite glorious the week before last.*

June turned away and began to think of the packing.

– Mr Cresswell, have you met Mr Teale?

Mrs Mills gave the feminine turn of her hand to indicate the hearty Mr Teale. As a young girl she had been to a garden party in the grounds of Sewerby Hall and she had a vivid memory of the hostess moving amongst the guests there, much as she was doing now, turning her hand in quite the same way, glowing in a bright dress, fully in charge of the whole affair.

– We've bumped into each other once or twice! said Mr Teale, exposing some unfortunate teeth in a wide-mouthed grin, and as the representative of heartiness he was, Mrs Mills allowed him rather to cut across her hostessing. At the social function this Friday evening was, she could not have all her guests as potentially tongue tied as Don Cresswell. Having allowed this, however, she reasserted herself: Mr Teale also works in mining she said. It was no more than an appropriate connection for her, the smooth link of any good hostess, she had neither the knowledge or the inclination to consider its ramifications; it was the same to her as observing to the Briggs family that the Phillips couple also came from Doncaster.

– Kellingley, said Mr Teale still with the wide-mouthed grin. I'm Deputy there.

Don nodded, feeling an intensification of the dislike he had already felt for this man, even as they had passed each other in the hallway, but particularly as he had listened to him holding forth at mealtimes, the loudest voice Don had ever heard in Rosedean's dining room, going on about his son who was going to university and about the old Jaguar he had restored himself, which he and his wife had driven here. Don had glimpsed the mash of food inside the man's big mouth as he went on, talking even whilst he was eating, and then he had seen the unmistakable leer on the man's face as its eyes, glistening as much as the big mouth, followed the young Irish waitress around the room. The man had even winked some male collusion at Don then and had seemed impervious to the cold stare he received in return.

– I forget which mine it is you work at, Mr Cresswell – Mrs Mills continued with her hostess interconnections: bringing people together in the sweet respite of a lovely setting and a relaxing holiday was a clear part of her role. At the same time, she glanced across to see if Mary was setting out the piano stool correctly.

– I'm at Glasshoughton, said Don and as Mrs Mills herself took a step to one side he would have turned away. June had already gone to the table where some drinks had been set out. Mrs Mills considered an outlay on white wine and some soft beverages a legitimate expense for the Friday Social. Although she never provided beer. It seemed, however, that Mr Teale was not yet ready to let Don go; something in him perhaps seeking retribution for the unreturned wink. Another man had made him feel leering rather than playful, vaguely grotesque rather than quite naturally driven, and he was not about to let this go.

– I hear production's down there, he said. I hear you are down a bit in Glasshoughton. Well, more than a bit!

Don had no response for this; other than as it related to his own bonuses, he knew little and cared less about the overall performance of the pit down which he worked. On the other hand, a certain squaddie rivalry stirred in him at the negative comment this was certainly meant to be.

– Sid Walsh is your manager there isn't he? Mr Teale went on, pushing his glistening face closer to Don's. And who is it? Randall? Is that the name of the Deputy? One of the Deputies there? Don nodded. He knew both of the mentioned names, although he had no particular contact with the men. His reticence only drew Mr Teale on still further. Sid Walsh was over with us just the other day, he said. He was over at our place just the other day, looking at some of the new stuff we've had put in. I think he's thinking of doing the same at your place. Going to the Board with it. Modernizing. Trying to get old Glassie back up to scratch. You on the surface? Upstairs or downstairs? This was an unmistakable provocation and Don took on rather more of his working-day manner, in which words came more readily.

– *Downstairs* he repeated and gave its silliness a seam of contempt and actually met the man's glistening eyes, his own suddenly harder and digging through, as if through superfluity, and finding nothing there worthy of his effort.

– Knickers and kneepads, he said. Ripping it out.

June appeared beside him with a glass of Dandelion and Burdock, but he did not turn to her. Nor did Mr Teale turn to his own wife who was offering something of the same service at his elbow. Both men held their ground and then Mr Teale leaned in still closer, en element of unrequited retribution giving a false, fixed quality to his continuing grin.

– So, everyone, are we ready for a little music?

Mrs Mills waved her hand for attention, slid the compilation song book from the top of the old upright piano and settled the book and herself into position. She did not practise during high season, but the tunes she played were those she had always played and the Fridays came around quickly enough for her to feel quite comfortable with what she was about to do. From time to time her fingers slipped, but any false note was covered, she thought, by what she considered to be the overall bravura of her performance. She had, however, abandoned her off-season attempts to update her repertoire; the currently popular 'Sidesaddle' for example, for which she had obtained the music, she had found too trickily fast.

– I'm sure you will all remember this one! She launched into 'A Wandering Minstrel', slipping a couple of times early on but then warming into her act. She was aware that there was someone with the same surname as hers who appeared on television playing the piano, one of her old friends had shown her an EP, although Mrs Mills liked neither the look of her namesake nor the bouncy music she played. Bounciness was not an aspect of her own playing, more a studied determination, which to her ear was clarity, just like the clearly printed notes on her notice board.

Flipping the page with the smoothness of habit she went from 'A Wandering Minstrel' into 'Moonlight Becomes You'. Crosby had been a particular favourite of her husband's and Henry's younger face always came at least vaguely to her as she played this song. Given this and the cocoon of focus performance entails she rather lost track of what the guests behind her were doing; she could not concentrate fully on the keyboard and her hostess role at the same time, but she was aware of some movements and then voices rising behind her. *Yes, you can sing along if you want!* she called over her shoulder, as indulgent as her concentration would allow. She preferred the singing to be after she had got through her own repertoire, but this was a Social and so she must allow an element of spontaneity. One of the voices she heard being raised was Mr Teale's so perhaps the hearty fellow had been unable to prevent himself from being drawn along early. Yes, join in if you know the words! she called, feeling wholly the orchestrating force, indulgent even with some definite whirls of movement. Were they dancing? She was not sure she wanted dancing. It was only when a shrill female voice, pitching up almost to a scream, cut quite inappropriately and unmusically into 'O What a Beautiful Morning' that Mrs Mills looked away from the keys and over her shoulder at the fight which had developed in her sitting room.

At its centre were Mr Cresswell and Mr Teale, the former with Mr Phillips trying to restrain him and the latter with his wife bouncing behind him, her hands waving as if for a minstrel show. Mrs Teale it was who had emitted the scream, a surprising loudness in one who had seemed so quiet, and in her own strange confusion this was Mrs Mills' first thought. She even looked away from the melee then and back at the keyboard as if resuming her playing would reassert normality. But then a couple of expletives rang out, swear words such as had never before been uttered aloud at Rosedean Guest House, and the landlady came to her feet and turned from the piano, seeking her usual presence, but finding it temporarily overwhelmed. She saw Mr Cresswell pull away from Mr Phillips' outstretched arms then and, taking advantage of the distance provided between him and his opponent, he launched a swinging blow which caught Mr Teale fully on the side of the face. Mr Teale himself received this blow noiselessly, but his fat, previously quiet wife screamed again as if she had taken it herself. Mr Cresswell followed this with another punch into an area below Mr Teale's heart, knocking out any last vestige of heartiness, and Mr Teale, with his wife bouncing around him but not touching him, went down onto his knees and then began to keel slowly forward.

– Do you want some more?! Mr Cresswell bent over this sinking figure and shouted at it in a voice Mrs Mills had not heard from him before, a voice the like of which she would not have believed he could have, and finally she found her own

– What are you doing?! What is all this?! She raised that voice in an attempt to match the shout from Mr Cresswell and the scream from Mrs Teale. *Stop this at once!* She looked at Mr Cresswell, but received nothing but a blind stare in return. Beyond him she saw that in the grappling which had taken place during her playing and the efforts of others to avoid it, a rubber plant had been knocked over and the glass door of the ornament cupboard brought open and some of the ornaments displaced. There was also some evidence of spillage from the drinks table.

– What?! I mean *what?*! Mrs Mills stepped fully away from the piano and towards Mrs Teale who was still not actually touching her husband, but holding on to her own head as if it were in danger of falling off, emitting noises which were now more high-pitched whimpers than screams. *What?*! *I mean what?*! The tableau held for a moment around the figure prone on the floor and then Mrs Teale finally knelt and laid hands on her husband and Mrs Cresswell also reached out and drew her own husband away, looking back from the doorway with what, had Mrs Mills been seeing things as clearly as she usually did, she would have recognized was a slight but recognizable smile.

The Cresswells' coach journey back to Castleford contained only a few limited familial exchanges, but somehow the mood was better than it had been on the journey out. The monks had been left behind in their bleak, coastal monastery. Apart from the father, all the members of the family were pleased in their own way to be going home and Don's own mood still had in it the release and the afterglow of a physical victory. There was no doubt Mr Teale had provoked the exchange. Mr Phillips and another man whose name the Cresswells didn't know had said as much. The Kellingley Deputy had been the first to raise his hand, they had agreed on that; he had been the one who started with the shoving and he had also been the first to come out with an expletive. The setting was inappropriate of course, the two men should have taken the matter outside as Mr Phillips had tried to say, but if Mr Teale was going to launch a shove and a swearing insult at another man then he could expect no less than he got. Moreover, in what was virtually an admission of this guilt, the Teales had left Rosedean before eight on the following morning, rousing the Irish girl to open the door especially for them. The old Jaguar was as conspicuous by its absence as it had been by its presence. In all, it was generally agreed that Mr Teale had started the fight, if of course, he had failed to finish it. Don felt the warmth of this collective judgement in his favour as well as a new and wary appreciation of his presence in the Guest House, but most of all he was feeling his wife's approval; he may have characterized this as less complex than it was, his simpler masculinity making something merely primal of it, but its reality and its warmth were unmistakable. He also felt there might be just a hint of respect from his son; Billy had been told about the incident by his mother and, although he could hardly be certain, Don felt there was just a hint perhaps of the old pride the son had felt in the physical prowess of his father; just a hint, but Don took even this possibility as another degree of the warmth which ran through him as June leaned into him on the coach seat as she had done when they were young lovers.

June herself could not say she had not been excited by watching her husband overcome another man, by watching his blows, nor that she was unresponsive to the muscled arm she leant into now, capable of ripping coal from the earth and sending another man to the ground; but even more than this her mood was lifted, her monk finally dismissed, by the certain knowledge that they would not be going back to Mrs Mills' Guest House. The old biddy had not even appeared for their, or for anybody's, departure on that Saturday. Nor for any of the new arrivals. The young Irish girl had been put fully in charge.

– She's locked herself away in her room she has, this young woman told June as the Cresswells passed through Rosedean's front door. – She's taking it quite badly, so she is.

And there had been a smile on the young woman's face which June felt perhaps had something in it of her own smile to Mrs Mills, something of a recognition of times changing, some approval of a blow being struck as a herald of this change, the sound of a new gong. Perhaps there was an element of retribution in it also (and envy for a strong partner?); June wasn't really sure of any of this, but as she stepped out of Rosedean for the very last time, she did clearly hear something in the goodbye the Irish girl offered, something Mrs Mills had never really managed in all her years of salutations, even though it was a goodbye: there was in it a note of true welcome.

The Wanderer

(*Dion 1962*)

What he needed, Brownridge was thinking, was to tie a serious one on. That or find some totty, or both, although he had to admit that lately the skirts had not been bringing him the release which at one time they had. The last few had actually failed him, particularly the last, playing Hermia to his Demetrius, although she was clearly too old for the part and had only got it because she had put up most of the money for the production. 'Betty Boop' he had belatedly found they all called her and when it all came down, when it all came off, there had been a wrinkled width which he had found himself contemplating even as he performed. There was a well-founded suspicion on his part also that the company was smirking at him behind his back. Belatedly he had seen that it was she and not he who had another notch on their gun. There had been nothing to it of his old days as the Conqueror, the Wanderer, the 'love 'em and leave 'em' reputation he had had in his youth. London was a more complex jungle where female predators could roam as far as any male. It was not a happy recent memory.

Nor was the still more recent audition at the Bradford Alhambra which had brought him north. The humped toad of a director, sitting in his isolated splendour just under the dead footlights, with his thick, crew-necked, toad-coloured beatnik pullover rising almost to his mouth like Wilfrid in *The Beano*, had, it seemed to Brownridge, already settled on his cast and was just seeing a few others to massage his humped-toad ego. He had not even delivered the thank you but no thank you himself, but sent out his mincing, cream-faced loon of an assistant to do the dirty work. It had been a complete waste of his time, thought Brownridge, and it had also dropped him into this home visit. Although with this there was the potential recompense of being treated as the famous, favourite son, taking time out from the whirl of a far more exciting and exotic life, to demonstrate he had not forgotten the people and the places amongst which he had made his start. The stage name he had adopted was Terence Cass, and although the use of the full Christian name might be noted (he had always been Terry at school), adopting the native colloquialism as his stage surname was undoubtedly appreciated. As with most outback towns, Castleford was always appreciative of having its existence acknowledged.

Brownridge caught himself in this snobbery and it added still more to his depression, a depression which not even the glow of pride on his parents' faces had worked to dispel. 'Charlatan' was a word he was finding increasingly hard to avoid. True, he had played in Shakespeare at Leeds Grand and then on the London stage; true he had had a role in an episode of *Z Cars* on television; but more recently he had been in *Charley's Aunt* in Bristol and on the disastrous *Dream* tour which on one engagement literally had more people on stage than in the audience. The Alhambra audition was only the latest of what was becoming a string of disappointments. So the pride on the old folks' faces and on Aunt Vicky's, who had called round especially to see him, only seemed to cast another spotlight on his Charlie charlatan role and he could not find the same glow in his heart or spring in his step which he had felt when he came back home just after the *Z Cars* episode and someone had asked for his autograph in the Co-op. That television appearance was more than a year ago and his *I'm concentrating on theatre, that's my real love, you know, with a real live audience, not just looking into some camera!* might begin to sound with some of the hollowness even here which it had in London, the hollowness it most definitely had in the honest moments in his own head. *No!* He shook that head. He could still get away with it here. But then the very idea he was *getting away with it,* acting everywhere, even about his acting, extended the depression. Yes, he needed to tie one on and he began the process even before his afternoon meeting with Snowy. He bought a half-bottle of Bell's at the Co-op (where he was unrecognized) and slid it into his jacket pocket as he set off on the walk to the Charlotte Hotel where he and Snowy had agreed to meet.

The first drinks, or hits as he might call them now, proved the validity of his assessment. Before any time at all, the softening but sharpening light of alcohol's true perspective began to spread around him and he walked up and along Broome Hill with an increasing relaxation. He paused in the welfare he had played in as a child and then went on so he could look down through the allotments, feeling their greenery intensified, both the random foliage of the hedges and the more orderly rows of vegetables. *Under the Volcano* came to mind, a quite poetic but for him rather rambling work dealing in essence with its protagonist's irreparably broken heart at his loved one's infidelity (not something Brownridge himself had suffered and to which his reaction was rather philistine: *just move on to the next one, you fool!*), but which also dealt with unquestionable accuracy with the details of drink. The well-known passage came to his mind of how but through drink could anyone find beauty in an old crone playing dominoes (or was it cards? For all its fine writing and its accuracy, Brownridge had not revisited the book). How else but with the assistance of Bell's blend could he look out across a patchwork of allotment gardens with their ramshackle sheds and lean-tos and garden implements and an old chair and a dirty strip of rug and find it all beautiful? How else but as a result of the distilled nectar could he gaze on a line of lettuces in the near distance and find them a row of green, unfurling wings? Or the ragged plastic protection for some other vegetable a gleaming cloak? A passage from Tolstoy also came from his wide-ranging, if superficial, reading, in which the rambling Russian had eulogized on manual labour and described how he had taken a pause from that labour to take a draught of water from some rusty receptacle and how this had been a great moment.

This literary memory was a step too far for Brownridge, even in the early euphoria of the Bell's, and the thought he had had when he had first come across the passage (in extract, the Russian books were far too big; finishing *Under the Volcano* had in itself been a stretch for

him) that this was the romance of someone who had never really
had to do a day's work in his life, let alone a year's or a lifetime's –
that thought came through like a real lettuce. Brownridge himself
had done some manual labour as a teenager and again as a drama
student and it had been enough for him to doubt any idealization
of the activity. And repetition and necessity will kill any romance. As
he took another drink, however, even this tougher conclusion was
softened: there had been times had there not when in the middle
of some irritating exchange between the cream-faced loons of the
theatre, the precious beings from planet Thesp, wearing neck scarves
in summer and prattling on about a gesture or an intonation, times
when he had felt he would rather be laying asphalt? What use was
any of it compared to building a road? The loons, the pastry cooks,
felt they were providing the service of entertainment and some of
them were, but the most precious and the most committed (and this
increasingly in Brownridge's opinion) felt their business was to make
a movement in their watchers' soul, maybe even (and this was far
more unrealistic) make some actual alterations in the world. Even
Charley's Aunt had found a director who believed he was making a
political statement.

Brownridge took another hit and his disenchantments became
playful observations and his own honesty seemed to shine through
like an Excalibur thrusting up through the soil of the allotments.
He at least knew why he had become an actor and why he took to
any stage and it was all to do with him. It was the same with the totty!
At heart he was honest about it, he thought. *He just liked totty! He just
liked the skirt!* He took another draught. He could deliver a line he
had learned as if it had just come into his head, he could get the
right emphasis and the right facial expression; he could move as if
the motion had inevitability, just as he did with the totty. His moves
and his lines were never forced, never incongruous, usually powerful.
At his best, he it was who could instigate some temporary movement
in the soul; he it was who could draw some response from the
heart. Glancing around to check he was not actually being watched,
Brownridge raised a toast to this and to the garden allotments rolling
out before him and to the place where he had begun.

The affection was not wholly fuelled by the alcohol; his had been a quite untroubled childhood, with a working father and a doting mother and for all the smoky undernourished images he had come across in the minds of various pastry cooks down south, he had some bright memories of his youth. He toasted them all now, the friends and the girlfriends, each face glowing like some perfect fruit or vegetable – the fruits the girls, the sturdy vegetables the guys – all of which some rich northern soil or some verdant northern tree had rejoicingly provided. The girls in particular. He lifted his half-bottle to them and looked back at the welfare and beyond it to the blazing green bushes amongst which he had lain with Catherine Slater.

Snowy was approaching the Charlotte Hotel from the opposite direction, but he also had set out feeling some disenchantment with his young life. The new baby was at the bottom of this; the wailing, screaming dumpling of flesh which he had carried back and forth the previous night, bringing himself into some kind of trance which allowed him to continue with his pacing of the bedroom floor, knowing that the minute he stopped, let alone attempted to put baby Sarah back in her cot, the eyes which at times seemed as big as the head would come open and then the screams would start. Why did they call it *crying?* he wondered. *The baby is crying.* He remembered childhood instances of crying himself and recently his wife had been crying quite a lot, and there was nothing in the baby it seemed to him which resembled this. There were no tears in the eyes or on the cheeks, no sobbing as some wordless expression of misery, no tailing off into sighs and intakes of breath; the noise the baby made seemed to him more like an insistent siren, spiralling up and down, designed to call out a fireman to lift it out of some invisible fire; the child seemed content then for a time, but soon came the blank concentration, watching for any attempt to return it to the flames. The siren might begin to wind up even as a warning against this. Much advice had been given, but none of it had worked. Leave her to cry herself out, his own mother had said, but this had had the dual negative of annoying his wife as advice and the neighbours as a racket. The screams of this tiny and supposedly vulnerable being, it seemed to Snowy, might actually bring down a wall. He would rather walk the bedroom floor in a trance, for this at least could be done in quiet and there was a possibility those watching eyes might reduce in size and even close and he could very carefully disburse himself of the load into its pink railed cot. Although more often than not this was a mere ruse on the infant's part to let him think he could sneak away and put his own head down and let his trance turn into sleep, for as soon as he did so the cot reignited and the siren began again. There were times he thought when, if the baby had been consciously timing it all for maximum irritation, she could not have done so with greater finesse; and finally for all the female suggestions and advice – his mother, his wife's mother and sisters and cousins and aunts – the only comment which had been any real help had come from his male senior at work, who said: – the first four years are hell in the night, don't let anyone tell you different, but in the end it's worth it. Snowy had felt some reassurance of an exit and a recompense in this, the prospect of a time when the weary fireman might rest, take off his helmet and wipe his flame-blackened brow and look with pleasure and pride at the person he had saved.

Another aspect of the problem of course was his wife's post-natal depression; the phrase was fairly new but known in the early sixties and there was in Snowy the element of a much later debate as to whether giving an emotional state a name helps to overcome it or simply makes it more real. Certainly, being told what she was suffering had seemed to be no particular help to Debbie, nor had the medication prescribed, and hers was a far more specific and darker depression than anything Snowy was feeling. The emptiness, as he imagined it, of someone who had been so full, someone who had been so primarily purposeful confronted by a purpose altogether less definite. This too he hoped would pass, as he had been reassured on all sides it would, but he hoped its passing would be quicker than the four-year timetable his senior set. His heart went out, as it always had, to his normally sweet-natured wife and it was almost a physical pain for him to see her as blank eyed as the baby, to see her usual brightness deadened and drained and to hear the uncharacteristic lifting of her voice, mostly against her own mother, who came around every day during the day, but also against him, her husband, as if her love itself had been lost in an emptiness. It was Snowy's hope that this also was a matter of transition.

– So you are going to meet up with Terry Brownridge?!

Debbie had made no attempt to conceal her irritation and her disapproval as he prepared to leave the house. *He thinks he is something he does! God's gift, he thinks he is!* Snowy had been looking for an appropriate exit point, like putting the baby down, but just like the baby it seemed his wife was not about to let him go easily or quietly. She handed the child, perversely asleep in the early afternoon, to her mother and pursued her husband to the door.

– I've told you about how he treated Paula Swales! And Lynne Fowler and her sister! Snowy caught a glimpse of himself in the hallway mirror, his chubby, amiable features showing their recent weathering, particularly around the eyes. His school nickname had come not just from the play on his surname, but from the almost white patch which even in his school days had been visible at the front of his wiry black hair. The school doctor had explained what it was and had said it was nothing to worry about. Looks quite distinguished, he had added, which had been no particular comfort to young Kevin, who once had even attempted to address the issue with black boot polish; this had been noted by his school fellows of course and had received more ribbing attention than the mark itself. So he had left it and whilst at twenty-four he could grasp a little more of what the school doctor had meant by 'distinguished', he would still have preferred his hair to be uniformly black. Certainly he did not want the patch extending as it appeared to be doing now. He did not want to be grey haired before his time. Youth is seldom a real consolation to the young and distinguished not a word which usually appeals to a young man. Nor was it a word particularly in time with the times. And perhaps he was not in time with those times, thought Kevin Day on that afternoon. There had been no dropping out of any educational institution for him; he had not taken off as Brownridge had to the brighter and more modern lights of London. He had remained stolidly in the Castleford area. Even in his three years as a student he had lived with his parents and commuted to the University of

Leeds, then after completing his degree he had taken what everyone agreed was a good job at the dispensing chemist, married his school sweetheart and moved into a house in Townville quite near to his place of work. He even wore a white smock at that place of work, like some doctor, although he would have been the first to explain the actuality of his pharmaceutical qualifications. *Whoa! It's the Snowman. It really is the Snowman!* Brownridge had exclaimed on his one and only visit to his friend's chemist's shop. *Look at you!* Ben Casey. Or is it the ice cream man? I'll have a cornet please! Snowy smiled at the memory. He had seen his old friend on no more than a few occasions since his departure for London, but he felt sure Brownridge would lift his spirits as he usually did. At heart Snowy knew that his state was temporary and that in his case medication would be useless unless it was moved to a level which involved clear pharmaceutical risks; he knew this was something which was better simply endured, seen through, seen out; but as, with a dismissive wave of her hand, his wife turned on her heel from his little escape, he felt in need of his old school friend's lifting energy, his difference, his freedom. He's only here today, he called after his retreating wife. He's going back to London tomorrow. And received nothing in return but another dismissive gesture and a catch in the throat which seemed a bubble from the void

– Well go on then! she called. *Get off and see your friend!*

Snowy tried not to seem hurried as he closed the door and went down the path of the little semi, but he was only a few steps away from breaking into a run, perhaps from taking off his jacket and whirling it around his head like the blades of a helicopter for his flight as he had seen Brownridge do more than once with his school blazer. Snowy smiled at the image and then at himself, knowing full well that for him such abandon would never be more than an image. 'Responsible' was a word which had appeared more than once in his school reports: *Kevin is a very responsible pupil. Kevin takes his responsibility as a prefect seriously.* And he had. And now he liked to wear the dispensing chemist's white coat and was pleased by the looks he received from those waiting for his careful preparations. It was probable he would take over from old Ross, his senior at the chemist's shop, but even in this Snowy was responsible enough to know – even to hope – old Ross would not take any retirement before his junior had fully accustomed himself to all that was necessary. He still lacked experience; Snowy knew this and he hoped he would be given time to gather it before anything like full responsibility fell upon him. Those same four years at least.

His sense of release then as he left the house was, as ever, soon muted; for all its wearying aspects there was that in him that would soon want to get back to the scene of domestic difficulty, the heart of the conflagration.

He shot the cuffs of the black shirt which, to his wife's clear disapproval, he had put on under his tweed jacket and wondered whether he should actually remove the jacket, not to whirl it around his head of course, but at least to hook it by a couple of fingers over his shoulder as of someone rather more abandoned. And in this way he could show off more of the shirt. On the last meeting with Brownridge he had felt the contrast of their clothes; his old friend wore a silky and quite brightly patterned shirt and tight trousers and what was clearly an expensive sweater which he draped over his shoulders in a style uncommon in Castleford. He had also had a slim but visible gold chain around his throat. London style, thought Snowy, and although any chain or any such sweater were out of the question for him, he hoped the tieless black shirt would at least provide some indicator of modernity. He glanced down at the brown Hush Puppies as he walked and they undoubtedly seemed the footwear of an older generation, but he agreed with Debbie that there was still wear in all his shoes and the Hush Puppies had not been cheap and they still showed some quality. And they were very comfortable.

The black shirt was his great hope and he had bought it despite Debbie's objections. Those objections he found a little suspect anyway; she had once admired someone's black shirt on television so he could not escape the suspicion that it was more that *he* was wearing it. Seeing a black shirt on others was one thing but seeing one on her husband had in it some vague threat to domesticity. But then Snowy recognized the similarity in his own reactions; he liked to see his wife in tight dresses, but he had no wish to see her go out in them. Not like Brownridge, who had always preferred his girlfriends to show themselves off. And there had been plenty of girlfriends. Again Snowy smiled to himself as he walked. The girls had always liked old Browny, even in his earliest days at school and certainly in the Sixth Form where he had had some legendary successes. Even Debbie, who had been two years below them at school, whom he had first taken out on a date when she was in the fifth year and he the upper sixth, had once admitted that Brownridge was attractive. Not her type she had said, but she could see he was attractive, if rather too full of himself. Did this worm of a thought wriggle its way in because of the current circumstances? wondered Snowy. There was certainly a wormy suspicion that his wife's recent tirades against his old friend were protesting a little too much. He remembered the other local girl, although the name didn't come to mind, who had done nothing but speak scornfully of Terry Brownridge then ended up going out with him. Was there something in the smell men such as Brownridge developed which drew women on? (Snowy had even mused on the chemistry of this.) Some residue each girlfriend left which grew stronger as it grew thicker, as if women found themselves pulled towards it by the traces of other women? In men such as Brownridge then it became a layered confidence which men such as Snowy, who had only really known one woman, could never have. Not that Snowy particularly wanted it. For all his lack of experience, he was quite cognizant of the likely side effects of any chemical excess. He had watched his friend with interest and amusement, but never really with envy. Was this changing for him now? Snowy could not but ask himself as much as he walked. *Would he rather be going off tomorrow to London?* Off to some stage or some television camera and something which had no smell of nappies and the cleaning fluid used for them (a smell altogether more cloying and murky than the cleaner, crisper smells of the chemist's shop), some place where the sense of female flesh retrieved its excitement from the dull hothouse necessity which was all he felt around him at present? Some place of *adventure*? Snowy shook his head at himself again as he approached the Charlotte Hotel.

– The Snowman! His old friend's greeting was everything Kevin had expected and he smiled pleasure and admiration at Brownridge, who was leaning with his usual casual confidence against the bar of the hotel's posh lounge. Here was the person Kevin had seen on the big stage in Leeds, the same person who had been on television. It had been strange to see him on that little screen, looking more or less just as Kevin knew he looked in real life, but become a member of the new elite of images millions could watch, those with an extra dimension for all their dimensions were reduced to two. Here he was in the flesh and that flesh knew him and greeted him as an old friend. – How are you buddy? Terence Cass, as Terry Brownridge called himself for the stage and the screen, extended his hand and Snowy took it and then returned the punch to his arm with a light blow of his own. *How is fatherhood treating you?* Brownridge showed his white, even teeth in the playful smile he had.

– You're looking well on it, kidder. Really. Definitely more mature. Definitely! Snowy smiled in return. Brownridge was wearing a dark blue suede jacket with a leather collar which he had turned up a little in the style of some pop star. A beautiful jacket, thought Snowy, no doubt acquired in London; a jacket which fitted and suited Brownridge so well. This had always been the case with Brownridge, he thought; somehow his clothes had always fitted him so well, somehow he had always managed to get the right touches whatever he wore. Snowy took off his own jacket to reveal the black shirt.

– So what chemical composition is it you are drinking?

Brownridge nodded towards his own glass of yellowed ice cubes and Snowy knew he could not ask for the shandy he preferred. He needed to commit himself to this brief escape, he thought, and although his wife and his mother appeared as ghostly but stern observers on either shoulder he said that he would have whatever his famous friend was having. Brownridge dropped a pointing finger towards him in approval at this.

– And here I was thinking it would be too early for the hard stuff for the Snowman!

– Well – Snowy grinned and tugged at the collar of his shirt. – Like you say, getting a bit older.

At which, Brownridge moved his face in closer as if he had just heard a deep-seated truth. *Wham, bamalam!* he said and smiled and Snowy felt an elevation, a brightness, even a carelessness inside him, rising like a song.

A barmaid came forward at Brownridge's beckoning, a pleasant-faced young woman with rather too much red lipstick for Snowy's taste, but one who in that moment seemed appropriate, some shapely model from an advertisement, programmed to simple indulgences. This is Laura, said Brownridge. And I've already told her I love her, so don't you start. He smiled at the young woman who tutted and blinked but returned his smile.

– It's Lorna not Laura, she said and glanced at Snowy and he was pleased to be part of this. This was *chatting up* young women. This was what young men did, although he himself had never really done it; this was young males in action and here he was in the company of one of its expert actors. Beneath the excessive make-up the young woman was quite attractive. – *Lorna* – he echoed the name and even met her eyes – Like *Doone.* He saw those eyes cloud a little.

– Like what?

– Like Doone. You know, like the book, *Lorna Doone. Doom* was what sounded for Snowy, however, and the song flattened out and all that faced him across the polished bar was the young woman's puzzled face.

– So, two whiskeys, Lorna Laura! Brownridge called the barmaid's eyes back onto him and clutched at his old friend's arm with his own song of affection. The old Snowman could still be relied upon, he thought, and a whiskey joyful memory came of years ago when the two of them had been talking to a pair of totties and old Kevin had gone into what the chemical formula for something or other was.

– Doubles. That's the deal isn't it? He had the barmaid's attention, although she did glance again at Snowy as at an alien presence which had offered a brief unintelligibility.

– We'll be over there in the soft seats ... Brownridge leaned towards the girl. – Would you bring them over to us? Please. I just want to see you in motion.

He held the young woman's gaze and Snowy remembered the advice Brownridge had once given him on how to talk to girls. Be simple and straight at first, he had said. Don't overdo it, don't put them off. Meet the eyes but don't stare into them, build up to that. It's like acting, let it all build up. And here was Brownridge, thought Snowy, building up. But then it helped if you actually looked like Brownridge; Snowy had thought this as he received the advice and he thought it again now; Ratty Leach or Big Ears Gamble could have had all the building-up techniques in the world, but their successes would surely still be limited.

He followed Brownridge to one set of the leather armchairs arranged around the tables of the lounge and they settled themselves into these as the barmaid brought their drinks with a flourish of mock irritation but then a consciously sashaying return to her post.

– So, kid, how's the old pharmaceutical trade? asked Brownridge then. Still the Sorcerer's Apprentice there? What was the old dickbrain in charge there called? Ross, yes, Ross. Is he treating you OK?

– Fine, said Snowy. He's fine really when you get to know him. And a good chemist. He took a sip of the whiskey, the very aroma of which was faintly repellent to him, but he must commit himself here, was his thought, just as he was committed elsewhere. Commitment was his nature.

– Well, that's good, said Brownridge. And I certainly like those coats you wear. *Middle and leg, umpire*! He lifted a finger and Snowy recognized that his old friend was already quite drunk and he felt the disapproving presences again on his shoulders. It truth he rather disapproved himself. It was not yet two in the afternoon.

– So how's London? he asked, lifting his glass and letting the more pleasurable sensation of the ice cubes hit his lips, taking in only the thinnest sip of the liquid.

– *The Smoke*! Brownridge shook the ice in his own glass. The big city! The concrete jungle. It's good to get away from it to be honest with you. It's good to get back to some real people. More honest up here, more straightforward!

Snowy saw the blur pass briefly through his friend's eyes but he could not deny that as someone who had decided to stay he was pleased by the comment. Other comments of a similar nature followed and then some happy and comic reminiscences and the whiskey began to seem less repellent to him and they had another although this time Kevin asked the sashaying Lorna for a glass of water to go with it, which request the young woman again treated as if it had come from a briefly visible Martian. Brownridge pointed a finger of approval, however. *Sensible stuff, kidder!* he said. Sensible. I remember you telling me how the drink actually dehydrates you. I remember you saying that and I remember old Deranged Grange casting nasturtiums on it, saying how could drinking possibly dry you up. But you were there with the chemistry, boy, you were there with *the formulae!*

– Well, it's true. Snowy could feel the alcohol running its softness into his own brain, but scientific fact is scientific fact. He said this. *You should always try to drink something with your drink.* He laughed then at what he had said, as loose and pleasant a laugh as he had given in many a day, and when Brownridge leaned in closer he mirrored the movement. *And what about some of the other stuff coming around?* His old friend winked. Some of this new stuff. It's less dangerous they tell me. The wacky backy isn't as dangerous as the old Capstans. Nor is the snow, Snowy, *snow.* The two young men leaned their heads together and laughed at this mere echo as if it were a joke.

– You can get it all in London, said Brownridge, opening the palms of both hands. *In the smoke, the smoke.* He whirled his long fingers upwards in a rendition of clouds, but then he pulled a greater focus out of them it seemed. He had always been able to do this, thought Snowy; there were other times he recalled when he and Brownridge had drunk together and he had felt the whirling pit beginning to open beneath him whilst his friend, it seemed, could always step around it, he could always pull at least some clear elements of sobriety from any fog. *So what do you think? Is this new stuff safer than the old stuff?* The question seemed a sober one and Kevin drew himself up to answer in kind. The new stuff as Brownridge called it had all been used before, he said, medicinally for that matter, and there was no hard evidence of any harm as there clearly was with alcohol and tobacco. But then as with anything, he went on, the best path is the tested and recommended prescription, otherwise the consequences will be different for different metabolisms, the issue more a matter of physiological chance. Snowy heard himself going on a little then and although he saw Brownridge's continuing smile he was happier when his old friend called out to Lorna again, although this time, emboldened by the whiskey he had drunk, he ordered a pint of his far more favoured shandy.

– And another glass of water, added Brownridge, laughing.

When they left The Charlotte to walk up towards Townville, Snowy recognized that it was he who was rolling a little whilst Brownridge seemed as steady as ever. His old friend even caught him on the edge of a roll and held him with an arm around his shoulders, dispelling the last of the ghostly faces which had been resting on these. Not really used to the whiskey, said Kevin, and Brownridge smiled.

– Sometimes you need a little help to see the beauty around you, he said and moved his hand as if across a screen in front of them, taking in a line of houses and the gentle rise towards Whitwood and the green strips of the sports grounds. Look at that! he said. *Beautiful!* And his finger moved towards the winding wheel of Whitwood Colliery. Even that! Even that, old Snowman. Even coal. Black, slatey diamond. Burning. Glowing embers! Snowy nodded, breathing in deeply.

– It's coming, kidder! Brownridge went on then, and Kevin could hear the power and the concentration his friend could invest in words; that he could invest in anything. This was his friend's secret, he thought, this apparent belief. – You watch – Brownridge made a more sweeping gesture – You see, it will all be about places like this before long. All that southern stuff will be gone, all that cocktail crap, all that *tennis!* Brownridge hugged him closer, more physical contact than they had ever had; something else learned in London, was Snowy's blurred thought.

– It will be about *real* people, buddy! About *real life*, that's what it will be. It'll be *coal!* It'll be about what's hard and bright and beautiful and can be set alight. That's what plays and shows will be about, not damn farces, not stupidity, but real dreams, buddy, the enchantment in reality!

Brownridge stepped away from him then and lifted both arms to the heavens.

The enchantment in reality. The phrase came back to Snowy as he walked with the baby that night. Inspiring, uplifting, he thought. It had not just been the drink; he might even argue the alcohol had prevented him from a full and clear appreciation of what his friend had been saying, what his figure had *represented.* Perhaps he should have stayed out with him as Brownridge had wanted him to. He had wanted to go the Great Wall as they had used to with Ginner and Lang. Snowy had promised Deb he would be back in time for tea, however, and in time for the evening operations with the baby, and he could not risk throwing his wife out of the precarious balance she was working towards. The outing itself had already threatened this and the fact that he had had a drink. And there was work at 8.30 sharp the following morning. Brownridge had been disappointed, but he had never been one to insist on anything. In another flush of affection and inspiration, Snowy recognized this; his friend had never been insistent, a hint of negative had always been enough for him and he had always been so aware of hints. People were drawn to him, but never through any insistence or attempted domination on his part – the women themselves should recognize this, thought Snowy – people were drawn by the *promise* Brownridge offered, by the sheer glamour of his presence. He never forced himself on the elements of the reactions, he was their catalyst.

– Yes, you get on back to the family, kidder, Brownridge had said. That's where it is really is. That's where the truth is.

Had he meant this? Snowy wondered as he paced the little bedroom. Brownridge had seemed as if he meant it. But then this was his secret as an actor, seeming to mean whatever he said. Whatever it had been, whatever mixture of alcohol and truth in whatever proportions, Snowy used the memory of the encounter to give a lift to his feet as he walked, to dispel the element of sluggishness of the residue of alcohol: *there was Terence Cass on a well lit stage and there again, a glittering, moving image in black and white.* And there – it was some time now since Debbie and Kevin had shared any full embraces – there was Brownridge with the short-skirted barmaid, perhaps in the alley near Burton's as he had once described his encounter with Gayle Tankard. Snowy let this particular image go as inappropriate to his present task. Nor had Brownridge been the type who had given many such accounts. Ray Grange, with far less basis, had been far more detailed in his stories, many of those details probably imaginary. Whereas, thought Snowy, if Brownridge told you, it would be true. For all his ability with performing, for all his speaking of parts, there was in him a real sense of truth. In tune with the times, thought Snowy; increasingly so as the lies and the facades of the past and of accepted ways and institutions were increasingly being revealed. Youth and truth were chiming together, he thought, and his last image of Brownridge was as some embodiment of this, standing with his arms raised against a backdrop of Townville, declaring how enchanted reality would soon be emanating from its depths and how individual souls would find their freedom in truth and their truth in freedom and how there could be beauty anywhere and everywhere.

As he walked with his child in his arms that night Snowy could not have known this image was to be the last he would have of his friend in the flesh. They had agreed he should visit Brownridge in London as soon as the home situation settled down and Debbie was back to something of her old self. They had agreed also that Brownridge would let him know of any plays he was in, any performances he was giving, which were in a reasonable radius of Castleford and Snowy would make sure he got to them; and Brownridge must also be certain to let him know of any television appearances so he, Snowy, could be certain not to miss them. Brownridge had assured him of all these things. Yet, after that afternoon in the Charlotte Hotel, Snowy heard nothing from his old friend, not even the occasional amusing postcard sent from some venue or other (writing letters to each other was not what men of the area did). There was no telephone call either, even though Snowy had made certain Brownridge had not only his mother's number, but the number of their own recently installed apparatus. And then some five months later came the news that Terry Brownridge had suffered an accidental death in his attic flat in London. The news did not appear on television, nor in any newspaper, either under the name of Cass or Brownridge. The *Pontefract and Castleford Express* did not report the matter until a fortnight later and later still there was a short article and a photograph, but this was well after the event was common knowledge.

Snowy learned of it from Neil Harris, who came into the chemist's shop specifically to tell him. Harris' mother knew Brownridge's and so there could be no doubts. The parents had been called to London to identify the body, said Harris. Snowy's first reaction was, of course, disbelief, the early inability to accept that a physical presence was no more, especially one as notable as Terry Brownridge.

– Burned to death apparently, said Harris. Set his own bed on fire somehow.

Snowy had looked blankly around the products on offer in the chemist's shop.

– He didn't really smoke, he said. Brownridge had tried smoking as they all had in those days, but Snowy remembered the conversations in which they had agreed that whatever the fashion the evidence against inhaling tobacco smoke was increasingly indisputable. Nor had Brownridge wanted his teeth discoloured or his lungs impaired.

– Well, apparently he was smoking that night, said Harris. Or doing something whatever it was. And set his bed alight.

For all the apparent concern of the delivery, Snowy recognized the messenger's standard pleasure in the drama of his message. Harris would have made a poor actor, he thought. And there was also discernible in him the comfort people feel in the sense of equilibrium which an elevated form brought down entails. Nor would Neil Harris be the only one who would be less than grief stricken, thought Snowy. Jealousy is a compound reaction. There might even be some women who would feel pleased. Kevin looked for this in Debbie when, still in something of a daze, he passed the news on to her, but his wife by that time had more or less recovered herself and whatever she had thought of Terry Brownridge, her sympathy for her good husband's shock dominated her response and her comment that he never really saw this particular friend these days was kindly in its intent.

Snowy, however, could not but replay the last image of Brownridge in his mind, his arms raised to heaven and his heartfelt, impassioned evocation of the enchantment in all things, and when he had finished listening to the news from Neil Harris he had gone in to ask Mr Ross if he could go home early, the first request for unprogrammed free time he had made since that Wednesday afternoon and the Charlotte Hotel. He had wandered out of the shop with nothing around him then, it seemed, but simple elements, basic preparations without their crucial ingredient, their catalysts, and he had gone almost two hundred yards from the shop and towards his house before he realized he was still wearing his chemist's white smock.

Big Bad John

(*Jimmy Dean 1961*)

So nothing of the gentle giant here?

The probation officer who had come out from Wakefield looked at Sergeant Powell, who inclined his head. *No, nothing of that.* And they both looked through the dissected panes of the door to the interview room at the mass of a back which it seemed had closed around the chair like a great hand. There was a tapering then to the head and the American-style crew cut. This head was almost motionless, its eyes fixed on the old photographs of Castleford centre which the sergeant had recently hung on the walls of the otherwise bare room. Whole family's like that, said the sergeant. In his day old Walter could fight with his shadow. The policeman looked at the thin young official and the thin excuse for a tie he was wearing with the condescension he used to prevent himself from feeling annoyed. This latter response he had found was bad for his digestion and his shift was almost over, and he could already smell the pork chops and the gravy he knew were to be his tea that night. All he had to do was ease himself through this last bit of nonsense he had been landed with and he could get on his moped and head for home.

– So a family history of violence …

The younger man pushed the metal-framed spectacles back up his nose.

– No doubt he was knocked about himself as a boy.

He shook the sandy mound of hair which the sergeant looked down on with distaste.

– We all were, he said, making the remark as light as he could. He had little time for the gathering climate of excuses, although he was aware his new Inspector was making some efforts with such initiatives; hence this young man's presence.

– But this one can be a real bad lad, he went on. Although his brother's worse. He's a good few years older, closer to thirty than twenty, and hunchbacked. Hunchbacked is Vic … The sergeant did at least stop himself from the humorous references to bell ropes and Charles Laughton which the constabulary had applied to the older Wells boy. He kept his tone as even and professional as he could: He's in Armley, he said. GBH. He watched the sandy hair shaking again, its fringe down to the eyebrows, strands of it reaching over the ears.

– So this one's following in a family tradition.

The young man nodded and the sergeant sniffed.

– You could say that. Although Sam here is twice the size of the rest of them. Vic, he's the one in Armley, is nothing like as big and the two girls are no height, big like, but no height. Old Walter was biggish but nothing like this one. The sergeant faltered on the local knowledge he had, but decided it might be appreciated as background detail.

– There was some talk Sam wasn't even his. There was some talk he was some merchant marine's Mavis took up with. The mother's from Hull and she's – well, let's say she used to be known, you know …

The young man turned his pale face towards him as if perhaps he didn't know and the sergeant left it at that. There were two measures of life in Sergeant Powell's philosophy, the straightforward and the hopeless, and as this youngster was clearly in the second category he could talk to him as he did to Grannie Grant who made almost daily visits to the station to complain about imaginary thefts. What he could not do, however, was leave him alone, or at least unobserved, with Sam Wells. If this official thought the big young man who was sitting with some reasonable calm in the interview room at present could be relied upon to maintain this calm, he was mistaken. The sergeant had already alerted the two constables on station duty, although the prime message of the alert had been to say that if Big Sam kicked off he would probably be intent on exiting the station and that he should be allowed to do so. Sergeant Powell hoped Constable Walters, who fancied himself something of a hard case, had taken this in. The constable was quite a tough kid, but he did not have the look the sergeant had seen in the eyes of those like Sam Wells. He glanced again at the probation officer. And this one would not have seen that look either, he thought, nor would he recognize it if he saw it; for him there would always be a line of reason, motivation as they called it now, which once found could be repaired and drawn upon like the string of a complicated marionette; he would have no idea that in some men such lines become so irrelevant they may just as well not be considered; in some men when the trigger is pulled, when the switch is thrown, violence becomes an entirety.

– I think I'll just have a word with him.

– Not really necessary, sir. Sergeant Powell, who had been in the army, offered the salutation as something which might work on youthful vanity. All the Inspector wanted, I think, was an observation. Young Sam may not even be charged on this one. The witnesses say the other man started it.

– The one in hospital?

– That's the one, sir.

The young official was insistent, however, and Sergeant Powell considered his options as he watched him go into the interview room. Calling out the constables would be a potential provocation in itself, he decided, so he simply made a visual check that the exit route was clear. He glanced up at the clock then. Sergeant Reeves would be on in half an hour and he could hand the whole malarkey over to him.

– Hello there, I'm Simon Morrison. I'm a probation officer with the West Riding Authority ... Sam Wells turned his dull, steady gaze from the photographs of streets onto the young man who had come into the room. He looked rather like the pop star he had seen on television, the one his sisters liked. 'What do you want' was his song and had Sam's brain been quicker he could have matched this title to a question of his own. The concurrence did at least come vaguely to mind, but it was soon overridden by the official's – I've just been asked to make a few observations – and Sam settled for his usual silence, taking in the last word with some suspicion, more for its length than its implications. He was always suspicious of any long words used in his presence, always ready to respond to anyone being a clever clogs. This had been the beginning of the bother at the Rising Sun where some clever clogs of a stranger had asked him if he had ever played in goal and then kept on at him, egged on by his mates. He had been the first to raise his hand, or a prodding finger. Also he, Sam, had been willing to take it outside as the landlord had called for them to do, but the man had kept on and finally he had had no choice and as they pulled in close he had got a good one in; he could feel the impact with some pleasure still. The opponent had barely got a blow in after that, and Sam had brought his big knee up into another pleasurable softness and then, unhooking himself from the desperate grappling, he had hauled his opponent around and got in a proper wallop. His knuckles still had a sweet residue of this and he could still feel the limbs falling from him and see the loose daze which made the face as soft as any girl's and wide open to another punch, which Sam had delivered as if into a pillow. *What they should recognize, however* – another slow but quite clear thought came – what they should all recognize was that he had then allowed people to pull him off. What they should realize was that he had not hit the man again as he would once have done. These days he was showing more restraint; at one time there had been occasions when he had been looking for it, in some ways he could see this now, but these days it was all retaliation on his part. *They should recognize that.* He looked through the probation officer's gossamer frame to the old sergeant. As he had told the sergeant, the other man started it. He had simply retaliated; this was all he did these days. The trouble was that in this increasingly flashy and clever clogs world there was so much which called for retaliation.

Sam's gaze came slowly back to the young man who was still talking and he saw the appropriate apprehension in him, the deference to a greater physical presence which he had become accustomed to receiving, and given this he allowed the man the leeway of a few questions and answers. Yes, he had been bound over after a previous provocation, but no he did not think today's lunchtime incident was a breaking of that bond; the man had laid hands on him first, what options had he had? Sam's thoughts moved at their usual steady pace; he did not consider himself slow or thick as a few, to their physical regret, had called him; he simply saw matters for what they were and saw also how others could use words to dress and present those matters as something they were not. He began to see something of this in the probation officer as he nattered on, particularly when a certain element of comfort came creeping in to replace the apprehension, and so Sam let his gaze fully become its usual mixture of emptiness and threat, quite indecipherable to such a man, not least because there was nothing in it other than threat to decipher. These days, thought Sam, he would probably not turn on such a feather; this should be recognized; not since school had he really taken on anyone completely unworthy of his size. As long as they offered him the appropriate deference of course.

– Can I get off soon, Sergeant Powell?

Sam turned away from the probation officer, turning his whole upper body which, given its bulk, was the easiest way for him to turn his head, and addressed the sergeant, who was also a biggish man, though old and quite fat. He had fought in the war and won some kind of medal and Sam had had a few acceptable talks with him, which had usually ended with the sergeant saying he should join the army: *Before you end up like your brother, doing something so they won't take you. Get a bit of order to it, lad!* And yet, thought Sam, his brother had done National Service and he had come back from it worse than when he went in; although they did say he had spent most of his service in an army jail. Sam had listened to the sergeant, but the steady thought had come into his head that he would have difficulty following the army's orders just as he had at school and then at John Lumb's and then at Poskitt's, although in the last case everyone agreed the Poskitt's pallet manager had been a clever clogs.

When he left the police station, which was soon after his appeal to Sergeant Powell, Sam lowered his head to go under Ticklecock bridge and out past the Railway Arms where a couple of men in the group waiting for the pub's bolt to go back hailed him and asked if he was coming in for one. He lifted a big hand in a no. Like Sergeant Powell he had begun to feel a real need for his tea and the Railway Arms would have nothing but scratchings and stale pies. He could get Diane or Paula to go out to the chip shop and there would still be some of the fruitcake left for afters. The mouth stretching across almost the whole of a face, which seemed the smallest part of his visible anatomy, moistened with this prospect and when Sam arrived back at the terrace on Glebe Street he was not pleased to find a visitor in the house.

– Go out to 'chippie for me, he said to his sister, who was squeezed into an armchair with the oldest of the household's dogs, and she retorted that he could go himself. The mother, however, who had been sitting at the table with the visitor, came to her feet and went over to the girl, reaching into her pinny as she went. Go on. Get twice, she said. And you can keep 'change. At which Paula looked at the proffered coins, made a calculation and detached herself from the armchair and the dog.

– Get scraps, Sam called after her and turned himself towards the visitor who was sitting at the sitting-room table in front of a mug of tea and an ashtray. He had seen the man before, an oily smear, who looked as if he used Brylcreem not only to hold the lines of hair across his balding head, but also to polish the knobbled highlights of the forehead and the big nose. He was drawing on a little cigar and as Sam looked at him he blew out a plume of smoke and then formed his mouth to blow out a ring. The man was far too much at his ease was Sam's thought, and he directed his usual blank threat towards him although this seemed rather deflected by the smoke.

– Mr Cox has got something to say to you.

Sam's mother, Mavis, went back to one of the three upright chairs which were set around the sitting-room table and lifted her own filter-tipped cigarette from the ashtray, drawing on it deeply, before looking across at her troublesome son. *Who'd have 'em!* she had been saying that morning to her own sister. *Nothing but bother they've been! Just like him!* This 'him', as the sister knew without elaboration, being old Walter, who had left home a number of years ago and whose whereabouts were unknown. Vic at least was out from under the mother's feet at Her Majesty's pleasure, but the son who stood before her now like a great upended sideboard left where it was because it was just too heavy and too awkward to move, seemed incapable of holding down a job or fixing himself with a girlfriend or doing any of the things which might result in getting him out of the house.

– That's it, chum. I've got an offer for you.

The greasy man sat back in his chair and blew out another smoke ring.

– As you know I'm the manager at the Star Picture House …

Sam gave no response, but watched the smoke ring rise and distend and curl into itself in a disappearing knot. What he wanted was his tea. He could already taste the chips and the battered fish and smell the salt and vinegar. He needed this stain of a man out from the table as it was where he usually ate and the ease with which he could physically effect the removal was like a slow, clear thought in itself. *Had they really recognized just how much he was restraining himself these days?* If Mr Cox caught anything of this he didn't show it. There was no deference in him, nor any appearance of being intimidated. In fact the only oppression the man was feeling was just being in this terraced house, which seemed to be a mound of poor possessions and pets. One of the daughters had been holding a rabbit as he arrived and apart from the old dog occupying the armchair there had been another tied up in the little garden and another which had passed through the room mad-eyed and barking until the mother grabbed it by the scruff, quietened it with a slap and slid it across the lino of the kitchen like a curling stone. She had shut the door on it then, emphasizing the claustrophobic quality of the sitting room. Cox had not examined the details, but he did feel as if he was occupying one of the few spaces in what was otherwise a haphazardly crammed storage vault. And then in came the ox of a son and the room had grown still smaller. The man might serve his purpose, however, was Cox's estimation, and he got on with his offer. He had no need of any sullen threat from any half-witted Bluto to make him want to get on and get out.

– What it is, he said, is I need someone to help out with the Saturday matinees. *Star Juniors* – he pronounced and repeated the title with all the bile it had come to entail for him. – They're the Saturday matinees we have, one in the morning, one in the afternoon, and well, what can I say, the behaviour of young people today ... Mavis nodded her head, plastic curlers on the fringe of her hair, in heartfelt agreement and drew deeply again on her cigarette. – It's turning into a madhouse! Cox blew out a less tranquil stream of smoke from his Wills' Whiff. There are some coming in now who are almost like Teddy Boys. Do you know what they did last week?

Sam was still staring blankly from his fixed position at the place at the table which should be his. He didn't like the look of this Cox man, but then he liked none of the men his mother took up with; he had even got hold of one who had clever clogged it with him once, realizing after a time his mother was punching at him from behind, shrieking as she did so. He hadn't really sorted that man out, although even Sam had recognized that from time to time he had taken his blank anger with his mother out on others, especially at school after his father took off and then at John Lumb's, although on that occasion there had been the clear provocation of someone calling her a name. None of this was of particular importance to him as he stared at the man at the table. As Sergeant Powell would have observed, the meaning of life is the next meal for men such as Sam Wells, a fact which others with bigger pictures would do well to remember when dealing with them.

– Do you know what they did?!

Cox stood and stepped away from the table, quite unaware himself of what his doing so signified. He had his own fish to fry. *A bunch of the little sods pulled the back off one of the seats!* He glanced at the mother's nodding recognition of the atrocity, then looked back at the featureless, but potentially useful mound in the centre of the room. That's right! he said, as if Sam had shown some interest. *They actually pulled the back off a seat and threw it up at the screen!* He let his glistening lips vibrate around the next exhalation of smoke. – Gene Autry was singing and up comes the back of a seat! He waxed a little more reflective then: he had told them those old Gene Autry films were not what they should be showing at the matinees. The more fighting the better, he had said, that's what keeps the audience involved, films with fighting and the cliffhanger shorts, *Flash Gordon* or *Captain Video*. He had even suggested the whole matinee programme be made up of those serials and cartoons. Any feature, he said, would be bound to have its slower sections. And showing films with singing in them was just asking for trouble, even if they were cowboys. Why don't we just go the whole hog, he had said on the phone to the distribution office in Wetherby. *Let's show a Mario Lanza and see how long it takes for them to burn the place down!* He had to put on what they sent him, however, and they were safe in Wetherby. He had tried to show some initiative, to demonstrate his managerial skills, but the skiffle group he had brought in to play between the shorts and the main feature had been half ignored, half abused and his turning on the house lights and appearing himself in front of the blank screen after the Autry incident had been ineffective; a lolly had even been thrown at him. No doubt – he had thought this as he surveyed the young faces from the stage of the illuminated cinema theatre – there were a good number, probably a majority, who would sit reasonably watching the picture, even if Gene Autry was singing, but the unruly element was definitely growing, he had seen it sniggering and gurning in the shadows, and as all the world knows an active minority can always characterize a crowd.

– So what I need – Cox came around the table and even thought of reaching out an arm to the big bugger in front of him, as in other settings would have been his management style, but he felt the force field which was an extra to the already substantial outline: *you touched this beast at your peril.* On the other hand, he thought, this was exactly what he needed. Cox himself had never been particularly intimidated by size, or at least not by the size of an individual, particularly one who looked as if he had the intelligence of a wooden beam. On the other hand, he had tried intelligence, both with his superiors in the cinema chain and with the Star Juniors themselves, and it had proved useless. Brute threat was what he needed, he thought, and he made his offer, which Sam took in, even though as it was being made he turned towards the front door wondering why his sister was taking so long with the food and whether, as had happened before, she had simply taken the fish and chip money and gone off with her friends. – What I need is someone on security for me at those matinees, said Cox. Someone who shows himself at the door and then walks up and down the aisles a few times during the picture. I've got a couple of girls who sell tickets and ice cream at the intervals, although after last week they're threatening not to do it at the matinees. Otherwise there's just me and another bloke upstairs working the projector and the old lad who looks after the building. I need someone who can, you know, make those little sods think twice!

Again Cox considered and rejected a managerial touch to the arm, but the mother weighed in with her support and just as the daughter arrived with the fish and chips bundled in a newspaper, they got a grunt of agreement from the son. For a ten-bob note, Sam would be there at the Star Juniors matinees.

And there he was the following Saturday.

– *Every morning at the mine you could see him arrive, he stood six foot six and weighed two forty-five* – Cox amused himself with the opening lyrics of the Jimmy Dean hit and then he waved the projectionist over to look down from the upstairs window at the big man who was staring at the cinema as if wondering if it was the right place.

– Look at him, said Cox. As much brain as an unmanned barge. If you went down now and told him this was a warehouse, he'd go home. *Big lad*, said the projectionist and Cox dropped his cigar stub into the fire bucket. That's about all he is, he said. But then that's what we need. Look at him. Like bloody *Gulliver's Travels* down there! The queue for the morning matinee had begun to form, a twitching, jabbering line, mostly boys, and all, it seemed to Cox, completely incapable of keeping any of their growing limbs at rest. – Right, he sighed. Let's open up.

He ended the morning matinee pleased with himself, however. He had positioned Sam next to the ticket kiosk as the customers filed in and this it seemed had had its intended effect. He had also given prominence there to a sign he had made himself saying that anyone causing any trouble would be put out of the cinema and he felt that even the twitching Lilliputians who filed past it made the connection that this was the big man who would be doing the putting out. He also had Sam make a couple of excursions down the aisles whilst the pictures were showing and had him escort and stand beside the ice cream seller at the interval. The whole thing went smoothly and Cox could not help but be pleased with himself as they saw off the last of the audience. He congratulated Sam also, although he was still smart enough not to make any physical contact, smart enough also to give his instructions lightly, more as deferential suggestions. He was aware, however, that the afternoon session, which drew a rather older clientele, would be more of a challenge. But he was in good enough spirits as he let Sam go off for his dinner – *Kinda broad in the shoulder and narrow in the brain* – he intoned for the projectionist as they watched the young man walking off, although no witty rhyme came to him to complete the amusing parody.

As for Sam, he was thinking of the ten shillings. With this in his pocket he could have a reasonable Saturday night with Hartley and Binns and them. He seldom went to the cinema himself; he liked neither the restricted space nor the darkness. He had seen a few war films he had liked, but too often, even in those, there was too much talking. To be earning ten shillings just for standing around was, as his mother had said, too good an opportunity to miss, however, and Hartley and Binns had both been impressed and envious when he told them and although he still didn't particularly like the look of Cox, the man had at least shown some appropriate respect and given him quite full and manly thanks at the end of the morning.

Sam arrived back for the afternoon matinee then in a fairly serene state, full of the beans and chips and the fruitcake which had been his dinner and contemplating a reasonable Saturday night. The trouble which started even before the ticket kiosk opened its sales for the afternoon session took him by surprise. – *Who are you?* came from the midst of a group of slightly taller boys, a couple of whom were in long trousers, and Sam dropped his blank and threatening gaze towards them, saying nothing, as he had learned to do with provocation, partly because he had found this effective and partly because no words of response actually came. *Bouncer!* he heard from another unidentified source. *Is that what you are, mister? Are you a bouncer?* As he had stepped forward from the group, Sam saw the boy who asked this; a grinning ball of a boy in a reddish-brown pullover. *Have they brought you here to sort out any bother?* Even in its boyhood state, Sam recognized a clever clogs. He had seen any number of them of various ages and sizes, but always with the same and usually grinning indication that they would be using words for their own sake, not to clear anything up, not actually to *say* anything, but to foment a completely unnecessary froth of sound which had nothing to do with anything but itself. The boy looked him straight in the eye, his smug security in his youth and his facility with words slicing through the threat. Also, he had his own audience. – Don't you talk, mister?

Cox, who was upstairs in the projection room, later regretted not having placed himself next to Sam for this initial reception; he could have fielded the verbal balls with Sam as a supporting presence. He and the projectionist had just found that the *Buck Rogers* episode had been twisted on the morning rewind, however, and straightening this out had been a priority.

– What do you call your haircut, mister! came from the queue and Sam, who was looking down on the figure which had stepped towards him, could not change his field of vision quickly enough to see where it had come from.

– Are you American? The cheeky face beneath him was not to be denied its protagonist role, however; although a whisper did run along behind him from a few who knew of Sam and his brother. The boy ignored this and lifted the bag of sweets he was holding. – Do you want a torpedo? Still Sam said nothing, as nothing was coming to mind, although the urge to swat at this irritation was gathering, with the back of his hand as he remembered his father doing to him when he was small; it was the strongest memory he had of the man. The cheeky boy glanced back at his fellows. Can't talk, can't eat, he said. Like whatshisname. Frankenstein. He looked back with a fully cheeky challenge. Is that it, mister? Are you Frankenstein?

Sam leaned over the grinning, upturned face. He knew of the names his brother had been called and although he and his brother had never got on, although they had spent most of the time fighting each other, he had once battered someone who had used one of these insults in his hearing. *What did you call me?* he asked finally, but the cheeky face retained its grin and its own belief that the empty, playful words would come; the grin even widened a little at the success of bringing out a verbal response to play with. – I didn't call you anything, mister, I was just asking. I mean, have you been in pictures? There was laughter from the queuing audience and the boy, as so many others have been, was urged on against the mountain. *Weren't you in that one where they had you in chains? Where you climbed up the building?* Sam had no idea what the boy was talking about and a sliver of confusion entered his usual glare. He recognized the name which came then, however, and it was the name of an ape – *King Kong!* Weren't you King Kong? – at which his control gave way and he grabbed at the reddish brown pullover and bunched it in his fist, lifting the boy towards him. The face was still not fearful, however, although the grin at least vanished in an indignant squeal: *Get off me! You get off me! I'll tell my dad, you big, daft bugger!* Sam found himself in the clearing he had found himself in before as others stepped away from the action. He was a little confused, however, as if he was suddenly back in the schoolyard. This was too small an opponent for him these days, a tiddler, a tadpole. It squirmed exactly like one such tiny ceature and Sam let go of the pullover.

– Look at that! You've torn it! The boy pulled out the frayed portion of the V neck. All right, you are not getting in! Cox would have said if he had been present. You can get off and take any friends you've got with you! Sam had no such words, however, and the boy in an angry blankness of his own lifted his voice into a cry: *I'm going to tell my dad on you, you big, daft bastard!*

At this Sam's simplicity became complete and he swiped a hand in a downward arc which only just missed its target. The surrounding children scattered fully then and the boy repeated his abuse before turning and running and, without any thought at all, Sam went running after him. Running was not his strongest point; he had never been particularly good at any sports; they had tried him at rugby because of his size, but found him fairly inept with the ball and far too ready to respond to the inevitable contact with violence quite outside the rules. He lumbered after this little boy, however – no-one could call him names like that and get away with it – and his longer stride meant he at least kept up with the quicker steps of his little prey. They kept the same distance between them as they went away from the cinema and across the frontage of the Airedale Hotel and towards Poskitt's pallet yard where Sam had worked for a time. *Let him go!* Cox would have shouted had he been present. The point was to get the troublemakers away from the cinema. Sam could have no such thought, however; his giant hands were going to extract revenge for each of the insults he had received, particularly the last; each provocation would have its retaliation. *And whose fault would it be?* If there had been no cheekiness, no empty words spoken only for showing off, for feeling smarter and superior, then there would be no reprisal.

The fleeing boy turned down the unmade ginnel beside Poskitt's yard and Sam lost sight of him. His local knowledge came into play, however, as he knew where this ginnel led and he was able to change direction and do no more than stride across the patch of waste ground beyond the ginnel and then double back alongside the brick wall of the pallet yard, which was closed on a Saturday afternoon. Sure enough, there was his target, crouched behind a ragged bush, peering back in the opposite direction to that from which Sam was now approaching. Too late the boy saw the big shadow fall across him and as he turned he was trapped against the bush and frozen in the headlights of the blank stare from above. He squealed like a little animal as Sam grabbed again at the reddish brown pullover and pulled the light weight up towards him. The little round face now showed nothing but terror and as his squeal died away Sam saw the tears coming to the eyes.

– *Don't kill me mister!* the boy cried. Please, mister, don't kill me! And Sam faltered at this.

– I'm not going to kill you, he said after a moment and he saw the terrified little face with more precision and felt his mind opening, if slowly, to a few thoughts. *Did the kid actually think he was going to kill him?* This came with a vague sense of admonition, not for the boy, but for himself. Surely this kid did not really think he was going to *kill* him? Like some murderer? Like one of those men who creep up on kids in deserted places? Did he not recognize a just and simple punishment?

– You shouldn't be … Sam found himself attempting to word his thought. You shouldn't be saying stuff like that to people, he said, although still he saw nothing but terror in the boy's face, nothing before or behind or beyond and a quicker and more reflective brain might have seen a mirror. You shouldn't be cheeky to older people … He found a real moment of clarity then: *Just to be showing off,* he said. Just to be showing off to your mates. He looked at the little wide-eyed face above his fist.

– I know, mister. I'm sorry. The tiddler was quivering above the stream and Sam let his hand relax and then release its grip. Remember that, he said and for the first time in his life he felt like a teacher or a magistrate or some other adult authority, making a point with words. The boy fell back to his feet, but he didn't set off running, calculating that he would still be in reach. I will, mister, I will, he said and Sam looked down on the figure which it seemed had grown still smaller and was staring up at him as a supplicant might at a god. Certainly all the clever clogs was gone.

– So get off home. Sam pointed into some distance. You can't go into 'pictures. Get off home and remember what I said.

The boy stepped away and turned and retraced his steps down the ginnel, walking at first but then breaking into a run. Sam returned to the cinema queue, which had gathered again and which was still buzzing with the incident. Cox had finally appeared and instructed the box office girl to start letting them in. When he saw his new employee walking slowly back, his first instinct was to ballock him as he would have done with anyone else. What in God's name was he doing chasing after a kid?! A threat would have done or at most a quick clout as in those days could be administered by any adult to any rude child, but again he thought better of saying anything but – did you see the young bugger off? – and accepting the slow nod as a reply. Also, he had to admit the audience going into the cinema was more subdued than usual and the performance passed off without incident. He needed to give this particular security solution more consideration, was his conclusion, however.

As for Sam, he found himself in a vague confusion that afternoon; extra thoughts intruding on the usual linear quality of his mind always brought on something of this and the feeling was intensified by the flickering darkness and the riot of artificial film sounds. He even received his ten shillings at the end of the matinee in this state, although the equally usual simplicity of his manner meant nothing of it showed. He found himself pausing on his walk home then, as he attempted to take some stock of these thoughts. *Did the little kid actually think he had been going to kill him? Like some murderer, like some monster?* Sam didn't like this thought and he sought consolation in another, that perhaps the boy had truly taken in the point he had made and next time he would think twice before being cheeky, before coming out with empty words and insults. Perhaps, thought Sam, he had actually helped. As he had been thinking recently, he was not the same as he had been. What had just happened that afternoon seemed decisive proof of this. *So perhaps* – these thoughts were the vaguest of them all – perhaps it was time for him to think about himself and about his future. An echo came of Sergeant Powell talking about him not going down the same path as his brother. Perhaps, thought Sam, he should give some thought to this; perhaps to the army. Or even the police force. Somewhere where he might speak with authority. It all became too much for him then, however, and as he set off again he looked up at the heavens as if seeking some clearer, lighter and more widespread guidance. *You are nearer to heaven than any of us!* his Auntie Pat, who went to church, had said to him once and this thought also passed through his head like a cloud.

Where the Boys Are

(*Connie Francis 1961*)

Dot Lomax was a Plain Jane; her mother had said this about her to others and even to Dot herself, although when she did the daughter had taken it with the non-reactive solidity – or stolidity – which was a notable aspect of her manner; moreover, she agreed and this agreement had quashed all but the faintest resentment that her mother should have said it to her at all. In fact, Dot's own conclusion had been still harsher; if not exactly ugly, she thought, she was very close: she had her father's square and heavy jaw, above which there were thin lips and a nose with a prominent white-boned bridge and a pinker, bulbous tip. Also, from being very young she had needed spectacles, the lenses of which grew thicker as she aged, although in 1962, as she reached her forty-second year, it seemed the condition was no longer worsening (or the spectacles were improving) and her close sight seemed as good now as it had ever been, which was advantageous for her work at Town Tailors.

– *Born to a father too old* – had been something Dot had heard about herself and her brother – *Seed like tatty water* – Cousin George said this, which when she overheard him say it she hadn't understood, but then when she did understand, she had resented it and she never really spoke to Cousin George again; the same quiet but persistent reaction her father would have shown. They all said that along with the facial features it was old Harry's personality Dot had inherited; she was a chip of his solid block, reserved to the point of inscrutability, methodical and considered in her movements and unlikely to allow too many smiles, let alone laughs, to crack and lighten the plain solidity of the face. By contrast, the younger brother clearly had more of the mother, being more likely to smile and to laugh and to speak with a greater variety of volume and tone. His face was generally more attractive also, even a little girlish, although his short-legged, rather stunted figure was attributed again to the father's age at his conception rather than another echo of the mother's own small frame. What the chorus of assessment (such as formed around anyone in that community) missed, however, was the romance in Dot. They missed it early on and they certainly missed it by the time she was forty-two; by then the lines and the lineage had been drawn and the conclusions reached and even Aunt Winnie, who had the reputation of being inordinately perceptive of the subtleties of female mentality, had not seen just how much of Dot's existence revolved around this romance.

– Are you on with those again?!

The mother pointed across at the mound of women's magazines neatly piled in one of the lower cupboards of the china cabinet and Dot shut the door on them; she had needed just a glimpse to get her through the moment; she did not even need to lift one out as their stories were so familiar. From time to time she added to their number, but increasingly she preferred to revisit the passages she knew; fresh approaches to romance seemed contradictory exercises to her and whilst she was willing to look at more recent reiterations, some altered settings, some from history perhaps, she had no wish to risk anything really new, particularly nothing with the greater licence of vocabulary and action which seemed to be developing.

She offered no answer to her mother and this had the effect of sharpening the old woman's tone. – *Those bloody magazines of yours*! I'm going to throw them all out one day! Throw them down the lav! Dot stood and went back across to the mother, ignoring rather than suffering the stare from the brown eyes which it seemed were growing daily bigger but more empty. When she did look at them, the daughter was in fact quite pleased she had generated anything in them which looked like attention. *Dressing up for photos*! The mother made one of the unsequential leaps which were becoming more common in her. *I remember doing that when you had to go*— as was becoming equally frequent, she lost the last part of her thought, although it was still the case that Dot could often provide it.

Given the length and proximity of their life together, the daughter might still even be able to follow the obscure leap, the single word, the assonance or the fragment of an image which led from one thing to another. She could do so in this case as she knew the scorn her mother had poured on the idealized illustrations of men and women in the magazines just mentioned and that the mother was currently being groomed to receive their Sunday guests. Also, Dot remembered the photographer's studio in Castleford where she had been taken as a child and where her mother and father, with great preparation, had gone on other occasions. The photographs from these visits still existed, brown with the technology of the times and browner still with age, most of them deep in the drawer of the bedroom dressing tables or of the same living room cabinet. The few photographs on show in the little terrace in Park Crescent were in standing frames (embroideries and landscapes were the preference as wall hangings) and were mostly of her mother as a younger woman, although there was one of the parents together, some thirty years ago, and a couple of Dot's brother and his wife and the two small children they now had. Apart from a distant shot of her mother and herself on an outing to Scarborough, there were no photographs of Dot. She had made sure of this.

What a rigmarole! the old woman went on, moving her head around as Dot brought the comb she was carrying back into the thinning, grey hair. It had been another and quite virulent comment about hair which had sent Dot for a moment's communion to the magazine cupboard. *That bloody bun of yours!* the mother had said. *Bloody, bloody bun!* Repeating the alliterative expletive as she knew her daughter did not like swearing. The mother's mental competence seemed to return more fully when it came to virulence, as if whatever annoyed her was far more sharpening than any praise or pleasure, which was more conducive to distraction. *That bloody bun on your head* – the mother had lifted a pointing finger at the tight mass into which Dot habitually formed her hair. It was necessary for her work, but she even preferred it at home. She had no wish to have her hair cut or styled (the few occasions she had tried this as a younger woman had, it seemed to her, been disastrous; hairstyling it seemed to her was not for the commitedly plain), but nor did she care to have hair falling around her face and tickling in her neck; even at home she preferred it ordered and held.

– Looks like somebody's just thrown a brown loaf at the back of your head!

The mother had laughed at her own joke, echoing something of the gaiety for which as a young woman she had been known. – Looks like – she had rummaged around then in the increasingly disordered souvenir box of her mind – *Looks like dog shit*! This had been faintly desperate and certainly too much and Dot had given her a scolding – *Mother*! – and the old woman, still capable of recognizing when she had gone too far, had subsided, only picking herself up again when she saw her daughter going over to look at her magazines.

– Do you want to see? Having returned to her post, Dot cupped her hand under the lowest wave of her mother's hair. It was better to move on quickly from unpleasantness; this had always been her way and now more than ever with her mother, who no longer had any tenacity with criticisms and whose mental state at least meant that such focus as she was capable of could be shifted quite easily. It was a long time now since she and not her daughter had been the manipulative force of the household. The men had gone, the father long since found dead in the little greenhouse he had constructed in the back yard and Dennis with his own council house and family on Crewe Road.

Dot lifted the hand mirror, but although her mother's eyes appeared briefly in its glass, she could see they had drifted away from the operation in hand. Dot herself was satisfied, however; the effects of the home perm she had used could still be seen in the mother's hair, but the softer and more rounded waves which had now come out of the originally tightly permed curls were, in Dot's opinion, altogether more pleasing. Unlike her daughter, the mother had been quite pretty in her youth (as the photographs showed) and from time to time, if not recently, Dot had included her mother and her father in the catalogue of stories in her mind: it had been a romantic courtship after all; the ordinary girl worker at the factory falling for her older supervisor, rejecting the more callow men of her own age. The young woman had recognized and pursued her love and he, seemingly heading for a middle age of gruff bachelorhood, had suddenly found this pretty, bright young thing enlivening and rejuvenating his lonely world. What the subsequent marriage had become was another matter, but Dot's stories stopped, as all such stories should, before anything like supposed reality or real time had any effect.

– Now, do you want to put the new necklace on? She lifted the beads from the quilted jewellery box and hung them in front of the mother's eyes. I think it'll look nice with that dress.

The mother stared and then shrugged. I don't like green, she said and Dot set her features with the patience of a good seamstress. The mother herself had picked out the greenish dress and the green and black cardigan she was wearing. The daughter lowered the beads and waited for the old woman's attention to turn to something else and then she stepped around and deftly clasped the necklace on. Have you put the meat in? the mother asked as her gaze settled on the kitchen door and Dot knew she had gone back to the days when there had always been a Sunday joint of beef, perhaps even as far back as when the father was alive. It was some years now since they had made such a Sunday dinner.

– It's *tea time*, Mother, she said. I've made some sandwiches. Dennis is coming. I've made some luncheon meat sandwiches. Do you want one now? As her mother's appetite was increasingly erratic, Dot took any opportunity to feed her. The only thing which really seemed to stimulate this appetite now was cream cake, although she had recently even rejected a slice of that. The nurse who called around had said attempts should be made to get something more substantial, as she termed it, into the old girl. And try to get her to eat some fruit, the fat, brisk woman had said, but although Dot kept two bowls of apples and pears and bananas, one in the kitchen and another on the living-room table, the old woman seldom ate any and some half-eaten fruit remainder could occasionally be found openly discarded or more slyly secreted. The mother might eat some of the tinned fruit served with evaporated milk, however, and Dot had readied some of this for the Sunday tea. On the few occasions they had visited, Dennis' children had also seemed to like this, although the sandwiches had not been equally welcomed. They were two podgy little bodies anyway, thought Dot, and they would undoubtedly bring the spice they always seemed to be eating.

She wasn't particularly looking forward to the gathering, which was an unusual one, arranged at Dennis' request, and she hoped it would not last too long and certainly that it would not extend into early evening when *Dr Finlay's Casebook* came on. This was one of the few television shows Dot liked. Some of the stories in it even reminded her of aspects at least of those in her magazines and but for the rather too pronounced aquiline nose, Dr Finlay himself could have been a character from their illustrations. Dot rather liked the organized and sensible Scottish housekeeper in the show also. On the other hand she did not like Dennis' wife, who was quite loud and common and who from time to time referred to Dot's mother as 'mother'. Dot had made no examination as to why this presumption irritated her, but it undoubtedly did and the wife also gave her quite clear versions of the look Dot had received many times; the look of pity for the unmarried woman, the old maid, the sad-hearted human ornament collecting dust on the shelf. *How you must envy me!* Dot had read this in the wife's looks, although she had suffered it all before and grown used to it and she did not even consider the counter as to what was there to envy in the ragged insistence both the wife and Dennis had to exert with the two dumpy children, who were by turns sullen and raucous; or the clear evidence of tension and even dislike which could be heard in the exchanges between the parents. Whatever romance there had been for them was probably over; Dot saw this, but she gave it no particular consideration, either as an observation or as a response to any looks from her sister-in-law. But there was certainly nothing of envy in her hoping that the visit would not be a long one.

– Where's that dog barking? asked the mother as Dot studied the plates set out and wondered if she should add some arrowroot biscuits to the digestives. She could put out some chocolate fingers also, but the children would definitely gobble these up and she had found she had fewer of these left than she had thought and her mother might eat a couple later on and Dot herself liked a plate of chocolate fingers with her late evening cocoa. If she could get her mother to bed early enough, it was one of the best times of Dot's day; a quiet late evening with one or two of her magazines; she would even give some thought throughout the day to which magazines she would take out so she could anticipate the pleasure and then she could go off to bed herself with the lovely stories still in her mind, letting them and those she read in bed run there until sleep came and then with any luck have them reach like chocolate fingers into her dreams.

– That dog. Can't you hear that dog?

– No, I can't, Mother. There's no dog next door now. It got run over.

The mother turned towards the daughter, her eyes sharpening again with some vitriol. *I'm not talking about next door!* she said. I'm talking about in here. Somebody's brought a bloody dog in! The mother had never liked dogs; Dot remembered the family having a cat in the very distant past and her mother being quite upset when it failed to come home one day. But she had never liked dogs. Nor, in particular, did Dot. There's no dog in the house, she said firmly and the mother's eyes sank away. She seemed to be hearing things from time to time. Dot had told the nurse how her mother had woken up in the night recently convinced *Forces' Favourites* was coming from the wireless, when the wireless wasn't even switched on. Getting old, had been the nurse's response, drawing on her wealth of training and experience, and Dot had looked at her as yet another example of how real life could never be her stories. There were nurses in several of these stories, but they were never the big, bull-necked woman who was standing before her, an overcoat over her uniform and a shopping bag to carry medication.

– What are you doing all that for? I don't want any of that!

The mother had turned towards the food set out on the living-room table.

– Dennis is coming, Dot repeated patiently. They're coming for tea.

– Who's coming?

– Our Dennis. For tea.

Dot looked again with some satisfaction at her mother's appearance. Again there had been no envy in her recognition that her mother, even into a later age, had looked decorative. Nor had she resented that it had been the widowed mother who had flirted with the few men they came across. Dot had been content to be the solid amanuensis and her resentment had come not at any comments the mother might make as to her daughter's spinsterhood, but at any attempts to draw her out of the role. It was the mother who had altered in the last ten years; the only change in Dot had been the extension of the care she had had to exert and now it was sufficient for the mother just to be clean and groomed. As Dot looked at her mother on that day, seated in the high-backed chair bought specifically so the mother might have less trouble getting out of it, she felt that she had achieved this aim.

– They're here.

Dot heard the key turning in the front door and made a final survey of her arrangements, before going to open the door to the little hallway. Dennis had come through the front door alone, however, and closed it behind him and was wiping his shoes more carefully than he usually did; he knew his sister was more house proud than his wife, to a fault both of them in his opinion, but also there was already something of contemplation and preparation in the minute he took marking time on the doormat.

– Where's Vivian? asked Dot, neither relieved nor disappointed her brother was alone; the late afternoon arrangement had been marked out for her like a working session at Town Tailors; it could be a single stitch, a double stitch or a cross stitch; all of it was simply what was necessary before *Dr Finlay* and then the equally necessary evening ritual with her mother, before her own evening and bedtime stories. Dennis hung his overcoat and his cap on one of the hall pegs and stepped back onto the mat for another moment of contemplative wiping.

– Brian's not well, he said. Gone down with something. And Keith might be starting with it as well. So Viv thought it best ... He came into the living room and went over towards the mother, who was looking at him as at a stranger. – How are you, Mam? Physical greetings had not been the adult norm in the family, so Dot was surprised to see her brother step still closer to the mother and then, after what seemed another moment of mental feet wiping, lean forward and plant a kiss on the grey head, disarranging one of its waves. The mother lost focus of the form coming in close then recoiled a little from the contact and looked from side to side as if seeking its cause. Are you feeling all right? the son persisted and the mother finally recognized his presence. She's made some sandwiches, she said and nodded in her daughter's direction. Right, said Dennis. Right-O, and he turned towards the arrangement on the living-room table. Do you want a cup of tea? asked Dot and her brother smiled. Don't suppose you've got any beer? The question was superfluous and Dennis turned the smile into a laugh as if he had intended the superfluity as a joke.

– There's some Tizer, said Dot, then, remembering a previous visit – There might be some of that ginger beer left. Dennis shrugged – That'll do – and went to the armchair of the three-piece suite Dot had had reupholstered, although she had hauled the other armchair upstairs to make room for the mother's special straight-backed seat. She went into the kitchen for the ginger beer then came back with it and the teapot and occupied her usual place on the sofa (although she didn't bring her legs up as she often did when she and her mother were alone) and poured herself a cup of tea.

– Wet out, said Dennis.

They sat for a time in a faintly awkward silence, which again was unusual; over the years they had sat many times without speaking in the same room together, the comfortable non-communication of siblings, but on this occasion Dennis seemed rather restless and he looked again at his shoes, even twisting his feet so he could examine something of the soles. It's quite a cold wind as well, he said finally, wondering as he had before why his sister didn't leave the TV or the radio on as was always the case in his own house; in his own house there were never any awkward silences, seldom any silence at all, too much racket in fact as he had been known to shout, but at least there were never any awkward silences. This was the thing with women, was his increasingly jaundiced opinion: there was always too much of one thing or another. He took out his Woodbines and lit one, putting the glass ashtray Dot had thoughtfully brought out onto the arm of the armchair. The times of objecting to smoking were some years in the future, but his sister did not particularly care for the habit.

– Aren't you going to have something to eat first?

Dot restricted her objection to this, although Dennis heard it. Again, he thought, it was always the case with women that one way or another they would make their objections known and it was hard for him to say whether he preferred his sister's veiled or what would have been his wife's far more direct approach (although not with smoking: if anything, Viv smoked more than he did). He could live without either, he thought.

– I've had a Sunday dinner, he said, then seeing the faintest shadow pass across his sister's face and recognizing the effort of preparation she had made, he added, I'll have a sandwich though, in a bit.

Dot sipped at her tea and looked at the mother, who had lifted the edge of her cardigan, possibly seeking loose threads which seemed an increasing fascination to her. Are you warm enough, Mam? she asked, largely for something to say. The fire was burning well, and when the old woman looked blankly up, Dennis took the chance to begin with the matter he was here to broach.

– I'm not sure she recognizes me these days, he said, lowering his voice and leaning in his sister's direction. Does she even know who *you* are all the time? Dot looked at her younger brother, recognizing a preamble. Usually Dennis was talkative to the point of gossipy or boastful, but if there were a more serious issue he could become quite furtive; she had seen this develop over the years and she had seen also that for all her brother's well-stocked life – the electrician business he had set up after he left the power station, the wife and the children, the rugby games he went to and the smoking and drinking friends – there was no real solid centre to him, no haven or retreat; he too would have poured scorn on Dot's magazines, had he considered them worthy of his consideration, but he had no equivalent; any one of the aspects of his life would be considered more worthy or more *real*, but not one of them provided a telling and consistent core and taken together, vying with each other for prominence as they did, they might well bring confusion.

– She's not so good today, said Dot. It varies. She was better yesterday.

– She's getting worse though.

Again the sister noted the unusual insistence. In those days it fell to females to give such care, but even given this, Dennis had shown little involvement. Dot didn't mind, not just because of her acceptance of the norm, but because, knowing her brother, she knew the help he could give would be poor. Nor did she want any intrusions from Vivian. The daughter had been quite happy to look after her mother, although she recognized how it might become increasingly difficult to leave the old woman alone whilst she was out at work. Nowadays the mother rarely got out of her chair and Dot railed off the stairs when she went to work or to the shops, but recently she had come home to find the mother had been in the kitchen and left the taps running and for some reason put the kettle in the sink. Perhaps, thought Dot, this was what her brother had in mind; some suggestion as to help whilst she was out at work. Although she would not be keen to have Vivian coming round. Her sister-in-law was undoubtedly the type who would go poking about in every drawer and every cupboard.

– Yes, but what I'm saying is, she's getting worse.

Dennis drew deeply on his Woodbine and held the comforting smoke for some time before the practised release. Generally I mean … He could see his wife's ghostly features in the smoke and hear the ghost of her voice asking whether he had done what they had agreed he should do, whether he had said what they had agreed he should say. That's what I'm saying, he said and Dot looked at him quizzically. She had never included even vague renditions of her brother and his wife in her stories, although there had been an earlier girlfriend who had come to the house when both she and Dennis were teenagers, a girl who Dot considered had a face worthy of her magazines: black, glossy hair and dark, mysterious eyes. Dennis had almost become part of a story with her, but this girl had soon vanished and Dot's stories had nothing in them which was not finally and happily resolved.

– It varies, she repeated. She's better in the mornings.

Dennis got on with his mission then, reaching out to take a sandwich as an acknowledgement of the hospitality, even though his Woodbine was unfinished.

– Anyway, what I'm saying is … we should give some thought to that brass. You know, the money Dad left her.

With some reluctance, Dot came fully into the moment. She had made herself capable of being party to any conversation, even the few she had outside work, whilst at the same time having part of herself in her stories; there were no specifics to this device, it was not a case of simultaneously re-running any one story or any particular scene or dialogue, it was more a generalized and cushioning glow as if her being had some unseen source of warmth and light and importance. At times, however, she had to give a more whole-hearted focus to what was happening and what she was being called upon to say; it had happened quite recently at work where Mr Hampson was attempting to make some roster changes and it seemed to be happening now. What do you mean? she asked, although she knew. She even had a suspicion then as to where the conversation might be going and although she would dearly have loved to give herself at least in part to a contemplation of the story she had marked out for that night, the one where the veterinary doctor and the apparently haughty mistress of the mansion are thrown together by the illness of a horse, where they recognize their love for each other by way of their both caring for an old animal others think should be destroyed … although she would have liked to do this, she focussed, letting the characters step as far back as they could, with just the occasional fine brow and bright eye visible.

– The brass, the money, Dad's … Dennis stubbed out the Woodbine into the ashtray and blew on his yellowed forefinger.

– It's in that account, said Dot.

– I know it is. I know it is. The brother looked at the older sister, seeing her focus and seeing also the solidity, or the stubbornness as he had called it. *Bloody minded* was his wife's description. The cow just doesn't want you to have what you could have! She'd rather have the money just lying there! She wouldn't use it. She doesn't need it. God, she gets half her clothes from 'Sallies. She never bloody goes anywhere. She never buys anything!

– She bought that chair – Dennis had felt a vague need to offer up some defence; he and his sister had been too different to be close, but he had no memory of her ever really doing him down, which was more than he could say for some others. On the other hand, his situation was becoming very difficult. – And she takes her to Scarborough ... he had rather tailed off with the defence then, particularly in the face of his wife's waving hands and piercing voice:

– She does *bugger all!* Vivian had snapped. Your mother just sits there all day and old Dottie Dewdrop just buggers off to work and then buggers back like some bloody tram on a track! Dennis had blown out Woodbine smoke as if to cocoon himself from his wife's hectoring, but in truth he felt she was right. He needed money now or the business was going under and there was money there; the old fella had been quite careful with his brass and there was the service pension and the widow's allowance which had all accumulated. There were those who had no money at all, those who did not have his option, but whether his sister would see it this way was another matter. *It's all right for her* – his wife had gone on – *no kids, no responsibilities, it's no problem for her letting that money just bloody lie there. She doesn't need it. She's got no bloody life!* Dennis had agreed he would talk to his sister that very Sunday. He faced her solidity now.

– Look, what I'm saying is, with her in the state she's in ... He almost whispered this last phrase and brother and sister both glanced at the mother who seemed to have turned her attention to the fire. With her as she is, he went on, we can actually get control of the account ... 'Control' was the wrong word, Dennis realized this as soon as he had said it; his sister's square jaw came up like a defensive ramp.

– It's her money, she said. It's in that account.

At which Dennis felt himself moving from awkwardness towards irritation.

– But what's she going to *use* it for? Dot had no answer to this, he felt, although Dot herself did not feel she needed one. – I mean we could *use* that money. The brother bit into his sandwich and chewed and swallowed quickly – I mean we could make some use of it, instead of just letting it just lie there. Instead of just doing that …

Dot gave no response. Her brother had hinted at the matter before, but as she saw it there was no debate, nothing more to be said, and the characters from her stories began edging their way back, some embracing, others with just the light first touching of hands. – *For Christ's sake, Dot!* Dennis' voice lifted. They used their names with others, always with the possessive characteristic of the area – our Dennis, our Dot – but they seldom addressed each other by name (very few had heard the sister being addressed as Dorothy, a few formal moments at work and the mother when they were all younger, although the mother used no name at all for her daughter now). Dot recognized the significance her brother was injecting with this, but it had no particular impact on her. I mean we could *use* that money, he repeated. That's what I'm saying. I mean, I'm only talking about *some* of it – The brother's tone changed again to one of quieter pleading and then again to a bleaker desperation.

– I mean, I could use it, Dot. I could really use it. I mean, I need it …

This last seemed a punctuation even to him and hearing this and seeing again the blank solidity of his sister sitting across from him, the brother came to his feet, his voice pitching up into anger. – She'd give me some if she knew what she was doing and where she was! He pointed at the mother. Wouldn't you, Mam? You'd give me some of the money Dad left you? The mother's eyes came away from the flames of the fireplace. Can you hear that dog? she asked and looked from side to side. There'll be shit all over the place! Dennis threw his hands open. *You see!* What's she talking about? What's she on about dogs? He stepped towards the old woman. What I'm saying, Mam, is you would help me out, wouldn't you? You'd help me out with some money?

The blankness in the mother's eyes was reduced by this last word, the relevance of which had been so persistent in her life. We've got

no money, she said. We never have had. Aunt Flo had money. So did
Sheila. Harry was diddled though. He was diddled … She stared at
the fragments of the past being moved and flipped around before
her eyes like the coins and cards of some malicious magician. *You see!*
Dennis turned back to his sister, who was taking another infuriating
sip of tea.

– She doesn't know anything about it! She doesn't know what
she's talking about. We may as well use it, some of it at least. I'm
told we can do that. Viv's brother said we can and he works in a
bank … Mentioning his wife's name was another mistake, Dennis
realized, and he clenched and unclenched his hands and swayed
back and forth on his rather stunted legs. He saw his sister would
never agree and without the solidity she had, without any core of
salvation, feeling himself oppressed on all sides, by circumstances,
by women and by men, he gave vent to something like the outbursts
to which he had been prone as a child. He even felt like a child as
he did so, wailing at the cold manners of the world. *It's all right for
you!* he cried. You don't need it! He waved a hand at his sister much
as his wife had waved hers at him. *You don't need it!* You don't have
anything you need it for! You don't have anything – but I do! I have
… He fumbled around in his own confusion and, again like a child
seeking the most hurtful things, he came up with echoes of what
he had heard said about his sister, things he had never actually said
himself before that day. *You're cold you are!* You're just cold. It's not
just that you're – he could not bring himself to say plain or ugly
although he had heard both, but the words sounded anyway and
they were nothing his sister had not heard before. – *You're just cold
hearted!* This came up through the brother like the heavings of sobs
– *I'm not surprised the boys never wanted you!* I'm not surprised there
were no blokes coming round! I'm not surprised you're on your
own! You're just too bloody …! He gave a last wave of his hand,
which delivered the half eaten sandwich back onto the table and
then he went through the door to the hallway and began to haul his
overcoat from the peg.

– Keep that door shut! the mother called. – There's a right
draught with it open!

Dot herself was quite surprised at the intensity of her brother's words and movements and for a time after he left the fictions in her mind retreated. On the other hand she could not see what else she could have done but sit there as Dennis banged his way out of the house. The money he had mentioned had been left by her father to her mother. It was in the mother's account. When the mother died it would be passed on equally to her and to Dennis. This was the arrangement and Dot did not see why it should be altered. Dennis must make his own way in the world just as their father had, just as she did. If he had a family, as he had, then he should look after it. There should be no need of any recourse to any money her mother had. Particularly where Vivian was involved (and without doubt the sister had seen and heard another woman's promptings in her brother's outburst, particularly its finale). Dot had no intention of letting her sister-in-law anywhere near her mother's money whilst the mother was alive. After the front door had been banged shut, Dot went out to latch it and to close the hallway door, before nodding some reassurance at the mother who was staring at the residues of the recent display as if some unusual force had just given an extra swirling to the fragments which were her normal contemplation. There was even a momentary clarity coming from this. What's up with our Dennis? she asked as Dot picked up the discarded, half-eaten sandwich from the tablecloth and placed it on the edge of a plate.

– Nothing, said the daughter. – You know what he's like.

The residue of the rather unpleasant scene and the echo of her brother's raised voice did stay with Dot as she cleared the table and sorted out what she was having for tea herself, but then the evening was quite a pleasant one. *Dr Finlay's Casebook* had a pleasing element of romance in its story and some nice comic moments between the crusty older doctor and the Scottish housekeeper. Dot also managed to get her mother to eat a full bowl of tinned fruit with evaporated milk; the old woman even dipped a slice of buttered bread into the milk and ate that and then some biscuits. Perhaps all this made her more ready to sleep and Dot had been able to get the mother upstairs and off to bed quite early, giving herself time for her cocoa and chocolate fingers and the magazine stories she had planned to read before she went upstairs herself.

Another echo of the brother's raised voice came as she readied herself for bed, and some thoughts as to work the following day where the roster issue was still ongoing, but she put both matters out of her mind as she made her 'last story of the day' selection from the pile of magazines in her bedside cupboard. She chose the one about the wounded army captain being tended in France by an aristocratic English lady who had gone over to help with the war effort. Dot had no memory of that war, but quite clear memories of its sequel when she had been a Land Girl. She had quite enjoyed being a Land Girl and there had been a soldier – no-one really knew about him and Dot had wondered from time to time if he too had been wounded, maybe even killed. Certainly she had never heard from him, despite his promise, but in truth she had known even then that there was an unreality to the relationship. Real people will let you down, not necessarily through any malice or any other emotion but because in reality, in time, it is simply too much to ask. You are better off with something made up, something which can stand against that time (the Bible was a consolation for Hilda, another spinster at Town Tailors, although Dot didn't find the Bible's stories sufficiently romantic). Yes, from very early on Dot had recognized that no actuality could ever match the true romance of the heart and there were no echoes of any real soldier in the story she chose that night, which anyway was from a different war.

She pulled on the winceyette nightgown and began to unclip her hair, then combed it out and back over her shoulders. She had tried a night cap but found it rather intrusive and when she slept was the only time her hair was loose. She bunched it into the back of her neck then and climbed into bed and, setting the bedside lamp so it gave appropriate light, she spread the magazine open in her lap.

A Little Bitty Tear

(Burl Ives 1961)

Airedale's Holy Cross Church had been built in 1934, using the stone and some of the pillars from the demolished Fryston Hall. The same stone from the same demolition had also been used for the font just inside the main door, but the stone used for the altar had been cut especially from Fryston Colliery, despite some lighter clerical opposition which was of the opinion that a stone altar was rather too medieval, rather more sombre and forbidding than it should be in modern times. The single slab at the top of this altar had even been incised, in the medieval tradition, with five crosses, one in each corner and one in the middle, as indicative of the five wounds of Christ on the Cross. J. C. S. Daly, the first vicar of the parish, had given some thought as to how coal itself might be employed somehow amidst such details, as an indication of the working and suffering reality of his parishioners, but nothing workable had presented itself and he had settled for placing a miner's lamp beside the sacraments in the aumbry, which lamp was later inscribed with his name.

A quarter of a century after this founding, when he was offered the parish, the reverend A. P. Gill had had an early conception of it which had also been somewhat cut in stone and lit imaginatively by a coal miner's lamp. Having grown up amidst the rolling downs of Gloucestershire and with no personal experience of the North of England, the newly ordained minister imagined his future parishioners as something vaguely Laurentian, the men with their dirt layers left in a tin bath, fitted out in church clothes which were poor but immaculate in their way, if a little tight fitting, the women the essential mothering salt of the earth, possibly wearing some kind of bonnet. There had been an element of missionary zeal in his accepting the post, a zeal which had been fuelled also by the socialism he had imbibed as a student. There seemed no doubt to him that Christ would have been a socialist, a bringer of equality in its purest form, that which leads to the equanimity of the soul whatever its surroundings and which promises the final, all-levelling judgement. During his student years the young man had perfected his thesis of how the Anglican Church had found the Golden Mean between an infallible Pope and a too literal, methodical reading of much-translated scriptures; this balance, this equanimity, was, it seemed to him, the means by which spiritual truth could be made coherent and perceived. Of course there was no mention of a church per se, let alone any ecclesiastical hierarchy, in the Bible, but much as the socialist party needed its organization to promulgate its beliefs and to achieve its aims, so a religion must have its rituals and its structure, for without these the undoubted needs of the soul can seem hopelessly confused or can be misdirected by soulless forces or worse, corrupted and used by evil ones.

A. P. Gill himself felt none of the exclusivity and bigotry of what he saw as the saddest part of churched religions, particularly in their turbulent and bloody schisms. Jesus, he was certain, would have had – would have – no bigotry; for all the sentiments of the psalm *except the Lord build the house, they labour in vain that built it,* for all Matthew 12.30, Christ Himself, thought Gill, would not finally have rejected any other means of recognizing the one true God. The Roman persuasion, for example, was simply misguided in its excess of structure, the Muslim faith wrong in not seeing Jesus as far more than a prophet, and the Hindu and others simply too disparate and too reliant on habits acquired before Our Lord actually walked this earth. The Buddhist faith he smiled at, feeling that for all its attempts to obliterate God, He was still at its heart. What, after all, is Nirvana but a final Communion with Him? And the young vicar had nodded and smiled on reading how more and more shrines and other such artifacts were creeping into this churchless way. What had happened also with the great atheist Lenin, but that he had become embalmed and enshrined like some relic of a saint for the undeniable spiritual needs of the multitude? Focus was needed, thought Gill, structure and focus, succour and guidance: people need external help for their eternal souls.

The reality of his parish had provided some challenges to all this: the Holy Cross, despite its stone columns and rather awkward bell tower, was lower and smaller than he had imagined, with a tiled sloping roof which reminded him of one of the large outhouse barns he had been familiar with in his youth. Also, set back as it was from Fryston Road, the church had less visual impact on this road than the isolated brick mansion which was the Magnet pub. The new vicar found the interior of the church a little more satisfying, with the pews and kneeling desks of gleaming wood, carved and constructed by 'Mousey' Thompson of Kilburn, all with his tiny but distinctive mouse emblem raised at some point on them. There was also a Holy Water stoup resting on another piece of stone with a late-Norman dogtooth pattern, which stone Gill learned had once been in Durham Cathedral. The simple pulpit was made of duller wood and had no mouse on it, but in all Gill was able to persuade himself that the interior had the balance of reverence and commonality which characterized his own faith and intentions.

He found more difficulty, however, in persuading himself he was communicating any of this to the congregation therein or thereout. The parish he actually found in Airedale, Castleford, had little of D. H. Lawrence to it, nor any great sense of the dignity of labour or of any worldwide community of socialist hope. The response to work in Castleford was of people who had to do it; men brought up knowing they would have to go out to it and women who expected to stay in doing it. Politically the parish was a solid Labour vote, but Gill found little fervour and, even as the new decade began, a continuing acceptance of station. The young vicar tried to find strength and stability in this and from time to time he did; from time to time he encountered a miner on his way to the pit or a worker heading for the small steel works or the bigger glass bottle factory and he saw the coal black or steely glint in their eyes of his own religious and socialist vision; the glint, the gleam, which could surely also have been seen in Our Saviour's eyes as he went about his own work. And yet as the honest man he considered himself to be, both with others and with himself, Gill could not but admit that at times there was also the glassiness to those eyes as of the robot or the slave, even perhaps behind the surface gleam the dull deadness of thoughtless stone.

And yet, few people in Airedale would have said they had no religious belief; the Communist heresy, that excess imposed on socialism which in Gill's opinion had been the great political tragedy of the first half of the twentieth century, had, he was pleased to see, made no real inroads. Hysterical belief was alien to Castleford; virtually all of its men would have called themselves Christians, but few of them actually came to church. As the intellectual he saw himself as being and given his own easy-going Anglicanism, the Reverend Gill was not too upset by this; on the other hand, he could not help but feel a certain professional concern for his limited and dwindling audience, nor, naturally, was he wholly indifferent to the opinions of his superiors in the Wakefield Diocese; this, after all, following in his father's footsteps, was the profession he had chosen and as with the best of workers he wanted to make a good job of it.

Women were the bedrock of the parish; that was undeniably the case and, as the Reverend Gill knew, it would hardly be unusual anywhere. Women formed the majority of the congregation and the backbone of his non-ecclesiastical assistance. Mrs Flowers and Mrs Johnson were the driving forces behind the Sunday School and, along with Mrs Hobbs, the jumble sales and other social gatherings. Mrs Cook worked as an unofficial secretary, typing and posting the messages for the church notice board, and Mildred Sidebottom, who seemed always to be carrying a Bible, was available for any appropriate task the vicar might choose to give her. Most of these ladies were at least middle aged and although there were some younger women who came to services, Gill had noticed that in the period of his incumbency the number of these had also fallen, as had the number of adults who attended with their children.

What was the most glaring absence for him from the beginning, however, was the absence of young men. And this, the Reverend Gill, in all his honesty, had to admit was for him the gravest concern of all.

As he looked up at the reproduction of a Zurbarán Christ on the Cross he had hung in the vicarage, he had to admit his actual conception of hope, his actual belief in how a final salvation could be attained. Christ had died at the very age he was now. Our Saviour had gathered around him a group of men who were equally lean and committed and it was on their comparative youth and strength, on their suffering and their efforts, that the church had been founded, and Gill could not avoid his honest feeling that any regeneration of this church, any expansion of it into the truly catholic, any joining of it with ideas of political equality and the redistribution of power and wealth, would necessarily be driven by a similar male cadre. As the modern intellectual he saw himself as being, he had examined the sexual bias of this, but in all honesty he could not escape his feeling that it was still the case that whilst women gave essential succour – Magdalenes and Madonnas – the drive of true unity, of expansion and change, must come from these males. He remembered A. P. Wesley, the head boy at his school (an unfortunate name, but no connection), whom he had watched making a winning caught and bowled at a house match, who had gone into the RAF and whose erect back and slight, confident but not conspicuous smile he had always tried to emulate; and Chambers, also at school, and the devout Maynard and the comedian Wright at college; each of them had aspects of manner worthy of imitation. This was what Airedale and perhaps the Church of England itself was missing, thought Gill: weighty older men could be found, but this very weight, it could be argued, was the fat of satisfaction, the weight of resignation. The Anglican Church hierarchy itself had the quality of a club for ageing men with bad eyesight; Gill had made this point in a letter to an old college friend, observing how he may be the only priest of any level in the Anglican Church who did not need spectacles. He was also (as this observation might indicate) one of the calling who had a genuine sense of humour. This at least was how J. P. Gill saw himself and certainly, just as with his internal debate on his designation of women, he was always ready to examine himself for any semblance of humourless pomposity, excessive intellectualism or undue self-importance.

This also had been tested in his two years in Airedale. It would be a number of years, decades perhaps, before ignorance fuelled by mass media would go on the offensive (what you don't know doesn't matter, what counts is who you are and what you buy) and the ignorance in Airedale and Castleford still had a defensive, occasionally apologetic, even decorous quality, but ignorance it was and Gill had found it hard to see anything of the Noble Savage in it. (He disliked Rousseau anyway, agreeing with his father that anyone who thinks unrestrained freedom will lead to freedom or that mankind will find the proper way without guidance was sadly mistaken.) Nobility there was in Airedale and Castleford, this was certain; Gill had seen it in fine, hardworking men and women, concerned to survive with something of dignity and to pass on such values to the next generation, but the truth was not many of these men and women came to church. They did not see the church as the sustenance, let alone the fount, of their noble dignity or their anonymous worth; indeed more and more, he concluded, they may be seeing it as an irrelevance or just another arm of the social, historical and fast-gathering capitalist forces intent on keeping them in their place and making them work hard in every sense for whatever dignity they might keep. And yet these were the people, thought Gill, whom the new disciples should reach out towards, the ones those lean, Zurbarán-shaded men should be trying to encounter; these and the young, before the increasing calls of simplicity and indulgence made young people unaware and then incapable of the true soul and the real salvation they could find. Judgement after all, as recorded in Matthew 16:27 and in Revelations 22:12, will be 'according to works'.

And yet – once again the young priest had to be honest with himself – it seemed all his efforts had fallen on stony ground. The committed were there, as they would be unto death, as were those drawn by ritual and habit. Sunday still provided something of a congregation and weddings and funerals were well attended, but the Reverend Gill had found himself unable to win over not just new churchgoers, not just young people, but the community at large. He himself was too young and too southern for their taste; he had tried to broach this in one sermon, telling how, after one Sunday

School, when a boy had told him he had lost his 'coyt', he had spent some time looking for a toy rubber ring rather than a jacket; the anecdote was directed at himself and related to the sermon's theme of differences overcome through Christ, but whether it was received as such (as he belatedly recognized) was another matter. Other attempts, such as pointing out that the strong northern 'u' in 'butter' was surely far more accurate than the tendency to 'batter' 'butter' in the south and that a 'roof' should never be a 'rough', he also recognized might have been received as condescending rather than complimentary. Also, although he was quite trim of figure, Gill had never been particularly good at or even particularly interested in sports and his attempts to reach out through an interest in rugby and cricket had proved fruitless, perhaps even counterproductive. Once he had called out 'O well played!' on the sidelines of one local match and received the stony glances of those around him and a few grins as of seasoned sailors watching a hopeless young officer drown.

So it was that after two years at his Airedale parish the Reverend Gill found himself feeling not only frustrated but rather depressed and he could not help but think of Proverbs 13:12: 'hopes deferred maketh the heart sick'. Suffering was necessary of course and this came clearly as an answer in his prayers, and he let none of his frustration or depression show in his outward manner. He tried to let what he considered to be his natural good humour dominate; and yet he was too young to be jovial and he had found it hard to align his own humour with that of the locals for whom wit and word play could be so readily identified with the 'smart Alec' (Alec was the first of the Reverend's Christian names and he allowed it to be known, trying to get it truncated to Al; the second name of Piers he suppressed altogether). Suppressing the wordy, the intellectual, tendency in himself was a cause in itself of his frustration and depression and the close and clever observer could have seen the ripples in the vicar's soft and still fleshily youthful features as a comment or a verbal concurrence came to mind only to be suppressed and dissipated as if a natural fountain was having the boot of experience placed firmly on it, whilst slower consideration was given to where the waters should be directed or whether it should be allowed to spring forth at all.

The young priest was increasingly aware that he had established no particular character or personality for himself which might help with his pastoral duties or his mission in general: he was the young vicar from *down south*, too posh and altogether too lightweight to be consulted by anyone other than the already terminally committed, and even they were wary. It was in the throes of this frustration and depression that Gill found himself turning more and more to the companionship of Ben Strong.

Ben Strong had appeared at the end of the first nineteen months of the new vicar's incumbency, to take over the management of the First Airedale Scouts. He had been a scoutmaster in York and then, having spent some time at Gilwell, apparently with great success, he had been asked to take over the First Airedale which, as he had been confidentially informed, was showing every sign of disintegrating, in part owing to the misguided appointment of a new and inexperienced young vicar. Unlike that vicar, the new scoutmaster, through word of mouth and some clever use of articles in the *Pontefract and Castleford Express*, managed even in a few months to engineer a revival in the local Scouting body. He also increased the Sunday congregation at the Holy Cross by insisting the Scouts attend and by reinstating the flag-carrying ceremony on the first Sunday of the month, which ceremony Gill, closely advised by Mrs Flowers and Mrs Hobbs, had put into abeyance after an unfortunate incident during its enactment soon after his arrival. Again, the young vicar had only belatedly realized the role he was supposed to play with the Scouts. He had rather presumed the organization would be managed separately, even though the Scouts used the church hall for their meetings. He was ambivalent anyway about the soldierly and nationalist aspects of the movement (with its echoes of the Cadet Corps he had unhappily been subjected to at school) and he even reminded Ben Strong in one of their conversations that the Scouts' founder's 'Be prepared' had been truncated and sanitized from its original 'be prepared to die for your country' to an imprecation always to have something to start a fire with. (Although he had been pleased by Strong's spirited riposte that this was only a rendition of how the Christian Church itself had adapted and grown: an eye for an eye becoming the turning of the other cheek.) The new vicar had of course shown some interest in the Scouts, but no more than he had in the Mothers' Union, which also used the church hall, and perhaps a little less than he had given to the threadbare Amateur Dramatic Society, which had managed a Christmas entertainment in that hall, but then engaged in enough internal disagreements and erratic attendance to falter and fold.

And there had been the unfortunate incident at the flag-carrying ceremony early on in his time, when the central Scout of the three marching down the aisle to the main door of the Holy Cross, having received the flag from the vicar, had become a little too conscious of his family watching from the pews and forgotten to lower the flag to go under the stone ridge of the organ loft, resulting in the flagpole jabbing sharply back into his stomach and he and the escort stumbling backwards down the aisle. Gill could still hear the clatter of the flag as it fell and the unfortunate swear word of the Scout involved, and although he had tried to make light of the matter from the altar steps (a reaction which in another setting, he thought, might have been considered quite expertly Christian), it had been another recognition on his part that it is difficult to make light of stone. He was altogether too subtle, too readily considerate and liberal, too intellectual and certainly too southern for the post.

When he recounted the incident to Ben Strong, however, the scoutmaster laughed. *Right in the breadbasket!* he chortled. I've seen it happen! And he told the story of the time when as a young Scout he had been a flag carrier in the same ceremony and a myopic vicar had been unable to hit the leather holder with the end of the flagpole: I was moving it as much as I could to one side and the other, said Strong. But he still kept missing it. It was the young groom's marriage night! Here, vicar, here … he mimed the movement of the holder … It was like somebody trying to kill a rodent. In the end I just grabbed the end and pushed it in myself! They had laughed together and Gill had thought this was the reaction as it should be: the balance, the equanimity, the forgiveness. Nothing of the church ladies' high dudgeon. *This was how Our Lord himself would have reacted; the true perspective, the light heart of a truly believing soul.*

In all he found Ben Strong a godsend; they seemed to share the same sense of humour and a delight in informed intellectual debate. The vicar discovered also that the scoutmaster was a history graduate of the University of Leeds, a Master of Arts in this discipline in fact, which rather knocked his own Bachelor of Divinity into second place; Gill was still young enough to consider the pecking order of qualifications, although Strong seemed less concerned and he only spoke of his university days when the vicar sought some detail. Nor it seemed had Strong made use of his academic background in the work he now did, which as far as Gill could gather was something to do with agricultural machinery; the scoutmaster was even involved in some actual farm work, he said, driving tractors and such and living in an old and, according to him, dilapidated farmer's cottage between Selby and Castleford, commuting back and forth on his Norton motorcycle. You must come out and see it some time, he had said. I'll take you on the bike. Although only if you wear your full regalia, I'd love to see those togs flying and flapping out on the back of the Norton!

Again, they had laughed together. Without doubt, thought Gill, this man would be one of the troop of brothers who could bring in the new world, educated and balanced, good humoured and doughty, unpretentious and competent; he had watched in admiration once at the speed with which Strong fashioned the sheepshank knot which had just defeated him. Moreover, the man had a face and figure which fitted his name, like the character of a Ben Jonson play: the high cheekbones, the strong chin and brow and a neatly cut crop of brown hair, the fringe of which fell more carelessly from time to time. Gill could even see this as something like the images used in the old socialist propaganda posters (and abused then of course by the Soviets), and the scoutmaster's short-sleeved blouse showed strong shoulders and forearms and the shorts (not obligatory for an adult troop leader, but which Strong regularly wore) revealed an extent of muscled thighs and calves and the lack of any unsightly prominence at the knee. A veritable Zurbarán in his shading, thought Gill. A genuine leader. Strong would be the Christ figure. This conclusion only came in the vicar's very private and, as he saw it, almost playful thoughts; he could never place himself in that role, not just for any element of blasphemy, but for his inability and unworthiness; witness his first performance in this, his first parish. No, he thought, he could be a worthy disciple, he could carry the message, break the good news, but he would never have the face and figure, the latent power and the proven competence of a Ben Strong.

There was of course something of a problem with the scoutmaster in this role (and more than once the vicar had smiled to himself about it). Ben Strong it seemed had some lightly expressed but seemingly quite deep-seated theological doubts and questions. These had formed the core of one of their liveliest exchanges in the Green Room attached to the church hall one Wednesday after the Scouts had dispersed.

– Here's to that great tea drinker, old Eric Orwell!

There were sink and tea-making facilities in the Green Room and Strong lifted the cup he had just poured himself. Although I'm not sure about old Eric's overall vision, he went on. He actually *believed* in the working class; just like all you public schoolboys. You never grew up with them, so it's a lot easier to wax hopeful about them!

Gill had heard this cynicism from his friend before, but heard it as no more than intellectually provocative. Not that he particularly cared to discuss the privilege in which he had undoubtedly grown up. Strong was equally vague about his own schooling, although there had clearly been no private education. Also, the vicar was more interested in following up the quite throwaway comment with which Strong had left him at the end of their previous conversation. – *Jesus*, he had said – *fine fellow but just another Jew prophet.* The vicar had agonized quite extensively on this after his prayers and into the night. It was not the anti-Semitic hint (he dismissed this: not in a fellow, he thought, so educated and balanced as Strong) but the mention, the almost dismissive mention, of Jesus. It was the one thing A. P. Gill could not live with; this had become clearer to him than it had ever been before as he thought the matter through, awake in his bed. All other attacks of the church, all other theological and Biblical debates, particularly those with regard to the Old Testament, he could accept, he could argue, he could *place* all those things.

He could readily recognize the metaphors and the parable qualities which were to be found more extensively in the Good Book than just in the parables themselves. But without Jesus it seemed to him there was nothing, without that divinity actually touching this earth and its people; without that, thought the young vicar, it may as well be nothing.

He had been impatient then to follow the comment up, especially from a man who it seemed to him could actually play Our Saviour in any mystery pageant; were his hair long and his blouse and shorts swapped for white robes ... Or with a simple loin cloth, his fine muscled arms and legs and torso could be stretched Zurbarán shaded on the cross. – *And Jesus?* Shall we drink to Jesus? The vicar asked quite slyly, lifting his cup, and Strong smiled, recognizing full well it seemed the impact his remark in their last conversation had made.

– Of course. Another fine fellow.

– I'm glad you agree.

– Something of a scruffy beggar perhaps.

Strong smiled and Gill, seeing the continuing and playful provocation, smiled in return. Also quite a hick, the scoutmaster historian went on. I mean, his ministry! Just a couple of short years wandering around the countryside. He never really ventured into the conurbations. He never really took on the sophisticats ...

– *What?!* Gill put his cup down quite noisily. He was Jesus of *Nazareth!* he said. He confronted the urban authorities, the Sanhedrin. Are you saying the high priest Caiaphas was not learned, not sophisticated?!

– *Hereditary Zadoks.* Strong was still smiling mischievously, playfully. – And Jesu only took them on in the end. Before then he just wandered around the countryside cadging off rural folk, spitting on one or two to heal their disfigurements ... Gill shook his head; he knew of course of this aspect of the Biblical healer's technique, but as well as being a mere indication of changing customs and possibly a mistranslation when applied to Our Lord, he preferred to think of the laying on of hands; this surely was how the current of divine power would have been transmitted.

– *He* had not come down to earth to dwell in palaces, he said. *He* had come down to be with the lowest, to elevate the most low. Like you driving your tractor instead of, I don't know, pushing a pen or managing accounts … As usual they had shared a few ginger biscuits with their tea and Strong flicked a crumb from one of these off the badge-laden pocket of his blouse.

– That's true, he said. He certainly stayed amongst the common folk.

Gill shook his head in some frustration, but the intellect must be allowed to go where it will. He *began* there, he said. As he should, but the message reached up to the Emperor himself – *in hoc signo vinces* (this carving could be found in the Holy Cross itself). How's that for a conurbation? A sophistication? An empire!

Still smiling, Strong took down the leather bomber jacket and the rather grubby trousers he wore to ride his motorcycle and put on the jacket before unbuckling and unzipping his shorts to make the change. Gill glanced away to offer a little privacy, but then thinking this was rather prissy of him, he looked back. For all he was no rugby player, he knew the conventions of young men in showers.

– And what was that remark about just another Jew prophet? he asked directly then. To his ingénue's surprise, he had encountered some anti-Semitism at college, often smartly phrased or subterranean, but still discernible. He had found none of this in Airedale, no mention of it whatsoever in fact (which had made Strong's remark still more egregious), although the vicar recognized that the complete absence of anybody Jewish might be a factor here. Real tolerance had not yet been tested in the area; the congregation at the time was exclusively white and the few Eastern Europeans there were still carried with them the sympathy felt for those who had escaped Nazi tyranny. Moreover, in those days there was still enough work for those who wanted it, tedious or back breaking or both as it might well be.

– What about it? Strong stood for some time in the swimming trunks he wore beneath his Scout shorts, shaking out the legs of the trousers and then sliding them on. Jesus was a Jew, wasn't he? Historical fact.

The young vicar still felt he was being toyed with, but he could not keep the edge from his voice; light hearted and wholly tolerant Our Saviour may have been, but final reverence for Him must be observed. *Of course, he was!* he said and Strong took the striped snake belt from the pocket of the trousers and began sliding it through their loops. – I mean what he proclaimed had been proclaimed before hadn't it? The scoutmaster gave a broad smile. – Others had proclaimed the coming elevation of the chosen people, the unification of the twelve tribes of Israel, that's a matter of history. And Jesus was in that line. And he meant it literally! Strong pulled the belt tight and smiled still more broadly. – *The Kingdom would come!* Israel would triumph. It was later generations of Gentiles who turned this into a timeless, non-historical promise. Although the fact the kingdom didn't come then or later left them little choice!

Ben Strong's smile finally became a laugh, but seeing the consternation in his friend's face and having heard the edge in his voice, he stepped towards him.

– Look, I'm sorry, he said. Really. Forget it. It's just me messing around. Don't listen to me. The ramblings of a poor historian. Time locked. What has history to do with revelation? What has poor reality and brainless time to do with a wonderful dream?! He lifted his strong hand to the vicar's arm, first in a slap, then in a firm grip on the bicep. – Don't listen to the nonsense of a sinner. I've told you before, I have nothing but envy for you and your faith, I have some of it myself I hope, or at least I'm trying, but for you and your faith I have nothing but … Unusually he seemed to be seeking words and his other strong hand came up so the vicar was held and then drawn forward.

– Nothing but respect for you, said Strong. Nothing but love.

Gill wasn't sure this last word had actually been used. As with the mention of 'Jew', the word was unusual in that community; it might be carved in silent stone, it might be part of the deep bonds there undoubtedly were, but it was more usually heard only in popular songs, seldom spoken outright. *Nothing but love.*

It was at this point that Mildred Sidebottom came into the Green Room, carrying her Bible and wanting to know if the chairs should be left until morning or whether it might be a good idea to set them out now in the way the Mothers' Union preferred. Surprised by the question, which Mildred had not asked before, Gill said to leave the chairs until morning and then on second thought agreed it might be better to set them out now. Mildred's brother, who acted as caretaker for the church hall, had recently been struck with a debilitating illness. Want help? asked Ben Strong, turning back towards the case in which he neatly packed his uniform, and Mildred Sidebottom, seeing something of the vicar's distraction, answered for him, saying quite sharply that there would be no need for that, thank you, Mr Strong. She rather disapproved of the Scouts' use of the church hall, particularly when it involved rough games such as Bulldog, or bringing in wood and leaves. She also seemed to dislike the scoutmaster himself, as Gill had already noted, as he had noted in general that for all her Christian commitment, the woman seemed at times to have little of any truly Christian manner.

He wondered later whether Mildred had even been eavesdropping at the Green Room door, and somehow this was part of the confusion in which he spent that particular night and no few nights afterwards. He prayed for clarification. *With what was he confused?* Frustration, depression, disappointment were all reasonably clear in their causes. Was it part of these weaknesses? What exactly was he feeling? And then on one terrible evening, following a poorly attended Evensong, when, still in his vestments, he had wandered down amongst the pews of the empty church and slid along one at the rear to face the distant altar and to test out the kneeling cushion provided, an answer came and he could not decide if it proceeded from the reverential space around him, the spare, silent and beautiful voice which his father had told him could only be Our Lord's, or from an interloping whisper of the Devil himself. *If it was the Lord's voice, it was a warning and a guidance, and if it was the Devil's it was a taunt.* Clarity came then it seemed and it was a terrible thing. What he felt for this other man, came the silent whisper, was no fellowship, no admiration, but a simple and dreadful sin. Romans 1:24–27, 1 Corinthians 6:9–10, Leviticus 18:22. *Spare me any modern doublethink on the sacraments,* as Gill's father had said, and as this clarity descended the vicar felt a nausea rising and his praying hands knotting together. When his eyes came open it seemed to him then these hands were a gnarled disfigurement, tainted and blasted by the limbs they had touched. For a moment in utter panic he felt he could not pull them apart as the interloping Devil spat his cloying evil onto them and sent a thin snickering all around the empty church. *I know*, the Devil whispered. *I know*. And Mildred Sidebottom knows. And others know. And still others suspect. Have you not seen their looks? It seemed to the young vicar then that he had seen those looks: the glinting, stony glances. Even the blanker and glassier stares were of condemnation not just for his youth or incompetence, but for a deeper and blacker matter, a matter as foreign to this community as any fancy word.

Gill pushed himself up and sat on the pew, his hands still fixed in their unsightly lock, his head lolling back, his eyes staring up at the arched and shadowy ceiling where for once he saw no assisting God. *Lord! O Lord!* he heard, perhaps from his own mouth, perhaps another imagined echo in the empty church. *Faithful servant* came – *Your true and faithful servant* – and Matthew 6:9–13, *Lead me – Deliver me. Me?* Me, you say? This was the Devil, it seemed certain to him then, creeping around like a thief in this sacred place, turning wine to dirty water, peaceful shade into threatening shadows and fine feelings for others into the rancid emanations of a physical self. Gill's eyes came down in thoughtless panic, searching for the Beast's movements in the shadows, and as his state briefly touched madness, he thought he saw the carved mouse on the pew slip forward. The rodent had slid along the wooden arm it seemed and its little hump was lying now, breathing and waiting for another chance to move. Yes, the tail flickered, it seemed to Gill, and he glanced insanely at the other mice on the other pews; all had made the same swift, liquid movement of their species, all directed by the invisible Devil, looking for the dirt, the detritus, the sewers even in the most holy of places.

Dizzily, the young man came to his feet, finally becoming more conscious of his state and separating his clenched hands so he could employ them to make an unsteady progress back along the pew and up the aisle towards his vestry. A more conscious thought came also of steadying himself fully and kneeling on the stone steps of the altar to make a better prayer, but he felt himself too unsteady to do so and the invading forces, dissipating though they were, were still strong enough to have him hurry along and out, like a slithering mouse himself.

The experience marked the beginning of the end of A. P. Gill's ministry in Airedale. He had already had some communication with the Bishop's office in Wakefield; there had already been some suggestions the placement had not perhaps been the most appropriate and now the young vicar found he was implying as much himself. Also he re-instigated his correspondence with Penelope Waddington, the Gloucestershire girl with whom, at his parents' instigation, he had kept in contact throughout college. She was a very clever girl who had studied literature at Trinity Hall and who, after a short time working for a publisher in London, had returned to Gloucestershire. Gill had let their correspondence lapse, but now, excusing himself with the travails and commitments of his first incumbency, he began to write again and received quite copious replies and a letter from his mother saying how pleased she was he had renewed the acquaintance. His father even added a postscript, hinting at the private man-to-man, retired priest to new priest, conversation they had had before his departure for the north, in which the elder had spoken of how much better it was for a parish if its pastor were a family man, obviating the clear folly of the Roman persuasion where men are called upon to advise on matters of which they can have no experience. Gill remembered the Bishop of Wakefield himself making a similar point, if rather more surreptitiously, when he had first welcomed the young bachelor to the diocese.

Duty was calling it seemed to Gill and as can be the case with duty it was necessary to make something of a blank of at least parts of the mind. The free questionings of the growing intellect are all well and good, thought Gill, but what he had recognized now, what Airedale and its Holy Cross had in themselves taught him perhaps, was that too much debate, too many recognitions of other ideas, will end in weakness. He had his belief, he had his own guide in Jesus Christ, and the rest was a mere juggling of detail, the sophistry of the Ancients, the negative, Socratic arguments for argument's sake of artificial intellectual victory. Gill had never liked the Greek philosophers; not a socialist amongst them, he had said, and, still more provocatively in one seminar, offered the opinion that Plato would have approved of Hitler, at least in the Fuhrer's early stages; the young man had even considered writing a book which would attempt to examine, perhaps even extirpate, Platonism from the true faith. He mentioned this old college project in a letter to Penelope (seeking ways to make his missives at least something like the length of hers) and received enthusiastic encouragement. As for his strange fit of seeming revelation after that Evensong, he consigned it to those new blanks in his mind and if it glinted a little amidst these, he saw it as no more than the barely glimpsed and no doubt illusory movement of a wooden mouse.

In line with his new conclusions about excessive debate and the merely provocative, the vicar reduced his contact with the scoutmaster, avoiding the Green Room conversations and any of the slow walks they had taken together along the pathways between the church hall, the Holy Cross and the vicarage. – *Are you OK., A. P.?* Strong had called to him once as they accidentally encountered each other on one of those pathways and Gill said he was fine, but hurrying to a Confirmation class. *Thought they'd stopped coming?* said Strong and Gill assured him this was not the case as he went on to his empty study. Once or twice he glimpsed not only the question in Strong's look when he did see him, but also the element of hurt. *Did I overstep the mark with my playful intellect? With your beliefs? Or lack of them? I am sorry, my friend. I am so, so sorry.*

The worst moment came, however, on the day when the young vicar actually left the parish. Having sent his cases on, he boarded a train at Castleford station which would take him to Sheffield, where he would change for the train to Cheltenham. Somehow he had thought the scoutmaster might turn up to join the little group gathered outside the Holy Cross to see him into the taxi bound for the station and then, when Strong had not been in this group, that he might appear at the station itself. *Why would he?!* came the internal dialogue's answer. After weeks of avoiding the man, after making

169

it clear in albeit indirect fashion that their dialogue was over, why would the man lower himself to the extent of offering a goodbye? This goodbye had already been made; the seeping away of the worst finales; the sad disintegration which echoes cold time itself; no embrace, no good wishes, simple inevitability. And yet Gill could not deny it was Ben Strong's face he would have liked to see and a word from him he would have liked to hear; he it was that the young vicar's sidelong glances were directed at discovering, as on the Evensong night when he had searched the shadows of an empty church.

Despite all this internal turmoil, he concluded that he had handled his departure well; he had learned from the parish, he said in his final sermon, and again in more colloquial terms to the little valedictory group; he had learned from their strength, even at times from their silence, and he would take with him memories not just of reverential or altruistic acts, but a better sense of humour, one based not on mere word play and flippancy, but one which comes from a wry recognition of life's suffering. He would remember, he said, Mrs Johnson's husband, bedridden, but always with a joke to tell. Life can be hard, but the spirit can always shine through: he had learned this here, he said, and he was leaving as far less of a soft southerner than he had arrived. It may have been his best sermon and his most effective communion, he thought as he stood on the platform at Castleford station. How ironic it would be if the most effective manner can only be found when the heart and soul are elsewhere. Mysterious ways indeed. But undeniably then as he waited on that station platform, an emptiness descended, as of a great empty church, an echoing mine, a pit. And beyond this emptiness there was stone. He tried to heed his own words and toughen himself against this, like the miner facing his shift, the female facing her drudgery; he had his path, he had his duty. He hoped, however, that it would be sooner rather than later when these would fill his surroundings with clear meaning and outweigh the great aching space he felt inside.

It was four years later when the vicar saw Ben Strong's name again and it took him by surprise. He was surprised even to receive a large envelope postmarked Wakefield, which contained the Holy Cross newsletter and a folded broadsheet from the *Pontefract and Castleford Express*. A couple of years previously, Mildred Sidebottom had sent him a few editions of the monthly newsletter the vicar who had replaced him had begun, but she had not kept up the practice, despite Gill's written response that he would always welcome news from his first parish, and then asking Mildred to pass on his condolences to Mrs Johnson, the death of whose husband had been one of the items in one of the newsletters. After such a considerable lapse, then, he was surprised to receive a newsletter again and had no idea what to expect in the folded newsprint in which, said Mildred's note in her cramped script on a single sheet of lined paper, there was an item which would be of interest to him (and expressing her hope of God's continued blessings). Another death perhaps, thought Gill as he unfolded the double newsprint page, or perhaps something which had put the Holy Cross actually into the local newspaper, some act of vitality by the current vicar about whom, in her cramped way, Mildred had been enthusiastic in her previous notes. The woman had put red biro lines around the news item of interest, however, and so Gill saw it at once: *Prison Term for Scoutmaster* was the headline and then the report.

Benjamin Roy Strong, 38, was convicted at Wakefield Assizes of an act of gross indecency, committed in the public toilets of Bradley Street, Castleford, on 12 September ... Gill refolded the sheet without reading any more, and before his wife came back from the kitchen to the breakfast table he had hidden it and the accompanying note by sitting on them. A newsletter from the Holy Cross, he said, and showed this to Penelope as she came in with the teapot. – Perhaps they are going to start sending it to me again – He could not let his clever wife see either the newspaper or the note. She had shown quite clearly in the thirteen months of their marriage how sharp she was with implications and her pregnancy was not putting her in the best of moods, although at least, preoccupied with her morning state, she seemed to miss or perhaps ignore the vague awkwardness with which her husband took himself off rather earlier than usual to his study.

– Don't forget the Heatheringtons! was all she called out to him as he went, not closing his study door fully, which she would have

171

noticed, and then taking out the newsprint page and the note which he had quickly crumpled into his pocket as the breakfast things were being cleared, opening them a little at first then squeezing them into a still tighter ball and looking for a means of disposing of this.

The Reverend Gill (now the vicar at Bishop's Cleeve, Gloucestershire) looked at the Zurbarán reproduction of Christ on the Cross on the wall of his study then, feeling the same emptiness he had felt those four years ago as he left Castleford and on a number of occasions since. As they always did, other thoughts tried to fill this or at least reduce it – *witness what licence will bring*, he thought, *word and thought become deed*! This was where a man could go who does not recognize the reality of Jesus Christ. Light hearted we can be, curiosity of the intellect we can have, but without His real salvation the Devil is waiting, the vermin will move. Gill stared at the reproduction and then at the rolling Gloucestershire hillside beyond his window. He had been *delivered*, he thought. He had been right in the guidance he had chosen to heed and the path he had chosen to take, whilst another fine and competent figure had been stolen away, tricked and robbed of all its potential, reduced to confusion and to shame. He had been *right*, he thought. *Undeniably*. Undeniably also, the great emptiness was still there, only bounded by some distant stone, and as A. P. Gill went down on his knees, careless for once whether his wife might look in and read his actions, he could not rid himself of its oppressive presence, nor prevent the tear which its chill brought to his eye.

Midnight in Moscow

(Kenny Ball 1961)

Is that all the heat we've got?

Councillor Hardcastle asked this of the old man who was setting the fire.

– Hell's freezing over out there!

– You could slide down Ferrybridge Road on your hobnails!

This was a lighter touch on his part, but the man gave no response and Hardcastle remembered being told that the Master at Arms, as he was referred to by a couple of the old guard, and caretaker by most others, was at least partially deaf. Nor could he remember the man's name, which displeased him as he prided himself on his personal touches. He stepped closer and repeated his question until the man turned and pointed at the red-fronted triangular box in one corner of the room. *Oil fire*, he said and even in those two words Hardcastle heard the flat tone of the chronically hard of hearing. There was some war story about the man, which again Hardcastle could not specifically remember, which story meant a succession of Mayors had insisted on him keeping his post.

– Have we got no … the Councillor let this question tail off; the expense of electric fires had been a heated issue at the last budget review. He went towards the oil apparatus, which seemed to be throwing out as much pungent paraffin smell as heat, but he did manage to thaw out his fingers on its tin sides and then he looked back to see the old man had got to his feet and was spreading a newspaper in front of the fire to draw the blaze. *You'll have the whole place on fire doing that!*

– Haven't you got a proper – he called, but the name for the handled metal guard used to draw fires did not come, although the Councillor remembered his mother using one over many years and he could still see it leaning against the wall beside the fireplace. Did it even have a name? *A drawer?* Surely not. He set off towards the caretaker to make his question and his warning heard, but as he did so the old man, with something of a matador's flourish, whisked away the news sheets, just at the final moment of impact, and revealed a substantial blaze. Hardcastle turned back to the oil stove whilst the old man nodded proudly at the flames he had raised and knelt again, with quite reasonable facility, to dig out some coal from the gleaming brass scuttle. Piling this on the screwed-up newspaper and wood with which the fire had been started inevitably subdued the blaze and standing again the caretaker brought his newspaper cloak back across the fireplace, letting it be sucked in tight against the rims of the aperture. *Was it even turning brown in parts?* Hardcastle peered towards it. Like the map of Bonanza? But then the Master at Arms whisked it off again to another bullish blaze. The old chap seemed to know what he was doing, the Councillor concluded, and if he didn't there were a number of rugs in the room as well as the large decorated carpet the committee table stood on and he could quickly lift up one of these, a matador himself, and win hero status by extinguishing a blazing old codger in its roll. The Councillor would have welcomed the opportunity to be thought a hero. His duties in the last war had offered him none.

Young Riley sauntered in. What the Glasshoughton ward was doing electing someone so young was a puzzle to the 41-year-old Hardcastle, although Riley senior was quite big in the local N.U.M. and had probably had some influence. *Brass monkeys out there!* said the young man, hugging himself in his rather short overcoat, and Hardcastle did no more than nod. Although hardly old himself, he had begun to feel a dislike for the attention increasingly being given to young people, especially teenagers, of which his own elder son was most definitely, quite defiantly, one. – Oh, good man, Charlie! Riley stepped towards the fire, pulling off his gloves and directing open palms towards the blaze. *Charlie.* Of course, Charlie, thought

174

Hardcastle as the old caretaker inclined his head towards the new arrival.

– It'll be needed today, sir, he said and Hardcastle glared at the oil apparatus under him as if it had given the salutation. There should be no *sirs* here was his thought, particularly for some stripling in his early twenties.

– What's on then, Ron? It'll be the protest march, I suppose.

Hardcastle gave no more than a shrug in answer. His friends and colleagues called him Ron, this young snot should be using a Mister. Probably, he said then, feeling the youngster's continuing gaze and turning to meet it, trying for the weightier presence which should be the due of his extra years, although any such manner bounced off young Riley like an arrow off a tank. The boy even offered full face to Councillor Wanglass, who had been a sergeant major and who still retained in his straight back and hard eyes the quality of someone used to obedience. Times were changing, thought Hardcastle, and not necessarily for the better. Witness his son.

– Yes, it'll be that. Young Riley turned back to the fire, opening up his overcoat to the blaze. The garment had quite a large collar which was fully turned up. What was it with turned-up collars for young people? wondered Hardcastle; it had been a recent point of conflict with his son, although this had been the collar of a shirt. Why would anyone turn up the collar of a shirt?! Other than as some gesture of defiance? The collar of an overcoat in cold weather perhaps, but the collar of a shirt! He looked at the younger Councillor's profile, the puce colour of its skin enlivened by the deep pink ripples of a shaving rash and a few other redder marks and dots. At least his hair was still fairly short at the back and the sides, he thought; unlike his elder son's. He hoped that when he next saw his son he would have been to the barber's as instructed. Otherwise …

– *Morning, gentlemen*! Alderman Bright came in, dressed in his usual Churchillian suit and waistcoat; the man had stopped short of a Homburg, but otherwise he made no apology for dressing as his hero had dressed and as he came in he took out the fob watch from his waistcoat pocket. – Others not here? *Clearly not*! Hardcastle sniffed away any sarcastic response. *Where do you think they are? Hiding*

175

under the table? And where was he? came an accompanying internal jibe. Standing between the new whipper-snapper and the old guard. Churchill had been the man for the war, Hardcastle had always agreed on this, but they had soon got rid of him when the war was over. Others had seen, just as he had, that the new world the war brought in needed other hands to shape it. He himself had been one pair of those hands; he had left the Forces on a tide of hope, a difficult tide, of course, with all the cross currents of any great aftermath, but his generation it was who had rolled into shore, come in on a wing and a prayer, looking around for what there was to salvage and what needed to be built. And yet now it seemed this generation's successors, its sons, could not even appreciate let alone continue these efforts. For all he had been born a nobody in the nowhere land of the north, Ron Hardcastle had grown up with *significance,* come to manhood amidst the undoubted importance of seeing off the most evil force in history, and he found it hard now to see this undoubted significance and unarguable importance sliding into what looked like ephemera. *Radio Luxembourg.* He had always allowed the necessity of recreation, but he had no way of conceiving of it as an end in itself.

– Is there an agenda? Young Riley looked across at the portly Alderman, who was an easy target for his own private mockery. The man had Churchill's plump figure, but unlike the great man, he had not accepted baldness or the absence of any matinee idol looks and there was an awkward concoction on the Alderman's head of greying, gingery brown hair parted ruthlessly just above either ear and drawn up to form some kind of harvest festival on top. There was a strange quality to his complexion also, as if an onion, relieved of its first layer, had been lightly rouged, and there were stories of the Alderman spending inordinate lengths of time locked in the Gents, preparing for any entrance. Not that any lack of masculinity could be part of any mockery, as it was said the man shared the reputed endowment of his hero but that, again unlike that hero, he had conferred the gift on a number of ladies, including a Town Hall secretary and the widowed proprietor of a jeweller's on Banks Street. Young Riley was attempting to flesh out the bones of such rumours. The more informed future he felt would be less tolerant of such matters in its leaders than had been the past. The Alderman's wife was said to be long suffering, but she wanted to be Mayoress as her husband wanted to be Mayor, an honour which so far his enemies had managed to deny him. Hardcastle was one of these enemies and young Riley smiled at seeing the subterranean hostility in the exchanges between the two older men: one some ten to twenty, the other thirty to forty years older than he was; both, in his private opinion, figures of yesterday.

– There's no agenda, said Alderman Bright. Though I've got Gwen getting some copies of the relevant details.

At that moment Councillors Grant and Beevers made an entry together, the first a boat hook of a figure, his long grey overcoat the pole to a thin neck and a sharp-featured face which seemed to be permanently angled forward seeking some detail onto which it might properly attach. Beevers was shorter and heavier and more known for cutting through, or ignoring, detail. He wore a flat cap on his balding head and thick black spectacles on a face which showed the pittings and paunches of both hard work and indulgence. His arrival alongside Councillor Grant had been mere coincidence. Beevers still lived in a terrace in the old Potteries district, whilst Grant had a big house on Sheepwalk and sported an altogether more pretentious trilby, although he was already holding this in his hand as he came in. Young Riley turned back to the blaze in the fireplace. How long before such characters as these were all consigned to the flames of time, was his thought.

– So what is this? asked Grant, his hooked features seeking a boat. Is it this sit-down thing?

– It's not a sit down it's a march, said Hardcastle, still standing over the oil heater.

– Well, they start off marching, Ron … Grant turned towards another possible target … but then they end up sitting down. Didn't you see that business in London?! Beevers took off his cap and adjusted his spectacles.

– Too bloody right, he agreed. With that bloody actress! Can't let stuff like that get going here, Albert! He addressed the Alderman who was looking again at his fob watch.

– They've got a right to protest. Riley turned from the fire towards the heat of disapproval from all the other men in the room. Primarily for his youth in his opinion, which was accurate, but also for their recognition that despite all the bluster and badges of old office, he was tomorrow and perhaps even today, which was more his own assessment.

– What are you talking about, 'right'? Councillor Beevers crumpled his flat cap into the pocket of his donkey jacket and directed his heavy step in the youngest Councillor's direction. They've got no bloody right to strew themselves across a bloody thoroughfare. They've got no right to do that at all!

– What specifically is the protest about? asked Councillor Grant, seeking another fixing place. Is it just Ban the Bomb or is it Polaris?

– *Polaris*?! Beevers paused in his movement and looked towards the heaven beyond the high ceiling of the Committee Room. That's up in Scotland isn't it? What's that got to do with bloody Carlton Street?!

Gwen Hicks came into the room with a sheaf of Roneoed papers and Alderman Bright pocketed his watch and motioned the secretary to set out the sheets in front of the chairs around the central table. – Let's have a look at the details and then we can take action, he said. *Action this day* as he had once written on a Public Works memorandum, much to the amusement of everyone else involved.

– We haven't got a quorum, said Hardcastle, still standing over the oil fire. We need two more.

– It's an extraordinary meeting, countered Councillor Grant, even with some relaxation in his manner as he found his first really appropriate resting place. We don't actually need a quorum at the meeting itself, although the rubric is that attempts should be made to contact all the other members of the committee. Proxy approval is sufficient and in special circumstances a simple majority of members present.

– Are you sure that's the ruling? asked Hardcastle, somewhat perfunctorily; he and Grant had clashed before on procedural matters, with Grant always emerging victorious; because, thought Hardcastle, he, unlike Grant, did not spend his time in a big house on Sheepwalk, calling in the occasional instructions to his home furnishings store and reading up on the dry minutia of local government. The man, in Hardcastle's opinion, had no common touch.

– Quite sure. Grant's sharp features gave off a silvery smirk.

– Reg Shaw is due, said Alderman Bright, but Jim Wanglass can't get. Family bereavement. He's in Cleethorpes. And you all know about Mr Liversidge. So, let's get on with it.

All the men turned towards the oval wooden table and Hardcastle briefly considered taking the chair at its head, to which he was nearest. The Alderman was the proper convening authority for the committee, but, particularly given the ad hoc nature of the meeting, there was nothing to say he should be its chairman. Although finicky fanny Frankie Grant could probably dredge one up from some bureaucratic tome or other, he thought, and after rubbing his hands once more in the pungent haze of the oil fire he made his way to a more central chair.

– Thank you, Gwen. Taking the seat at the head of the table, Alderman Bright waved at the exiting secretary. And some tea? which instruction the woman took with no response. The caretaker, with a final look at the flames he had brought up, followed the woman out and the heavy, polished wood door was closed, although rather than shutting in the warmth of the fires, this seemed to emphasize the coolness of the room; the dark wood panels of its walls and the high, arched and carefully corniced plaster ceiling seemed weightily designed to keep out any warmth and light and the one window in the room looked out only onto the dull and unheated interior of the Town Hall's first floor.

– What you have in front of you then is the proposal for a march and a meeting and what Jack Aubrey and Assistant Chief Constable Bottomly have to say.

Alderman Bright took the reading glasses from his top pocket as he waited for the others to peruse the document before them.

– Who's this chap organizing it all? asked Hardcastle.

– Some doctor or other from the University of Sheffield … Bright placed the spectacles carefully through the lower arrangements of his hair to check the name. A Doctor Hirst …

– *Sheffield?*! Beevers lifted his own thick spectacles up onto his forehead. Who is this bloke when he's at home? Is he a Castleford resident? What are we doing with a proposal made by some pillock from Sheffield?

– He lives in Fairburn, said young Riley.

– You know him?

– Yes.

– I thought you were a Glasshoughton lad?

Riley gave the indulgent smile of coming youth for ageing insularity.

– He's a PhD in chemistry at the University of Sheffield. He wrote an article in the *Yorkshire Post* this week. Didn't you see it? He teaches chemistry at the university.

– A *teacher?*! Beevers gave this the same intonation he had given to *Sheffield*. Then he should know better than to be setting off this kind of doowacky!

– I think he believes we need to make some protest before it's too late!

Riley's sudden injection of a more urgent note into his previous indulgence was something of a confusion for Hardcastle; the lightweight teenager's sneer of the latter he could attack, but the note of urgency was more in tune with his own dark mood. *The world is teetering on the brink of annihilation.* Hardcastle could not help but feel then that it was Beevers who gave the teenager's dismissive shrug.

– As Doctor Hirst said in his article, Riley went on – unless something is done to reduce and control nuclear arms then civilization itself will be destroyed! We need to act now to force our government to be the first to stand up for sense and for safety!

Hardcastle looked around at the other men sitting at the Committee Room's table and wondered if they shared the subdued terror in which he found himself living. *It could happen!* His time at war had taught him this: the same men who had sat in the briefing room, those to whom he had brought the maps he had been given to bring, could be gone the following day; their lips had words, their minds had thoughts, their limbs had movements and then no more. And the same structures which seemed always to have been there, like this Committee Room with its portraits of old dignitaries hanging like extra shields, could suddenly be transformed by ordnance into ruins. Hardcastle knew this and he knew also that the weapons now could be so extensive, so *inclusive* ... with them there would be none of the lucky survivors to mourn and to carry on, no element of sweepstake with each of those involved secretly believing they would be lucky, that the God who had given them the only life they knew would somehow not wish to have this handiwork expunged. Despite all the external evidence to the contrary. *There would be no fortunate ones now*, thought Hardcastle, no lucky escapes, no heroes; it would all fall like a great thick carpet. He had acted the reassuring husband and hero for his wife when she had asked him directly if he thought there was going to be a nuclear war and he had found some fortitude in responding to her more openly expressed fear, but he could not deny that which was unexpressed but so insistent in himself. It even played its garbled part in the trouble he was having with his elder son. *How could significance be so easily lost,* was his question, insistent and deadening like the cold of winter; how could meaning be so readily gone?

– Well, it's clear what the Assistant Chief Constable thinks.

Councillor Grant had finished his close reading of the document. He considered this to be a trick anybody could learn, but which few actually did. *Actually read* what you have in front of you would have been his advice if he had not also considered it something of an advantageous secret. People think they have done so when in fact they have only taken in the gist or picked out what they thought was relevant to them (as Cliff Beevers had just done). Frank Grant prided himself on his full and thorough concentration; before him at present was a simple document, but he would have applied the same hooked-on focus to a more complex or a thicker tome. It was, he thought, his great strength. – He says there will be a public order issue as the local force is insufficient to police it properly.

– He also says there could be reinforcements brought in from Wakefield. Hardcastle pointed at the Roneoed sheet and Grant turned a sharp look towards him.

– I know, Ron, I read it, he said. What it doesn't say is who's going to *pay*! Close reading will also give you the omissions, he had found.

– Why Castleford anyway? asked Beevers, who considered himself the most local of these local men. Frank Grant hadn't even been born in the town and Hardcastle was seldom to be seen in its public houses. What's Castleford got to do with any of this? He glanced at the door, hoping Shorty Shaw, another proper Castleford lad, would soon appear. They were the ones, it seemed to him, who could truly speak for the town.

– I don't think Castleford will be excluded from a nuclear attack!

Hardcastle tried to convey something of his support for what Riley had just said with this, but Riley offered no acknowledgement as he made what he considered to be his own younger person's point.

– Its part of a whole series of marches and protests, he said. There's a coordinated effort on the same day, a real sign of the strength of feeling. There's going to be one in Pontefract as well.

– What about Featherstone? Beevers rubbed at his bald pate, which, as those who knew him well would have recognized, was the signal for a witticism. That could do with bombing!

Young Riley gave a slight smile at this opening. These old men gave him so many, stuck as they were in their John Wayne pictures; problems solved with a punch. In essence these were the men, he thought, who had conspired in the doomsday scenario. – Well, if you are going to be *facetious*! he said and Alderman Bright, who had rather drifted off from the discussion into wondering where Gwen was with the tea, which he knew had already been brewed, was brought back by the young man's tone.

– I think we're getting off the point, he said as he usually did, not always certain what that point was, but knowing action needed at least one. We've got to decide whether to approve this march.

– And whether we pay for the extra police to police it, said Grant.

– Well, that's why it's this committee I've called in.

– So, it's just a money issue! Riley shook his head: It just comes down to money!

– *Public* money. *Public* funds. Bright turned a full Churchillian glare onto the young man and Riley settled for another shake of the head. The Alderman should know all about public funds, would have been his reply in a different and better, and undoubtedly coming, world. Bright and his firm and his brother's subsidiary business had benefitted enough from such funds. *And why bother with this meeting anyway?* he would have added. Why bring people out on a freezing Saturday morning when it was clear that if Wakefield's Assistant Chief Constable didn't want them to agree to the march then this would be the decision. The Assistant Chief Constable and Alderman Bright were both trouser rollers, fellow bib and sash wearers, and what they decided over drinks at the Lodge would undoubtedly be what would happen. Young Riley said none of this. He would bide his time, he thought; it would not be long now before his time came, if of course they were not all annihilated beforehand by John Wayne and his Flying Leathernecks.

– I think they have a right to protest.

Seeing the young Councillor seemingly silenced, Hardcastle spoke up.

– I mean, unless something's done we're all going to end up …

He felt his private terror beginning to show a little and he flattened it out with a dismissive hand gesture, looking quickly around the other men. Each one of them must surely feel some trepidation, he thought; genuinely fearless men were few and far between. The Guy Gibsons. And most of them quickly end up dead. Perhaps what was happening here was that they were talking about such issues as finance in order to obscure the more terrible possibilities, like playing darts before an op. He looked blindly back at the Roneoed sheet.

– You call this *doing something?* Councillor Beevers had had an animated exchange just the evening before with his sister's husband, a Mancunian. All this does, he snorted, is tell the Russians there's no bloody unity in this country! They'll be jigging around all over the shop in Moscow seeing what's happening here. Folk strewing themselves across bloody thoroughfares!

Young Riley had resolved on a period of silence, but this comment shattered his resolution. *Russians!* he echoed Beevers' snort. *You think it's all the Russians?* It's the Americans you want to worry about. They're just dragging us along into it all. Macmillan's just a pet poodle for Kennedy! Alderman Bright was brought back to concentration again by this attack on a gentleman of the old school, a junior minister or something for Churchill himself if memory served.

– What are you talking about, Mr Riley? He glared at the young man. We've still got the best army in the world. The Americans learn from us. Look at our boys out there in what's it called? Kuwait. And in Berlin. Still the best damn forces in the world, young man! The young man's sceptical exhalation at this almost brought the Alderman to his feet and even the secretary's final arrival with a tray of five mugs of tea did not fully calm his annoyance, particularly when young Riley, despite this decent woman's decent efforts, said no tea for me thank you and deliberately left his mug standing alone on the tray. The Alderman barely managed his own thank you and the secretary, with an ill-tempered look for them all, pulled the heavy door quite noisily shut. The pause which her presence and her exit instigated reduced the moment, however, and Councillor Grant was able to offer some cooler details after she had gone.

– There is a need for a deterrent, he said. I wonder if Dr Hirst and his people have really thought this through. And Polaris will provide us with some independence in this field.

– *Polaris?* I thought it was the Skybolt thing. Beevers was fumbling for his cigarettes and Hardcastle looked at him as at a hopeless case.

– Skybolt was cancelled he said, noting with the slightest pleasure that he had beaten Grant into saying this. Grant carried on as if he had in fact said it, however.

– We're getting the Polaris missiles, he said, and they will be under *our* control. The Americans can't tell us when and where to fire them … Again young Riley was drawn out by the utter mess of aged stupidity which it seemed was surrounding him.

– *And what are we going to fire them from?* he snorted. A rowing boat on Ponte Park lake?!

Grant's thin, hooked smile glittered at the riposte this offered.

– Now who's being facetious? he said.

– I think we're getting off the point, gentlemen.

Alderman Bright brought two pudgy hands towards the document in front of him as if he were kneading it as dough, but the youngest

Councillor actually came to his feet as the Alderman himself had almost done.

– On the contrary, I think this *is* the point! the young man said and tapped a finger hard into the wooden table, his eyes and his shaving rash taking on the glow of flames. We need to see the stupidity of it all! The *madness*. Someone needs to lead the way in showing this, otherwise it will all go up, otherwise …!

For the first time Hardcastle detected a clear element of his own terror in one of these other men and he was surprised it was in the one who was by far the youngest. Younger people like his elder son, he thought, had no conception of what could happen; like all young people they had the subterranean expectation of immortality. Riley might be a little older and more responsible than his son, but it was still a surprise for Hardcastle to see an element of himself in this younger man. He had grown up in a world which looked up not down for its examples. He also recognized how the young Councillor flattened out the revelatory moment, just as he had flattened out his own, although Riley chose a different verbal strategy.

– *Otherwise we are all potato crisps!* the young man said with something of a forced laugh. – Because don't tell me anybody has control of it all! His voice rose again as he went on. – As soon as you get two sides facing each other like this then they both go mad. *Always!* And don't give me age and experience! Don't give me Macmillan (he avoided saying Mr Pastry as he and his friends routinely did). *Don't give me him!*

Beevers, who had little time for any national politicians, was watching the young man with interest. On the previous evening, albeit quite drunk, he had developed an argument that no-one under fifty should be allowed into public office. Before this you still have mistakes to make. Ask anyone over fifty. The lad spouting forth here it seemed to him was validating his argument. – What about Kennedy? he asked. How old is he? Grant was about to give the American president's age, but his detail was lost in Riley's heated response.

– *Don't give me him, either!* he snapped, rather misunderstanding the weighting of the question. Don't give me *the Americans*. Look at them with this space race. Look at the money they've spent there when it could have been better spent elsewhere. *Just to keep up with the Russians!* Look at the money they've just wasted sending whatsisname on an orbit.

– Grissom … Grant was able to get this detail in and Beevers looked genuinely puzzled. *Grissom?* he queried. Wasn't he part of a gang?

Young Riley turned away in something like despair then and Hardcastle's heart went out to another in fear. Also he agreed with him and whoever this university Doctor was. The government he had seen at local level and what he knew of it at national level gave him no reassurance. They were just men, word bound and emotion infested, just as they were here, and in the final analysis he could not see any of them guaranteeing safety.

– I think we are getting away from the matter in hand, said Alderman Bright. The Assistant Chief Constable needs an answer this day.

– Surely he can make a public order decision off his own bat.

Not thinking with any particular clarity, Hardcastle allowed Grant an easy score.

– I think you're missing the point there, Ron. What he needs to know is whether we are willing to pay for the overtime and so on to police it all.

Hardcastle dropped his gaze back to the Roneoed sheet, thinking how little it could matter. The thick walls of this thick room and its thick old building could at any moment come crashing in as the nuclear wind, hurled out from its bright-centred mushroom cloud, obliterated everything. They had all seen the images. And unlike Grant, he thought, he could not bury these under a mound of bureaucratic detail. There was a silence, punctuated only by some slurping of tea and a few snapping sounds from the flames in the fireplace and then, fingering out a match from his Swan Vesta box, Beevers asked – So what's it going to cost? Smelling the pleasant and comforting smoke of the John Player Full Strength Beevers lit, Hardcastle wondered if he too should light up, although he was trying to reduce the habit he had acquired in the Forces. Alderman

Bright had a box of panatellas in the pocket of his jacket, but he had recently been made aware of some comments about the size of his cigars. The bigger kind, such as Churchill smoked, were not easy to get hold of, however.

– I don't suppose it'll be cheap. Beevers blew out smoke from both nostrils. With overtime and specials and all. Especially when they start getting their helmets knocked off carting folk to the Black Mariah.

– There's a projected cost given. Grant pointed at the Roneoed sheet and Beevers blew more smoke down onto it.

– Christ Almighty! he said, adjusting his spectacles so he could make out the figures. Where are they bringing these bloody specials from? The Bahamas?

– Sending them there on holiday more like! Riley was unable to resist this, unable to maintain a meaningful or even a sulky silence. *What's going to be your share?* He did not ask this of the Alderman, however, settling for a glance at Hardcastle, not unconscious of the common ground, however vague, which the nuances of the exchange had exposed.

– I mean, are they wearing gold helmets?! Beevers forged on with a search for comic images which would at least please him. The blunt but rich comedy of a true Castleford lad.

– That's the cost of things like this these days, Cliff, said Alderman Bright. Do you think the Assistant Chief Constable doesn't know what he's doing?

This question hung like the smoke and the smell of the paraffin stove for some time with not even young Riley giving a qualified response; nor was there any detailed questioning from Grant, who had seen the way the matter was going. Hardcastle also recognized the mere rubber stamp nature of the meeting. This happened too often in his opinion: committees were formed, talks were held as a mere semblance of involvement. Beneath them the usual powers, the old vanities, just carried on, defining matters as freezing cold defines a day. He looked for young Riley to share this conclusion, perhaps even to express it, but the young man, though still on his feet, was staring into the fire. – Well, it's going to be approved isn't it?

This was the best indication Hardcastle could make of his perception, but at least, he thought, amidst those age-old features and fiddling they would be approving some kind of protest against madness. His war experiences had taught him there are always those who will find benefits in conflicts, although the nuclear wind might be just too ill even for those. We're just here to rubber stamp it, he said, which brought Alderman Bright into at least a semblance of irritation.

– We don't do rubber stamping, Ron! If you're not in favour say so. We're not in Russia. Everybody's free to say what they want here.

Hardcastle let his eyes fall blankly back down to the sheet again and Bright looked with faint contempt on the man's weakness. He turned to the youngest Councillor then: And you, Councillor Riley? Are you in favour?

– *I am!* came the abrupt response.

– Well, I'm not sure I am, said Beevers. Not at that price. And – he addressed Councillor Grant – like you say we're going to end up with people sitting strewn across the road. Grant shrugged, however; part of his sharpness was to recognize which boat was best to hook on to.

– This isn't London, Cliff, he said. We've got a bit more sense up here. I'm sure it will be a peaceful march and then a meeting with a couple of speakers, as it says here.

Beevers lowered and then lifted his spectacles and then also shrugged. The Cas match would be frozen off, but he could still have a pleasurable anticipation of the Smawthorne Club that Saturday night. This was what his fellow Councillors and a number of other folk he knew should do more of, he thought; these protest people themselves. Would you rather sit at home or go marching up and down waiting for the bomb to drop or be caught by it in the midst of a good pint and good company? He had said as much to his idiot Mancunian brother-in-law, jabbering on about the situation in the world the previous evening. – Even at that bloody cost? was his final gesture, addressing the remark again to Grant, although he could see where Frankie was going.

– If that's the Assistant Chief Constable's estimate, said Grant. He's the expert here. I see no reason to dispute his figures. Beevers looked beyond him to the door, wondering if Shorty Shaw was going to make it; if he did they could get in the Smawthorne for a lunchtime.

– All right then, he said. Let 'em march. But let's sort it out quick sharp. It's bloody freezing in here.

– *All right then*. Alderman Bright echoed the phrase, asked for a show of hands and seeing the unanimous vote sat back in his chair with some satisfaction; this was how action was taken. That's a majority, he said. I'll let the other members know of course. And I'll inform the Assistant Chief Constable. He began then with some of the remarks he always used to finish off meetings, but even as he did so young Riley pulled his eyes from the flames of the fire and set off for the Committee Room's door. Hardcastle watched him go and then on an impulse set off after him, although he let his own movements coincide more with the Alderman's rounding off. *Thank you, Ron!* the Alderman called after him, but Hardcastle ignored the vague gloating in the pseudo-Churchill's tone. He should ally himself with the younger rather than the older elements was his conclusion. The old guard might gloat, they might sit comfortably in their chairs, but they were ending; the nuclear wind, the modern wind, even if it did not actually blow them away, would blow them finally into the past. Whatever ulterior motive they had in matters such as this, whatever sop they thought they were giving to transient disruptions of old and inevitable practice, their day was done. They had after all just approved a public protest; they had just allowed the first movements of the giant which would devour them all. Hardcastle turned at the door and offered his goodbye.

– *Good morning*, he said, and went off after the younger Councillor.

Beevers and Grant came to their feet after the two younger men had left and Alderman Bright spoke to them as to adults relieved of children: Johnny Bottomly will keep a lid on it all, he said. Don't worry. You can count on him. And both the other Councillors nodded as they went to the open door. As they did so a figure appeared there wrapped from head to toe in thick dark clothes, serge trousers rising to an old navy overcoat which in turn rose to a dark blue woolly balaclava.

– *Bloody hell!* said Beevers. It's Captain Midnight!

– What? Are you done? asked Reg Shaw, pulling the damp wool away from his mouth then dissolving into a fit of coughing and drawing the aperture of the faintly steaming balaclava still further down so he would not take in any of its moistened fluff. Overjoyed to see his friend, Beevers reached out the hand which was not holding the cigarette to slap at the little man's arched back.

– You'll not be here at Christmas, lad! he chuckled and Grant, stepping around the two friends, smiled sharply.

– None of us may be, he said and all three set off along the Town Hall corridor leaving the Alderman still sitting at the head of the committee table, reaching into the inside pocket of his suit for his cigars and beginning his usual contemplation of the mayoral portraits hanging on the Committee Room's wall.

Blue Moon

(*The Marcels 1961*)

Eileen Barnes – née Goodall – was a deeply artistic woman. She had felt this even as a girl growing up on Tennyson Avenue, although the setting and the atmosphere in which she had grown had not been conducive to any fostering of the feeling. Her youthful talent for sketching would have been more remarked upon – perhaps even acted upon – had she been a male, but as it was, if it was considered at all, it was consigned to the vague accomplishments of the female, alongside needlework (which at that time and at that social level would have been thought far more useful), and in truth it was not accompanied in her by any consuming appetite or pictorial drive which might have had it blossoming anyway. It was difficult to tell how far this was a failing in her talent or the result of her setting. Her mother died of tuberculosis when Eileen was only three and she and her brother had been raised, if such a term was worthy of the operation, by her father's Great War widowed sister in something of the dutiful but grudging stereotype of such arrangements. The father himself, his spirit in essence destroyed by the loss of his young wife and by his work as a miner, retreated into a comparatively even-tempered but irretrievably bleak and undemonstrative manner. Both he and his sister would praise the little girl's sketches, but the praise was perfunctory, particularly on the part of the guardian aunt, who had other work for female hands, and Eileen soon left off seeking their appreciation and began simply to store the works in her own private books and boxes.

Her feeling for music fared rather better as the guardian sister had brought an old upright piano with her when she moved in, which she played in faltering fashion herself and on which she gave, if still grudgingly, some lessons to her young niece. Again it was hard to tell whether Eileen's own later limitations as a pianist were a result of this half-hearted early exposure or whether they were the limitations of the ability itself. All a Mozart needs is access to the instrument, but there is a vast realm of possibilities between him and the wholly talentless and no-one could say for certain what Eileen might have done had she been born into privilege and true artistic encouragement.

Certainly, as a mature woman, Eileen felt there was a realm inside her which had not been explored, possibilities which had not been allowed, expressions which had not been made. A not unattractive face and the vitality in her personality had allowed her to marry well (everyone agreed on this), but looking back it seemed to her this marriage (albeit not unwelcome or unhappy) and the two daughters which followed had ensured that the barriers to her artistic nature were extended, that her life had entailed a long and seamless curtain drawn across this internal realm. And yet, in the late 1950s and early '60s when she found herself with her daughters past childhood, her husband a faithful if rather dour success at Barclay's Bank, and with time and resources to remove these barriers and draw back this curtain, nothing in particular was revealed: it was a brightly coloured landscape, infused with fine but vague music and sweet songs, but it had in it not only the promise of its horizon, of some great and satisfying discovery, but also the bluish light and melancholy distance of something lost.

Eileen's continuing vitality came to her assistance here and after a few years of faint depression and confusion she made herself seek out at least some recognizable shape to her deeply artistic nature. She attended the painting classes given by a local artist who had been at Castleford Grammar School with Henry Moore, who had gone on with him to Leeds College of Art, but not then on to The Slade and international fame; he had stayed with the real people, the local artist said, where real scenes could be found for his work, although as Eileen realized after no great time under his tutelage, the work based on this reality was really quite dull. She wanted to put something *more* into her own efforts, but the water colours with which she seemed most comfortable kept forcing their usual effects on her and when she actually painted an angel into the River Aire landscape she had copied from a photograph, the result, she had to admit, was faintly ridiculous. She tried oil paints, but found them somehow too substantial and the pastel and crayon pieces she produced tended to the condition of the water colours. Nor had she any particular subject matter; the realm inside seemed too wide (or too little explored in the years when exploration has the intensity of youth) and she could find no motif which might capture its extent and offer it framed as both an encapsulation and a portal as the best paintings and poems do.

As for poems or any other creative writings, these were never an option for her and this time she could quite definitely blame her background. She had left school at fourteen to start work at United Glass, although her presence and vitality had kept her out of the most menial tasks for women there and seen her placed in the reception offices. She was always aware of the limitations of her vocabulary, however, and she had kept a secret list of words she had not understood or met before and a large dictionary at home in which she looked them up, adding for good measure each night at least three new ones she had only encountered in that dictionary. She was lucky enough also to have as a fellow receptionist at the glassworks an equally vital and more confident, if far less artistically inclined, older woman who had been born in Chelsea and only come north as a wartime bride; from her Eileen learned how to modify her northern accent, but not in the artificial fashion of some as, with this woman's help, she took in the basic trick of such modification, which is to speak with grammatical accuracy; the reductive markers are to be found more in weak idioms and actual mistakes than in the accent itself; Eileen learned this (she was consequently both rather dismissive of and rather disturbed by the fashion for weak-idiomed and mistake-ridden northern accents which began to take some hold in the sixties) and by the time of her visit to her elder daughter in Leicester where the young woman was at university, Eileen had made something of the finished article of herself with regard to verbal presentation. She could even be rather intimidating. There are those who make deficiencies the cause of further deficiencies and those who use them to find strength and Eileen, at least with regard to her personality and her presentation of herself, was one of the latter. There was a security in her manner and a vitality which still shimmered in a face become handsome. Her husband was certainly no verbal match for her and again without any great show (and after a more subservient demeanour early on) she affectionately dominated him.

There was still not enough in any of this, however, fully to calm or finally to satisfy the artistry within. Appearances and behaviour were like words for Eileen, they served more practical purposes – they were so *diurnal* – and even those arrangements of them which seemed to touch on that greater realm were, it seemed to her, compromised by *thought*. Even the great poems and novels she had made herself read seemed to do no more than provide a few instances – a rainbow here, a pool for a courtship or a suicide there – in a realm which was still numinously beautiful and specifically elusive.

Music was her best option. Eileen came to recognize this. Poems and paintings need the daily language of words and images whereas music is an *otherness*, just like the artistic realm inside her. No painting or poem had ever brought Eileen as close to feeling herself truly within this realm or recognizing its true forms as had music. The actuality of this music was a little more problematic; it would have seemed more appropriate had it been music of the highest brow, but she had to admit this was not the case (again what else could be expected of a woman with her background?). There were moments in Tchaikovsky and some Chopin, but although she had tried him, Mozart remained too complex for her, as was anything baroque or 'modern'; Beethoven was too heavy, like oil paint, Stravinsky unintelligible and Wagner … With some reluctance Eileen had to admit that any glimpses of anything specific in her great internal realm had been afforded to her through songs such as 'I'll be Seeing You' and – perhaps her favourite – 'Blue Moon'. Not that either of these, or any song or tune, spoke to her of loss or longing, of some man or other; what she would be seeing when she looked at the moon was some rendition of the realm inside. What would appear in its light was a clear moment of the soul.

She responded in this way also to some musical shows and films, not particularly to the shows and films in general, which, for her, were often contrived in their stories and laboured in their dialogue, but to particular moments of melody. Again there was no resonance with regard to love relationships, as there would have been for others; Eileen loved her husband with the straightforward affection with which she would have loved her father if he had given her the chance and a son if she had had one. She had not felt drawn to other men, nor any longing for anything or anyone past (most of this past she was glad was gone), nor did she feel particularly drawn to exotic lands and places, recognizing, with something of the insistent practicality and realism of her upbringing, that however different these lands and places might be, in the end they would not be *other*. People still lived their own diurnal lives in them, perhaps even dreaming of the places their visitors had come from. None of this was at the heart of the matter for Eileen, there was no particular face or place evoked for her in these melodic moments, only that great and still-mysterious realm which they briefly seemed to reach into and illuminate.

Eileen's involvement with Legiolium Amateur Operatics then was yet another attempt on her part to find some shape for this deep-seated nature. The group had begun as a Gilbert and Sullivan Society, founded in '55 by a local insurance agent and another, rather more theatrical, figure who had served in the Forces' entertainment operations alongside, it was said, a couple of others who subsequently became famous on radio and television. When the insurance agent was rendered invalid by diabetes and his co-founder went off south to seek a wider audience (although he was never heard of again) Eileen took over the running of the Society. She had seen its first two productions, *Iolanthe* and then *Pinafore*, which were rather too built around the comic urge of its more theatrical founder (she had disliked his Joseph Porter quite intensely), but there had been a few moments of true melody in both shows which had reached into her. She had been persuaded to sing in the chorus of the second of these productions, but her voice, as with her piano playing, she recognized would bring more disappointment than satisfaction; any musical performance on her part was more likely to make the internal realm more distant than distinct. What her vitality allowed her to do, however, was to keep the Society alive just as, whatever the difficulties, true painters keep on with their painting, writers with their writing and composers with their music. When, after the indisposition and the departure of its co-founders, it seemed the group might disband, Eileen organized a more limited concert performance (allowing her to listen to her favourite Gilbert and Sullivan song, 'The Sun Whose Rays', without the difficulty of mounting a whole production of *The Mikado*). Following the minor success of this and mostly at her instigation, the Society decided on a production of *Carousel*; a promoting factor in this (as has been argued for the bear in *A Winter's Tale*) being the availability of an old fairground roundabout which had somehow come into the possession of one of the members and which, under Eileen's supervision (and at no little expense on her part), was disassembled and reinstalled on the stage of the Civic Hall. Eileen also ensured there was a small but reasonably competent band of musicians brought in to accompany the members' voices (the Gilbert and Sullivan shows had survived with only piano accompaniment) and this time, for all the vocal and dramatic limitations exposed, the Society enjoyed a real triumph. Even the *Evening Post* sent a reporter, who gave a glowing review.

For a couple of years then, as the new decade began, Legiolium Amateur Operatics concentrated on Rogers and Hammerstein, with Eileen making up any shortfall between the box office receipts (and the fees the members paid) and the cost of performance rights, the hire of the hall and other aspects of any such productions. Her husband was a great help in this as his position at the bank meant that more than a few local dignitaries and commercial figures could see benefit in keeping his favour and the financial losses involved became notably reduced. The public success of *Carousel* was followed by a concert involving its songs and others advertised as 'worldwide favourites' and this concert also went well. The Society's membership expanded and reasonable to good audiences could be anticipated, and *South Pacific* came next, trading on the surprising number of men who had now become members. Eileen liked this production less than the more soulful *Carousel*, particularly as the female lead had none of her vitality, let alone that of Mitzi Gaynor, and the male chorus grew altogether too full of itself, shouting rather than singing about the virtues of a dame and each of its members seemingly intent on finding his own bit of business at every possible opportunity. Others may well have had similar reactions as, at a well-attended General Meeting, some feeling was expressed that it was time for the Society to return to its roots and put on another Gilbert and Sullivan. *Pirates of Penzance* was suggested by the local manager of Marks and Spencer, who had seen D'Oyly Carte's most recent production at the Savoy and who spoke with some passion about how this was easily the best G and S, working at every level, dramatically, comically and musically. Eileen, however, had other thoughts.

– I think we should do one more Rogers and Hammerstein, she said. Complete the trilogy as it were. I think we should do *Oklahoma!*. She was not unaware of how much sway she held within the group. *Production supervised by Eileen Barnes* had appeared on both the *Carousel* and the *South Pacific* programmes (she had declined to be referred to as 'producer', but there were few in the Society who did not recognize that without her shaping vitality – and also without at least some of her money – the Society's activities would be lessened in both smoothness and scale).

– I think we should do *Oklahoma!*. Everybody knows it. Everybody will have seen the film. I think we should complete the trilogy with *Oklahoma!*

There were a number of factors in this suggestion on Eileen's part: she herself preferred the more modern shows, but she also had the feeling the Society's potential audience would be more enthused by the work of the more recent music and lyrics pairing. Also *Pirates* to her mind rather spoke of a reprise of the mob of *South Pacific* sailors wandering around at will on stage, slapping each other's behinds and double taking like music hall stooges. There would be a more limited

197

chorus of cowboys in *Oklahoma!*. Without doubt, however, although of course she made no mention of this, the greatest factor in her championing this show was the possibility it offered her daughter.

Eileen's younger child, Shirley, was at the time in the Lower Sixth of the Grammar School and for a number of years it had been agreed she had a very nice voice. She had sung in school concerts and in the female chorus of *South Pacific*, where it was also generally agreed she had looked particularly good in shorts. She was in Eileen's opinion perfect for the teenage female lead of *Oklahoma!*. In this the mother was not unaware of the possibility she might be using her daughter to give some actual shape to her own internal realm; she was not unconscious of the grand tradition of parents using offspring to have the experiences, achieve the successes they themselves had missed, but this it seemed to Eileen was outweighed by the actuality of her daughter's voice and her suitability for the part. Harder eyes might still have seen a self-deception (although the sweetness of the girl's voice could not be denied), but the mother's need was just too great and the means just too close at hand. Rationalization is frustration's great ally and parents are always to some extent the products of their children.

Marigold, the elder of Eileen's two daughters, had arguably suffered from this already, not least in the Christian name which the mother to her husband's muted horror had insisted upon. It was not a Christian name common in Castleford (unheard of in fact), but the new mother, amidst the mix of the brutally physical and the dreamily universal which is pregnancy, was adamant, even for a time feeling she could see some specific and lovely flower in her realm and that perhaps offspring after all were its nature and its fruit. This feeling passed. Nor did the child offer Eileen many other such opportunities as she grew; the girl rather favoured the father both in looks and in the capacity for detailed diligence, which was a great help academically; and although Eileen was proud of this, she was never able to make anything of it in her own realm, particularly when the daughter decided to pursue the emerging discipline of economics, about which Eileen knew nothing, but which she found impossible to equate with art. (The beauty of numbers eluded her as they simply recalled practicalities. And money was only what it could buy, or, more importantly for her beyond those earlier years, what it could *instigate*.) Marigold then, although Eileen loved her with the same straightforward bond which tied her to her husband, had provided little help and no resolution for the great internal space. (Although the mother noted with some pleasure how the girl had grown to like the unusual name she had insisted upon; how it had begun to chime with some developing mood.)

The younger daughter it had seemed to Eileen, whilst similarly loved, would be similarly useless in this regard, perhaps even more so, as although Shirley (Eileen had bowed this time to her husband and avoided another egregious Christian name) had a still more attractive rendition of her mother's not unattractive face, she had none of the academic capacity of her elder sister. Again it was not disappointment Eileen felt in this, only that she had to conclude finally that, unlike some women, she could not people her internal realm with children. And then Shirley's voice appeared and developed and Eileen began to doubt her conclusion and to wonder if, after all, her younger daughter might be a star by which at least something of her own internal realm could find its path, by the light of which at least something of its landscape might be illuminated.

There could be no doubt the young woman's voice was pleasing; this was no mere parental bias. It was a voice which was not unlike the voice of the young woman with the same Christian name who had appeared in the films of both *Oklahoma!* and *Carousel*, a voice as pure and clear as any pure, clear spring in any imagined landscape. The two even rather looked alike and Eileen acquired a number of photographs of Rogers and Hammerstein's particular starlet and was overjoyed to learn that for all her lovely voice, Miss Jones was musically untutored (which again fitted with Eileen's own Shirley, who had shown neither desire nor aptitude for music lessons). Rogers and Hammerstein's Miss Jones had stumbled into stardom by chance, a casual audition performed whilst she was on the way to some obscure college or other, and then suddenly there she was, the picture of youthful prettiness, with the voice of an angel. A true angel it seemed to Eileen, with none of the complexities of opera nor the limitations and crudities of a Saturday night television songstress, it was the beautiful *rightness* of an angel, with songs neither too high or too low in their content and always lovely in their tunes, genuinely placed between heaven and earth, the true hope of intercession.

So it was that when the Society agreed on *Oklahoma!* as its next production, Eileen felt that her daughter taking the female lead was just another part of a seemingly inevitable process. Even the lesser and more human issues seemed to be falling into place. As with all such societies, Legiolium Amateur Operatics had nothing of the hard-hearted selectivity of the professional theatre. Members after all were seeking comfort and continuity in their club as much as any final product and there were those such as Mary Lightowler and John Pope who had appeared in the chorus of all the Society's shows despite their remarkably poor singing voices. (One of the positive aspects of *Carousel* had been Mr Pope's suffering a throat infection during its run and not being able to undermine the sound of June busting out all over as he had in rehearsals. He had returned with something of a vengeance for *South Pacific*.) Sentiment and fellowship must play their parts in such organizations; Eileen recognized this and also how a quite considerable number of the audience was made up of those who had come along as much to see a relative or an acquaintance as to see the show itself. She was not dismissive of any of this. She had no wish to reduce what would later be called the sense of community which it all entailed, nor in any way to undermine one of the few regional artistic endeavours which could be counted as thriving.

– *Despite some Southern viewpoints, there have always been feelings for artistry here!* Eileen had made this point on numerous occasions, usually adding a recollection of seeing a tear on her father's cheek as he listened to Paul Robeson on the radio – 'Just a-Wearyin' For You' – and her aunt's love of the piano, for all the tragedies and hardships of her life. It was true, thought Eileen; there had always been enclaves of artistic appreciation in the setting in which she had grown and which in some ways she had grown to dominate, but she knew also that just as with her own life's experience, curtains of harsh reality as well as those of easier sentimentality could so readily be drawn across these, or even brought down on them completely.

Her desire to see her daughter elevated to the teenage starring role in *Oklahoma!* posed no threat to Legiolium Operatics' community character, however, and involving the incorporation of youth as it did, it would work towards maintaining and extending artistic involvement in the area. It began to seem to Eileen that the whole matter was shaping up in a way in which none of her previous artistic ventures had, and with the true soul of the artist, she began to feel a vaguely divine hand at work. Did her daughter not even have the same Christian name as the now famous film star and star of *Oklahoma!* (her first film)? Did she not even have something of that young film star's appearance? And at sixteen going on seventeen was she not exactly the right age for the part? Was her voice not good enough? Whether it was strong enough posed more of a question; Shirley had never had to carry a starring role or sing so many songs before, but Eileen felt she had answered this when, to her accompaniment, she listened to her daughter singing all Laurey's part during one evening in their Hightown home. Her husband agreed. Also – another piece fell into place – it was generally acknowledged *South Pacific* had been Biddy Foster's swan song as female lead. She had been in fact rather too old for Nellie Forbush, looking at times more like the mother than the ingénue target of Adam Singleton's De Becque, and her voice had cracked on more than one night during 'Cock-eyed Optimist'. (This as well as, in Eileen's opinion, performing 'Wash That Man' as if painting by numbers.) She could not play Laurey and the Society's whisper was she herself had recognized as much and she would not be putting herself forward for the part. She could consider the role of Ado Annie, thought Eileen, although Olive Pratt might see this as more appropriately hers (she had more comic talent than Biddy) or perhaps (no doubt with a great amount of make-up at her insistence) the mothering aunt, which would allow Biddy to dance, at which, despite some visual evidence to the contrary, she considered herself gifted.

All these were minor issues for Eileen, the kind which usually appear in such societies, although as is also usually the case in such societies, other placements were quite readily apparent. Bernard Cooper would be Curly. The competition for male roles was far less than for the female roles, most of the group's men were more inclined to take undemanding chorus parts (*all of the fun and none of the work or worry!* as John Pope had once put it) and there were only a couple with anything like the necessary solo voices and only Bernard Cooper with a nice tenor. He would be Curly, just as he had been Billy Bigelow and Lieutenant Cable, whilst Archie Weatherall, who had half talked his way through roles in all the Society's previous productions, would be as right as he had ever been for the role of Jud. Nor was there a problem with who would direct, as the new member Adam Singleton had been elected by a virtually unanimous vote even before the next production was confirmed. The young man had other amateur and some semi-professional experience in both Coventry and Huddersfield and his efforts at helping Nicky Ledbetter with the direction of *South Pacific* had been universally noted and appreciated (although even he had failed to keep the sailors in check). The problems of *South Pacific* had led Nicky to announce that two shows were enough for her as a director, particularly as her husband had been complaining about the amount of time it all involved, and so there was no opposition to the new man. *All shaping up*, thought Eileen, and as a part of the process she must make sure her daughter played the young lead.

Shirley herself seemed quite keen to do so; she had been in school plays and sung to general enthusiasm in a recent Grammar School musical evening (although Eileen had not particularly liked the songs she was given). Above all, she was right for the part, was the mother's thought, the whole matter was *right*, with all the strands coming together, all the pieces falling quite naturally into place as happens with the greatest of artistic works. Finally it seemed there would be something specific in her realm, something which had a real face and figure and voice, something of radiance which would draw the otherwise nebulous surroundings into their shape and send this shapeliness ringing back out again with the clarity of a lovely song.

Given this feeling, Eileen was rather thrown by Adam Singleton's reaction when at the end of the Tuesday evening meeting in the Civic Hall annexe she put her daughter's name forward.

– Has she ever sung a leading role before? he asked, his tone quite recognizably dubious.

– No, Eileen replied, but there has to be a first time for everybody. She watched the man then, scratching at his faintly bristled cheeks and chin; unlike her husband he clearly did not shave carefully and diurnally.

– She has the voice for it, Eileen went on. You've heard it. She had that part in *South Pacific*. This isn't just a mother speaking out ... She gave the newly designated director her most handsome smile. As with many of her time and background she had been forced into dentures in early middle age, but they were an even and attractively white top set and she was never seen without them, not even by her husband. She received a little grin in response, but she could not help but feel irritated at having to touch on justification. The man after all was a comparative newcomer, with some stage presence and know-how but with no great voice of his own, and although he had seemed rather too young for the French plantation owner in *South Pacific*, without the stage lights and the make-up on him Eileen began to think that he was actually somewhat older than she had thought. Only a few members of Legiolium Operatics were close outside its Society and all Eileen knew about the man was that he lived in Knottingly, nearer to Pontefract than Castleford, that he was married with no children and that he worked for the Gas Board (for all she knew he was the lowliest hand there). Nor – this came alongside her irritation – did she particularly care for the way he dressed, which seemed to her altogether too young for a man of whatever years he was. A married man. She began to wonder whether she should have so readily and fully supported his elevation to director. Not that there had been any obvious alternatives.

– I'm sure it's nothing of the sort, said Singleton after a pause. Of course not. Your daughter has a very nice voice. He was pushing a hand into the wicker shopping basket in which, rather artistically, he carried his dramatic paraphernalia. He let the moment extend again and Eileen was further irritated at having to take up this slack with still more reasons for the obvious.

– She can deal with the score, she said. I've heard her. I've listened to her sing all the songs. And, well, she is the right age and she does look the part ... Eileen let her smile become a half laugh, hinting again at the real objectivity of what she was saying, although this half laugh was rendered faintly hollow by Singleton receiving it with yet another pause.

– This isn't just a mother talking, Eileen repeated. I just really think she is right for the part! (She made no mention of the coincidence of Christian names with Rogers and Hammerstein's starlet, recognizing this to be her own more ethereal sense of shape.) *Don't you agree?* She faced the man directly then, stepping some way around him to do so and instigating her own pause as she waited for his eyes to come up from the wicker basket. Those eyes were smaller and shiftier than they had seemed in the spotlights, she thought; the wrinkles around them seemed to set them further back than they should be, like pencil lines giving perspective. Nor was the face as open or at least partially handsome as it had seemed as lovelorn De Becque. It was not a face she would have wanted to sketch, thought Eileen; the features were altogether too bland, no real characteristics for the artistic sensibility to seize upon.

– What it is, Eileen – Singleton straightened up from his basket, realizing that here was one of the myriad moments any director must deal with; even in this amateur field there were nettles which would have to be grasped. – What it is ... I was thinking of someone I know who sings with the Huddersfield Chorale. Absolutely top-class voice, with a great range. She saw *South Pacific* and she's keen to join us. She would be so good. She has played a number of leads. The Belgrade in Coventry. She's been in *Guys and Dolls* and *The Pajama Game.* Top stuff. She would be absolutely spot on ...

He looked back into his basket. He was perfectly conscious of this woman's weight and status in Legiolium Operatics; he had even been impressed with her at meetings, and (as directors are always impressed by those who facilitate their work without wanting to share it) by her relative absence from rehearsals and backstage at performances. She was a little blue rinse perhaps, was his thought, a little too much the representative of an old order, but she was also something of the true theatrical angel, one of those who simply make certain talent such as his own has its day. It was a pity she had a mother's interest in her daughter. It was not that he thought the suggestion outlandish; the daughter was a pretty little thing with a nice voice, who could be made to work. Lord knew, he thought, he could no doubt get her to work better than the options he had for Ado Annie. The girl would probably not be his biggest problem in the show. On the other hand, if he could just bring Geraldine in, she would provide him with a fixture, a security, around which he could build the rest. She would inspire the designated Curly and offer him some help with his reasonable tenor, whilst he, the director, would smooth out the man's stilted stage movements. This duo, thought Singleton, would be a virtual guarantee of acceptable success, with all the rest (and this at worst; Singleton was not short of confidence in his abilities) afforded the leeway audiences give to such productions. And yet the woman facing him now was insistent.

– *Bring an outsider in?* she asked and Singleton heard the strength Eileen had made of her disadvantaged beginnings, the vitality she had brought to sharper edges. *Someone from outside the group?*

– Well, no, she would join the group of course. She would become a member.

– So a new member straight away given a leading role?

– Well – Singleton stared into his basket, realizing that here was a nettle which might well have to be left ungrasped.

– We're not really that kind of group, Mr Singleton. We have always drawn the leading roles from existing members and I know Mrs Foster doesn't want to do it.

The Society's neophyte director made another unnecessary rearrangement of the things in his basket. The young girl could work, he thought. She had a nice voice and she was certainly younger than Geraldine. And his own ability was surely fixture and security enough. *Of course,* he said, looking up again at the woman confronting him, so fixed herself and complete it seemed in her self-made position and strength.

– I'm sure your daughter would make at excellent Laurey.

Eileen went directly up to Shirley's room when she got home after this exchange, feeling as if the deepest part of her inner life was for once rising fully into the heterogeneous exterior. The new curtains she had recently chosen for the upstairs windows, still open to the evening as they were, seemed themselves to be indicating this and not just another example of her tasteful, artistic eye. The chandelier lamps were giving back deeper gleams from each of their glass drops and the golden rods which she had decided on to fix the stair carpet delineated a stairway to higher things. She faltered a little outside the room, hearing voices and knowing how many other times, without the knowledge of anyone else, she had found such wider, deeper hope reduced to good taste and nice colour, reduced and accommodated into some lesser satisfaction. But then the exciting *rightness* of it all drew her on and the very blue of the door of her daughter's room seemed an invitation from heaven. A blue which would turn to gold.

Even as she knocked, however, the devils of the diurnal, the Yahoos of the real world, made themselves heard in a sudden and awful cacophony of noise from within the room, a babbling bass and then some half shrieking as if these devilish forces had seen her approaching and were setting up their barriers. Nevertheless Eileen went on in, looking at the source of this noise which was her daughter's Dansette record player, open lidded in one corner. Two young girls were sitting amidst the flowered eiderdown of the room's bed: Shirley and her friend Danny, which friend Eileen did not particularly care for. She liked neither the corruption of the interesting and pretty Christian name of Danielle into something only a young Irishman should use, nor the other extreme of the excessively bright nail polish and lipstick to which the girl was prone. It was Eileen's hope her daughter would outgrow this friend, although the girl's father was a local magistrate. She gave the girl a civil greeting, not unaware of the disapproval in her daughter's look for having entered the room after a knock but with no invitation. Unusually, the mother still went on. Usually she would have turned away as soon as she heard voices and music from inside the room. Somehow, however, it seemed she must take on the devils which were trying to block her off from realization.

– Lord above, what a noise! Eileen indicated the Dansette. She knew of course this was not the best of openings. It gave some validity to her entry, but it might also help the devils with their work, forcing her towards a standard parental complaint. Excitement and determination do not always offer the best of strategies, however, and Eileen heard herself follow this with another standard question. – Can you hear yourselves talk? – a rendition of her husband's *hard to hear yourself think* on other occasions when the sound from the record player had reached too far into the spacious house.

– O, *Mother!* Shirley shook her head as she went across to lift the needle from the 45 disc. Both younger women glanced at each other then and waited for the elder to declare her business.

– I've just been talking to Adam Singleton, said Eileen. You know the one who's going to direct *Oklahoma!*. He thinks you will be just right for the part of Laurey. He thinks you should do it. You would make an excellent Laurey, he said.

For all the fairy-tale colours of her daughter's room, Eileen could not help but feel some greyer reality boxing her in, which feeling was intensified by her daughter's reaction which, just like Adam Singleton's earlier, was not infused with the excitement and enthusiasm Eileen wanted to see. And the curtains of the room were already drawn. – What it is, Mum, said Shirley, after going back to her seated position and with the slyest of glances at her friend (Eileen had made sure the more colloquial *Mam* had not appeared in her Hightown home). What it is, is I'm not sure I want to be in that show. I know you really like it and some of it's OK, but I don't know, I'm not sure I want to be in it.

Eileen almost looked through her daughter to the flowered wallpaper. She had seen fields recede too often, however, watched too many flowers become indistinct not to recognize when it was happening again. Also, she was too artistically intelligent to think that mere insistence would be enough. She saw the reality quickly and clearly as she had always done and with the strength which had got her through her own girlhood she accepted it. Labour, especially artistic labour, can go on for years, but it may only take a moment to see its failure: Adam Singleton's friend would play the part.

– I thought you wanted to do it, she said. I thought you liked the songs. And this was all Eileen offered as the daughter hugged her knees up into her chin, an element of apology in her voice but playing for two different audiences.

– Well, I do like some of the songs, but everyone's so much older than me – she went quickly on over the names her mother might give to counter this, although in essence it was true – And (this to the daughter's other audience) you have to admit these days it's all a bit *corny*.

Eileen nodded and even smiled, her strength and her vitality coming to her aid yet again. *As high as an elephant's eye.* – Well, the chance is there if you want to take it, she said and turned, and there was no retribution in her – and don't play that too loudly – as she closed the blue door behind her. Nor was there any head shaking as she set off back down the stairs. It had after all been too much the mother in her perhaps, someone too ready to use another for their own dream. In the end such searches may always have to be solitary. And after all, it was just another pathway which had petered out and her nature could not let her think there would not be others. Her search would continue and one fine day the inner realm would be rendered beautifully clear. Meanwhile, there were still the moments, the songs themselves, whoever sang them.

Eileen paused on the stairs as the cacophony began again in her daughter's room, its volume somewhat reduced. It was, she realized then, a version of 'Blue Moon', the lyrics and even something of the tune unmistakable, and she did shake her head a little at this as she went on down.

Dreamin'

(Johnny Burnette 1960)

Lambert's memory of the preamble to the accident was piecemeal. He remembered coming out of Bradley Street bogs and something of the progress his group made through the town centre, the quiet of which had been broken by Rutherforth and Morgan singing 'Rock-a-hula Baby' and, owing to the drink, laughing more than he otherwise would have at their version of the opening lyric – *the way she eats her chips and licks her finger tips* – at which response Rutherforth repeated the lines again and again as was his wont when he had had a bevvy. Lambert remembered Peters hushing them all then and pointing to the cop car parked near the river bridge and the group stopping on the tessellated paving outside Pennington's whilst they lit up the cigarettes Clarkey handed round. He could not recall the walk up past the fields of the Secondary Modern, however, or Smales and Briggs breaking off from the group as they usually did on a Friday night. He had been suffering a gathering nausea as the ale thickened behind his eyes and became less of a jolly inner companion and more of a weight. Nor did he particularly care for the cigarette, but he knew Clarkey, who was something of a purist in this regard, might not be too drunk to comment on anyone not inhaling properly. He remembered fighting hard with his nausea as the climb up Park Hill made this nausea shift and spin and he recalled looking at the closed main gates of the park and thinking he could hold on to their rails whilst he puked, but then struggling on. He had no memory of Duggie climbing half way up the side of the park's exterior slope, nor why he had done so, only of the shouts

209

around him as Duggie came running back down and tried to stop himself from going on into the road.

Lambert's memory of that moment was vivid, as if the weight in his head had made a sudden shift to its outside and become a miner's helmet with a miner's lamp switched on to pierce through the blur his drink-sated eyes had been making of things. The nausea was similarly reduced by the clarity which a sudden recognition of the inevitable has. The old van was labouring up the hill (if it had been a newer, faster vehicle then the consequences would surely have been worse) and it was the only traffic on the road, but its driver, who had also been drinking, was not alert or able enough to avoid the figure which came stumbling into its headlights. Peters' high-pitched shriek of *Duggie!* was another vividity, sounding alongside the squeal of brakes and the more muffled thud of the impact as Gordon Douglas at first seemed to drape himself over the bonnet of the van and then went back onto the road, his head bouncing like a badly inflated ball.

They all gathered around the prone figure then and Lambert recognized that he had been the last of the group to do so and that he had remained standing whilst others knelt, partly because he had felt this might bring back the full effect of the drink, but also because he would have liked to ignore it all (he could not avoid admitting this to himself even at the time); he would have preferred to step into the shadows, even to go back fully to the nausea, which was at least a blurring. He had no desire for this kind of vividity. And yet he was more of a pal to Duggie than either Clarke or Rutherforth, who both seemed to have quite the opposite reaction to his, rushing towards the event like two athletes towards a tape; there was even a hint of excitement touching on enjoyment as they bent eagerly over the victim. This at least was Lambert's feeling; Clarkey may even have been disappointed the injuries and the consequent drama were not greater as Duggie was quite obviously alive, if quite definitely stunned. Lambert could not separate any such suspicion from his own guilt, however, and so he let both reactions slide into the shadows. He did recall seeing Duggie's rather puzzled expression and then the gaze seeming to come up quite directly onto him as he leaned in on the ministering group and then the weight of nausea sagged back inwards and he had to turn away to throw up into the weeds at the foot of the man-made slope.

The following day he went along to Pontefract General where Duggie, bruised and concussed, had been kept overnight. *What larks, Pip!* he said with a grin after the more obvious how are you's. He and Duggie had both liked Dickens at school. His pal seemed disinclined to take up the lighter tone, however. His big-featured face was unusually bloodless and the features themselves somehow reduced; the line between the thick, rather corrugated lips was tighter than usual and the normally bright, if faintly baleful, eyes were made narrower by an unusual hooding of the lids. This impression was intensified by the lopsided bandage drawn tight across his forehead to the top of one ear. The thin, brown hair was half hidden, half flattened by this, only showing at the back of the head resting against the pillow, as of some dusty residue hanging over whatever had happened below.

– I was going to bring some grapes – Lambert opened his hands as if the grapes had actually been there – but I didn't know if you'd be allowed ...

He looked at the little bedside cupboard which had nothing on it but a glass of water and a crumpled handkerchief, then over his shoulder at the rest of the ward, the echoing quality of which was only partly reduced by the quiet exchanges of the other participants of visiting time. – Clarkey said he was coming. Lambert looked towards the grey double doors at the far end of the ward, then turned back. – Have your folks been? He actually knew they had, having seen Mr and Mrs Douglas coming out of the hospital as he approached it. He had slipped into Woolworths' doorway so there would be no actual encounter.

– They were in earlier, said Duggie mechanically.

– Did you get a bollocking?

The lids on Duggie's eyes came fully down in a slow blink. His pal seemed completely preoccupied, thought Lambert, and he would have considered this the continuing effects of the concussion if what was visible of the eyes had not seemed quite intense. This intensity turned towards him then and Lambert's shadowy guilt whispered that perhaps Duggie was wondering why his best pal had been so peripheral after the accident, why the faces of lesser pals such as Rutherforth and Clarke had been closer before the ambulance men arrived and pushed theirs in front, why his voice had not been heard in the roundel of concern and reassurance sounding through the fog of concussion. (Lambert had also stepped back from the semicircle around the two policemen who arrived and took details. Having thrown up he had felt less nauseous, but he had still wanted it all done.) He was here now, however, which was more than could be said of Clarke or Rutherforth or Peters, although they would probably turn up at some point if Duggie were kept in for any length of time. *The speed of your visit is just further evidence of your guilt* retorted the whisper and then it deepened into an older voice: *if you want to be a solicitor, young man, if you want to study the ass that is the law, then you must begin by studying the ass that is yourself.*

– I thought I was dead, said Duggie and Lambert was relieved to let his own thoughts go.

– Well, kid, if it had been a bus … Still he tried for the lighter touch but Duggie was having none of it; the face beneath the angled bandage was as serious and intent as Lambert had ever seen it.

– I thought I was a goner! he said.

– Well … Lambert rummaged around for another bedside comment; one which would take them both to a lighter periphery, but his pal went straight to the dark, centre. *Do you think there is anything after you die?* For the first time since his arrival, Lambert saw the eyelids fully lift so his pal's face looked more as it usually did, although it was the face as he had known it at its most baleful, when, for example, Anita Nichols had two-timed him; it was nowhere near its most Dickensian, readily amused and amusing, light hearted and occasionally reckless.

– Do you think there's a life after death?

Lambert brought his shoulders up and let them fall, looking over them again at the hospital ward's doors.

– I mean, do you think this is it and after it there's nothing?

Duggie moved his head on the pillow to bring his intensity still closer.

– I remember you saying that. You said all this life after death stuff was just invented to console people. They are just afraid when they are going to die and so somebody says, don't worry, you're just going on to another life. You said that.

Lambert remembered saying it. It was what he believed.

– Well … he was taken by surprise by the outburst, which came in the same restricted, even hushed tones which the other hospital visitors were using. Fortunately, he thought, the bed immediately next to them was empty and a curtain had been drawn across the bed on the other side. Someone dead perhaps. *You are in a hospital!* Lambert accused himself then. Your pal has just suffered an accident which could have been fatal and yet you are taken by surprise by his question. *Are you sure you have the mettle for the law, young man?* Are you sure you have the solicitor's, the advocate's *agility?* Passing a few exams is no final indication of that!

– Well, you were nowhere near *dead!* Finally he came out with this, although he tried to gather up his manner: the comment after all was not making light or offering mere reassurance, it expressed a fact.

– The ambulance man said straight away you'd be all right. *How would you know what the ambulance man said?* whispered the accusing shadows. *You didn't even put yourself close enough to hear this verdict.* Duggie seemed not to be considering any of this, however; his eyes, fully opened now, were wholly fixed on his issue.

– I really thought I was going, he said. I really thought I was going to die. That it was, you know, that moment. And there was just … there was just … His eyes lost something of their intensity … there was just *nothing!* The eyelids became hooded again and the gaze dimmed still further as if going some way back towards the void they had seen.

Lambert recounted the exchange to Rutherforth and Smales on the evening of the same day when they got together in Rutherforth's house. There had been some suggestion of going to the pictures, but young men of their age doing that on a Saturday night without female company smacked of pathos. Besides there was nothing much on. So they stayed at Rutherforth's, who was lucky enough to be an only child with a bedroom to himself and parents who were indulgent beyond the average. He also had a notable collection of records, particularly Duane Eddy, about whom he was something of a fanatic. Smales' taste was turning more towards old jazz and unknown American blues singers, mostly on 78s. Outside his presence, this was considered a pretention (Rutherforth in particular was an exponent of this view), based on Smales' desire to be different and specialist. Smales still found Duane Eddy acceptable, however, and it was an LP of his they were listening to as Lambert described their injured friend's state. Said he thought he was going to die, he said. Actually experienced the moment.

– Shock, said Smales.

– Kept saying it, said Lambert. There's nothing there. Nothing beyond this life.

– Well there ain't, said Rutherforth.

– You don't know that, countered Smales, typically. Not for sure.

– O but I do, said Rutherforth. *Frogman Henry.*

– How can you know it for sure?

– Of course I can! It's all bollocks.

Lambert took a sip of the shandy they had agreed on after the previous night's excess. Clarke, who would have considered this unacceptable, was out with his girlfriend and not there to monitor. Morgan had said he might get along depending on what happened with Jill Thompson. The late-teenage group was beginning its natural disintegration. Lambert was still commuting to Leeds, but Smales would soon be setting off for university in Dundee, the distance and the four-year course of which would almost ensure his separation. Rutherforth was bound for a PE college in York, whilst Duggie, who, for all a certain literary bent, had the worst academic record of them all, would be forced to work in his father's haulage firm, no doubt in some office position although he said he intended to pursue a heavy goods licence. Clarke was still undecided as to his future, Morgan was considering the Fire Service and Peters had recently announced his intention of joining his brother in Australia. Briggs, although he was staying in the Castleford area with an apprenticeship at Whitwood Tech, had never been more than an intermittent intimate.

– You just don't *know* that! Smales was shaking his head at Rutherforth and Lambert nodded more readily than he might previously have done. The empty extent of Duggie's stare had left its impression on him.

– I suppose no-one knows for sure, he said.

– No-one does, agreed Smales. You have no more proof there is no afterlife than anyone has that there is. Less perhaps if you listen to ghost stories and things about séances and such.

A vague memory came to Lambert of old Tordoff at the Grammar School telling his class about Dr Johnson saying 'I refute it thus!' and with it a mental image of a very real boot kicking half a brick into a completely imaginary cloud. He gave this no expression. Quotations or any references to recorded wisdom were difficult to deliver without a hint of showing off, which hints at that time in that area were sought out like pests, a search which even a younger and more intellectually inclined group had not managed to avoid. They were less averse to dialectic, however, particularly Smales, although it might be seen as just another urge on his part to be different, alongside the old 78s.

– Do you know it is the only question in this world which has a definite yes or no answer, he went on. Everything else is never so black or white. As old Wittgers says, you don't solve a question, you dissolve it (this was the way to introduce learning, very lightly). Every other question in this world has a messy answer ... could be this, could be that, depends what you mean by ... etcetera. But an afterlife? Either there is or there isn't.

– It could be death and nothing until resurrection, said Lambert, knowing what his mother would think, although probably not say; she would have considered all this the prattling of youngsters.

– Well, that's a yes! exclaimed Smales. That's obviously a yes. It's hardly a no. If you get resurrected, it's an afterlife. Of course it is. You see, you can't get round it. It's either yes or no. You can't treat the question in the same way as you can the meaning of life. That does depend ... meanings get made up and they are different for different people. But whether this life, whatever its meaning for us whilst we are living it, is all there is for us, that's a damn yes or a bloody no.

– So you might come back as a cow or a blackbird? said Rutherforth. Like the Indibobblers say ...? Lambert saw Rutherforth was not treating the debate with any particular interest or seriousness; his mind was made up on a no, although the example of a blackbird had a faintly strange resonance.

– Well that's a yes, said Smales. You come back as a cow, then it's obviously a yes ... Rutherforth lowered the cover of the Duane Eddy EP he had been examining.

– You mean to say you think we are going to come back as somebody else? There was the glint in his eye of the practical athlete about to show the academic the irrelevance of his mind. *Can I be Elvis then?* With one of those women in Hawaii?

– Or Ann-Margret! Lambert joined in. He wasn't sure he wanted to go on with Smales' discussion, not certain that somehow it did not bring the fearful, baleful look he had seen from Duggie still further into his own being. Or Ellie May. Or what about whatshername – he pointed at the little poster on Rutherforth's wall, which was actually of Bardot – in that series, you know, the one who sings 'Don't Bring Lulu'? I quite like her.

– Dorothy Provine – Smales threw this quickly and academically in; there had been some twenties Dixieland in the television show Lambert was referring to, but he was not about to be taken away from his central philosophical point. *It's either a yes or a no,* he insisted. Either this is all there is, or it isn't. Can't get round it. Can't dissolve it. Only question in the world you can't!

Lambert turned his eyes fully to the picture of Bardot. She was wearing a sweater and a skirt. (A bikini might have been acceptable for a pin-up, but anything less probably not, even though Rutherforth's parents were more liberal, as it would come to be known, than some. Lambert didn't even want to think of his own parents' reaction if he had pinned up something similar; it was also unlikely any other parents of their group would have allowed their son's bulky friends such access to a room in their house.) Smalesy could be a pain at times, he thought, certain at that moment he would rather contemplate the tight lines across Bardot's skirt than any tight line of reasoning. *Another escape?* whispered the shadows, their penumbra taking on something of Duggie's most recent expression.

– Well that's it then, said Rutherforth. No debate. It's either nowt or summat and for my money it's nowt!

– You just can't be *sure*, persisted Smales.

– O I'm sure, said Rutherforth. I'm bloody positive.

– Well there's no logic to that. No logic at all.

– Of course there is.

– No there isn't.

So what about ghosts? Lambert was conscious not only of impasse, but of potential confrontation such as Rutherforth and Smales had had before, even arguing about the saxophone on Duane Eddy. He needed a quiet evening after the drama of the previous night and its shadowy aftermath in his hospital visit that afternoon. Before long they would be on about the Bomb. Ghosts it seemed to him might lighten the mood, whilst retaining some relevance.

– *Ghosts?* Well, that's a clear yes, said Smales. If there are ghosts there's clearly something after death.

– Bollocks! Rutherforth's dismissals could be limited and repetitive. No such thing. Old wives' tales. Just superstition and imagination. No such bollocks as ghosts.

– You're *positive* about that? asked Smales irritatingly. You are quite certain?

– Abso bollocking lutely, said Rutherforth.

– So you could spend a night in a haunted house?

The shadows themselves seemed to be speaking for Lambert then, whispering and nudging amongst themselves and then giving him the words as their spokesman. They had gathered around Duggie's drama, they had been less obvious but still present in the hospital ward and now somehow they had gathered even in this casual setting. He of course had made no mention to the others of his own night-time fears, such fears as should have gone with childhood, such fears as should all have been identified and placed in a young man his age, a potential solicitor. He should not still be thinking that something ghostly could actually come out of the shadows, that something might suddenly be glimpsed in a mirror; he should not secretly be avoiding ghostly movies or wherever possible still closing his eyes at their ghostliest moments.

– Of course I could! said Rutherforth. What do you think is going to happen? Some bastard in a bed sheet come floating towards you?

– What about Marley's Hut? Could you spend a night there?

The shadows were playing with Lambert now. He and Duggie had given this place the name it had for their group. It was known more generally as Cemetery Shed, a disused outhouse standing on the higher edge of the burial ground which lay between the Grammar School's cricket pitch and the walls of Queen's Park. It was widely reputed to be haunted: a recently buried corpse had once been found in the hut (which may or may not have had its basis in the grave robbing which was still a means to remuneration at the beginning of the twentieth century, which was when the building's reputation began); then, just before the Second World War, a woman's body had been found in it, which body had not been interred, but had been strangled. This was a matter of fact, as was the murder remaining unsolved (a soldier had confessed in a letter home, it was rumoured, just before being killed himself). This poor woman's ghost haunted the building, it was said, calling woefully for others departed to come to her aid. Wailing had been heard from the building at night and there were some eyewitness accounts of shadowy figures entering and emerging, even more graphic stories of corpses disinterring themselves to enter the building as one of their number had once done or of the sad form of the murder victim emerging to find herself a resting place. There was a good vantage point for the observation of all this from the wall of Queen's Park, amidst a clearing in the copse beneath the old playground, and Lambert, Douglas, Smales and Rutherforth and some others of their extended group had ventured to this spot a number of times as schoolboys, daring each other on as schoolboys will, although even in daylight the disused building, half brick, half wood, had a forbidding aspect, looking down the graveyard's sloping path as its badly boarded window did, and at night it was a veritable toll booth for those spirits hauling themselves up by their headstones and trooping mournfully towards it.

Older as they now were, it was some time since any of them had even occupied this vantage point, let alone gone towards the doorless building itself as they had done a few times in earlier years, daring each other on, laughing uncertainly at the imagined sounds of wails and chains. Paul Briggs even alleged he had persuaded Janet Price to go in there with him one evening, but there were no witnesses to this and no-one really believed him, although it was agreed Janet Price was quite a strange girl. The building retained its reputation for the group, however, and at night it would still be a place which all the money in the world would not have tempted Lambert into. He would never have said so, of course, but without doubt his challenge to Rutherforth was a translation of a challenge to himself and to all the shadows hanging and playing around him. A challenge even to Duggie's baleful question.

– I bet you couldn't spend the night there.

Rutherforth had followed his gaze to Bardot and back.

– What, in that old cemetery shed?

– That's it. I bet you still couldn't spend a night in that.

– How much? asked Rutherforth.

The amount was set at five pounds, the bet was on and despite all Lambert's attempts to delay or even prevent what he himself had instigated, it was on for the following night. *Screaming Lord Sutch!* said Rutherforth. *Shazam! Forty Miles of Bad Road!* Lambert felt then like some agent of the shadowy forces in and around men, elected by them to speak and then drawn on helplessly himself by their momentum, not the first to feel how readily the internal can become the external, the word the deed. He learned that Duggie had climbed the slope on Park Hill after a dare from Morgan and the whole succession of events began to take on something of the preordained quality of literary tragedy. He tried to shake this feeling off, Aladdin's lamp it away with images of Bardot and Ann-Margret and Lucy Green, but the retreat was rather desperate and the relief short lived. He was

Pip going to a graveyard or, as in a still darker story from his A level literature, one of Chaucer's young men going out to deal with death and finding it.

Also, talking to Smales as they walked away from Rutherforth's that Saturday night, he recognized, perhaps for the first time, just how potentially bitter the rivalry between the two young men was and this led him to consider how ambiguous many of the ties within the group had been and to feel, again perhaps for the first time, the necessity as well as the loss of loosening those ties. And yet, even amidst this development, it seemed there were those sad, half-mad aspects which would always be the same; as if those same shadows would always be there to make certain death was not the only inevitability.

– He's such a simple-minded sod!

Smales waved his hand back at Rutherforth's house.

– He thinks he sees it all, but he only sees the *obvious*. If he can't score a try with it or eat it or shag it there's no possible reality to it for him! Smales' tone had never been so harsh, there was no vestige of boyhood playfulness here. *God, I hope some bloody ghost does appear!* he went on. Frighten him out of his prospective PE teacher's wits!

Lambert began by wondering which of the two he preferred as a friend, but he ended by recognizing his desire to step away from them both.

Yet of course, he was there with them the following night, with Clarke and Peters and Morgan, just after eleven o'clock, positioned at the old vantage point by the park wall to watch Rutherforth clamber through the section where the bricks had been knocked lower by more hooligan groups, and march on into the cemetery grounds, taking the overgrown path through the headstones towards Marley's Hut. It had been agreed that staying all night was unnecessary, that the bewitching hours between 11 p.m. and 2 a.m. would be sufficient for the bet (one pound per hour, plus two for luck), facilitating also the witness operation, although even then, Peters said he would have to set off back home soon after twelve as his parents still had a curfew of sorts even for their young-adult son. Lambert would have liked to make a similar excuse; he even contemplated crying off altogether, going out to a phone booth to tell Smales, who had a telephone at home, that he or his mother or his sister was unwell, but any such story would have been quite transparent. And so he turned up with the others, trying at first to generate some lighter sense of the lark of it all.

The night did not help in this respect, being a night such as ghosts would surely relish. The almost full moon was visible amidst some higher, spectral cloud which never did more than make its light equally spectral, which light served by contrast to deepen the darkness and blacken the shadows beneath. A veritable film set for ghouls and ghosts. There was no more than the occasional breath of breeze, coming only as another animation for the dark, a whispering from its shadows, and even the coolness of the night seemed muted and waiting. There were no more than faint wisps of human breath to accompany the group's words and even the cigarette Clarke lit up seemed to produce less smoke than it would have done in a room, as if the darkness were sucking off any homely comfort. This at least was how Lambert felt and in his estimation, Peters also. Smales was more involved with the bet and perhaps the experiment of it all, Morgan vaguely diffident as ever, whilst Clarke seemed quite excited, watching Rutherforth go off as he might watch the early exchanges of a sporting fixture, all anticipation. *There he goes!* he said and rubbed his hands together.

– Free as a bird, daft as a brush! added Morgan. You wouldn't catch me doing that for a lousy fiver! Lambert wanted to agree with what at first seemed to be the honesty of this, but the shadows which had led him to word the instigation of it all now seemed to be weighing silence on him. Talking too much would also be a clear indication of anxiety and as Morgan went on about how he would never do such a thing for less than twenty quid, Lambert did not even nod.

– See if he thinks it's all bollocks at midnight, said Smales.

Peters, betraying his nervousness with half a laugh, said, You don't really think anything is going to appear do you? Smales' face, made ghostly itself by the moonlight, turned back towards him.

– Nothing *we* will see, he said. But we're not in there in an environment loaded with suggestions. (Smales would be studying

221

psychology in Dundee.) What I'm saying is you just can't say for *certain*. You just can't go mouthing off about being absolutely sure when you can't be. Although if there is anything I'll be surprised if it's as clichéd as ghosts. They're obvious projections. Out of the mind.

– I'm not sure that makes them any less real, said Lambert, whispered at somehow to speak again, but without any clear idea of what he meant.

– *Exactly*, said Smales. That's what Ruthers is underestimating. Just what the mind can do. Just how much the mind can have him see. *I thought you said his was a simple mind!* Lambert did not say this.

– So if you don't think there's any such thing as ghosts why did you bet him? asked Clarke.

– I didn't say that, said Smales

– Yes you did.

– No I didn't. What I said was we can never be certain. And certainly we can never underestimate the mind. I mean you saw the look on Ruthers' face when he set off. He wasn't so certain then. He wasn't mouthing off then! Lambert had seen this look, he thought, if faintly, but Clarke was dismissive:

– Rubbish! he said. He was all right. He'll see it out and you'll be five quid down, Smalesy!

They all looked towards the silhouette moving closer to the hut, which owing to the shadows of the nearby trees was in complete darkness, its form only visible as something still blacker. The silhouetted figure soon took on the same aspect and it was hard to tell if it had paused before vanishing or merging. He's gone in, said Clarke and then in a cod spook voice, *There's only thee and me here –* they all knew the old Yorkshire joke, but Clarke completed it anyway *– And in a minute there'll only be thee!* There were some smiles and animation at this and Peters began to bat his arms as if it were colder than it was. They were all well wrapped; Rutherforth himself had seemed a veritable mound of clothing; he had even lined the inside of his pullover with newspaper he said, a trick he had learned on a survival course, and on top of all this was a knapsack containing a blanket and some sandwiches. He had wanted to take a torch and some reading matter, but this had been adjudicated against, any artificial light being unacceptable to the wager as it invaded the natural setting of manifestations. Beer had also been disallowed as it might provide Dutch Courage. Matches to go with his cigarettes had been permitted, however, and Rutherforth said he would have a couple of fags and then he might actually get some sleep if he could find a comfortable spot amidst the rubble in the building. – It might well be you lot will have to come and wake me up when it's time, he had said. *If any of you dare!*

– The aboriginal Australians don't think anybody dies …

As much as anything, Peters spoke to break the silence which had fallen on the group. They were all speaking in muted tones, Lambert noticed, much as the people had in yesterday's hospital ward. Clarke had raised his voice to a more normal volume earlier on, but this had seemed inappropriate and might be construed as a confrontation of fear and so he too had dropped below the daylight norm.

– It's all a dream the aborigines reckon, said Peters. With his prospective emigration in mind he had been doing some reading about Australia and its history. That's what they call it, The Dreaming. It's all in lines, song lines they call them, criss crossing everywhere. You come out of the land and then you go back to it …

– Ashes to ashes, said Morgan.

– How many beers have we got? Lambert felt himself wanting to retreat again from anything which made the shadows more real. *Is it after all not a reality that any afterlife entails both hope and fear? When all is said and done are souls not ghosts?* Morgan lifted the off-licence bag, Two more each, he said.

– Shit! Is that all?! Lambert released some of his irritation against the shadowy trees, their dark leaves each a whispered word, their trunks at once flattened and solidified into half-human substance. In that moment the old wall itself seemed not to have been built, but to have grown, as the headstones in the cemetery had risen from the ground rather than being shaped and put into it by people. Everything seemed to be growing around Lambert then, arching over him like some forest, with even the moon no more than a fruit. And it was not consolation he felt in this, but an equally ubiquitous and rooted fear.

Smales had been nodding at Peters' Australian information as if he knew it already. It's like water, he said, glancing quickly back at Peters, not wanting to take his eyes off the black outlines of the hut for too long in case Rutherforth made a sudden or sneaky exit. – There has always been the same amount of water in the world. It's a constant amount. He had heard this recently on a TV programme for young scientists, along with the enlivening illustration he gave next: The water you drink was drunk by dinosaurs ... Bollocks! said Lambert in Rutherforth's absence.

– What's that got to do with aboriginal Indians? asked Morgan, prompting the correction from Peters.

– They're not Indians, they're aborigines. One of the oldest known people in the world.

– Well, all right, but what has dinosaurs and water got to do with them?

– Well, dinosaurs are old.

Smales exhaled some extra wisps of exasperation.

– The spirit Peto's on about, he said, is like water. It's a constant, it just takes different forms. It just comes out into one and then goes back into another.

– Yes, that's it, agreed Peters, pleased both with his research and his enlightening contribution.

– But what's that got to do with Johnny Burnette?

Again in Rutherforth's absence Lambert felt the urge to adopt his postures, as a good lawyer might for a client, and Rutherforth's capacity for relevantly and amusingly inserting the names of current songs and performers into any conversation was much admired. Both Peters and Morgan looked puzzled, however, and so Lambert had to make the insertion more specific. This and the bad planning of the beer increased his annoyance with the whole setting and what things around him were making him say and do. '*Dreamin*'! he said. Johnny Burnette. What has water got to do with that? Water's not dreaming, water's real. You're not dreaming when you drink some water.

– Or pass some, said Clarke, and Lambert welcomed the reduction. Smales kept the matter up, however, although this time his eyes stayed fixed on the setting of his wager.

– It's a metaphor, he said. Christ, Ian, you're the one who did English. It's all a dream and all that. Dreaming's a constant, just like water … Smales was definitely wishing Rutherforth's dark form would come running out of the damned hut sooner rather than later and he could, without any gloating, win his bet and they could all go home.

– So we're all just *dreaming* now? This time it was Lambert who persisted. He had been mollified to some extent by Smalesy's use of his first name as opposed to 'Lamby', which he disliked, but he was still being prompted somehow.

– We might be. This was quite lame from Smales, everybody heard as much, and Lambert himself gave the big sniff Smales himself usually afforded clichés.

– I refute it thus! he said and kicked at a shadowy stone at his feet.

– What's it got to do with dinosaurs? asked Morgan, but Clarke lifted a hand and shushed them. *Hear that?* In the quiet of the night there did seem to be a faintly human voice, a distant and indecipherable call which soon wove away into the rustling of the trees. The darkness cushioned even this then and the great and spectral night both opened and closed around the breathing human forms of the little group. All the young men were pleased not to be alone. It'll be somebody in the park, said Smales.

– *Somebody shagging!* said Clarke and Lambert returned his grin and found himself trying to project something of Bardot onto the dark.

– It'll be whatshername and one of those weightlifters she goes with, said Morgan, and Clarke's grin went from one to the other of his fellows.

– *Or all of them!* he said and all the young men found some comfort in this sexual image. The vaguely human cry came again then, however, and it did not fit with any pornography, too plaintive a moan.

– It's probably a cat, said Smales.

– Or a badger. Peters was betraying the greatest nervousness it seemed to Lambert and although he was thankful this position could not be given to him, he was still moved into a tone of castigation.

– What are you talking about *badgers?* he snorted, although he gave some unnecessary repetition to the word, adding a few bloodys.

– Whatever it was, it will be something real, said Smales, but Lambert turned quite sharply on him also, increasingly recognizing, it seemed, the fragility, even the superficiality of Smales' intellect.

– *You say that as if it's a good thing!* he said.

– Might be Mad Mick Layton, said Clarke, enjoying the discomfort of others as was his tendency. They reckon he wanders around here at night with his pickaxe.

– Bollocks, said Lambert, but Clarke insisted.

– They do. He was arrested once in the park up there, for getting on the bandstand and pretending he was conducting with the pickaxe handle.

– Is that true? asked Peters.

– Is it bollocks! said Lambert.

– Well, he was arrested.

– I know, but not for that, it was out by Benny's Beck. It wasn't in the park and there was no axe on his handle.

– He still clouted somebody with it though.

– Yes, but not in the park.

– It might be Flasher Fisher, said Morgan. He *was* arrested in the park.

– And what the hell would he want with us?!

Lambert's annoyance was gathering enough perhaps to allow him to turn away for home in impatient and justifiable rejection of it all before long. Peters would probably come with him, maybe even Mogsy, he thought, and they could leave Smales and Clarke to see out the witnessing operation for their own different reasons.

– That's true, said Morgan. He'll be looking for some more girl guides. *Take this salute girls!*

Morgan's image and accompanying mime lightened the mood. There was some chuckling and they each took another can, and the moonlight seemed to gather around them in a faint globe of companionship. Also when they did all listen again there was no discernible human cry. Various girls were discussed then, until Smales lifted his watch close to his face and announced it was midnight.

Lambert began to give more detailed consideration to how he could actually engineer an early departure. He would go with Peters when Peters made his already announced exit. *But why?* What reason could he give for doing so? He began to curse himself for not having laid at least some groundwork. *In the law as in life, young man, preparation is all!* the adult voice came. *You must never be caught without it.* Perhaps he had made the wrong choice of profession, he thought, like Franz Kafka; perhaps in the end he was just too imprecise, too much of a dreamer.

What in God's name is that?!

Drawn on by the witching hour, Clarke had leaned beyond even Smales' observation point and he pointed and brought the whole group's focus onto Marley's Hut, the blackness of which had suddenly come forward from the blackness around it. A faint yellow light in the badly boarded window was the cause of this effect, a light which intensified and then began to swing around, it seemed, beyond those boards. *Jesus Christ!* exclaimed Morgan and for a moment all maturity was gone and they were all credulous children and this was a ghost: the murdered woman called back into form by the ongoing atrocities of men, perhaps even their own male talk, the avenging female spirit returning to frighten the most muscular of their number to death. Or the snatched and desecrated body returning to teach the greatest unbeliever a lesson, perhaps even to carry him off to the grave.

– I'm going to get a closer look! Predictably Clarke was the first to gather himself back into manhood; his technique had always been more confrontational.

– Are you out of your bloody mind?! exclaimed Peters, whose tendency was quite the opposite. I'm off! It serves bloody Rutherforth right this does.

Clarke began to clamber through the wall, but then he and all the others were held again, staring at the ghostly light which could now be seen swirling in the doorway of the hut. They saw the figure of Rutherforth come running out then, beating it seemed at the bright ghost hanging onto his back, trying to pull him again into the deadly hut. *Hey! Hey you lot!* they heard Rutherforth yell – *Hey!* – and in more laudable, if thoughtless, action they all followed Clarke through the wall and towards what was clearly a cry for help. Lambert even found himself running towards the figure which was only kept in evidence at first by the pulsating aura it was trying to rid itself of and then by a patch of moonlight as, still yelling and flailing, Rutherforth threw himself down amongst the gravestones.

In the next few days there were two possible hospital visits for Lambert. As they were working days, St James' would have been easier for him as he was already in Leeds. The hospital was something of a walk out of the centre, however, and although he knew Rutherforth had been admitted to its Burns Unit, he had no idea where this was exactly in that extensive medical campus. He left the matter until Wednesday, thinking Duggie might be out by then and perhaps they could go together to see Ruthers as Clarke and Morgan had already done. Yet for some reason Duggie had not been discharged and Lambert argued to himself that finding out just what this reason might be gave a visit to Pontefract General priority. Also he had a tale to tell to one friend of another setting fire to himself in Marley's Hut whilst trying to win a stupid bet about ghosts. Perhaps another of the group had already been in and told him, but Lambert hoped he could give some Dickensian quality to his own telling: Rutherforth stuffing himself with newspaper like a Pickwick and then being daft enough to let a cigarette fall down the neck of his pullover causing him to steam out of Marley's Hut like a ghost train for a signalman. There was certainly enough material: Peters taking off his overcoat and swinging it at Rutherforth as if he were putting out a bush fire. His own throwing the quenching contents of a can of beer which he found was still in his hand. Helping the victim down through the cemetery then, with Rutherforth cursing every corpse, hauling him over the cemetery wall and going along past the Grammar School to the nearest telephone box, trying to quieten him, trying to get him to sing away his pain – *Rock-a-hula Baby* – and then when he stumbled amidst the assisting group and lay rolling and shouting abuse, Morgan slinging him fireman style over his shoulder and carrying him on like a moaning sack. They had made lark stories of far lesser stuff.

And yet there was still a dulling quality to it all for Lambert, a confusion as to whether he wanted to talk about it at all. It had been no ghost in Marley's Hut, but perhaps there had been something more terrible; real flames, real injuries, real deaths. He could imagine Duggie reacting this way in the state he had last seen him in. This was Lambert's thought as he made his way slowly up from Monkhill station to Pontefract General. There was no real clarity for him even in this, however. After the ambulance had taken Rutherforth off, Smalesy had tried to insist he had won the bet, that Rutherforth had not spent the designated time in the cemetery outhouse, and when he was faced with the general response that the accident had nulled the wager, he cited the strange look on Rutherforth's face as they had all first seen it, before the pain of the burns to his chest and his shoulders really made itself felt. There was something in that look, said Smales, something which indicated fear over and above these burns. Rutherforth had seen something, he said, or projected something; he even implied Ruthers had lit the newspaper under his pullover deliberately as an excuse for running out (although he had underestimated its effect). Scorn was poured on this, but despite his own – *Bollocks!* – Lambert could not but silently recognize that he too had seen something in Rutherforth's face.

He shook his head at it all as he walked up towards the hospital and even paused in the bus station where he could catch a bus back to Castleford. When he thought about it, it seemed likely Duggie's parents or some other relatives would be availing themselves of the evening visiting hours. It had been a working day for him after all and he could reasonably leave the visit until the weekend, by which time Duggie may well have been discharged. And he had already visited him once. Lambert found himself turning towards the bus station rather than going on towards the hospital. Whatever it all was, he thought, it was certainly time for him to move on. This was a clear yes. He went towards the timetables in the bus station. It was time for him to commit himself to a wider, older future, time to involve himself more fully in the real details of life and the law. Time to leave behind such childish nonsense as dares and ghosts, dreams and nightmares. It was even time perhaps for him to start living in Leeds.

More Than I Can Say

(*Bobby Vee 1961*)

Joy was Joyce in Castleford. She had only taken to shortening her name as a student in Liverpool and that at the instigation of a fellow first year, who had felt it altogether more modern, even fully in tune with the times (the same fellow insisted on 'Sandy' for her own Sandra). It was also a rendition of the brightness and prettiness of the face it designated. Joy had not sought to introduce the abbreviation with the friends she still had in Castleford, however, and certainly not with her family. In fact during the recent days of the Christmas she had spent there she had found a vague pleasure in hearing the full name used again, perhaps as another touch of the fond memories she had tried to allow in unexamined. And there had been some old Christmas moments for her, some magical touches in the highlights of a silvered ornament, the sound of fingers on glossy wrapping paper, even the smell of food, although on the eve of the year which would bring her twenty-third birthday, she could not help but feel she was finding these with a certain self-consciousness (one day she would be able to avoid this perhaps, she thought: through children of her own, or still older, as her grandmother did, through glorified recollections). The Christmas piece she had been charged with writing for the *Echo* about the increasing commercialization of the season, the mercenary drive behind it all, had truth to it and had been well received, and yet when she re-read it in print she felt somehow that its own hard-headed tone leaned more towards the very thing it was attacking than the values and the magic it was arguing were being lost. She had not sent it as a clipping to her parents as she had with other pieces, and quite why she hadn't she wasn't sure. Her sister certainly brought the new baby along as a clear indication of success and Joy had mused on the subtle ways in which even older offspring can continue to do this. Could a lifetime be spent bringing renditions of good reports to parents?

With some reluctance, she lifted herself out of the bed. There was a long radiator in the room which she had heard clunking into action early that morning, but there was still a chill which made faint clouds of her breath, particularly when she gave out a deliberate, testing exhalation. The bathroom was warmer. Jonathan had already showered and shaved, leaving not only the mist of the hot water but also the cloying residue of his bodily presence. Joy spread out the towel he had left bundled on the rail and felt at another of the larger ones to check he had not used both provided as he had in another hotel room they had shared (the casual inconsideration of the higher born had been a surprise to her in her time in a Hall of Residence). She wiped the condensation from the mirror then and looked at the neatly arranged features looking back, seeing, as she had over Christmas, just how much they were her mother's: ageing is an inversion of the sculptor's art and if the reflected face could have had less definition, could have been pressed and spread part way back into the moulding clay or the block of wood or stone, then it would be her mother staring at her now. Joy dropped her eyes from the idea, for the stare would be one of condemnation: a young, unmarried woman spending the night in a hotel room with a man … There would be ambiguities to this, but in that moment Joy did not feel like invoking them or running through the litany of new freedoms as she had elsewhere. In that moment she simply dropped her eyes as a sinner might. It was in fact only the third time she had done it and she knew of others her age and younger, who …

Her eyes fell on the sink and she saw Jonathan had not swilled it out properly after his shave and there was a thin crust of black bristles in its bowl. She rested her hands on either side of the thick porcelain then, feeling a faint element of repulsion as she had at the thought of the breakfast which was on offer and which Jonathan had wanted her to join him for. You could just have some tea and toast, he had said. You don't have to have the whole bacon and egg bang shoot … She had been adamant, however: she wanted no breakfast and, with a shrug, he had gone off alone. For all the intelligence he could bring to his academic work, she thought, the man had something of the simple beast about him. For all his diatribes against the old military ways there was still something of these ways in him. He ate like a man on manoeuvres; he would be doing so now, taking in gobs of bacon, thick eggs, sturdy coffee; he preferred wine to beer but he still drank it in notable draughts, and there was an element to him of the straight-backed, substantial soldier (or fully grown ape), blocking out the light. His hair had an unkempt, modern length, but it was reiterated too fully on his chest and on his forearms and, as she had recently discovered, in thin clusters in the small of his back. *Oh dear*, she thought. *When you start picking out such things …* It had been a mistake perhaps to bring him along, but he had been keen to come and there were still moments when his extra years (and the kudos of the postgraduate beginning a doctorate he had been when they first met) still pleased her. This and his pure physical presence, which she now recognized she may have transferred too readily into a similar mental presence. There were more old forces in play perhaps than she had thought. She had seen some of these again over Christmas. Women must be careful their new demands do not paradoxically give still more freedom to men so that the gender mismatch is rendered different, but stays the same (as mismatches tend to). Everyone must be careful, thought Joy, with age-old forces, whatever the ideas they surface in, whatever the words they use.

She decided against a shower and gave her face and arms no more than a light wash before going back into the bedroom of the en suite, suddenly keen to be fully dressed before Jonathan returned from his breakfast. *Jonathan* – unlike Sandy he insisted on the full rendition of his name and although Joy could understand how the extra syllables softened as well as offered a little more distinction to the surname of Dodds, somehow she found herself feeling altogether less sympathetic about this insistence than she had. *Castleford again?* Clarifying snobbery for her? *Oh dear*, she thought. It would soon be time for *the conversation*. The dread exchange of relationships ending (people have got married, she could see now, just to avoid having these). It could be done in stages perhaps or even ducked out of completely, which last she recognized now might not be quite *the epitome of emotional cowardice,* as she had once described it. Admittedly she had formulated this phrase with regard to a rejection coming the other way; the Gregory beast, the boyfriend of her early years in Liverpool, who had simply taken to averting his eyes and even once making a cowardly dash out of the JCR when she came in; skulking and spineless and then bumbling like an inarticulate idiot when she confronted him. It had been some time before that confrontation had not brought heat to Joy's cheeks, although increasingly it was as much for her own shame as from indignation and rejection. That young man had proved a complete failure anyway, associating himself with the most vacant of bumpy brunettes and dropping out before taking his degree.

She took down the red dress which she had decided would be appropriate for the mixture of engagement celebration and New Year's Eve party and examined its hem for threads and looked with resignation at the creases which had appeared despite her laying it out with only two folds in the boot of Jonathan's car. There was a day to get through in it anyway and there were no ironing facilities provided in the room of the modest hotel. Moreover she was still enough of a Castleford lass not to seek out any such facilities from the hotel management. Jonathan would probably do so if she mentioned it (he was from Kent and of an age when he was keen to show his worldly domination of such matters), but Joy herself knew that instigating any such operation would be another of the unbearabilities which in all honesty she had to admit she still suffered from. The couple who managed the hotel (and whose assistance would have to be sought with any ironing) was a case in point: Joy had to admit she had flushed at the looks they gave her; the man's had been easier to bear, a tubby goblin in a threadbare suit and a garish tie, his was just the half-hidden smirk of the lascivious, but the woman, even at a distance, had managed to communicate a subtle contempt and it had been all Joy could do not to hide behind the man she was with and whom she was allowing to do all the talking.

She must overcome such reactions, she thought. She must not be so affected by old forces and old ways.

Hearing a sound in the corridor, she hurried to pull on the dress. She had considered jeans and the new flowery blouse she particularly liked, but this was Castleford and for all they were on the eve of 1966, people still made more formal efforts with their clothes for such occasions. During Christmas, Joy had even taken out the old petticoated frock she had worn when Bob Allen took her to the school dance. Would Bob Allen be there tonight? He had stayed in Castleford and Glynis still knew him, and the party, Glynis had said, would be more or less an open house. (*Free and easy* had been her phrase – *none of the stuffy old invitations and such.*) Joy looked at herself in the long mirror attached to the inside of the old wooden cupboard and hoped Bob Allen would not be there; of all the conversations marking the end of relationships which she had known (which she suspected were rather more than some others had known at her age, certainly those in Castleford, certainly her great friend Glynis) – of all those conversations, the one she had had with Bob Allen on that late-teenage evening had been the least bearable.

The door to the hotel room swung open and Jonathan came in, his big form bringing the tight space still further inwards so the wooden fittings and the brown blankets and the coffee-coloured walls became something of a wardrobe in itself for Joy. Even the window, the curtains of which Jonathan had partially opened, had its light made still duller, even coffee coloured. Could she spend another night in this place? This was the plan; they would return here after the party, after seeing in the New Year. Joy saw Jonathan's big face rise like a dull planet over her shoulder in the darkened space of the wardrobe's mirror.

– Missed a treat with breakfast, he said. Beans. The whole bang shoot!

The rugby clubhouse on Pinfold Lane where the New Year's Eve party was being held had at first been no more than a hut providing changing facilities for the teams which used the rugby pitches there. Subsequently it had been extended and then the whole edifice solidified with bricks and mortar courtesy of a few better-off Castleford benefactors who wanted to see the Union code of the game take a greater hold in an area far more committed to Rugby League. At that time the two versions of rugby were mutually exclusive: the thirteen-a-side version was confined to northern and poorer areas and its best players and teams played for money (although not even the best of these earned enough from playing to make it their only profession), whilst the fifteen-a-side game was more widespread, harshly amateur and still had evidence of its public school roots: doctors and pilots could be found running and scrummaging amongst a fifteen, whilst The Lord's Supper version was the province of the humble labourer. Castleford's Grammar School aped Rugby School by playing Union and thus excluded perhaps the greatest player of handling football England has ever known as soon as he ventured down Wheldon Lane to play Rugby League (and even before he took a penny of appearance money). Roger 'The Dodger' Millward could occasionally have been seen during the early sixties on the touchline of the playing fields of the Grammar School at which he was a pupil, passing a Saturday morning watching his fellows lose a game which, had he been playing alongside them, they would undoubtedly have won. Glynis and Barry, the couple whose engagement party was being thrown to coincide with the New Year celebrations, both knew Roger and Barry had invited him to the party, although Glynis suspected the Dodger was unlikely to appear in the venue they had chosen.

That venue had begun to seem more generally as if it might not have been the best of choices to Glynis as the party got under way. There were others whom she had expected who had not appeared: Pinfold Lane was some distance out of the centre of Castleford, on the edge of Methley and the farmland which spread out past Oulton to Rothwell. She had been told the Christmas decorations put up inside and outside the clubhouse would be left there for her function, but the strings of bulbs draped on the outside had proved too great a challenge for the local post-Christmas vandals and all but those hanging over the entrance were now haphazard in their arrangement and dead of light. The trimmings inside were intact, although to Glynis' eye at least they had a certain dilapidated and sagging quality, particularly under the modern strip lighting which was a little too clinical for a party. (Glynis had only previously seen the place in daylight.) Also there was a definite chill to the interior (some of the guests had as yet not taken off their overcoats), one of the beer barrels was refusing to offer up anything but drips to the tap to which it had been connected and the sandwiches, cakes and pastries which she and her mother had spent so long producing had at least half disappeared into the maw of an early group of Barry's friends, who had arrived in a removal van owned by one of their number as if direct from a desert island. Glynis had tried to instigate some restraint here and even forced Barry into calling out – Hey lads, leave some of it for someone else! – but the ramifications of *Free and Easy* were being increasingly indicated to her. Had it been a sit down or something a little more formal she would not have had to witness Brian Tennant lifting a whole plate of carefully cut sandwiches as if it were his personal helping, or Raymond Hicks with a slice of pork pie in both hands. A plate of chipolatas had gone onto the floor also (Glynis thanked goodness that, ignoring her mother, she had decided on paper plates) and a few of these which had not been retrieved were still beckoning her glances like little fat digits.

Also, the love of her life was already inebriated, as was his brother. The first posed no great problem: Barry was a pleasant drunk; his wide and affable face simply became a little wider and still more affable, the usual pinkness of the cheeks deepening to a rosiness which moved over his features like setting sun on water. Glynis knew the only danger of her fiancé continuing to drink was that this suffusion would become so sweet and deep his eyelids would go down, the sun might actually set, and Barry would nod off. He seemed capable of doing this anywhere and any time after he had been drinking; she had once found him contentedly asleep on the floor just inside the porch of his parents' house, hugging a half-removed jacket, his foot still in the gap of the open door. His brother, however, was another matter: the redness which came with the drink to Stan's face was neither rosy nor suffused; it quickly concentrated into blood spots on the cheekbones, which spots kept their shape as they intensified and spread until they reached up into the lower rims of the eyes.

There was no rose tint in this for Stan, more a bloody vision of all things, a potential for aggression which might become physical (although this was unlikely in this setting and this company, thought Glynis), but which would almost certainly become verbal. In the sometimes inverted manner of such matters, Barry, who usually had something to say when he was sober, became more blandly receptive in his cups, whilst his normally more reticent brother became prolix, even provocative.

Glynis had one eye on this situation and another moving across other aspects of the party. The DJ recommended by one of her fiancé's friends had as yet, it seemed to her, failed to generate any real party atmosphere; he seemed to be spending as much time messing with the back of one of the strangely shaped amplifiers he had brought with him as offering a continuous stream of music. Nor had he any Twist records. He didn't like that crap, he said when she asked him, but he would play it if somebody had any discs of their own. The other potential entertainment was a problem also, Glynis recognized now; her own brother had brought along his guitar. It had been in another mood altogether in which she had agreed Phil could sing at the party; he sounded quite good in his bedroom, but now she had begun to wonder whether the folk songs or protest songs or whatever they were called that her brother sang would work in this setting. Perhaps later. She was somewhat concerned also at her brother's Donovan-style cap and the scruffiness of the long-haired friend he had brought along, with the tambourine. She had already noted Stan's blood spots turning in their direction. And yet there were only young people here; she looked around and saw this: those over thirty she had felt obliged to make mention of the party to had either not appeared or had appeared and vanished. There were no parents here to mess with youthful communion. *Or to call order*, Glynis could not avoid thinking this also, with another glance at the chipolatas, but then she thought they had all reached an age now when they must do things for themselves, when younger people should show that it was their time. This had been her idea from the start: the party would be of truly young people welcoming in a New Year and celebrating a union of two of their number, both of which occasions would be signs of fresh beginnings, of youth. For all her immediate concerns, Glynis still felt this, but she was not the first to feel also how a concept made flesh can be a concept obscured. Thank God, she thought, that Joyce was here.

She glanced across the room at her great friend, looking nice as she always did in a black velvet jacket over a red dress and wearing light brown, very modern boots with just the right amount of heel, standing next to the big boyfriend she had finally brought along for them to see. Her friend looked as calm and contained as she always did and the straight fair hair, which she had never coloured and which now she didn't even wave or curl, seemed to fall with still more indisputable modernity. Glynis knew she could never get her own frizzy mop to do anything like that, but as ever there was no envy: the shorter, plainer young woman took nothing but pleasure in her best friend's looks and abilities; it seemed no more than appropriate to her that Joyce should have gone to university, whilst she had done teacher training at Bretton Hall. It was no more than the way things should be that her clever friend was writing for a newspaper (the essays Joyce had written at school had been very good; Mr Robinson had even read some of them aloud to the class as a whole). Joyce Lee would quite properly go on to greater things, thought Glynis Anderson, who, for all her greater homeliness, had a good instinct for appropriate placements and potential destinies. This had served her in her relationship with Barry and in her thoughts of the future, as those who feel that what life has given them is appropriate are probably the happiest people there are. Such security can only be really challenged by major disruptions, but it can be obscured from time to time by specific contexts and this party, Glynis recognized, was becoming one of those.

At least the main room seemed to be getting warmer as more people came in and then a better party throb was instigated by the DJ's selection of some Rolling Stones records. Glynis herself did not particularly care for this group as they always looked as if they had just come from doing something quite dirty, but she was grateful for the throb. Glynis and Joyce had always preferred softer, sweeter pop. As sixth formers they had called themselves Bobby's Girls (which had even locked in with Bob Allen, the boyfriend Joyce had had at the time, although he had not liked to be called 'Bobby'): Bobby Rydell, Bobby Darin, Bobby Vinton and of course Bobby Vee, who was almost the same age as they were (only seventeen when he performed as a substitute for Buddy Holly after that terrible plane crash). Both she and Joyce had pictures of him on their bedroom walls, so sweet, so full lipped and clean and exotically American. Glynis herself had wavered towards Ricky Nelson at times, but as far as she knew Joyce had always been for Vee. *So what was she doing with this large and quite long-haired man with no tie, who looked nothing like any Bobby?* Glynis glanced at the big figure standing beside her friend, holding a plate which was nearly as full as Brian Tennant's. But then, unlike her, she thought, Joyce would really change with the times, she would really *move on*; and it would be a pleasure to watch her do so, to see in another actions and achievements for which she herself had no destiny. The organizer's eye which made Glynis a fine teacher of little ones moved on from her friend then to the verbal exchange between Mick Pollard and Pete Gibbs which was making itself heard even amidst the Rolling Stones. Politics, thought Glynis, as was usually the case with Mick Pollard; and one thing you don't want at a celebration is politics.

– It's going to end up with a full bloody invasion! Pollard was saying. Johnson is just sending in more and more troops …

– Invasion? That's just cow dung! Pete Gibbs shifted his feet rather unsteadily and reached for the drink he had put down amidst the dishevelled remnants of the food on the long trellis table. – Johnson's got to do something, otherwise the Chinks will just take it all over! South Vietnam and then Thailand and Malaysia …

– *Malaysia*! Pollard was a short, thick-set character, who had been known as Duane Doberman at school (after a character in the *Sergeant Bilko* television series); he had grown a little taller and straighter and certainly more opinionated thereafter. He had also developed a quite telling scoff, perhaps as a reversal of some earlier sufferings of his own. What are you talking about, *Malaysia*?! he scoffed. The Yanks just want to invade the country just as they did in Dominica. What are you talking about Malaysia?!

– I'm talking about Malaysia, retorted Gibbs, waving his beer so that a flat slice came away from its top. My brother's a soldier out there and he should know. He says the commies want to get in everywhere.

– The *commies*?! Pollard gave the abbreviation his fully ironic scoff. It's Johnson who's the problem. If he has his way you'll be joining your brother before long. It'll be a call-up before you know it. We'll all be heading for bloody Vietnam. They've already got Anzacs out there.

– Wilson won't let that happen. Dick Rountledge came into the exchange and Pollard turned towards him.

– Don't you be too sure! They support Johnson. They'll follow the Yanks just as they usually do.

– *Dung*! said Gibbs as if it were the bell for another round and he stepped closer to the ally he took Rountledge to be, allowing him to take up the argument.

– The Labour Left Wing doesn't support it at all, said Rountledge. Besides we've got enough on with Rhodesia.

– *Rhodesia*?! Pollard's scoffing tone even briefly overpowered the Stones' driving beat. Are there any nuclear weapons in bloody Rhodesia? he scoffed. Is it likely to start a Third bloody World War?! It's bloody Vietnam that's the bloody problem!

Glynis saw other young men turning towards the exchange and the potential for it spreading like hostilities in South East Asia. She even saw her future brother-in-law move his blood spots in its direction. Will you stop with the politics! she called, going towards the group and looking for assistance from Barry, although the rosy, dreamy smile he gave her, told her she would probably get none.

– This is supposed to be a party not the House of Commons!

– They have parties there, said Titch Townsend, grinning, and the little joke helped to re-establish a more appropriate mood, thought Glynis and she smiled gratitude at Titch.

– Wilson did propose a Commonwealth Peace Mission to Vietnam – came from another source then and Glynis looked with real displeasure at Joyce's boyfriend moving his big, faintly saturnine face towards the debate. What was her lovely friend doing with this

241

gormless southerner? This came as a crystallization of a number of earlier reactions when the man had been introduced and made a few comments he presumably thought were smart. What was her great friend doing with someone incapable of seeing what she was trying to do here, incapable of taking the cue of a joke at a party?

Perhaps Joyce read this in her look as she also stepped forward.

– Are the Rolling Stones all this DJ is going to play? she asked and the two young women shared a smile of old intimacy. Women in control, thought Glynis; as they had been in some of the old ways and as, with her friend at the helm, they would more obviously be in the New Years to come.

– Ay, that's it – Titch Townsend continued his unconscious role as saviour of the mood. Hasn't he got any Lonnie Donegan?

– *Lonnie Donegan?*! Despite his world political preoccupations, even Mick Pollard added his scoff to the chorus of disapproval this suggestion brought and Glynis nodded in the direction of the DJ. Go tell him what you want to hear, she said – *Go tidy your trays now, please* – the organizer, the arbitrator, the educator. She glanced again at Joyce and received a very fond smile in return. Both young women turned away then from the large southerner, who, showing no particular concern or even awareness, lifted a sausage roll from his paper plate.

Yes, thought Joy, it was quite clear now that she would have to have *the conversation*. Somehow Castleford had finalized this clarity, as home environments can. Seeing Jonathan in its context in the tour she had given him that day, seeing his big and foreign shape against the familiar buildings and streets, had convinced her this was not the man for her. *Was there any man for her?* She had left teenage presumptions behind, she thought, and now she could not but give such a question at least some consideration. She liked the company of men. She admired some, she was attracted to some and the exercise of estimating their thoughts and feelings was always of interest to her. She had grown up a girl, grown into a young woman, and with no more conceit than Glynis felt at her capacity for recognizing appropriate destinies, Joy felt that after any worthwhile exchange with any woman she could probably guess what they were thinking. This was fellowship more than anything else: the giddier, fluffier female traits she found rather annoying, but any subservience, quasi or deep seated, only activated the helper in her; the urge to clarify, to lift consciousness from the false to the true (this was what she would write about, she thought, this was what she would *communicate*).

Just like Glynis and the immediate aspects of her party, however, Joy had to give specific attention to her more immediate issues. It might well be that Jonathan needed a very direct approach – she looked back at him finishing his sausage roll – he had already failed to pick up on the changes of emphasis she had hoped might serve; the perception he showed with sociological analysis seemed to fail him in actual relationships. And there was the specific of the second night in Oulton, which Joy was not certain she could find bearable. Poor timing, she thought; poor and perhaps weak management of a situation on her part.

She lifted the glass of cider she had been sipping at for some time, quite unhappy with herself. Would she ever find a man who could match up to the increasingly exigent tick list she seemed to be formulating? Can anyone hold romance through a lifetime? Have it undulate and alter, but somehow keep its indestructible heart? She looked at Glynis, who had gone across to Barry and put her hand on his shoulder so she could lift herself a little and speak into the ear of the sunset of a face inclining towards her. These two might manage it, thought Joy, although who can say what other factors life might bring, what other weights and blows careless fate might direct even at a strong centre. *Oh dear ...* This was hardly the mood of a beginning; this was hardly the party mood and for a moment as Joy looked again at Jonathan she did feel for all those women who have sought security in marriage. In truth, she thought, there was nothing inappropriate for her in this man and with some deliberate effort she could recreate moments of romance and satisfaction whilst letting him be her shield. In some ways, ironically, she might need this more than her friend: the world and its politics were not lost on Joy as they rather were on Glynis. The new movements, the new media, affected her as they would never affect her friend; Joy was even proposing some kind of a career amongst them, but she could not help but recognize how much easier it would be to avoid their front lines, even as mere image and word. *Let the men inhabit those as they had in the past.* And yet look at the idiocies their front lines have resulted in, witness the danger zone men have made of the whole world. No, Joy could not reconcile herself to anything but some front line. So she must have that conversation with Jonathan; *man to man* – the phrase came to her as half joke, half taunt, but as she finished off the cider and turned with a clear resolution which she hoped would enable her to get through the evening smiling, congratulating and even dancing, she saw another face which sent clarity back into a still greater turmoil. Another room closed in on her then, it seemed, because of a man, although this time there was no walled firmness, more the claustrophobia of a dream dissolving the surroundings into the miasmas of the past. *Don't you love me any more?* Bob Allen had asked on that late-teenage evening. *How can that happen?* He had not asked this, this had been Joy's own thought. It isn't that, was what she actually said. It isn't that. It's just that ... She had tailed off and looked out into the twilight.

– Have you met somebody else in Liverpool?

She had, of course she had; she had met a number of bright and interesting people.

– It isn't that ... was the repetition she gave.

– So what is it? asked Bob Allen and Joy had felt the faintest irritation at his inability to recognize an obvious development. But then did he not have emotional logic on his side? How can two souls be joined and then separated, two halves made one and this oneness once again divide? If this can happen are there in truth only single souls, only separate, perhaps deluded, selves? There were no impositions on eternal love here, no worldly obstacles, no warring families to keep them apart, no soldier going off to war or the wasting expiration of a bohemian girl; this was just mortal change acting on a seeming eternity as wind acts on a glistening mist or sleet on perfect snow.

– *I can't believe it!* Bob Allen had said then, with a catch in his voice Joy could still hear, a catch with which it may be all things end.

– *I just can't believe ... you don't love me any more.*

She had looked at his fully lowered head: the carefully combed fair hair she had once taken so much girlish pleasure in, the sweet face no more than a pale, filled V, with its chin pressed into his chest. His hands fluttered up like the last attempts of dying birds and then he was still and she could see the dampness around the lowered crescents of his eyes. Mothering instincts had risen in her then and it was all her mind could do to avoid that trick. (This was the word which came as part of her effort. How many women, she would think later, have fallen for that trick? How powerful biology is, mindlessly seeking persistence and camouflaging this simplicity with siren sounds and bright images. In another article many years later she would mount a diatribe against advertising for using the same techniques without even the propagation of a species as its excuse, just money.) Her own hand had fluttered towards Bob Allen, but she had held it in check. It would be a dishonesty on her part, she thought, as would a continuing profession of love; there was still love of a kind, but undeniably she no longer wanted to see this man, she no longer wanted to exchange words with him, and had it been possible for her to snap the fingers of her restrained hand and transport herself away into her bedroom she would have done so. Something of her heart would have gone back to his still, seated figure, just as something of her heart went out to it as she sat beside it, but it was not the whole heart, it was not the heart of magical touches, it was not the heart he wanted.

– We should write to each other.

Yes, she had said they should write to each other. Joy felt her face flushing a little even now at the memory, for the letter he had written to her she could not help but receive as some awkward, underqualified visitor amidst the dreaming big buildings of a university and she had not replied. Nothing she could phrase had seemed capable of salving any wound or instigating anything but false hope. And yet she could take only intellectual comfort from the fact that he had not responded to this suggestion on that evening and that his letter had come as a surprise. They had not *agreed* they would write, she told herself. In fact Bob Allen had said nothing more on that evening, not even responding to her – we should go back inside – and her last sight of him had been on the old seat in Glynis' garden on the occasion of her friend's nineteenth birthday.

There was an element of recrimination in Joy's next look at Glynis. Here she was at another of her parties and here again was Bob Allen. It was a momentary feeling; Joy could see how he could not have been excluded, although perhaps he could have had the sense to dodge it, as had Roger the Dodger, but again, particularly given what was facing her that same night – or more specifically in the early hours of the New Year – Joy could not help but feel something like guilt, which her bright mind was soon able to override with clearer estimations of the way things are and the way things go.

– *What about some Beatles?!* came a cry from somewhere in the rugby clubhouse then. *We've had no Beatles!* The DJ looked out at the crowd with resignation. In his opinion this group was altogether more lightweight than the Stones, particularly with those silly suits, but he had to respond to his public and of course he had brought some Beatles records along. They would be asking for the Shadows next, he sneered, and wondered whether anyone here actually knew what the initials R and B stood for.

– They're from Liverpool, aren't they, The Beatles?

Maggie Wild came up beside Joy with this question and Joy nodded and forced herself into a chat. In yet another piece she would write many years later she tried to convey something of the innocence of popular music before the Beatles, particularly before they became not just a tight little band with a quite happy balance of toughness and melody, but a movement directed at the mind and the soul, before the world itself began to take on a dialogue of revolution, which dialogue would peter out as all such dialogues have into more basic and persistent human forces. It would be a long time before Joy found herself even railing against words themselves and the ways in which they could be dishonestly used. Still for her on the eve of that New Year, it seemed that complexity, subtlety and clarity would develop, analysis and dialogue would bring salvation. And this despite the awkward conversations which remained for her to have. Not just the foolish gabble of Maggie Wild or the brainless, drunken argument Barry's brother instigated with the DJ, which but for Glynis might have ended in blows; not even the other quite heated exchange between Glynis and her folk-singing brother, where Joy's opinion was sought, and which ended with the brother saying that if he was not going to be allowed to sing inside he would do so outside (the strains of 'Catch the Wind' could be faintly heard by those closest to the windows); not just the exchanges with Jonathan where Joy tried to convey coolness, in which she even used the word 'patronizing' to definite effect. Not just all these ... Bob Allen finally came across to exchange a few words with her.

– How are you? he asked and she replied that she was fine.

– Have you finished at university now? She knew he knew she had, but she went along, saying she had indeed finished there and now she had a job as a journalist and nodding at his description of the roofing and maintenance business he was running. He had always been good at woodwork. He had even fashioned a few wooden sculptures for her. I started it up with Tony Wilson, he said. But then he dropped out and now it's just mine. Got a couple of youngsters working for me and three vans. *Robert Allen Roofing and Maintenance* – he ran a stretched thumb and forefinger over the imagined logo – Tony was the roofer really, but I picked up enough.

– That's great, said Joy, trying not to hear any echoes or undertones or even to consider how her old boyfriend's appearance had changed. Some might have said he was better looking now, his sweet boyish good looks had solidified into handsome, but she wanted to give none of this any thought. That's really great, she said and then she had no choice but to introduce Jonathan and seeing the look Bob Allen brought onto him, it was all she could do not to add that she intended to discard this man also in a few hours time. *What was she*?! she wondered. Hardly a *femme fatal*. She had known her own miseries. But had she ever felt as Bob Allen did? Words had helped her, she thought, as they could have helped him if they had come to him with sufficient clarity. She shrank from his wordless look, however, using Jonathan rather as she might the shelter of a wall. As Bob Allen gave an awkward valediction and stepped awkwardly away she had found herself stepping into the other man's shade.

247

– Old boyfriend? asked Jonathan, grinning, and she smiled a yes and listened to his accurate assessment of the inevitabilities of moving on from a home town and then some less accurate assessments of the sociological realities of a working-class community. Fortunately, the party was gathering momentum, particularly as the last hour of the old year began. The beer on offer, which Barry had organized, did not run out as had Glynis' food – to great cheers and applause two new barrels were brought in from the removal van – and Glynis looked at her good-natured partner with pride. She did prevent him from making a speech, however, suspecting he was being egged on to this by those who simply wanted some memorable and probably comic moments. She would have liked Joyce to do the honour, she knew her friend's capacity for finding the right phrase, but in that company, in that setting, this was not really a possibility. Nor had Glynis missed the little exchange with Bob Allen or her friend sliding into the shadow of her new man. The engagement toast, such as it was, was left to Charlie Walters, who would be Barry's best man, who managed to call the clubhouse to something like quiet and, after some catcalls and some incoherence on his part, asked everyone to lift their glasses to the newly engaged couple.

Joy looked at these two then as at a single sunrise, the deeper rosiness of the bigger face absorbing the fainter flush of her old friend, and yet again she wondered if she herself would ever find such a union. The persistence of the question began to irritate her and by the time the New Year was counted in and 'Auld Lang Syne' sung and balloons knocked towards the strip lighting, a few popping to great acclaim, she was more than ready to get away.

– Did you have a good time? asked Glynis as Jonathan went off to get their overcoats and Joy said it had been great. Great to see everyone again.

– That's good. I'm really glad you could get here and it was nice to meet – Losing the name was not deliberate, Joy knew; it was not her friend's way.

– Jonathan.

– Yes, Jonathan, nice to meet him. The look they exchanged contained at least an element of a wish on both their parts that they could go back to the old bedrooms and talk as they had so often done. Glynis may even have read something of the new boyfriend's fate and Joy would certainly have liked to discuss it; explain it, excuse it perhaps, to a sympathetic ear. But they were older now, with the obligations this entailed. Glynis had not even had time to seek out the details of the Oulton Arms Hotel. *I saw Bob Allen come over* ... she did start with this but Joy's smile became both fixed and sinking and her old friend took the cue and said simply – He always calls himself Robert these days – and left it at that. Unspoken understanding settled like the fully gathered warmth of the room on the two old friends and as Jonathan came back with the overcoats they embraced and turned quite quickly away, Joy to Jonathan's car and Glynis to deal with Barry's brother who was arguing again with the DJ as the man tried to pack away his equipment. There was some negative potential also in the horseplay and raucous singing of a group of young men determined to prolong a party mood.

– How are they all getting home? Jonathan asked as, following Joy's directions, he turned his Triumph Spitfire out along the main road through Methley towards Oulton. He had already noted how few vehicles there seemed to be outside the clubhouse and how incapable most of those inside would be to drive them. With nothing but fizzy wine on offer he himself had drunk no more than a couple of beers.

– There are some taxis coming, I think.

Joy looked out at the dark and increasingly rural countryside.

– And some of them are just walking.

– But it's quite a way into Castleford, isn't it?

Joy closed her eyes, thinking how little she needed conversation at that point and then how much of conversation was at the same time pointless and useful. She felt no brief for those who allege they say nothing unless they have something worth saying, nor those who profess persistent truthfulness, or the downright idiots who want to talk everything out. On the other hand ... She allowed herself a yawn and then a moment of useful irritation at Jonathan's inane: *Tired?*

– You must be as well, she said. Given the amount of food you've put away today. She saw nothing but a bland grin on her driver's face, however.

– Growing boy, he said.

– They seem a pleasant couple … he went on after a pause. Seem right for each other.

– Yes, said Joy, considering a *carpe diem.*

– They all still call you Joyce, I see.

How would you *see* that? She tried to bring some energy into her manner, but Jonathan smile was nothing but kindly. *Joy* suits you better, he said and she knew she could not have the conversation that night with this decent, intelligent, but separate, soul.

Her mind turned instead to how she could avoid the specifics of the bedroom. The pleasures she had found in these had rather surprised her, but she knew they could only really come as part of a mood which she saw no possibility of finding that night and probably also as part of a more general warmth of feeling for the partner involved. She had heard other women arguing that their own sexual activities should be just as basic and heartless as they could be in men, but she was suspicious of such arguments. The women she had known trying to equal men in this way had, it seemed to her, always been working out other matters at the same time. Moreover, as she had written in an as yet unpublished piece, why would women want to find liberation in aping such simplicity? Why not find this liberation in the greater depth and complexity to which her sex was prone? On the other hand polemical gestures may well be necessary. She was not particularly happy with the analysis Jonathan had afforded an abbreviated version of during the discussion of the Beatles which had developed at the party … Saw them in '62 at the ABC in Blackpool, Jack Shawcross had said. Just paid at the door. But it was as the screaming and all was getting started, so you couldn't really hear them that well. What gets into these girls? He had addressed the question quite mischievously to her, but it was not an opportunity Jonathan could allow himself to miss; he was making the phenomenon part of his sociological studies.

– *It's religious,* he said and Jack Shawcross looked at the big southerner with interest. – There are mass factors – Jonathan warmed to his theme. Group suggestion and so on, but also all women are seeking their Jesus. The hysteria you see, the screaming, the swooning, is religious really; in a modern context; whereas men still can't allow themselves to do this and anyway they are looking for the Virgin Mary and you don't swoon over her, you protect her, you seek her comfort.

– You think? said Jack, pushing out his beer-wet lips in thought.

– They're not just a bunch of daft buggers winding themselves up?

Jonathan had laughed heartily and genuinely at this and Joy shook her head at both of them. So could you get to *swooning*? Jack Shawcross had asked her then, rather taken by the word, and the question came back to her in the Oulton Arms Hotel as she lay with her eyes open in the lumpy double bed feeling sleep had probably passed her by. Jonathan's advances had been dealt with easily enough; they had in truth been a little mechanical, the big man was actually tired and although a clear desire on her part would have enlivened his own, he had been ready enough to accept that she did not feel too good as she had put it and now he himself was deeply asleep, his breathing soft and regular, his large form quite still. Joy might have preferred to have him snoring and scratching like some great hibernating animal; she might have preferred bad odours, all validating the conversation she still needed to have. In fact, there was only a quite pleasant, fleshy warmth, and it was an undefined motivation which had her roll away from this and out of the bed and tiptoe across the cool room with its cold radiator to the curtained window.

One of the large white bath towels set out ready for the morning was all that came immediately to hand to wrap around the shoulders her nightdress left exposed and she pulled its soft, rough material tight around her as she parted the curtains and looked out across the fields towards Castleford. There had been some rain earlier, perhaps even a little sleet, but as she looked out the night was quite still and clear with frost hanging as no more than a faint ringing. In the distance she could see the lights of the town she had grown up in and after a time she picked out the silhouette of its highest ground and the still less distinct detail of winding wheels (only because she

251

knew they were there, she thought) and then the cooling towers of the power station and the tiny winking red light of the taller chimney in their midst. *Could she get to swooning?* She shook her head at the question and at herself, but as she did so a vague swoon did seem to come, sounding through that bell of a night and passing into her as something more substantial. Following its movement she leaned further towards the glass and bent her head to look up at a night sky which was darkening from its empyrean – blackness billowing down like ink being slowly poured into water.

Bob Allen would be lying awake, she thought; he would be thinking of their meeting, thinking of her and of what he imagined might have been, his heart breaking all over again. Her heart went out to him and the swoon took her still closer to the window until her cheek touched its glass and then it seemed her own heart was breaking and spreading. *Perhaps she too would never love again as she had loved at sixteen.* Never again would it be that mindless, that wordless and complete! *Take comfort in this my one time love, my one time world. All endings and beginnings. Only on a page can you fix a moment, and that only for others as transient as yourself.* This came and went in the space which it seemed had been made. And then more sweeping and somehow related hopes: *let there be no killing in this New Year* (in this year of the Beast as Jonathan, grinning, had reminded her), *let hatred be controlled and aggression subdued, and let empathy abound; the smile of a friend, the forgiveness of an enemy, let it be, let it become; let us truly feel for each other's fate and rise soaring above old forces.* These were Joy's swooning wishes, the outpourings of her open heart, in the earliest hours of that New Year. *And let Bob Allen find some other joy.* She splayed a hand on the cold glass, pressing as if the fingers and the thoughts could go beyond the pane. Yes, it would be words, she thought, giving forms and names to everything. Only words can truly clarify and uplift, enlighten and inspire. And yet as the dark sky came still further down, she could not help but recognize how they might also impede and misdirect, frighten and inhibit; how they and their images might spread until they were as the spreading night itself.

A sigh came through her as if it were the last exhalation of the swoon and then feeling a more tangible shiver, she pulled the towel tight to her shoulders and turned away, trying, as she went across the room (the chill following her like a ghost) to feel only the sweeter traces and touches which had been left. She slipped back into the warmth and curled up foetally, fond memories, dear faces, sweet songs running though her with that warmth and also, as another life began, something more likely to come as a more indefinite, timeless swoon (perhaps more than God's creatures, she thought, we are God's memories), more even, probably, than can be written and certainly more than can be said.